Praise for *A Reluctant Belle*

"Featuring flawed characters desperate to fight for equality, this intense historical romance will make readers wrestle—as Joelle does—with questions of what the Christian faith says about freedom, truth, and justice."

Publishers Weekly

Praise for *A Rebel Heart*

"*A Rebel Heart* features characters with depth, a gripping plot with thoughtfully researched authenticity, and unexpected twists."

Booklist

"*A Rebel Heart* checks all the boxes on my wish list for a satisfying novel. It brings a lesser-known slice of history to life and deals honestly with our national past. The characters are colorful and compelling, the setting richly painted, and the high-stakes plot carries the reader to the end without ever slowing down. Full of intrigue, grit, and grace, *A Rebel Heart* is Beth White at her finest. I can't wait to read the rest of the series."

Jocelyn Green, award-winning author of *A Refuge Assured*

"With great skill, Beth White combines intriguing history with inspiring romance, and then adds a good measure of mystery and suspense to her newest novel, *A Rebel Heart*. From the first page to the last, readers will be wrapped up in Selah's quest to restore her family's stately Mississippi home and charmed by the touching romance. Levi's investigation to solve a series of robberies and find out who is behind the mysterious incidents that threaten Selah and her family will keep readers guessing and turning pages until the very end. Well done!"

Carrie Turansky, award-winning author
of *Shine Like the Dawn* and *Across the Blue*

"Pinkerton agent Levi Riggins stole my heart, beginning with his valiant rescue of Selah Daughtry after a train wreck in the opening scenes of *A Rebel Heart*. Selah couldn't help but lose her heart, too, although she has more than one reason to be wary of the former Yankee officer. Beth White's careful historical research shines throughout this novel, as do her wonderful characters. Highly recommended."

Robin Lee Hatcher, Lifetime Achievement Award–winning
author of *You're Gonna Love Me*

A
RECKLESS
LOVE

Books by Beth White

GULF COAST CHRONICLES

The Pelican Bride
The Creole Princess
The Magnolia Duchess

DAUGHTRY HOUSE

A Rebel Heart
A Reluctant Belle
A Reckless Love

RECKLESS LOVE

BETH WHITE

Revell

a division of Baker Publishing Group
Grand Rapids, Michigan

Published by Revell
a division of Baker Publishing Group
PO Box 6287, Grand Rapids, MI 49516-6287
www.revellbooks.com

Printed in the United States of America

Library of Congress Cataloging-in-Publication Data
Names: White, Beth, 1957– author.
Title: A reckless love / Beth White.
Description: Grand Rapids, Michigan : Revell, a division of Baker Publishing Group, [2020] | Series: Daughtry house; 3
Identifiers: LCCN 2019056019 | ISBN 9780800726911 | ISBN 9780800738587 (hardcover)
Subjects: GSAFD: Christian fiction. | Love stories.
Classification: LCC PS3623.H5723 R44 2020 | DDC 813/.6—dc23
LC record available at https://lccn.loc.gov/2019056019

Scripture used in this book, whether quoted or paraphrased by the characters, is taken from the King James Version of the Bible.

This is a work of historical reconstruction; the appearances of certain historical figures are therefore inevitable. All other characters, however, are products of the author's imagination, and any resemblance to actual persons, living or dead, is coincidental.

The author is represented by MacGregor Literary, Inc.

20 21 22 23 24 25 26   7 6 5 4 3 2 1

This book is dedicated to the best
of neighbors and friends—
Danny and Kim Carpenter.

PROLOGUE

April 27, 1865
North of Memphis, Tennessee

Zane's first thought when he came to was that the world was coming to an end. Lying flat on the ground, hearing muffled, mud up his nose and in his good eye, he turned his head to squint against the giant boiling, roaring flare on the Mississippi. Fire on the water—how could that be?

But then he'd seen hell in all its various forms over the last four years. Maybe God had decided to start over, like he did with Noah's family. Zane wouldn't quibble with the Almighty over the need for a fresh start.

He pushed to his hands and knees, shaking his head to rid himself of the sensation of battle aftermath. The war was over. He was on his way . . . somewhere upriver. Maybe St. Louis or Cairo. Not home, because he didn't have one. Mainly he wanted to get beyond Mississippi and Alabama, a place where a man could live in peace.

Sounds began to come and go—small explosions, inhuman

screams, the roar of the flames—and he fought the urge to curl up on the ground, arms over his head, knees drawn in. No. He was here for a reason. Left behind for some purpose only God knew. If he didn't believe that, he'd have given in long ago.

Dragging in a breath that pierced his lungs and launched a spasm of coughing, he forced himself upright on his knees, wiping the slime from his face, spitting grit out of his mouth. His ears cleared long enough to distinguish—

The screams were real. Human. In a flash of recall, he remembered what brought him here. The man he'd followed by horseback along the river. The explosion—

Right, the steamboat—the boat he'd been aboard from Vicksburg to Memphis—had exploded, knocking him unconscious.

He stared in horror at the inferno on the river. There were people everywhere, floating past on doors and shutters and tree stumps, calling out, drowning, burning, shrieking like demons, the scene comparable to the worst wartime engagement he'd experienced.

As he staggered to his feet, something dripped into his good eye. He reached up to wipe it away, then stood looking at his hand by moonlight and the flickering fire, rubbing the sticky moisture between his fingers. His head was bleeding, though the patch over his bad eye remained miraculously in place.

He took off his coat, ripped off one of his shirtsleeves and tied it about his forehead, then put the coat back on.

By now his senses had straightened enough that he could think. He took stock of the tragedy around him and began to formulate a plan. That was what the Provost Guard of the

Indiana Iron 44th did. Take any unorthodox situation, assess the most critical problems, and deal with them step by step. It was how he'd survived the last eight months in prison. It was how he'd made it to Vicksburg mainly on foot, how he'd secured a berth on that hell-bound steamer.

It was why he wasn't on it when it exploded.

Step by step, Sager, he told himself. *There are people in the water worse off than you. Help them.*

Before he could act, voices pierced the chaos—not from the survivors on the river but from somewhere just ahead, behind a stand of trees near the top of the muddy, flood-torn riverbank. Though Zane's hearing still came and went, he thought he distinguished two voices. One of them had him crouching, reaching for the pistol he'd bought in Memphis.

Jones. He'd know that high-pitched raspy voice anywhere.

He froze. So he'd been right that the saboteur on the *Sultana* seemed familiar. His instinct to follow the man had saved his life, and now he had a choice to make. He could apprehend Jones with no proof—other than his own word—that he'd done anything wrong. Or he could dive into the river and save as many lives as possible.

As the screams of burning, drowning men and women and the crackling roar of the blazing vessel splintered the night, he reeled with the pain in his head. Maybe he wasn't strong enough to accomplish either task.

Suddenly he could hear the judge's voice in his head. *Vengeance belongs to the Lord, Zane. Don't take that on yourself.*

The judge. Judge Teague had been on that boat—in Zane's spot on the upper deck. It seemed impossible that he could still be alive. But Zane had never bowed to the inevitable in his life.

Praying for strength, he turned back toward the river.

The explosion jerked her awake. Aurora sat up, heart slamming in her throat. The second-floor bedroom was dark and quiet, but she could still feel the iron bedstead quivering. Cousin ThomasAnne lay beside her, snoring a prosaic, ladylike purr. How could she sleep after that concussion? For that matter, Aurora herself seemed to be the only one awake in the house.

Everyone always said she had the hearing of a bat, but had no one else felt the reverberation, the shudder of the house? Some nights she lay awake long after everyone else slumbered, listening to the hoot of the steamboats pushing upriver from exotic places like Natchez, Vicksburg, Baton Rouge, New Orleans. Now that the war was over, the Mississippi River had opened to civilian traffic. The daily symphony of sounds from the landing below the bluff had thickened with longshoremen calling to the crews of boats docking or steaming away, loaded with passengers, cotton, and other crops headed north. Nighttime was quieter, with a rhythm and music all its own: distant foghorns, the call of night watchmen, perhaps a drunken sailor singing a bawdy song on his way out of a waterfront saloon.

Now—only muffled silence, as though her ears had suddenly gotten stuffed with cotton wadding.

Shoving aside ThomasAnne's bony knees, she lay back and pulled the quilt under her chin. With spring slow to arrive this year, the night was sharp and cool for late April. The river had been roiling with snowmelt for weeks, overflowing its bounds, flooding the plains of the delta on the Arkansas side and across the state line in Mississippi. Though Memphis, high on its bluff, remained safe from the angry water, she breathed a prayer for the roustabouts below.

She lay awake for a long time, unable to shake the feeling of unease. Maybe that disturbance had been a dream after all. She hoped it had been. But sometime later, her eyes flew open at the sound of feet on the stairs just outside the bedroom door. The room had lightened, but shadows still lingered in the corners. Then, oddly, a flare of light penetrated the blackness beyond the open streetside window.

Scrambling out of bed, Aurora ran to lean over the windowsill. Lamplight flickered and swam along the street like giant fireflies, all headed in the direction of the river. A wagon rattled by, then a couple of horses, then more wagons. Suddenly the street was alive with chaos and noise, men pouring out of their houses, calling to one another.

"Steamboat exploded!" The words came clear at last in the melee. "Fire! People in the water—"

Craning to see beyond the mad activity pouring toward the bluff, Aurora spotted a stream of boats backing out into the river. Impossible to distinguish individual vessels from amongst the various sizes and shapes, but the US military packet *Pocahontas*, a midsized steamer charged with rounding up Confederate blockade runners and habitually moored at the foot of Beale Street at nightfall, was no doubt among the rescuers. That very day, Aurora and her sisters had been at the Soldiers' Home, serving members of the *Pocahontas*'s crew, along with paroled Union prisoners from the steamboat *Sultana*. Stopping in Memphis to unload a hundred tons of sugar and nearly as many barrels of wine, the *Sultana*'s pilot had allowed the passengers to disembark for supper. The ladies of Aurora's church had brought blankets and food, tea and conversation, to men so gaunt and ill from incarceration at Cahaba Prison over in Alabama that they hardly seemed human.

The men, clearly giddy with joy at the knowledge that they were on their way home, had seemed grateful for feminine kindnesses. Some had had the means to purchase new clothes in town, but others remained in stinking uniforms so black with grime that the original color could no longer be discerned. Aurora had held her breath and bravely smiled at each man she encountered, some who seemed hardly older than her own fourteen years, some aged beyond reality by their travails. All but blinded by pity, Aurora had ignored the revolting of her stomach and sat beside a poor man with an amputated leg and a ferocious head wound while a troupe of opera singers from Chicago, also traveling on the *Sultana*, had performed a program of comic scenes.

Could the *Sultana* be the afflicted vessel?

She thought it likely, and if so, the disaster could not be overstated. The steamboat had been monstrously over-loaded—so much so that it nearly capsized while passengers ganged on one side to pose for photographers on the wharf. Everyone at the Soldiers' Home had been talking about it this afternoon.

Or, more properly, she supposed, that had been yesterday. Dawn could not be far away now.

"Aurora?" came ThomasAnne's soft voice. "What's the matter?"

Aurora looked over her shoulder and found her older cousin

sitting up in bed, nightcap askew over curly, reddish-brown hair straggling in plaits over her shoulders. "I'm not sure." Aurora turned back to the ruckus outside the window. "Sounds like a steamer up the river exploded and caught fire. Those poor people . . ."

"Oh mercy! Come back to bed before—"

"Tom, it can't reach us here." Aurora squelched her own anxiety to reassure her cousin. "It's almost time to get up anyway, so I'm going to get dressed. I'm sorry I woke you. Go back to sleep."

"Heavens, no, you can't . . ."

Ignoring her cousin's bleating protests, Aurora shucked out of her nightgown. Feeling her way in the dark, she found her undergarments, stockings, and day dress lying across the cedar chest at the foot of the bed and quickly put them on. "Go to sleep, ThomasAnne," she said soothingly, slipping out into the hallway, carrying her shoes—and stopped in her tracks at the sight of her grandmother mounting the stairs. "Grandmama! What are you doing up?"

"I might ask you the same thing, young lady." Grandmama reached the landing with a thump of her ebony-head cane, an accessory which Aurora suspected was carried mainly for effect. "Turn right around and get back to bed." Once a famous titian-haired beauty, the old lady had not lost the raised-eyebrow expression of one used to commanding a retinue.

"I'm not sleepy." Aurora tipped her chin, imitating the autocratic tilt of Grandmama's well-coiffed head. "Besides, it's very noisy outside. What is happening out on the river? I heard the explosion."

"You *heard* the . . . You couldn't possibly have—" Grandmama buttoned her lips, then sputtered an exasperated breath.

"Pish. I told your grandfather we might as well wake you girls up. Go on down to the breakfast room and find something to eat. We'll need to start making bandages and send them on to the hospital. I'll wake the other girls—oh, ThomasAnne, you're up too? Good, then. Hurry and put some clothes on."

As Grandmama stumped past Aurora to knock on her sisters' bedroom door, ThomasAnne ducked back into the room from whence her white, freckled face had briefly appeared like a lace-frilled daisy.

Aurora hurried down the stairs to the breakfast room. Finding the table laid and an array of breakfast foods—bacon, biscuits, grits, fried eggs, and fig preserves—already spread on the buffet by the window, she marveled at the servants' ability to pull together such a bounteous meal in the middle of the night.

Thoughts of the unfortunate souls who had undoubtedly perished in the accident killed her appetite. She had gone to the buffet to pour a cup of coffee when a sudden banging on the front door startled her into dropping the coffeepot. Jumping up to deal with the spill spreading over the Aubusson carpet, she heard the butler, Alistair, go to the door, tut-tutting at the racket.

"Hold your horses," Alistair muttered, and Aurora heard him jerk open the door.

"Doc McGowan sent me!" came a rough male voice that Aurora didn't recognize. "Said tell the mistress to get ready for an emergency 'cause the hospital's already full—"

Aurora hurried into the foyer. "Grandmama's upstairs. I'll take the message."

The wiry young Negro at the door snatched his cap off. "Miss—Doc said not to—"

16

"Pish!" Aurora said, again in deliberate imitation of her grandmother. "How many?"

The man looked over his shoulder, then back at Aurora and apparently decided he'd better deliver his information fast and get back to the hospital. "As many beds as you can find, miss. Some going straight to the morgue, of course—excuse my bluntness—and the surgical cases will stay at the hospital, but the ones can easily be treated will need nurses and simple comfort. Blankets, bandages—"

"Yes, yes, we'll take care of it. I'm sure you're needed elsewhere. Thank you."

As the man ducked away, Alistair shut the door and turned to Aurora. He looked at her with reluctant respect glimmering in his dark eyes. She'd known him all her life, and he and his wife, Vonetta, the family cook, had half raised her. "Well done, little miss. I'll start down here rounding up blankets and laying out pallets, move some furniture around."

"Good. I'll go up and help Grandmama with bandages." She headed for the stairs, then hesitated, a hand on the newel. "I'm sorry about the mess in the breakfast room. I dropped the coffeepot."

Alistair responded with a grim smile. "I got a feeling we gon' have more to worry about than spilt coffee 'fore this day's over, Miss Aurora."

She nodded, then pattered lightly up the stairs, praying.

God, give me strength to be useful and kind and coura-geous.

Adams Hospital was a madhouse. Screams of pain ulu-lated over the shouts of medical personnel, the grunts and questions of volunteers, and a general roar of disaster. The iron smell of blood and stench of burned flesh permeating the hallway would have knocked Zane to his knees—but he'd already sagged against a wall outside the ward where he and a freedman named Lucky Tolbert had just left Judge Teague.

Tolbert and his dugout fishing canoe had saved his life.

By the grace of God, Zane had managed to pull five victims to safety before the current yanked his tired body under and nearly swept him downriver. But just as he feared he'd lost the will to fight, he caught sight of a dark-skinned arm reaching for him. Tolbert dragged him into the canoe and pumped the water out of his lungs, then the two of them set to work ferrying as many as they could safely carry to the Negro's island fishing camp.

Zane knew he shouldn't have been surprised that the judge was one of those survivors floating along on a door from the pilot house. It was a night of disasters and miracles. He closed his good eye and let his head fall back against the wall. He was so weary, and he wanted to sleep. Yet he dreaded what he knew he'd dream of—the nightmare of what he'd seen this night would haunt him for years to come. Maybe he'd never forget it. Maybe he'd never sleep again.

"Son, get up from there and let's find you a bed," ordered an aristocratic Southern soprano located somewhere above him. He felt a gentle, gnarled hand rest on his head. "Where are you hurt?"

Zane peered upward, his vision oddly doubled. He couldn't tell much about the woman, other than that she had once been beautiful. And she was willing him to do something he was incapable of accomplishing. "I'm fine," he said. "Just resting. I'm about to go . . ." Where was he going? He had no place to go. Besides, he had to stay and make sure the judge recovered. "I'll just stay here, if it's all right with you."

"It is not all right," she said imperiously. "Never mind. I'll send someone for you—"

"No, ma'am." Forcing his exhausted legs to support him, he stood up, tottering. "I need to stay here. Judge Teague is in there—"

"Judge Teague is in the hands of the best surgeon in Memphis—my husband, Dr. McGowan. I might let you check on him later—after you've gotten into some dry clothes and had a meal and a good sleep." Her blue eyes twinkled. "Now, since you seem to be ambulatory, come with me, before I have to call an orderly to haul you out of the way."

Recognizing a stronger will than his own, Zane pushed away from the wall, ignoring the arm she extended to assist him. Hanged if he'd let an old lady serve as a crutch.

By midmorning, McGowan House had been turned into a makeshift hospital. Aurora stood in the doorway of the dining room with a basin of clean water propped against her stomach. She watched her sisters—tall, gangly Joelle and no-nonsense Selah—work together to bring comfort to some poor burned soul. Frankly she wasn't sure if it was a man or a woman, as every bit of hair had been burned from the blistered head, and the body was covered by a blanket.

It was a hopeless cause. Selah closed the sightless eyes and brought the blanket up to cover the person's face, then sat back on her heels and stared at Joelle. "I'll get one of the men to come for the body," she said and rose.

Joelle nodded and moved to the next patient.

Aurora wanted to weep with exhaustion and sorrow, but there wasn't time for such maudlin selfishness. For once she could be grateful for her upbringing under Grandmama's spartan philosophy. She had been trained to cope with hardship when necessary.

At the moment, it was necessary.

Joelle, her strawberry-blonde hair hanging in messy disorder about her face, looked over her shoulder. "Is there any water in that bowl?"

"Yes." Aurora approached her middle sister and knelt beside the pallet. Ladies from the church benevolence committee had brought over piles of blankets first thing after the alarm had gone out, along with stacks of red flannel shirts and drawers. Many of the survivors of the disaster had been stark naked when brought in, having stripped off their clothes in an effort to avoid being dragged under by the current or drowned by other desperate swimmers. Aurora's initial shock had quickly turned to numb stoicism. In the emergency there was no time for missish sensibilities.

She held the bowl while Joelle dunked in a clean cloth and wrung it out. Joelle began to methodically wipe the dirty face of a man who had somehow, miraculously, escaped anything more than a severe chill. Eyes squeezed shut, he lay trembling and moaning.

"I'm glad I can't see what's in his head," Aurora blurted. "Can you imagine what that was like—being blown out of your sleep into fire and cold floodwater? Everyone around you drowning or burning?"

Joelle looked at her, blue eyes bloodshot, lines of fatigue bracketing her mouth. "I know. We've all seen awful things in this war, but this . . . ." With a sigh, she laid the cloth gently across the man's creased forehead. "These men were on the way home. I don't understand God at all sometimes."

Aurora hadn't even considered God's thoughts on this situation. But then everyone called her the Princess of Rainbows. Joelle was the deep thinker of the family.

Suddenly the front door slammed open. Male voices echoed from the foyer, along with the sound of boots on the marble floors.

"Hello the house!" someone shouted. "Doc McGowan sent us."

Leaving the bowl on the floor, Aurora sprang to her feet and ran to the dining room doorway. "Here we are. What's the—" The rest of her sentence splintered. Four men carried the corners of a litter on which lay an injured fifth man. There was blood everywhere, but it seemed to originate at his blood-soaked bandaged left hand. Aurora put her hands to her mouth in an effort to collect herself. Maybe she hadn't seen the worst yet. "Come this way," she told the man at the head of the litter.

"Yes, ma'am," he said, and the men tromped behind her into the dining room.

As two servants removed the deceased burn victim, Aurora took a clean blanket from the stack on the dining room table and arranged it in the empty space on the carpet. The litter bearers carefully rolled their unconscious burden onto the pallet, then helped Aurora settle him on his back.

She made herself study the patient so she'd know how to help. His plain bearded face was oddly veined, as if from drink, and he seemed generally healthier than the other paroled prisoners who had come up from Vicksburg on the *Sultana*. An unattractive specimen with greasy, graying brown

21

hair, he was short, barrel-chested, and perfectly dry. His only real injury seemed to be the bloody hand. "Did Grandpapa give you any instructions? How was he hurt?"

"Knife fight at the Soldiers' Home. Nobody knows who he is nor where he come from." The man shrugged. "Your grandpa's coming right behind us."

"Grandpapa's coming home?" Her grandfather had been gone since the alarm went out in the middle of the night, and she hadn't expected him back before nightfall, if then. One of the few trained surgeons in town, Belmont McGowan, MD, drove himself hard during emergencies, his family and his own well-being coming in a distant second and third to patients who needed his care.

The litterman nodded. "Yes'm. The hospital didn't have no more beds, so Doc said make this man comfortable here and he'd sew up that hand when he got home."

Aurora nodded. "What about my grandmother?"

"I don't know, miss." The man shrugged. "Judge Teague was brought in around six this morning, and I think she's been caring for him."

Aurora's hand flew to her mouth. "Judge Teague? Was he on the *Sultana*?" She knew how much Marmaduke Teague meant to her grandparents. The judge might be a Unionist, but he and Grandpapa had been friends since childhood and owed one another enough favors that even a civil war hadn't been able to strip their mutual devotion.

The man nodded. "Yes'm. Apparently so. The judge got burned pretty bad in the explosion but got away on a door from the pilot house. Young fellow with one eye and a colored man with a log canoe rescued the judge and couple others hanging onto some tree branches out in the river. When they got to the little island where the Negro had been camping, the young fellow knew enough to cover the survivors' burns with flour. Your grandpa says that's what saved the judge's life. Not too long after that, the *Pocahontas* stopped to take everybody to the hospital in Memphis."

"Well, thank the Lord for them both." Throat tight, Aurora dropped to her knees in a floof of skirts and started unwrapping the nasty bandage about the ugly man's hand. "All right, I'll get him cleaned up so Grandpapa can deal with him when he gets here." Casting aside the bandage, she reached for the bowl of water Joelle had abandoned before attending to some errand that took her out of the room.

Grandpapa treated saints and sinners, heroes and traitors, without regard to their deserving of his care. The least Aurora could do was to follow his example.

One

Five years later
June 1, 1870
Oxford, Mississippi

What a waste, Aurora reflected, that the most brilliant, extravagantly beautiful woman below the Mason-Dixon line lacked the sense to come in out of the rain.

Irritated, she eyed her sister Joelle, who stood in front of a full-length mirror, reading the ingredients of a receipt for calamine lotion she'd picked up at the pharmacy. With her chin-length red-gold hair caught up at the sides with ivory combs, cheekbones like a Botticelli angel, and full lips pursed, she could have been posing for an illustration in *Godey's Lady's Book*.

"It was such a shame about the fire over at Daughtry House." Mrs. Clancy, the bridal shop couturier, buzzed around, twitching at the lace, ribbons, and ruffles adorning the massive white skirt of the dress Joelle had reluctantly agreed to try on. "Especially after y'all had just had such a

lovely house party with the Forrests and the opera singer—
what was her name? Delfina Fabulous or something like that?
Weren't you all just scared to death? And I could hardly believe my dear friend Mrs. Scully's husband—that would be
Mr. Scully, you know—was involved in the tragedy of your
father's death, God rest his soul. Poor Mrs. Scully having to
keep her head up, with her husband charged with . . . something. What was it? Arson? Train sabotage?"

Aurora did her best to ignore the woman's gossip. Maybe
a shopping trip so soon after all the traumatic events of the
spring had not been such a good idea.

"I'm going to get Wyatt to mix this up for me when I get
home." As Joelle stuffed the leaflet into the front of the dress,
she caught sight of herself in the mirror and gasped. "Pete!
Have you lost your mind?"

Joelle's horrified use of her childhood nickname jerked
Aurora back to the subject at hand. "What's the matter?"
she asked.

Joelle grabbed the front of the dress. "I'm not wearing
this monstrosity! I look like an unbaked lemon meringue
pie! Schuyler would hurt himself laughing."

If pressed, Aurora would confess to some doubt as to
the likelihood of the dress passing down Tupelo Methodist Church's center aisle without knocking someone's eye
out. But one should never concede wholesale in a battle of
wedding fashion. She reached up to jerk the cap sleeves off
Joelle's creamy shoulders. "You're right. It is entirely too
conservative."

Mrs. Clancy gave Aurora a doubtful look. "Miss Joelle is
already exposing a significant amount of décolletage. Are
you sure—"

"I'm sure this is not the right dress." Aurora moved her hands, mimicking Joelle's tall, hourglass shape. "Haven't you anything that clings more to the body?"

Joelle yanked the sleeves back up. "I do not plan to expose any décolletage at all. And the shape of my body is nobody's business but mine—and eventually Schuyler's," she added with a smug glance at the sapphire adorning her ring finger.

Aurora laughed. At least the goddess had a sense of humor. "Touché. But we came all this way to—"

"—to see our lawyer," Joelle said, with one of her whiplash reversions to pragmatism. "You dragged me in here against my will."

Aurora sighed. What was the use of looking like a mermaid out of a fairy tale if one refused to take advantage of it on the most important day of her life? "All right, all right. Let's collect Sky from the music store and go up to see Mr. Greene." She gave the proprietress an apologetic look. "I'll talk to her and bring her back when—"

"I'm sorry, Mrs. Clancy," Joelle said sweetly, "but we won't be back. I promised my dear friend Charmion that she could make my wedding dress." She dipped a curtsey. "Thank you for your time. You have a lovely shop, and I'll be happy to send you any business it's in my power to influence. I'm going to change now." With a vague flutter of her hand, she darted into the changing room before Aurora could argue.

Exchanging a harassed look with the dressmaker, Aurora hustled after her sister.

Already skinned out of the wedding dress, which had been kicked into a giant pile of fabric in the corner, Joelle looked up from straightening her stockings. "You're not going to make me go back in there, are you?"

The idea that she, the youngest and smallest of the three Daughtry sisters, wielded any influence at all over her elders continued to secretly astonish and gratify Aurora. "If you promise to let me go with you to choose the fabric for your wedding dress."

Joelle dropped her simple blue-print dress over her head and began to do up buttons. "You do have good taste. Though I warn you, I'm not baring my cleavage, even in the interest of high fashion."

"Consider me schooled, Miss Daughtry." Shaking her head with a smile, Aurora helped her sister finish dressing.

As they bid good day to Mrs. Clancy and left the shop, Aurora looked regretfully over her shoulder. She'd been looking forward to shopping in Oxford, a much bigger town than poky little Tupelo. She hadn't been back to Memphis since early April, and though she didn't precisely miss Grandmama's constant interference, rural life had become rather slow of late. Ah well. Maybe she could come back another day. She skipped to keep up with Joelle's long stride. "What do you think Mr. Greene has to say?"

At Aurora's breathless tone, Joelle blinked and looked down at her. "Sorry, Pete." Slowing her pace, Joelle let Aurora catch up. "I've no idea, but he's not going to be happy that we came without Selah."

The girls' visit to Oxford today resulted from a very peculiar and cryptic telegraph they'd received three days ago from the family lawyer, requesting that they call on him at their earliest convenience, as he had some news of interest to the entire family that he wanted to impart in person.

Their older sister would normally have been the designated representative, but Selah had been feeling poorly, and Levi

Riggins, her husband of barely six weeks, balked at putting her on a train. Joelle, next in line, flatly refused to go anywhere without Schuyler Beaumont, to whom she had become affianced two weeks ago, and who followed her about like a lost puppy. However, his unchaperoned escort would be inappropriate until the two of them were actually married, so Aurora had volunteered to go along, braving the half-day trip by train from Tupelo to Oxford in hopes of luring Joelle into the mercantile for fittings.

A hollow victory, as it turned out. Since becoming a schoolmarm and an engaged woman (twice in one month, of all things, to two different men), Joelle had developed an alarming tendency toward stubbornness and keen observation. It was getting harder and harder for Aurora to coax her formerly absentminded sister to fall in with her excellent plans.

With a mixture of exasperation and affection, Aurora glanced up at Joelle's serene, flawless profile. During those long years of separation during the war, while Papa was away in the Confederate army, Aurora had resided in Memphis with her grandparents—for her own safety, they said. Meanwhile, Joelle and Selah had been permitted to stay with their mother at Ithaca Plantation. Oh, how she had longed for her sisters' company.

Now even she recognized the irony that their reunion for the purpose of holding on to the family property had resulted in both her sisters finding the love of a lifetime and ultimately going their own ways. Against all odds, at the advanced age of twenty-seven, Selah had married a Yankee-born Pinkerton detective, while Joelle had jilted the preacher and snared the heart of their longtime family friend and business partner.

Aurora didn't begrudge them their happiness, but when

the excitement of Joelle and Schuyler's wedding passed, she would be left alone. Again.

Well, so be it. She had always been capable of creating her own fun. She would just have to work for it a little harder than before. Grandmama or no Grandmama.

They quickly reached a store with big plate-glass windows, lettered J. A. SPENCER, FINE MUSICAL INSTRUMENTS AND PIANO TUNING. Schuyler had elected to pass the time with the large, friendly family of Justice of the Peace Spencer, while Aurora and Joelle went to the bridal shop. ("I assure you, Schuyler, you have no interest in this procedure," Aurora had informed him when he asked plaintively why he couldn't come along. "Your part is over, until you see Joelle coming down the aisle.") Now she braced herself for the inevitable saccharine outpouring that ensued whenever Schuyler and Joelle had been apart for more than ten minutes. It was enough to give one a toothache. Hopefully, the spooning would dissolve into the normal rhythms of their previous bantering relationship.

As she opened the door, Aurora was bombarded by a brassy wall of music, overlaid by a couple of flutes and clarinets, with percussion clunking along underneath. Following the cacophony to the back of the store, she found the community wind ensemble in its weekly rehearsal, conducted by Mr. Spencer himself. Schuyler, never one for sitting still when there was noise to be made or mischief afoot, had confiscated a bass drum and mallet and joined in. With little regard for tempo and less for dynamic sensitivity, he whaled away at the drum as if it had committed some heinous sin. Though he was clearly having a grand time, the second he saw Joelle, he dropped the mallet and went for her.

Rolling her eyes, Aurora waved at Mr. Spencer and headed for the stairs. Shortly she found herself at a second-floor landing in front of a brass doorplate etched with D. VAUGHAN GREENE, ESQ. When her knock was answered by a deep, firm "Enter, please," she turned the knob and pushed open the door.

"Mr. Greene?" She smiled at the genial, well-dressed gentleman who rose to greet her. "I'm Aurora Daughtry."

"Miss Daughtry! How nice to meet you." The lawyer covered a startled glance by hurrying to pull a chair out and indicating that she should sit. "I was, er, expecting Miss Selah—or rather, Mrs. Riggins. She has been the one to handle our business dealings in the past."

"Yes, I know." Aurora folded her hands in her lap and tucked her feet under her dress as her grandmother had taught her to do during the course of many agonizing deportment lessons. "Selah wasn't feeling up to traveling, so Joelle and I came in her stead. I assure you, I have both the intellect and the authority to deal with whatever information has come to light."

"Forgive the question, but have you reached your majority, Miss Aurora? Perhaps we should wait until Miss Joelle has joined us."

Aurora bit her lip. The poor man was staring at her in bemused embarrassment, as if he might offer her a box to sit upon. "Well, here's the thing. Joelle is extremely bright, of course, but she couldn't care less about money or legal obligations, and she'd go off into a brown study the minute she sat down. At the end we'd have to repeat for her everything that was said anyway. So it's best if you and I take care of things, then I can tell her what we decided."

Greene's florid face became even redder as he mopped a handkerchief across his high forehead. "My dear, I didn't mean to be insulting. It's just that you look so—"

"—young, I know," she finished with a grin. "I'm aware that I come in a small package, and the dimples are somewhat deceptive, but I am fully nineteen years old and quit playing with dolls some time ago. I have a letter from Selah, if it will make you feel better." She produced the document from her reticule and passed it to the lawyer across his desk.

He took it and cast a skeptical eye over Selah's neat script, his expression relaxing by a fraction. "I see." He cleared his throat and looked up at Aurora. "That is, I do apologize for my initial hesitation. You understand that I am bound to be very careful—"

"Never mind, Mr. Greene, I am completely unoffended. And as you can see, even Selah agrees that Joelle won't have much to contribute to the conversation—she's downstairs with the musical people, much more to her interest, I assure you—so let's you and I deal with whatever this mysterious business is, and I'll be, as they say, out of your—" She caught herself, noticing that Mr. Greene looked a bit glassy-eyed. Grandmama was forever telling her that she spouted more words in thirty seconds than most people used in a day. "Never mind. Please. Carry on."

Folding Selah's letter, the attorney nodded. "Very well. I'm happy to hear from your sister's hand that your business arrangement with Mr. Beaumont is about to be altered slightly by his marriage to Miss Joelle. I will consult with your grandfather to make sure the Daughtry interests are protected, particularly yours. With your two older sisters joining their thirds of the property to their husbands' holdings, I strongly advise that you continue to invest your share of the earnings so as to provide a stable income."

Aurora nodded, restraining herself from burbling further.

Greene rewarded her with an approving smile. "All right. With that said, let me come right out with it. I needed to inform you and your sisters of some property your father owned in town."

Aurora waited. When the lawyer sat back as if he had nothing further to add to that bald statement, she said, "Mr. Greene, my father has been dead for over two months. We thought he was dead long before that—in fact, the plantation came into our possession five years ago. Why is this just now coming to light?"

Greene removed his spectacles and polished the lenses vigorously with his handkerchief. "This property is somewhat different in nature than a plantation. It's more of a . . . business."

"A business? What kind of business?"

Greene mumbled something.

"Excuse me," Aurora said. "It sounded like you said 'saloon.'"

The glasses resumed their perch upon Mr. Greene's eagle nose. He sighed. "I did."

Aurora blinked. "Well, it's not a crime to own a saloon, though I understand why he wouldn't want my mother to know about it. But I can't say I'm surprised. Papa was a complex man, and everybody knows he liked both earning and spending money. What I *don't* understand is why the existence of this business has been kept from us, when we've been struggling with the debt on the plantation all these years. Presumably the saloon has been earning a profit, no?"

Evidently taken aback by her willingness—and perhaps her unladylike ability—to discuss commerce in such frank terms, Greene stared at her. "As a matter of fact, it was quite lucrative. But to keep you girls and your mother away from the somewhat shady nature of the Dogwood—"

"The Dogwood?" Aurora said. "That's the one across from the train station, the first thing you see when you come into town. No wonder it's lucrative."

"Yes. That's the one." The leather chair squeaked as Greene shifted. "Anyway, your father was a silent partner in a rather convoluted arrangement with Romulus Oglesby. Oglesby took complete ownership when your father died."

"Well, then why—"

"Let me finish, Miss Aurora. Perhaps you knew that Mr. Oglesby has recently passed to his reward?"

"I'm sorry to hear that, but I've spent most of my growing-up years in Memphis. This is the first I've heard of his existence."

"Fair enough," Greene said, "though I imagine the male members of your household would be conversant with his name. In any case, he died without issue, and as I represented him as well as your father in the terms of their partnership, it devolves to me to inform you that, according to Mr. Oglesby's last will and testament, you and your sisters are joint heirs to the Dogwood."

"So Selah and Joelle and I own a saloon." Aurora contemplated all the implications of that fact for a moment, then began to giggle. "Grandmama is going to have a hissy!"

Two

June 1, 1870
Memphis, Tennessee, Department of Justice

"I found this in the balcony of the courthouse." Zane tossed the spur he'd brought all the way from Tuscaloosa onto the massive seaman's desk in front of him.

As Lucien Eaton, US Marshal of the Western District of Tennessee, picked up the spur, Zane took the opportunity to study his new boss. A handsome, dignified man some ten years Zane's senior, Eaton possessed an impressive résumé which included a degree from Dartmouth and promotion to the rank of colonel under Sherman.

Zane admitted cautious respect for the marshal, but if Eaton balked at assigning him to the Jefcoat trial, the US Marshals Service was going to lose one of their most experienced guards and trackers. Nobody was going to keep him from finding the owner of that spur.

"Let me see that, Eaton."

Zane had almost forgotten the third man in the room,

Pinkerton agent Levi Riggins, who had recently brought in the high-profile murderers of Schuyler's father, Alabama gubernatorial candidate Ezekiel Beaumont. Spread thin due to lack of congressional funding, the Marshals Service often contracted detectives like Riggins for specific operations.

"I was in the courthouse the day of Judge Teague's murder," Riggins said, examining the spur, which Zane could have described in his sleep. It was constructed in a one-piece Texas style with straight shanks, a star-shaped rowel, and a round pin cover. "I heard the shot, but in the commotion I didn't see the judge die—I was trying to get one of my witnesses out before he got hit too." Riggins glanced at Zane as he handed the spur back to Eaton. "What makes you think this thing is connected to the murder?"

"I know who left it there." Zane hadn't been invited to sit, which was just as well. The images that clogged his brain since he'd visited that courtroom—blood staining the wall behind the judge's bench, splintered railings around the witness stand, Teague's gavel fallen to the floor—

He didn't think he could have remained in a chair.

"Someone connected to our case, I assume," Eaton said when Zane didn't elaborate.

"Yes, sir." Zane's habit of addressing authority with respect had been well-ingrained by five years of military service, followed by five more of training with the judge. "It's kind of a long story."

"You in a hurry?" The marshal raised an eyebrow at Riggins.

"Not any more than usual," Riggins said with a grin. "Give us the condensed version, Sager. I'll get the details during the trip down to Tupelo."

Zane nodded. "I came by that spur and its mate after the battle at Moscow, Tennessee. Trophy from a dead Rebel. It's valuable because of the Boone family marking on the heelband, but the mounting I added is what makes it unique."

"You rode for the Pony, didn't you, Sager?" Eaton tapped the famous Pony Express emblem on the pin cover.

Zane wasn't surprised that Eaton had investigated his background. But he hadn't been that wild-eyed, horse-crazy kid in a long time. "Yes, sir. Believe it or not, Theo Redding did that mounting for me. We were in the same Provost Guard unit." Though his fellow deputy now served the Marshals Service in Mississippi, they'd ridden together for a long time. "Anyway, I wore those spurs until I was taken prisoner in Mississippi in the summer of '64 and the Rebs sent me to Cahaba."

"The prison in Alabama?" When Zane nodded, Riggins gave him a straight look. "Is that where you lost the eye?"

"Yes." Zane resisted the urge to adjust the patch over his mangled face. No hiding the obvious. "I'd given the spurs to a Rebel guard who was kind to me on the march. By the time I got to Cahaba, Sherman had cut off prisoner exchanges. Rations and medical supplies were all but nonexistent, and the Rebs were just plain vicious. The second-in-command was a sadist named Sam Jones. One day in mid-October, I saw him strutting around, wearing my spurs. To this day I don't know how he got them, but as you can see, they're unmistakable."

Eaton gave Zane a sardonic smile. "I take it you asked Jones to give them back."

"Yes, sir, I did." This time Zane touched the patch over his eye. "Turned out he had a knife."

Eaton returned the spur to Zane. "So let's say Jones was in the Tuscaloosa courthouse at some point. That doesn't mean he pulled the trigger on the judge."

"Except he had good reason to hate Judge Teague." Zane spun the rowel on the spur. "And me. Not only was Cahaba a lice- and rat-infested swamp, it was a cesspool of brutality and corruption, led by Jones. Teague got the muggers and thieves under control and formed a prisoner police court. He served as judge and appointed me a sheriff of sorts. Jones lost a lot of income because of that court."

"I spoke with the judge on the morning of that trial." Riggins sounded surprised. "I didn't know he'd been at Cahaba."

"It's not something you bring up in conversation," Zane said.

Eaton stroked his impressive mustache. "But why wait five years to go after the judge?"

Zane hesitated. "Sir, I know you don't have much reason to trust my word. Not yet, anyway. But this wasn't the first time Jones tried to kill Teague. I just can't prove it. I guarded the judge the best I could for five years—as much as he would allow. Then he sent me to DC to testify before a congressional committee investigating the Crédit Mobilier scheme."

The judge's theory had been that the assignment would increase Zane's standing within the new Department of Justice, maybe even result in a promotion. Because Judge Teague had saved Zane's life on two different occasions, he'd quit arguing and got on the train.

But he hadn't been happy about it.

Turned out his gut was right, as usual. While Zane was in DC, the judge had been shot through the head while presiding over a race-riot hearing in Tuscaloosa, Alabama. Under normal circumstances, Zane would have been there to ensure Teague's security. All he could do now was bring the killer to justice.

Zane clenched the spur hard enough to bruise his palm and gritted out, "While I was in DC, Jones had the opportunity he was waiting for."

Eaton looked thoughtful, but he clearly wasn't a man to jump to conclusions.

Zane had to respect that. But as time slipped away, so did his chances of capturing Jones. "Marshal, I have a suggestion. This is the first tangible lead we've had in this case since Riggins brought in Jefcoat and Moore. Jefcoat has indicated he's open to turning on his accomplices, so what if you assign me to escort the two of them down to Tupelo for the trial? Use me as bait. I'll make it known that I have evidence leading to the identity of the judge's killer. Maybe we can lure Jones out."

Riggins released a whistle through his teeth. "That's not a bad idea, Marshal. We'll need witness protection down there too. Might as well be somebody familiar with the case."

The marshal studied Zane for a moment, then nodded. "Solid plan. Make a list of everyone who needs to be interviewed. We've got two murders, a kidnapping, and at least two other attempted murders, not to mention arson and vandalism. I want results for Congress's investment, otherwise we'll never get another dime out of them."

"Yes, sir. I want Jones. Bad." Zane hesitated. "There's a lot about this case I'm not familiar with. I assume I'll be briefed."

Eaton nodded. "To protect the witnesses and the judge, the Attorney General has decided to hold the trials in Tupelo instead of Oxford. That's why Riggins is here. He's got family in the Tupelo area and is already familiar with the particulars. He'll catch you up as you travel." Eaton stood, ending the meeting. "I don't have to tell you this is a high-profile case, Sager."

"Yes, sir. I know it is." Zane shook hands with both Eaton and Riggins. "Got a few things to tie up, Riggins, so I'll meet you at the jail in the morning to collect the prisoners. I suggest we take the first train out."

Riggins nodded. "Of course."

Zane was already at the door when Eaton stopped him. "Wait, Sager."

Zane turned. "Yes, sir?"

Eaton's expression was grim. "If this man Jones is hunting you, you'd best double your guard. I can't afford to lose you."

Zane chuckled. Nice to know he was valuable. "Yes, sir. I'm pretty attached to my own hide. I'll be careful."

Three

June 3, 1870
Tupelo, Mississippi

"Aurora, I'm sorry, honey, but that is no boardinghouse."

Aurora stood arm in arm with Selah on the overgrown muddy path leading to the Dogwood Saloon, preparing to walk through their new property. She had to agree. Calling this place a boardinghouse would be equivalent to tying a ribbon on a pig's tail.

"Oh, Papa," she sighed. "As if our reputation in this town wasn't bad enough already, let's add a saloon to the mix." She studied the huge wooden sign over the front door. The dogwood branches painted in each corner over a blue background had flaked off over the years until the flowers looked like dirty snowflakes surrounding that offensive word. *Saloon. S-A-L-O-O-N.* Even spelling it didn't take away the sordid sound of the word in her head. "Let's start by taking down the sign. I'll get Nathan to make us a new one, and Charmion can paint it."

"I suppose." Selah looked doubtful. "I still think we should sell it. We've already got enough debt sunk in the hotel."

"Selah Daughtry—I mean, Riggins!" She still hadn't gotten used to her eldest sister's married name. "You were the one who had the grit and persistence to get Daughtry House off the ground—over the objections of Grandmama and Grandpapa and everybody else you knew. Are you going to let a little problem like money scare you away from this gift that has fallen into our laps?"

Selah shrugged, and Aurora studied her. Come to think of it, she looked a little pale, though she claimed to be feeling better than the other day when she'd declined to travel to Oxford. Still, Aurora wasn't so sure Selah had truly been up to the bumpy wagon ride into town.

"It's not just the money," Selah finally said. "It's spreading our little staff even thinner. Honey, this place is going to take a lot of work to even make it livable, let alone fit for the public."

Aurora bit her lip. Yes, the porch sagged in the middle. For certain, several of the boarded-up windows were cracked and needed to be replaced. All right, and the scabby-looking roof probably leaked.

And that was just the outside. They hadn't yet even set foot inside the front door—which was shut tight behind the traditional swinging doors of a saloon. Maybe it had been profitable at one time, but clearly Mr. Oglesby's death had led to a steep decline.

Aurora stepped away from Selah and fisted her hands at her hips. "I'm not afraid of hard work. But if you and Joelle don't want to get involved, feel free to sign the whole thing over to me, and I'll take on the debt and the renovations. I'm sure I can sweet-talk Schuyler into backing me. And we don't need to use the Daughtry House staff. There are still plenty of folks out in Shake Rag who need work."

Shake Rag was the little community out near the tupelo gum swamps, where most of the freed slaves had migrated after the war. A lot of them had originated at Ithaca Plantation—now Daughtry House—and had returned to work for the Daughtry sisters at a decent salary. But there were many more still subsisting off laundry work and other menial jobs. The rest simply starving.

And why? Because white people wouldn't hire them. Aurora was aware that she was thinking the unthinkable. That her family made everyone else in their community uncomfortable in their guilt or outrage or whatever made them so certain of their superiority over a large chunk of the human race.

During the last three months, Aurora had seen Selah and Joelle suffer abuse and laughter from people who had known them all their lives. She had watched in horror as their kitchen, schoolroom, and blacksmith shop burned to the ground. Even Grandmama allowed that Christian people shouldn't behave with such meanness and spite.

Aurora wouldn't have said her liberal outlook happened overnight, because she'd long been aware of the effects of her sisters' education. Of course she loved them and would have forgiven all sorts of unorthodox and eccentric notions. But the night Aurora cut Joelle's beautiful curly strawberry-blonde hair, after chunks of it had been singed off when she went into Charmion's burning house to rescue her friend, something had shifted in her heart and soul. That kind of courage was beautiful and worth imitating.

Selah just stared at her, dark-brown eyes narrowed. "You

are bored, aren't you?" She sighed. "All right. Let's go inside and see what you have to work with." She hooked arms with Aurora once more and tugged her toward the porch, brambles catching at their skirts as they walked. "Admittedly, Daughtry House was a mess before Levi got hold of it."

Aurora would have said that the project of turning their family's ancestral home into a resort hotel had taken all of them working together, but Selah thought her husband walked on water, so she simply nodded. "Did you know Mr. Oglesby? Papa's partner?"

"Not well. Mama didn't approve of taverns in general, you know, and our trips to town with her were limited to the mercantile and bookstore. But Papa would always speak to Mr. Oglesby on the street, and one time when we met at Whitmore's, he bought us each a lemon drop. You were probably little more than a baby at the time."

Aurora shook her head. "I don't remember. So odd that Papa could maintain a business arrangement like that without anyone knowing."

Selah sighed. "Papa had lots of secrets. Mama adored him, but I don't think she really knew him."

"How well do you think you know Levi?" Aurora's conversations with her brother-in-law had been necessarily limited by the demands of his profession, which of late entailed a good bit of travel and withholding sensitive information. She couldn't help wondering what that meant for a healthy marriage. After all, Selah and Levi had only met in late February. Their courtship had been short and intense, followed by a quiet family wedding and a working honeymoon in New Orleans.

"I suppose I know him as well as any new bride knows

her busy husband," Selah said with a smile. "We have lots of years ahead to get better acquainted, and we both have deep faith in God to build on. That's what you look for, Petey." She squeezed Aurora's arm with affection as they climbed the warped porch steps together. "Find a man who serves Christ first. Then his love for you will fall rightly."

Aurora tucked that advice away to think about later. How would she know if any man really served Christ? Except for Levi, she didn't know any men who mentioned or referenced God in run-of-the-mill circumstances. Judging by Joelle's miserable first engagement to the pastor of their church, those who incessantly talked in spiritual terms couldn't be trusted to walk them out in practice. Even their grandfather, the kindest man of her acquaintance, never directly quoted the Bible, except in prayer over the meal.

"It will be a long time before I find someone like that," Aurora said with rare seriousness. "You and Joelle are very lucky." Taking a breath, she reached into her reticule for the key Mr. Greene had given her. "In the meantime, let's go on a little adventure, you and me. Just think! Two ladies walking into a saloon . . ."

Selah's laughter cheered her, and by the time she'd inserted the key into the lock of the ugly, unpainted old door, Aurora was regaining her usual optimism. And curiosity. What would they find? The saloon had been closed since Romulus Oglesby died nearly three weeks ago. She hoped there wouldn't be rats or other vermin—

Suddenly the door opened inward with a loud squeal of hinges, dragging across the floor in jerky spasms. A pale, blowsy face, curly blonde hair spiraling around it from beneath a lace nightcap, appeared in the opening. Red-rimmed green eyes squinted at the sudden sunlight, and a small freckled nose wrinkled in clear dismay at the sight of visitors. "Sorry, ma'am. Didn't realize we were so loud. Quiet as a mouse we'll be." The door started to close again.

"Wait!" Aurora put her hand against the door. "What do you mean? Who are you?"

The green eyes looked confused. "Rosie was playing the piano. Mrs. Whitmore complains all the time."

Aurora looked at Selah. "Did you hear a piano?" When Selah shook her head, Aurora turned back to the young woman in the doorway. Well, maybe she wasn't young. It was hard to tell in the murky dimness of the saloon interior. "We were talking and didn't notice. I'm Aurora Daughtry, and this is my sister Selah. Could we come in, please?"

"I don't think that's a good—"

"Look, miss." Aurora sought for patience, surprised that Selah hadn't taken charge as she usually did. "We have just inherited the—the—boardinghouse. Saloon. We need to come inside and inspect it. We weren't expecting anyone to be here."

That earned her a blank stare. Then a grin curled the woman's full lips. Amusement lit her round face and turned it into that of a girl of maybe sixteen. "Oh, that's—that's— tell him he got me this time!" She doubled over in laughter. "I fell for it, sure as my name's Bedelia O'Malley!"

"Tell who?" Aurora demanded, but the blonde woman just kept giggling.

Selah nudged Aurora aside. "Young lady, we have no idea what you're talking about, but I assure you this is no joke. Here's the deed, and here are our names. Are you Mr. Oglesby's . . . daughter? Granddaughter? If he left you out of his will and there's been some mistake, we'll sort it all—"

"G'way outa that!" Bedelia exclaimed, flinging the door wide to snatch the deed from Selah's hand. "Selah Daughtry, Joelle Daughtry, Aurora Daughtry . . ." She looked Aurora up and down with great suspicion. "Where's the third one? Joelle?"

Of all the questions to ask, that one seemed the least pertinent.

"She's at the bookstore," Aurora said. "Could we please come inside? If Mrs. Whitmore happens to come along, our business will be all over town in five minutes flat."

Bedelia seemed to comprehend the common sense of that observation, for she stepped back. "All right, ladies. But don't say I didn't warn ya. Careful of the swingin' doors on the way in, they'll whack ya in the bum."

Safely inside the saloon with her bum intact, Aurora looked around. The common room was lit by oil lamps in sconces along the back wall. To the left she found the bar and its wooden stools, made of thick, dark mahogany the same color as Selah's hair, squaring off a wall stocked with an array of colorful bottles. Tables and chairs, shoved into awkward arrangements, took up the space opposite. Above an upright piano on the other side of the room rose a giant lurid painting of a woman emerging from a bathtub, bubbles strewn strategically over her curvaceous body. Aurora stared at it. What imagination it must take to create a work of such stunning, hideous improbability.

Selah cleared her throat. "Well, isn't this nice?"

Aurora found her sister regarding her with a mixture of disapproval and amusement. Cheeks stinging, she lifted her chin. "What did you expect from a men's establishment? No wonder Mrs. Whitmore has been trying to shut it down."

"That woman is a menace to society." Bedelia flounced toward the stairs, which presumably led to living quarters on the second floor. "Sit down, Rosie, it's not the gorgon. It's our new landlords—ladies, I mean." She giggled at her own joke.

For the first time Aurora noticed another young woman in the room. Dressed in a green-striped dressing gown, she stood on the bottom step looking like she might bolt up the stairs at the least provocation. As dark as Bedelia was fair, with long black hair streaming loose over her slight shoulders and Asian features as delicate as jasmine petals, she offered a shy smile and whispered, "Good morning."

"Well, good morning!" Aurora said brightly as Bedelia tugged Rosie down to sit on the stairs. Squatting rights, undoubtedly. "My name is Aurora, and this is Selah."

"Daughtry," Bedelia clarified for Rosie's benefit. "There's another one named Joelle at the bookstore." She made a face, as if bookish people weren't to be trusted. "Ain't you the ones had the party for General Forrest and the opera star a couple weeks ago? Out on the plantation?"

"That's right," Aurora said. She summoned the manners her grandmother had smacked into her with a ruler on the back of the knuckles. Bedelia and Rosie had been living here, even after Mr. Oglesby's death. Which meant there were at least two women currently out of work. Whatever that had been. Aurora glanced at the painting. "We don't mean to keep you from your . . . music rehearsals. We only came by to look the place over before we make renovation plans—"

"Renovations?" Bedelia straightened, wide-eyed, her mouth a pink O of exaggerated outrage. "This is our home! You can't just come in and—and—renovate it!" She put a protective arm around Rosie, who looked confused and frightened.

"Actually, we can," Selah said in her no-nonsense manner. "You saw the deed. We are the owners. But since we had no idea you ladies existed until five minutes ago, I can understand why you might be taken aback by our sudden appearance. It seems Mr. Oglesby didn't inform you of his intentions before he, um, went to his reward."

Bedelia made a rude noise. "The only reward old Rom earned was a permanent voyage on the lake of fire. I was never in my life so glad to hear of somebody cashing it in."

Aurora exchanged glances with Selah, who had pressed her lips together. Personally, Aurora hadn't had such an entertaining morning since she and Grandmama arrived at Ithaca to find Joelle, dressed in boy's clothes, carting a giant beehive from the cupola out to the woods. "Miss O'Malley—may I call you Bedelia?—I admire your forthrightness. Could Selah and I sit down and discuss our plans with you? I think we can come to some sort of agreement here that will not involve casting you and Rosie out on the street."

Bedelia gave her a shrewd stare from narrowed green eyes. "You can call me whatever ya want, and Rosie and me be willin' to listen, sure we are. Make yourself at home," she added with a magnanimous nod at Selah.

Clearly repressing a smile, Selah dragged over two chairs, then sat in one while Aurora took the other.

"Now," Selah said, folding her hands in her lap, "since this is Aurora's baby, so to speak, I'll let her carry on from here."

Aurora's mouth fell open at this sudden transfer of leadership. Recovering, she cleared her throat. "All right, then. What I—we, that is—have in mind is a boardinghouse for war widows. Women who find themselves without a safe place to live, but who have a little income to live independently." She'd actually thought this out. What if ThomasAnne had not had family to move in with? She could not have survived the privations of growing older without a husband to support her. And goodness knew it was too late for her to attract a mate now.

Bedelia shook her head. "What respectable lady is going to come live in a place like this? We're directly across the way from the train station, and there be noise up and down the street at all hours." Her extravagant eyebrows lifted. "I assume you do mean respectable women?"

"Obviously," Aurora said. "Which means you and Rosie will have to be respectable too. No men allowed. Well, except for the ones working on repainting and whatnot." She looked around. It was going to take a lot of repainting, beginning with that awful thing over the piano. Charmion was going to enjoy covering that huge canvas with something pretty. Perhaps some flowers.

"No men?" Bedelia was looking as if Aurora had just announced that there would be no more breathing. "What d'ya think Rosie and me do?"

Aurora felt the blood climb into her cheeks but refused to look at Selah for rescue. She was a grown-up now, mistress of a new business establishment. But she was *not* a madam. "It does not matter what you did in the past," she said. "If you don't need a job, fine—there's the door. But if you want to stay here, what we need is an upstairs maid, a cook, and a serving woman for the dining room. If the business grows, perhaps we'll have other positions open. But that's what I'm starting with."

"I will be the cook," Rosie said unexpectedly.

Bedelia snorted. "You don't know how to cook."

"I always wanted to learn." Rosie's soft voice was defiant. "My parents own a grocery store in Canton."

"China?" Ignoring the blonde's skepticism, Aurora addressed the Asian girl with interest.

"Mississippi," Rosie clarified. "They settled there after the railroad was completed, and I was born there." A little smile curled the corner of her small mouth. "But we are of Chinese descent."

Aurora beamed at her. "Of course you can learn to cook. I'll send you out to Daughtry House to study with Horatia. She's the best in the South!"

"That's fine for you, Rosebud," Bedelia said, "but I'm not inclined to be learning a new trade at my age." She reached out to put a hand on Selah's knee. "You don't look too good, mistress. When's the babe due?"

Aurora laughed. As non sequiturs went, that one was a doozy. "There's no babe—"

"Probably next February," Selah said wearily. "I wasn't sure, so I haven't said anything." She rounded on Aurora. "So don't you either! I haven't even told Levi yet."

Aurora wiped the shock off her face. "All right." She gave Bedelia a respectful look. "How on earth did you know that?"

Bedelia shrugged. "Long story. None o' your business, come to that."

Hurt by the rebuff, Aurora stiffened. "Fair enough. I'll look forward to hearing that story as our acquaintance goes forward. Well!" She clasped her hands. "Selah, perhaps we should give Bedelia and Rosie a chance to straighten a bit before we complete our inspection. Meantime"—she leveled her best Grandmama stare on the Irishwoman—"you'll have two days to make up your mind whether you wish to take advantage of our offer." Bouncing to her feet, she extended her hand to Selah. "We'd best go. Joelle will be wondering what's happened to us."

"No, she won't," Selah said with a grin, ignoring Aurora's offer of assistance. "She'll be happy as a goat in clover, curled up in some window seat in the bookstore. It's been a pleasure to meet you, Bedelia. Rosie." Dipping a curtsey to each young woman, she returned the chairs to their table and accompanied Aurora to the door.

Out on the porch with the door shut and locked behind them, Aurora stared at Selah. "Are you really going to have a baby?"

Selah cupped her hands over her flat stomach. "I'm not sure. Probably so. I certainly don't feel right. I'm going to wait another couple of weeks to see if . . . nature takes its course. Then I might ask Dr. Kidd to take a look at me."

Aurora felt bizarrely proud to be in on such a momentous secret. "All right." She pursed her lips. "Did we just take on two fancy women along with a saloon?"

"I believe we did." Laughing, Selah took Aurora's arm and tugged her down the steps. "The Lord certainly works in mysterious ways, doesn't he?"

Four

THE HOURS ON THE TRAIN from Memphis gave Zane plenty of time to ascertain details of the case from Riggins, as well as a bit about the Daughtry family. But he waited until the two prisoners, Jefcoat and Moore, had both dozed off before he addressed the Pinkerton agent.

"It would help," Zane began, "if I knew exactly what we're involved in. I've told you why I'm after Jones in particular. But if he's connected to Beaumont's murder, as well as the riots in Tuscaloosa and atrocities in Tupelo—well, there's more going on here than Eaton indicated."

Riggins shrugged. "It's no secret President Grant is set on bringing violence in the South under control. It's why he pushed for the Enforcement Act and appointed Amos Akerman as Attorney General."

"I'd heard that," Zane said, "but I'm not familiar with Akerman."

"He's a good man," Riggins said, "in favor of protecting Negro voting rights. He's convinced these Mississippi church burnings, newspaper vandalisms, intimidation, and murders are connected to similar events all over the southeast, so the President commissioned him to identify the leadership of those rings and bring them down. Akerman is friends with Pinkerton and brought him in to help, which is how I got involved."

"Marshal Eaton says you managed to infiltrate the Mississippi Klan." Zane gave Riggins a skeptical look. "Passing yourself off during the war as a butternut soldier while on a flash raid through the state with Grierson was one thing. But this investigation seems to have taken several months. I have trouble believing they'd accept a stranger with a Northern accent as one of them."

Riggins responded with a grim smile. "Schuyler Beaumont volunteered to be our spy."

"Beaumont?" Zane couldn't control his surprise. "Related to Ezekiel—the one who was murdered in the Tuscaloosa riot?"

Riggins nodded. "His youngest son, engaged now to my wife's sister. You'll meet him when we get there. After his father was murdered, Schuyler agreed to use his somewhat wild—and, I might add, well-deserved—reputation to become a member of the local Klan organization. That stratagem resulted in these indictments in Tupelo. The Klan isn't happy about it, obviously, which is why we're preparing for all-out war." He paused. "I hope it won't come to that."

Zane nodded. "Since the trial's in Tupelo, who's the presiding federal judge?" He was familiar with the Alabama and Tennessee departments of justice, but Mississippi was new territory.

"Robert Hill will be coming over from Oxford. He's experienced and moderate, from what I hear. Prosecutor will be US Attorney Wiley Wells."

"And the defense?"

"Headed by Alonzo Maney, a lawyer from Tennessee. Ironically, it's common knowledge that Maney is a Klan muckety-muck of some sort, if not a Grand Titan. During the course of the investigation, his name has surfaced over and over."

"Maney?" Zane shook his head. "Sounds familiar."

"It should," Riggins said. "Maney was a Confederate general, and intel indicates he's been a guest at the Forrest plantation in Memphis on multiple occasions."

"Confederate General Nathan B. Forrest, I assume—the one they called the 'Wizard of the Saddle.'"

"The very same." Riggins flipped notebook pages backward. "Forrest and his wife were staying at Daughtry House when the kitchen and blacksmith shop burned. He was probably directing events, though we can't prove it yet."

"Hmm. Interesting. I meant, the reason Maney's name sounds familiar is because he's named in the money-laundering scheme I investigated for Congress."

"Exactly. Maney seems to have gotten suspiciously rich during his stint in the House. They're building quite a case, though it may be a while before they can bring him up on charges. Documents surfaced in the hands of former employees of the Maney family—an interracial couple who were the governess and tutor of the Maney children. Schuyler's father wound up with those documents, and they could be a motive for his murder"—Riggins glanced over at the sleeping Jefcoat—"despite the fact that Jefcoat claims to have hit him by accident."

Zane felt as if he'd just tried to drink from a waterfall. It occurred to him that if Sam Jones was involved in this web of criminals, he had gotten himself into more than he could handle alone. Even so, he set himself to memorize what Riggins had just told him. Every detail would add up, he was sure.

He just had to stay alert and focused.

Two hours later, the train pulled into the Tupelo station, and Zane angrily folded the copy of the Jackson *Weekly Clarion* that he'd picked up to read after Riggins finished with it. He stuffed the small, fat square into the inside pocket of his coat. He would burn it if he could. The last paragraph would remain imprinted on his brain for the rest of his life, one of the drawbacks of having a memory with total recall.

Men have been dragged from their homes without knowledge of the cause of their arrest, at the suggestion of malicious and procured perjurers. Many a farm is uncultivated, many a wretched wife is in rags, and many a helpless child has suffered intolerable pangs of hunger because those remorseless villains and adventurers sent down by Grant to ravage and destroy would secure rewards for convictions to be effected by Negro perjury.

Remorseless villain. Adventurer. Indicated the sort of welcome he could expect.

He glanced at Riggins, who was already gathering his belongings. The fellow actually looked eager to be arriving in this hornet's nest of rebel extremism. Well, no wonder—he'd married a Southern belle and planned to stay. On the day Zane brought the judge's killer to justice, he would shake the dust from his boots and return to the tranquility and isolation of the Western prairie. Nothing but horses, cattle, and grass, with maybe a few Indians to add interest to the landscape.

Getting up to check the prisoners' manacles, he smiled at Jefcoat's grunt of discomfort. "You did this to yourself, partner," he reminded the hulking, bearded young man. The son of a Mississippi dirt farmer, Jefcoat had once caroused all over Oxford and Memphis with the son of the man he was charged with killing. According to Riggins, the influence of older members of the Ku Klux Klan had sent Jefcoat down the road to destruction. By his own admission, in the middle of a riot Jefcoat had been aiming his gun at a successful Negro politician. He'd shot white rail baron Ezekiel Beaumont by accident.

Manslaughter? Zane doubted it. There was arrogance and bitterness in the small eyes regarding Zane so resentfully.

"Where we gon' stay?" asked the fourth member of their little travel group. Harold Moore had the distinction of being Jefcoat's accomplice, although there was clearly no love lost between the two. A light-skinned black man a few years older than Jefcoat, Moore had grown up in slavery to the Jefcoat family, and rumor had it the two were half brothers.

Riggins paused in the act of checking his revolver. "Jail," he said laconically before sliding the gun into the holster under his armpit.

Moore's dark eyes widened. "They gon' be after me, sir." His gaze cut to Jefcoat. "Him too. They don't tolerate nobody talking against 'em."

"'They' who?" Zane spoke over the squeal of brakes and huff of steam as the train ground to a halt.

"You know who." Lurching to his feet, Jefcoat scowled at Moore. "We're not saying anything else until we're under oath. And protected by a judge."

"Thanks to your friends, even a judge isn't safe in these parts," Zane said. "Come on, Moore, you'll have a bed and three squares a day. That's a pretty good deal for an accused murderer." He took the Negro by the arm and walked him toward the car's open door, leaving Riggins to deal with Jefcoat.

Leaving the train station, they walked down Front Street along the railroad tracks, passing a couple of saloons, a hotel, and a boardinghouse. As they filed through an alleyway into the town square, the prisoners' chains jangling with every step, the four of them received quite a few stares from curious Tupelo citizens. The courthouse, a two-story clapboard building with a small cupola and adjacent jail, seemed to be in the center of a business district. Across the street to the west, Zane noted a bank and a boot maker's shop, with a row of other small shops behind him to the south. Levi had told him the town had only recently incorporated as the new seat of Lee County, though it had existed as a community since before the war and already had a slightly tired look created by flaking paint and warped boards.

During the first four years after the war, Zane had gotten used to the relative bustle of Montgomery, Alabama, where he'd assisted Judge Teague in his role as a deputy marshal. Serving warrants, escorting prisoners and witnesses, keeping track of court expenses, and a host of other daily minutiae of the federal court system had kept him engaged in the life of a Southern capital—and simultaneously given him little time to dwell upon his personal isolation. With some misgiving, he'd made the move to Memphis in February, subjecting himself to the exacting supervision of US Marshal Eaton. Even so, Zane had to admit that the intellectual stimulation and greater physical demands of the new Justice Department had been good for him.

Now, for an unspecified length of time, he must adjust once more to the status of an outsider in a small town. Still, he supposed he had endured worse.

"You hungry?" Riggins asked as they passed the Gum Pond Hotel. "Once we get these fellows situated at the jail, we could eat before we head out to Daughtry House."

Zane shrugged. "I can wait."

"Good." Riggins grinned. "I confess I'm anxious to see my wife."

Zane couldn't help a pang of envy. It had been so long since anybody missed him when he was gone, he couldn't even remember who that would have been. "How long have you been away?" He wasn't good at making conversation, but Riggins was easy to talk to. Undemanding, friendly, considerate—probably why he was a successful agent.

"Nearly a week. Selah wasn't feeling well when I left."

"You been married long?"

"Since April 22nd—just long enough to really miss her when we're apart. We met in late February." Riggins glanced his way. "Remember that train wreck outside Oxford that was in the papers?"

Zane whistled through his teeth. "A lot of people died in that wreck."

"Yes. I believe God protected us and brought us together. I was on a case related to this one. Selah's father—" Riggins shook his head. "He blew up the trestle of that bridge. I'm pretty sure he was working for somebody else, but he died before I could get to the bottom of it."

Zane jerked to a stop, causing Moore to stumble against him. "Your wife's own father nearly killed her?"

Riggins paused, eyes somber. "Jonathan Daughtry wasn't right. Had some kind of brain injury, and he'd been held in Douglas Prison for a couple of years for war crimes. And in his defense, he didn't know Selah was on the train."

Zane slowly started walking again. "I know something about being a prisoner of war. What makes you think he had a partner?"

Riggins glanced at Jefcoat, who was walking along in stolid silence. "This is all common knowledge, so there's no harm in talking about it. A man named Scully—wartime friend of Daughtry—followed him here and got caught in the trap we'd laid. He's in Oxford, awaiting trial there."

"You said Daughtry's and Scully's crimes connect to the murders and burnings here. How so?"

"Scully came all the way from Oxford to warn Daughtry he had been traced, and to talk him out of continuing to hunt down Union sympathizers who pillaged their commanding officer's plantation during the Chattanooga campaign. I dug around for information about that inciting incident, and it turns out Scully and Daughtry were under the command of General Alonzo Maney."

"Maney? The man had a finger in everything!"

"Seems so." Riggins spread his hands. "But unfortunately, Daughtry didn't live long enough to tell me much about him—and his testimony would have been unreliable anyway. He was about as close to madness as a man can get without falling over the edge." He released a long, sad breath. "That was a bad business, Sager. Daughtry literally hunted me, thinking he was back in a battle zone, tracking a Union spy. Well, I *was* Union, but you know what I mean. The old man was living in a terrible past. He'd hidden in the Daughtry House attic, there was a scuffle over my gun, and he—" Riggins's deep voice broke—"he fell from the cupola window. My wife saw it happen. Nearly ended our relationship, as you can imagine. But God . . ." His steps slowed as he shook his head in a wondering fashion. "I have to believe God intervened. There's no logical reason that woman would have forgiven me, let alone married me."

"I'll take your word for it," Zane said dryly. He believed in God. But figuring out which events the sovereign Lord of the universe chose to get himself involved in seemed far above his ability to comprehend. "I'm looking forward to meeting Mrs. Riggins."

"You'll like her." Looking more cheerful, Riggins picked up his pace and they soon arrived at the jail.

Inside, a constable with a mustache bigger than his face sat behind a desk, gnawing a chicken bone. "Riggins," the constable said, wiping his mouth on his shirtsleeve, "you're back."

"I see your powers of observation are as keen as ever, Pickett." Riggins tipped his head toward Zane. "This is US Deputy Marshal Sager. We brought two witnesses from Memphis who need to be supervised for the next few days."

Pickett reluctantly put down the chicken leg. "We're mighty short-staffed right now. The sheriff's out on a family emergency."

Zane noted the three empty cells behind the desk. "Do you feel these two are beyond your ability to control?"

"'Course not," the constable blustered. "What're they in for?"

"I'm not at liberty to say." Zane led Moore to the far right cell. "Where's the key?"

"Over there." Pickett abandoned his supper with a sigh and got up to retrieve a set of keys hanging on a wall hook. While he locked Moore's cell, Riggins installed Jefcoat at the opposite end of the row.

Zane rattled both doors to check the locks, then turned to study Pickett. Muddy eyes. Lazy. Probably incompetent. He turned to Riggins. "I'm staying here tonight."

Riggins didn't answer for a moment, then nodded reluctantly. "I was going to put you up at Daughtry House, but if you want to stay, you should at least go to the hotel for a meal first. I'll sit with them—"

"I'm not hungry," Zane said. "But if you could go back to the train station and have somebody send my gear here, I'd appreciate it."

Riggins eyed him. "Certainly. I'll have to go to the livery for my horse anyway."

As Riggins left and Pickett returned to his meal, Zane spotted a ladderback chair over near the cells. He sat down and tipped the back against the wall. Composing himself for one of the long stretches of boredom that had checkered his life, he dug in his coat pocket for his Pony Express Bible. Back in his days as a rider, when he'd been an adventurous young kid, he'd mainly used the Bible as a code book for leaving his sister messages they didn't want their drunken father to read.

Now he took it in daily as the bread of life.

"I told you I could handle these fellows," Pickett said.

Zane didn't even look up. "I got nothing better to do." Nothing but sleep on a bed in a luxury hotel. Eat a meal that wasn't canned beans and salt pork. Engage in conversation with the pretty Daughtry women.

He focused on the fat little Bible open in the palm of his hand. Reading was a struggle, but this was worth the trouble. One of the many valuable things Judge Teague had taught him.

His gaze drifted to his prisoners. There might be a little fear behind Jefcoat's angry, discontented expression.

Zane hardened himself. Jefcoat was going to testify, if it was the last thing either of them did.

Five

Daughtry House

Aurora walked around the dining table with her mother's crystal tea pitcher, filling goblets, catching snatches of conversation as she went. She didn't have to serve, but it reminded her of her mother's gracious way of making people feel at home in *her* home. Mama would have loved seeing her daughters presiding over a lovely table set with the best china and silver, fine linen cloths tucked into each lap.

"The influenza is crawling all over Ackerman, and I'm afraid it's headed here next," Doc was telling Cousin Thomas-Anne, who listened with her wispy reddish-brown head atilt, blue eyes bright with interest.

Ew. Disease and birthings—that was all those two talked about anymore. ThomasAnne had become Dr. Kidd's de facto nurse since she'd all but single-handedly delivered Nathan and Charmion Vincent's little Ben. They were a proper pair of ghouls.

Moving on to Schuyler and Joelle, seated elbow to elbow

at the corner near the window, Aurora leaned close to whisper in her sister's ear as she poured her tea. "Your collar is wrong side out."

"Why didn't you tell me that before I sat down?" Joelle tugged at the crocheted lace tied at her throat with a blue ribbon.

"I like it that way." Schuyler's smile was both amused and indulgent as he kissed Joelle's cheek. "Leave her alone, brat," he said to Aurora.

Fine. Nobody was looking at Joelle's collar anyway.

Aurora set the sweating pitcher on a tatted doily protecting the buffet. On the wall above it hung the portrait Papa had painted when Aurora was about four years old. She couldn't remember sitting for it, but looking at it she could almost smell the lavender scent on Mama's yellow dress, feel the comfort of her mother's arm about her waist. Her own hair was now almost the same copper red as Mama's had been then. Joelle's had brightened to brilliant strawberry blonde over the years, while Selah's had darkened to a deep mahogany. So many tragic events had blistered their lives since that happy painting went up on the wall.

With a sigh, she sat down next to Levi. His arm casually draped across the back of Selah's chair, her handsome brother-in-law sat watching his wife sip on plain water. His hazel eyes drooped in concern—or perhaps exhaustion. He'd just returned from a trip to Memphis that he wouldn't talk about with anybody but Schuyler. He'd probably tell Selah all about it when they retired after dinner.

The whole world was pairing off, leaving her bumping along on her own like a wagon tongue dragging between the front wheels of a cart. These people were all so driven, going somewhere important. It was a good thing she now had the saloon to keep her busy.

She caught Levi's gaze. "Did Selah tell you about the women we met at the boardinghouse?"

The hooded hazel eyes came awake. "They're still there?"

Selah put her hand on his arm. "You *knew* about Rosie and Bedelia?"

Schuyler grinned. "Everybody knows Rosie and Bedelia." Catching Joelle's kindling eye, he sobered. "Well . . . not *everybody*, obviously."

"Yes, they're still there," Aurora said. "I think they're going to make fine employees."

Now Schuyler laughed out loud. "She's joking," he told ThomasAnne, who looked as if she might slide under the table in horror.

"I am *not* joking." Aurora aimed her best Grandmama stare across the table. "Rosie wants to learn how to cook, and Bedelia is going to—" She paused, not at all sure what Bedelia might be good at, besides the obvious. She improvised. "She's going to manage the cleaning staff. Tell him, Selah."

Selah hid behind her water glass and mumbled something.

Beside her, Aurora could feel Levi's chuckle erupting before she heard it. "I don't know what I did for entertainment before you girls came into my life." The engaging crease in his cheek took the sting from his words. "Pete, I'm putting my money on you turning those women into upstanding pillars of the community before this is all over. But if you get Bedelia O'Malley even remotely involved in mopping floors or cleaning chamber pots, I'll personally subsidize your next investment from the ground up."

Schuyler rolled his eyes. "I told her she should just send them packing and hire some of the girls from Shake Rag."

"I *am* going to hire them too." Aurora folded her arms. "But there's no reason we can't help Bedelia and Rosie. I gave them two days to decide if they want to stay." She glowered at Schuyler. He had turned into a regular sobersides since his engagement to Joelle. "And I hope they will."

"I hope they will too," Levi said in his peacemaker fashion. "If you want, I'll go by there tomorrow morning when I'm in town, maybe encourage the idea."

Selah set her glass down sharply. "I was hoping you'd stay home tomorrow."

Levi picked up her hand and kissed it. "You know I would if I could. But I left the deputy marshal at the jail in charge of a couple of prisoners. I feel like I need to relieve him, at least for a little while. In fact"—he sighed and pushed back his chair—"I really ought to go back tonight, take him a plate of decent food. Not fair for me to be dining here with y'all, while poor Sager has to watch Alfred Pickett gnaw on greasy chicken bones."

"'Y'all'!" Schuyler hooted. "Yankee-boy said 'y'all'!"

Laughter rounded the table, but Aurora latched on to the interesting news buried in Levi's explanation. "What prisoners?" She looked at Joelle, the reporter of the family. Joelle might not talk much, but she read and listened well outside the general scope of most men, let alone sheltered single women. "What do you know about this, Jo?"

Joelle gulped, exchanged glances with Schuyler. "I dunno."

"Yes, you do!" Aurora rapped her spoon against the table. "What is he talking about? Levi, who is Sager? Is he one of the prisoners?"

"No, Polly Pry, Sager is not a prisoner. He's the deputy marshal." Levi abruptly stood. "Selah, I promise I won't be long. I just need to take dinner to Sager, then I'll be right back."

"I have a better idea," Aurora said, intrigued by Levi's warning look at Joelle. "Schuyler and I will go."

Though Schuyler's mouth opened and closed, he seemed to realize how churlish he would look if he refused. "Of course we will. Levi, you're dead on your feet, and your wife will cry if you leave again."

Aurora jumped up, took Levi by the arms with exaggerated force, and tugged until he sat back down. As Levi laughed, she said, "Schuyler, you bring around the carriage, and I'll go find Horatia and pack up some ham and potatoes or whatever she has left. I'll meet you at the front porch."

Schuyler saluted. "Yes, ma'am. On your orders, ma'am."

"I promise, I'll bring him back in one piece," Aurora said with a wink at Joelle, then skipped out of the dining room and headed for the small kitchen at the back of the house.

For the past month, Horatia Lawrence, the hotel cook, had been forced to improvise family meals. Ku Klux Klan marauders, angry that the Daughtrys hired former slaves to help launch the hotel—more so that Joelle exercised what the KKK deemed the bad judgment to found a school for them—took the extreme step of burning the roof off the freestanding brick kitchen. The attached wooden storeroom, where the schoolroom had been located, was now completely gone. Fortunately, they'd been able to salvage the iron cookstove and move it to the butler's pantry, where sinks and a pump had been installed when the main house was built.

Aurora found Horatia wiping down the new butcherblock

table built last week by her son-in-law, blacksmith Nathan Vincent.

Horatia looked up with a smile. "Y'all ready for dessert? I got a lemon meringue pie—"

"Ooh, don't mention meringue," Aurora said, wincing as she remembered Joelle's comment about the frothy, rejected wedding dress. When Horatia's eyebrows rose, Aurora waved a hand. "I mean, everybody else will love it. But Sky and I have an errand in town. We need to take food to a—a hungry law officer."

"We feeding the law now?" Horatia propped her hands on her hips. "Ain't we got enough hungry mouths don't contribute one penny to the hotel coffers?"

Aurora laughed. "This one is special. He's a friend of Levi's."

Horatia's scowl cleared. Levi was her favorite by far. "In that case, let me find you a nice basket with a linen cloth." She began to bustle about, collecting delicacies that would have made the most exacting of gourmands weep with pleasure. In short order, she handed Aurora a heavy, aromatic basket. "Y'all be careful now. It'll be dark pretty soon."

"We will. Thank you, Horatia." After kissing the cook's caramel-colored cheek, Aurora hurried back through the house to the front door, pausing only to wave as she passed the dining room. "That was fast!" she called to Schuyler as she navigated the porch steps, lifting her skirt with one hand and balancing the basket hooked over the other arm.

He'd already pulled the carriage to a halt, wrapped the reins around the cleat, and jumped down to assist her onto the seat beside him. "Tee-Toc was feeding the animals when I got to the barn, so he helped me with the carriage." He took the basket from her and stowed it behind the seat. "That's an awful lot of food for one person."

Taking Schuyler's hand, Aurora stepped into the carriage, settling herself on the squabbed seat with a sigh of pleasure. The red velvet still looked new, and Tee-Toc, their ten-year-old stable boy, did a good job of caring for the horses and equipment. "Horatia insisted on sending enough lemon pie for you and me, as well as Levi's friend."

He set the horses into motion down the drive path. "I'm always ready for pie. But I want to know what's behind this virtual kidnapping. You're up to something."

"Not really." She hung on to the side rail as the carriage bounced over a rut in the drive. "But I want to know what Levi's covering. He never tells the whole story of anything."

"Sometimes it's better not to know the whole story." Schuyler's upturned mouth flattened to a grim line.

"Better? Or safer?" She made a skeptical noise. "And for who? Why do we have prisoners and a deputy marshal in Tupelo? Does this have anything to do with the fire? And if it does, don't you think the rest of us need to be informed so we can protect ourselves?"

"Whoa, whoa, whoa." He gave her a sideways glance. "If Levi chooses not to share what he's working on, it's not my place to blab, no matter how many questions you fire at me."

"That's not fair. Joelle's obviously in on it."

"How do you—?" He shook his head with a sigh. "Never mind. You women have some sixth sense I'll never figure out." With that, he clamped his lips together and refused further comment.

Aurora maintained a resentful silence for the remainder of the trip to town, while Schuyler whistled some off-key tune that would have set Joelle's musical teeth on edge. Well, fine. Schuyler, thanks to Joelle, was no longer susceptible to Aurora's particular brand of management, so she would have to content herself with reordering the lives of two saloon girls—and possibly this poor deputy marshal Levi had dragged to Tupelo. If he was anything like the constable or sheriff, he'd be a sad case indeed. The least she could do was cheer him up with a decent meal.

She brightened as Schuyler slowed the horses and turned them into the hitching lot.

Zane faced the plate of beans in his lap with resignation. His two prisoners had already finished a similar meal, provided by an errand boy from the train station, also carrying Zane's travel bag. Riggins had been as good as his word.

Jefcoat and Moore now sat in their respective cells, reading old newspapers and carrying on a desultory conversation about the likelihood of their mutual sire attending the upcoming trial.

Listening with half an ear, Zane still found it hard to believe that these two had sprung from the same family tree. Moore had apparently risen to the status of overseer on the Jefcoat farm, while the legitimate heir had, in the process of trying to prove himself to his father, managed to get himself caught in a maelstrom of post-war violence. Why Moore had been willing to throw aside his own position to protect this inarticulate young lout was a mystery Zane intended to untangle—as soon as he had satisfied his rumbling belly. Grimacing, he scooped beans onto his spoon.

The front door opened again, and he looked up, expecting

Pickett, who had stepped outside with a brown bottle he'd taken out of a desk drawer.

Zane's chair fell away from the wall with a thunk as he surged to his feet, a hand instinctively going to his holster. "Who are you?"

The tall young dandy in the doorway glanced at the gun, then the plate of beans. "Don't worry, I'm not here for your supper. In fact, we brought you something better, if you'll, uh, calm down."

Zane noticed the man shielded someone behind him—someone very small, wearing a fancy yellow dress, which was about all he could see of her. "I'm perfectly calm. State your name and your business, and we'll get along just fine."

"I'm Schuyler Beaumont, and right behind me is Miss Aurora Daughtry. Riggins sent us, but he neglected to say we'd be feeding a madman."

"Riggins sent you?" Zane set his plate on the sheriff's desk. He did not like surprises. "Did you happen to see Pickett out there?"

The answer came from behind Beaumont. "He's sitting out here smoking a smelly cigar and eating my lemon meringue pie." The voice was bright, feminine, magnolia-cadenced. "Move, Schuyler, he's not going to shoot me."

"Not unless you gave away all the pie," Zane said, surprising even himself with a rusty attempt at humor.

That elicited a delightful giggle, and by the time Beaumont stepped inside, Zane had braced himself for the pint-sized beauty who lit the dark room like a ray of sunshine. A concoction of straw, flowers, and ribbons sat atop hair that glinted like the lucky penny in his pocket—Judge Teague had insisted there was no such thing as luck, but Zane believed in hedging

71

his bets—and the yellow dress outlined a curvy little figure
with a waist he could have spanned with his two hands. And
of course she had deep dimples in a heart-shaped face, big
golden-brown eyes, and a shallow dent in her pointed chin.

He saw all that in one paralyzed second. If she hadn't
been blocking the exit, he would have taken off running.
That right there was trouble in spades.

Wait.

He looked at Beaumont. "Is this your fiancée?" Riggins
had mentioned that Beaumont had recently gotten engaged,
under somewhat unorthodox circumstances, to one of the
Daughtry ladies, but he couldn't remember which one.

"Gadzooks, no," Beaumont said, laughing. "Joelle would
make two of her. This is Aurora, the baby. You can call her
Pete."

"He most certainly cannot," Aurora said, pushing past
Beaumont. She plunked a large, cloth-covered basket on the
desk beside his pitiful plate of beans. "Ew." She nudged the
plate aside and twitched away the cloth. "Here, Horatia sent
this for you."

A heavenly smell set Zane's stomach to roaring, drawing
him toward the desk. "Who's Horatia? Never mind. Is there a
fork?" He pulled out Pickett's chair, all senses attuned to the
food. "I'm sorry for my manners. It's been a while since—"
That was no excuse. Jacqueline had taught him better. Removing his hat, he looked down at Aurora Daughtry and
forced himself not to shield his one good eye against the
onslaught of that smile. "Thank you," he said simply.

"You're welcome." She beamed. "Schuyler, go keep Mr.
Pickett company. I want to talk to Deputy Marshal Sager."
She snapped her fingers as if she were the Queen of England

72

commanding her footman, and to Zane's astonishment, Beaumont decamped with barely a grumble of protest. As Zane sat down, she rooted around in the basket and started laying out his meal. "Yes, there's a fork. And I think there's a . . ." Muttering to herself, she arranged a sumptuous array of delicacies in front of Zane. Finally she placed a finger in front of her berry-colored lips and frowned at him. "I forgot to bring anything to drink. I'll send Schuyler—"

"Never mind," he said hastily. "This is great. I'll get some water later."

"Are you sure?"

"I'm sure." He tried for a smile, looked down at the plate full of slices of cured ham with a beautiful, crisp glaze at the edges, accompanied by roasted potatoes and onions. There was also a hunk of crusty sourdough bread. Trying hard not to drool, he said a quick blessing, then picked up the heavy silver fork and knife and cut a slice of ham. He put it in his mouth and all but slithered under the desk.

Looking pleased, she dragged over Zane's wooden chair and sat down across from him. "Horatia is our cook, out at Daughtry House. What happened to your eye?"

He choked on the ham, and it took several seconds of coughing behind the fine linen napkin to recover. Ladies did not ever mention his deformity. Still wheezing, he said, "There was an accident."

"Well, obviously." She waved a hand. "I mean, is it gone completely? Has anyone looked at it? My grandfather is a doctor in Memphis, and I'm very good friends with Dr. Kidd—"

"It's still there, but cut through the nerve," he managed. Suddenly his appetite was gone.

"Oh, I'm sorry, I've made you uncomfortable." She reached across the desk and touched his hand, which had commenced to strangling the fork. "I'm in such a habit of talking about medical things with Grandpapa, I forget other people aren't used to my being so forthright. Please forgive me, Mr. Sager." Her eyes were wet with compassion.

Zane felt as if someone had upended him and shaken his brains out. "My name is Zane," he said stupidly. "There's nothing to forgive. In fact, I hate it when people pretend not to notice. It happened a long time ago, and I'm used to looking like a pirate."

She tilted her head, studying him. "Doesn't everything look sideways?"

He laughed, and it was such an odd feeling that he did it again. "No. And you are the kindest and most brutally honest person I've ever met, except for—" He'd been about to say "Judge Teague," but Judge Teague was dead, and he had to find the killer. There was no time for flirting with dimpled Southern belles, even if he'd known how. So he started to eat again.

"Zane," she said thoughtfully. "That's a good name. I guess you can call me Pete after all, if you want to. It's sort of babyish, and I don't know why Papa thought that would be funny, but it stuck and now I can't get rid of it. I wish they'd called me 'Rory' or something like that, but it's either Aurora, which is hard to say, or Pete, which makes no sense . . ." She squinted. "What do you think?"

He swallowed, wishing he had something to drink after all. Maybe something with some alcohol in it. "What do I think about what?" He wasn't used to talking much to anybody, let alone blinding young women who chattered like a telegraph wire.

"About my name. What do you want to call me?"

"I—I'm pretty sure I should call you 'Miss Daughtry,'" he said. "We've barely known each other for five minutes."

She blew an inelegant raspberry. "That's just silly. Levi is my brother-in-law, and you're his friend, so there." She sat back and folded her hands in her lap as if it were settled. At least she didn't snap her fingers. He might have come to heel like a hound dog.

He wouldn't have said Riggins was his friend exactly, though he respected the fellow. But he did not wish to offend this lovely young lady who had brought him a feast fit for at least a duke, if not a king. "How about we compromise, and I call you Aurora in private"—which was not likely to ever happen—"and Miss Daughtry in company. Otherwise, I might be sacked for unprofessionalism," he added when she opened her mouth to protest. He was rather proud of himself for his tact.

Aurora regarded him from narrowed eyes, then finally nodded. "Very well, I don't want to get you in trouble. Now eat up while I fix your pie. Then we're going to talk about those two fellows in the cells back there."

Six

As SHE SLID A SLICE OF PIE onto Zane Sager's empty plate, Aurora wondered if she might have overstepped the bounds of propriety. But the deputy marshal clearly needed some intervention into his barren existence. Even Grandmama would not fault her for showing kindness to a stranger. Angels unaware and all that.

And he was about as alien a personage as she was likely to encounter.

She sat back down and nibbled at the sliver of dessert she had left for herself, covertly watching her companion. He was a mass of contradictions. Judging by his nice white teeth and unlined skin, he must be young—under twenty-five, she'd guess. The dark hair, falling over his forehead from a deep widow's peak, bore not a trace of gray.

But the cynicism in that one deep green eye bore testament to a life of hard experience, and the leather patch over the other told its own story. His face was all angles and lines, the jaw like tensile steel. His clothing was functional and plain but well-made, and there was something of the military in his straight bearing.

Despite his tough appearance, though, he did not wolf his food but ate with fine manners and deep appreciation. What a puzzle.

"Why didn't Levi bring you home to dinner?"

He wiped his mouth with the napkin in his lap. "I'm working." There was a warning in his words and tone.

Anyone in her family would have told him that she did not respond well to caution. She laid down her fork. "As far as I know, no one has ever escaped from this jail. Are you really going to spend the night here?"

"I am."

Bald, unadorned facts. All right then. "I'm trying to figure out your accent. You're not Southern."

"No. Born in Delaware."

She blinked. "Then you're Union. Yankee."

He sighed. "Do we have to discuss this, Miss Daughtry? The war is over."

"It would be helpful to know where you've come from."

"Why? I told you I have a job to do. I am not coming to stay at your resort hotel. Beaumont should not have brought you here." He pushed back his plate, leaving half the pie. "Thank you, I'm finished. I'll help you repack your basket. You should get home before dark."

"Mercy, we're prickly. I'm just making conversation. When does the trial start?"

"Miss Daughtry—"

"Listen to me, Deputy Marshal Sager." She got to her feet, plunked her hands flat on the desk, and glared at him. "One of those men back there sat at my table, eating my food and sleeping in my home for two weeks, all the while conniving with people who tried to burn down our house. Naturally I'm interested in their trial. My sister Joelle will be called to testify, so you'd better believe I'll be there."

He returned her stare for a long moment. "I have nothing to do with the trial except guarding judge and witnesses. But I take the assignment seriously. And I will not talk about it."

Leaning in, she stared into that cold green eye. "That is commendable and will make me sleep marginally better at night." She lowered her voice to a whisper. "But I am not stupid, and I am not some weak clinging vine. I'm worried about my sisters and Schuyler and Levi—and my employees, who are all targets of the Klan. You may not think it to look at me, but I'm capable of picking up lots of information that people drop without realizing it. I'm willing to help you—or whoever is prosecuting those cowards. I just wanted to make sure you weren't hiding some motive to help them escape."

His gaze did not waver as he growled, "I assure you I have no intention of letting them miss their day in court. And I appreciate your concern, but your help is not needed. Let me make myself clear, Miss Daughtry. Stay out of my way."

Aurora jerked upright, entertaining the urge to slap his handsome, ravaged young face. She would not give him the satisfaction. Instead, she began to methodically load dishes back into the basket, ignoring Zane Sager's awkward attempts to assist. "Thank you," she said sweetly. "I *don't need your help*."

Looking stung, he folded his arms across his chest. "Touché."

When at last she hooked the basket over her arm and headed

for the door, she couldn't resist looking over her shoulder and dipping a curtsey. Something about his guarded expression made her throat close, but he'd done it to himself. She'd entertained a stranger, but he was no angel.

"Nice to meet you, Deputy Marshal. I'll be careful to stay out of your way from now on." She jerked open the door, prepared to go looking for Schuyler. "Uh-oh."

A crowd of men advanced toward the jail, and she did not think they were coming for pie.

"Now what?" Trying not to look at the red-haired blight in the doorway, Zane returned the ladderback chair to its spot against the wall.

He had hurt her, but he told himself he didn't care. How many times had he seen otherwise effective agents and officers lured down the primrose path by pretty girls? And she had as much as admitted that that was her "strategy" for assisting him. Well, he wasn't falling for it himself.

"I think you'd better come see this," Aurora said, then stood on her tiptoes and shouted, "Schuyler! Where are you?"

"What the—" Zane hurried to the door, saw about twenty men coming down the street, and yanked her back inside behind him. He recognized an angry mob when he saw one. "Get back to the far wall," he told Aurora. Pulling his gun, he stepped outside, shut the door, and looked around. Pickett was nowhere in sight.

Maybe that was just as well.

Waiting for the leader of the pack, a portly fellow with a bad toupee, to get close enough to hear him, he called out, "You men stop right where you are. I'm Deputy Marshal

Sager, and I need you to state your business before you come any closer."

Mr. Toupee slowed but took another experimental step or two. "You're not welcome here, Deputy Marshal. Our constable and Sheriff Gere, plus the citizens of this town, don't need the federal government's help in running our local justice." He looked over his shoulder to make sure his companions agreed. Receiving a loud grumble of approval, he smirked at Zane. "We suggest you get back on that train and go back to Washington, or wherever you came from."

Zane felt a cold, familiar calm pour through his veins—the one that had sustained him through a multitude of heinous situations over the last ten years. He kept his voice as steady as the gun in his hand. "I don't believe you gave me your name, sir. I don't want there to be any confusion when I make my report to the US Attorney when he gets here Monday."

"The name is Whitmore." The man's tone implied that he was a man of such importance that Zane should have recognized him on sight. "Behind me is my son-in-law, Bowen Nester."

Taking his gaze off Whitmore long enough to acknowledge the pockmarked young thug carrying what looked like a bricklayer's shovel, Zane scanned the rest of the crowd. He counted eighteen men in a variety of ages, shapes, and sizes. All but two were armed with either a rifle or a holstered pistol, and they all seemed to be spoiling for a fight.

What if he'd been stupid enough to leave his prisoners with Pickett? Sometimes his suspicious nature stood him in good stead. Just as often it left him facing unpleasant circumstances all alone. Now he was going to have to get creative.

"Mr. Whitmore," he said, "I'm not going anywhere until I've finished the job I was given authority to do by Federal Marshal Eaton."

"We didn't vote for your boss." Whitmore took a belligerent stance. "And you can't strong-arm us into housing and feeding federal prisoners."

"I'm not here to usurp local law enforcement," Zane said, striving for a reasonable tone. "In fact, Constable Pickett himself helped me lock my prisoners up. I'm just borrowing the jail until the judge can get here and sort out—"

"Judge?" A handsome middle-aged man in a neat frock coat—one of the unarmed men—stepped forward. "What judge would that be? Not that lily-livered liberal Bob Hill, from over in Oxford?"

Zane gritted his teeth. "Please state your name, sir?"

"Why?" the man sneered. "Am I going in your report too? I'm Frank Brown, owner of the Gum Pond Hotel."

One by one, the other men gave their names, moving forward until the whole gang had approached to within a few yards of Zane's position on the porch.

Refusing to give way, he tried to identify the leaders. He didn't want to shoot anybody, but he was sorely outnumbered, and he had a defenseless female inside the building, not to mention the prisoners.

Unfortunately, the defenseless female chose that moment to open the door behind him. "Mr. Carpenter!" Her clear soprano carried over the rumble of male voices. "Have you brought me a telegram?"

Without looking over his shoulder, Zane froze. "Get back inside!" he hissed through his teeth.

"You're taking too long," she whispered with sunny

obstinacy, then said more loudly, "Mr. Carpenter, did you hear me?"

A slight gentleman with sandy-gray hair stepped away from the crowd. He was unarmed, and he looked embarrassed. "No. There's no telegram, Miss Aurora."

"Then what are you doing here?" She sounded genuinely puzzled. "Is the station closed?"

"No, actually—"

Whitmore pushed Carpenter aside, cutting short whatever explanation he'd been about to provide. "Miss Daughtry, I might ask you the same question. What are you doing here alone—in the jail—with this interloper? Where is your escort?"

Zane would have intervened, except some of the hostility had seeped from the crowd with Aurora's sudden appearance. He could almost hear the long eyelashes flapping as she sashayed around him.

"Schuyler was right here a minute ago." She cast a bewildered gaze to the right, then the left. Then up at the sky, as if he might have flown away on a chariot of fire. Innocent brown eyes returned to Whitmore. "Have you seen him?"

"No, I haven't seen him," blustered the fat man, shoving at his toupee. "My wife is right. You Daughtry girls have no sense of propriety—"

"Stow it, Whitmore," came a deep drawl from the back of the crowd. "Unlike my betrothed and her sisters, your wife has no sense of charity—which, it seems to me, is more useful and attractive than propriety on any day of the week."

As the gang parted, Zane saw Schuyler Beaumont casually nudging people out of the way with an elbow and the barrel of a .46-caliber Remington revolver. Behind him came a short, rumpled gentleman with rimless spectacles stuck atop his balding head and a businesslike shotgun under his arm.

Aurora waved. "There you are, Sky! And Mr. McCanless! See, Mr. Whitmore? Everything is perfectly respectable. We just came to demonstrate a little Christian *charity*." She lifted her arm to display her basket. "You know how Pastor Reese says when we visit those who are sick and in prison, it's like doing the same to Jesus?" She turned to Zane. "I'm sorry about this, Mr. Sager. It's just a big ol' misunderstanding."

Zane's senses were alive to every source of potential danger in the situation. The restless mob, whose tension seemed to be defusing by the moment. Beaumont and McCanless ready to assist him. The prisoners in the jailhouse cells. Mainly he was aware of the perilous position into which Aurora Daughtry had thrust herself. One glance at her white face told him she recognized it, but was either too stupid or too brave to care.

He suspected the latter. And he was going to have to respond. He couldn't just stand here and let a girl dressed like a daffodil take over this confrontation. He moved in front of her in a nonthreatening stance, keeping his gun unholstered but pointed at the ground. "Gentlemen," he said with intentional irony, "I'm afraid your welcome committee visit has run its course. Nobody wants trouble less than me. Your concerns about my presence should be addressed to Judge Hill when he gets here. Until then, you should know that I'm here to protect you as well as my prisoners. Please let me know if I can assist you in any way." He waited, expecting the crowd to disperse. Most of the time bullies only needed a show of resolve before their bravado crumpled.

To his surprise, Beaumont and McCanless came to stand on the porch, one on either side of him. Aurora was now shielded by three guns, which made Zane feel a lot better. He hoped she'd have enough sense to stay where she was.

Whitmore's jowls shook. "This isn't over, so you'd better watch yourself, Deputy Marshal." He cast a mean look at Beaumont and then McCanless. "Things don't turn out so good for people who turn against their neighbors, do they, Wimus?"

When the little bald man looked ready to jump off the porch, Zane gave him a warning hiss. "Let 'em go."

To his relief, Whitmore revolved his arm in a gesture that called off his pack of dogs. With a low growl, they moved back in the direction they'd come—all except the man who'd introduced himself as Brown, the hotel owner.

Brown took a threatening step toward the jailhouse. "I want to know what those men are on trial for. I hear the federals are coming down on Klan activities in Mississippi, like they did in Georgia and South Carolina. Gonna send troops down here to put their Yankee boots back on us. That true?"

"I'm sure you know what I think about the Klan," Beaumont said in a friendly tone. "I hope somebody's planning to do something about it."

"You're a rat, Beaumont," Brown snarled. "We exterminate pests around here."

"Aw, now, Mr. Brown, you're just showing your jealousy over the success of Daughtry House. I'm sure I could get General Forrest to stop one night at the Gum Pond, if you're serious about getting rid of the bedbugs."

"Why you—" Brown raised his fists as if he might rush the porch, but since Beaumont's gun remained lazily pointed in the general direction of the street, the hotelier contented himself with fuming for an impotent moment before wheeling toward the business district.

Zane laughed and put away his gun. This was turning into a regular farce.

Then he turned around and found himself face-to-face with one smug Mississippi belle. "See there, Mr. I-Don't-Need-Your-Help? That's how we do things the Daughtry way. Creativity and brains, not hardware."

Seven

AURORA AWOKE THE NEXT MORNING to the familiar sound of hammers banging on one of the outbuildings that seemed to be under perpetual reconstruction. The roof was going back up on the kitchen and storeroom, Joelle's school was being rebuilt, and Nathan and Charmion's new house had been framed on the ashes of the little cabin that had burned along with the blacksmith shop.

It seemed like every time they got the hotel rolling toward solvency, something else happened to kick it down.

But, praise be to God, the main house hadn't been touched, and the manager's cottage—where she, Joelle, and Thomas-Anne lived—remained in good shape. Her natural optimism surged. It was going to be a good day.

Stretching, she looked out the open window, where filmy new curtains made by Charmion floated in a summer breeze, and caught a glance at the mantel clock. She'd slept through breakfast! Why had no one awakened her?

Jumping out of bed, she hurriedly washed her face, then began the tricky business of brushing her hair.

She supposed she shouldn't be surprised that she'd overslept by two hours. They'd all been up late, discussing the ramifications of her encounter with Deputy Marshal Zane Sager. Her family seemed convinced the whole thing had been her fault. But really, she'd been the only one with the sense to prevent what had promised to be a nasty, maybe even lethal, confrontation. *She* hadn't brought that bunch of men over to threaten the lawman. *She* hadn't stood alone on a porch with a loaded gun, goading one of the most arrogant, self-important fools in town into proving his manhood.

Men.

She pictured Zane Sager's face as he'd turned around after Mr. Brown slunk away. Mercy, that slow grin had scrambled her brain. And she had probably blurted something inappropriate. She couldn't remember what it was, but his smile had faded and that cynical twist came back to his fine mouth. So she'd hustled Schuyler over to the hitching lot where they'd left the carriage, and she'd jumped in without waiting for assistance. And she'd managed to ignore Schuyler for the remainder of the drive home, despite his aggravating insistence on taking all the credit for dispersing the mob.

Of course Schuyler had to relate the whole thing to Joelle, who stomped around like a mama bear (did bears stomp?) until Aurora begged her to stop because she had a headache. Thank goodness Jo decided not to bother Levi and Selah, who had already retired to the old overseer's cabin, but ThomasAnne had been predictably overcome with postmortem vapors.

ThomasAnne had a genius for making one feel guilty for nothing.

She stopped brushing. It was nothing, wasn't it? She'd lain awake until the wee hours, nursing the headache and thinking about the coiled-spring muscles in Zane Sager's back when he'd moved protectively in front of her on the porch. Yes, she'd managed to distract Mr. Whitmore and keep him from rushing the jail. But her presence had also given the deputy marshal one more thing to worry about.

Something very odd took root in the pit of her stomach. Probably hunger.

Finishing with the hairbrush, she twisted her mass of red curls into the most mature knot she could manufacture without a mirror, encircled it with a yellow ribbon, then put on a two-piece summer dress of dark blue calico. *First things first*, she thought. *Food.*

She accomplished the short walk to the back porch of the main house in less than a minute, slowing only to admire the peacock strutting past the chicken yard with his gorgeous fan on display for the benefit of the plebeian fenced poultry. Something about that imagery bothered her, but she'd have to trace the source of her discomfort later. She wanted to catch Levi before he headed for town this morning.

She found the kitchen abandoned, the counters cleared and wiped down, breakfast evidently long past. Resigned, she poked through the little corner pantry and discovered a couple of leftover biscuits with burnt bottoms wrapped in a napkin. Pulling off the tops to eat, she returned to the chicken yard and tossed in the burnt bread, laughing as she watched the hens peck and flap with squawks of joy. "Everything is relative, isn't it, ladies?" Dusting crumbs off her hands, she followed the sound of voices to the front of the house.

Neither of her sisters was anywhere in sight, but Schuyler held the horses while Levi loaded the boot of the carriage.

"Wait! I want to go!" She hustled around to the passenger side.

"Where do you think we're going?" Levi's dimple appeared as he came around to boost her onto the seat.

"Obviously you're going to town." She settled herself as Schuyler gathered the reins and vaulted up beside Aurora, while Levi climbed onto the rear seat. "I wanted to talk to you both anyway, and I need your help."

Schuyler gave her a sideways look. "I take it you're not angry with me anymore."

Aurora sighed. "I knew you were going to tell Joelle what happened last night. I'm sure Levi knows by now too." She glanced over her shoulder. "Don't you?"

Her brother-in-law hesitated before he said in his measured way, "Aurora, I've advised Schuyler not to leave you alone like that again. The times we live in—"

"I wasn't alone! I was with an armed US deputy marshal. Besides, if Schuyler hadn't gone after Mr. McCanless, we'd have been in a real pickle."

Schuyler released an exasperated breath. "But if you hadn't been there in the first place, the situation might not have escalated."

She wasn't giving in on this one. "From my perspective, I *kept* things from escalating. You and Levi weren't there, so there's no way you'd know. Anyway, I don't want to rehash that. I stayed awake last night, formulating a business plan for the new boardinghouse. Schuyler, I want you to send Shug

Pogue over to look at it and give me an estimate of how much it will cost to renovate, and how long he thinks it will take."

"Shug's already busy with rebuilding after the fire." Schuyler sounded obstinate. "Tell her, Levi."

"Don't put me in the middle of this," Levi said.

Aurora felt like exploding with frustration. "If Shug's not available, I'll find someone else. Why are y'all being so difficult?"

Schuyler exchanged a look with Levi. "I think you've got to tell her, or she's going to go off on some half-cocked plan to restore soiled doves to polite society."

"That's exactly what I've got in—What do you mean, he's got to tell me? I knew there was something funny going on. Levi?" She wheeled in the seat as the carriage tilted after a teeth-jarring bump over a rut. "Schuyler! Watch what you're doing!"

Once Schuyler had the carriage settled into a comfortable pace again, Aurora released the side rail and frowned at Levi. "All right. Enough cloak and dagger. What is he talking about?"

"You remind me a lot of your grandmother," Levi muttered.

"Doesn't she?" Schuyler glanced at Aurora. "I think it's the eyebrows."

"No, it's the bulldog refusal to let anything go once she's set her mind on it. I thought Selah was bad . . ." Levi chuckled. "All right, Pete, so I've got plans for your saloon, and a boardinghouse doesn't fit in with them right now. Though eventually—"

"You've got plans? Excuse me—you might have married into this family, but according to Mississippi law, a woman's inheritance does not pass automatically to our husbands. And even if it did, Selah's part is only a third. Joelle and I could outvote her."

"Joelle has already agreed," Schuyler said. He almost sounded apologetic.

Aurora stared at him. "My sisters colluded against me? I don't believe it."

"Pete," Levi said gently, "you're nineteen years old, a single female. You can't operate a boardinghouse on your own, even if you had the money and resources to do it. You know I think you're one of the three smartest women in Mississippi— probably below the Mason-Dixon line—but there are just certain facts of life we can't get around. Selah's going to have a baby, and I can't add to her physical stress. Joelle's busy planning to marry this chowderhead—"

"Hey!" Schuyler yelped.

"—plus she's running a school and writing a book. Nobody has time to keep running back and forth to town, checking on you."

"ThomasAnne does." Now that she thought about it, the sudden inspiration struck Aurora as pure genius. Nobody was more genteel and upright than her older, unmarried cousin. Nobody had more time to spare than ThomasAnne. "She would adore living in town, where she could assist Dr. Kidd in his office as a nurse. But before we get into all that—*tell me what plan you had for my boardinghouse*. Don't think you distracted me into forgetting that part of the discussion."

Levi pressed his lips together. "All right. All right, you win. But this has got to stay right here among the three of us. Well, five, counting your sisters. I want to use the saloon to hide Sager, Jefcoat, and Moore until the trial starts. Pinkerton has been hired to increase security for these Klan trials, and that scene last night worries me a lot. Certainly Sager managed to get out of it without violence— admittedly with a little assistance—but next time things might not end so easily."

Schuyler nodded. "Tempers are hot, especially in close little towns like Tupelo. Most of that crowd—you saw them, Pete—have been involved in one or more Klan activities. I saw them myself! People are scared they're going to get caught up and prosecuted. And when people are scared, they're dangerous."

Levi leaned forward. "Aurora, I need you as far away from the trouble as possible. And can you understand why I want to move those witnesses out of sight?"

"I can understand, and I appreciate you taking time to explain it to me." Chills walked up Aurora's arms as she realized the peril she had so blithely flirted with yesterday evening. But now she also knew, with eyes wide open, exactly what she'd been given to do. Both her sisters had risked their own lives and reputations to help others. Now it was her turn. "Let me posit my own suggestion. It may surprise you to know that I agree—moving the deputy marshal and his charges into the saloon is a good idea. But what if we start the renovations as a way to cover their presence? If Thomas-Anne and I are there, directing the activity, workers coming in and out during the day, no one would imagine we'd have male guests. You could even make a production of Sager taking the men out of town, then bring them back under cover of darkness and install them upstairs." She chanced a look at Schuyler and found him remarkably thoughtful. "And if you're still worried about society protocol, Schuyler could come stay too, as our male protector. I know you're tired of sleeping in the barn, Sky."

There was a brief electric silence as the two men considered her proposition. It could go either way. If Levi thought it was too complicated, or Schuyler resisted leaving Daughtry House and Joelle, Aurora was going to have a hard time defending the idea. She didn't know why she felt so strongly, but in her very spirit she knew this was something she had been born to do.

Finally Schuyler exhaled sharply. "I need to leave Daughtry House until Joelle and I get married. I've been putting it off, but I have to admit, I don't have any real objections. What do you think, Levi?"

Levi smirked at Schuyler. "I think you understand why Selah and I had such a short engagement. And I also think our little sister would make an exceptional tactical officer." His smile for Aurora contained a gratifying note of respect. "All right, you win this round as well, on the condition that Sager has no objections." He held up a hand to forestall her whoop of victory. "However, you're going to let me propose it to him. Otherwise, I can guarantee you'd be shot down without a second thought. Agreed?"

She meekly nodded, though she felt her grin spread from ear to ear. "I'm going to be the first landlady jailer in the modern South! Just don't tell ThomasAnne."

Zane had had about enough of this hick town jailhouse and its low-information constable. He kept himself from throttling Pickett by whittling a raccoon from a birch twig he'd picked up during his dawn trip out to the privy. Before that, he had not slept well in the ladderback chair; but then, he rarely got a full night's sleep anyway.

Consequently, the arrival of Levi Riggins and Schuyler Beaumont midmorning found Zane not only hungry but testy.

"I hope you've brought food again," he said when Beaumont opened the door without knocking and poked his head inside.

"Not exactly." Beaumont entered, followed by Riggins. "But if you'll trust Pickett to keep an eye on your folks for half an hour, we'll treat you to breakfast at the Gum Pond. Brown may be a hothead idiot, but his cook knows his way around a stack of hotcakes and some Andouille sausage."

"That's just a block away, right?" Zane let his chair drop onto all fours and glanced at Pickett, sitting at the desk reading an old newspaper. He needed to talk to Riggins and Beaumont, but he did not want to discuss this case in front of the constable. Two negatives did not make a positive in this case. Either choice might result in serious trouble.

"The sheriff will be in this afternoon," Pickett said, rattling the paper. "He'll expect you back by then."

Zane scowled at him. "I'll get back when I get back. You stay put and don't let them talk you into anything stupid. Anything happens to either of those men, I'll hunt you down."

"That was diplomatic," Beaumont said as the three of them walked the short distance to the hotel.

"Diplomacy is not my main job." Zane realized he probably could have spent the night at the hotel. Both prisoners had slept just fine, and the town had been quiet, including the train station two streets over. The first train had ar-

---

rived at eight this morning. But he suspected the hotel's owner might have instructed his clerk not to house the "interloper."

"No," Riggins said, "but it would go a long way to getting you to your goal, which is keeping those two fellows—and yourself, I might add—free of bullet holes."

Beaumont opened the hotel's front door. "Do you think Jefcoat or Moore will talk to the sheriff? What have they told you?"

"Not much, beyond what I had already learned from Riggins on the train. I know Jefcoat was once your good friend, and that he's deep in the Mississippi Klan."

Beaumont nodded as he led the way to a corner table. "Jefcoat was connected to the Klan through his father, who served as a Confederate soldier. He's a racist, dead set against the election of Negroes to Congress—and a proponent of voter intimidation. By his own admission, he was aiming at Reverend Thomas during that Tuscaloosa riot when he shot my father."

The three of them took seats. By this time of the morning, the restaurant was relatively quiet, most breakfast customers having come and gone. Zane gave Beaumont a curious look. "When did you discover how far he'd sunk?"

Beaumont's face was set, voice gritty. "He kidnapped me and would have killed me if I hadn't claimed to know Lem Frye's location."

Zane tipped his head. "That's a name I haven't heard." He sighed. "And there are a lot of names to keep up with."

Riggins nodded. "It's a nasty, sprawling nest of vipers. I'll provide you a list. Lemuel Frye is the white schoolteacher I mentioned on the train—the one who married the Maney children's Negro caretaker." He leaned in. "Follow this. Mrs. Frye grew up on the Jefcoat plantation and was sold to the Maneys. There are lots of ties between those two families. And Maney knows the Fryes have some incriminating evidence against him. They're in real danger, and we've got them in a protected location."

"I've talked to Jefcoat since he was caught, and he's scared," Beaumont said. "But I can't get him to break. Jefcoat said 'the general' sent him to stop me from going to Tremont. I suppose that could mean either Maney or Forrest. Or neither. I know one thing, though. I addressed Maney by name the night of the newspaper attack, and he instinctively responded. I never saw his face, but that voice is one I'll recognize if I hear it again."

"How much of your involvement in this mess is general knowledge?" Zane asked. "Does the Klan think you're with them or against them?"

"Wait." Levi reached into his coat pocket for a leather notebook and pencil. "I want to take notes on what we know in orderly fashion. Then we can look at it all and make connections, catch lies, eliminate suspects."

"Good idea." Schuyler glanced at the menu posted in chalk on a blackboard next to the doorway and waved to a woman in an apron, who bustled about straightening chairs. "But let's get those hotcakes rolling first. Mrs. Brown!"

The woman approached, smiling. Apparently her husband had failed to inform her of his humiliating rout last evening, for she took their orders with no noticeable prejudice against any of her three customers. "Hotcakes and sausage it is," she said and backed into the kitchen.

Levi opened his notebook to a fresh page, looking around

to make sure they were not likely to be overheard. "All right," he said, keeping his voice low, "the question about Schuyler's involvement in the local Klan was apt. Sager, you should know I sent him undercover with the intent of tracing the leadership."

Zane's respect for the young dandy rose. "That's a pretty dangerous assignment."

Beaumont shrugged. "I was the only one in the right circumstances to make it work. I announced a run for the Mississippi legislature as a conservative, knowing that would attract the attention of the contingent we're after."

Zane folded his arms. "You still in the race?"

Beaumont glanced at Riggins. "Probably going to drop out, since circumstances have changed. The election will take place this fall, and I'm inclined to throw my support behind a Negro pastor I've come to know quite well. To answer your question about the Klan, I'm assuming that everyone at the two meetings I attended—plus the mob who vandalized the newspaper—knew who I was. I can give you some names, some I can only guess at because everyone was disguised with either a hood or a mask or blackened face."

"All right, start with those closest to you," Zane said. "Jefcoat first. But there's another one still running around loose, right?"

"Yes. Jefcoat, Kenard Hixon, and I were college fraternity brothers and remained close after graduation. My father put me to work negotiating some railroad land deals, which is how I reconnected with the Daughtry family. All that wheeling and dealing suited me and my two friends perfectly. And when I landed the deal with Daughtry House, the two of them followed me here. Pretty girls, good food, hunting and fishing, you know?" Beaumont looked sheepish. "Then my father was killed and everything got serious."

Zane started to press Beaumont, but Mrs. Brown chose that moment to return with a tray full of food, and the conversation necessarily became more general until she went back to the kitchen.

By the time the three of them had knocked the edge off their hunger, Zane had formulated his line of questioning. He pushed his plate aside. "Beaumont, so far you've named Hixon and Jefcoat, plus maybe the two Confederate generals, Maney and Forrest. Anybody else you could identify from your involvement with the Klan?"

"Whitmore for sure. That toupee is unmistakable." Beaumont looked over his shoulder at the hotel desk, where the proprietor worked. "And Mr. Brown. They were at the first meeting I attended, as were the barber and two deputy sheriffs from Tuscaloosa—although they both left town the minute the deputy marshal showed up to take away Jefcoat and Moore. You might be surprised to know I talked at some length to our pastor, Gil Reese."

"The one who was betrothed to your fiancée?" Zane couldn't help a little grin.

Beaumont winced at the dig. "The same. Poor fellow claims he only participated in the attacks because they threatened to come after members of his church if he stood back or protested. I don't know." He threw his napkin down in disgust. "He demonstrated a mighty callous attitude toward good people who don't deserve his scorn."

"I wonder if there's a way to get him to testify against the higher-ups," Riggins said. "There are two strategies for putting a halt to this pack of wolves—taking out the low-level minions like Jefcoat, one by one, or leaving them in place and using them to get to the alphas. There's one more I'd add to the list of sympathizers—the Tupelo telegraph operator, Daniel Carpenter. He's friendly to your face, but I know for a fact that he was in communication with Scully, who was his counterpart over in Oxford."

Zane nodded. "We'll find a way to pump him for what he knows as well."

Riggins looked at Beaumont with quiet respect. "Schuyler got a lot of information in a short amount of time. It's too bad he can't stay undercover."

Beaumont rubbed his jaw. "Now that Joelle is in the cross-hairs as a liberal Negro-lover, and I'm betrothed to her, I'm not sure I'd still be believed as an insider."

"Lots of men put up with soft-hearted womenfolk," Zane said with a shrug.

"True, but I haven't tried to hide my friendship with Yankee-boy here." Beaumont toasted Riggins with his coffee cup. "He's known to be my attorney, and we'll soon be brothers."

Zane hadn't seen his sister in nearly nine years, and he mistrusted most friendships. But he appreciated it when he saw it. "Then it's out of the question. We're pulling you out as of now. Besides, once you stood with me last night, you made yourself persona non grata with this bunch." He smiled. "Not that I'm not grateful. Miss Daughtry created quite a scene."

Beaumont chuckled. "She thinks she defused it."

"I suppose that's a matter of perspective." Zane looked around for someone to pay for the meal. "I need to get back to the jail."

"Wait." Riggins stuffed his notebook back into his coat

pocket. "Speaking of Aurora, there's another reason we brought you away from Pickett's big ears. We have a suggestion for a safer place to put your prisoners and yourself."

"All right. Let's hear it." But Zane had a cold, gut-level suspicion he wasn't going to like the idea.

Eight

AURORA SAT ON THE FRONT STEPS of the Dogwood Boarding House, elbows on knees and chin on her fists. Some might say—her fretful cousin ThomasAnne amongst them—that her second visit with the saloon girls had not gone smoothly. Short of a blast of dynamite, Bedelia refused to be moved out of her room at the front of the house ("squatter's rights" seemed to be the linchpin of her psyche). Furthermore, Rosie's idea of a career in fine dining seemed to consist of rice and congee.

But not for nothing did Joelle call Aurora the Princess of Rainbows. She was going to make a success of this venture if it killed her.

Bedelia had introduced some logistics of the scheme that she hadn't honestly considered until now. Both women needed a place to stay while the place was being renovated—during this short period it would be used to hide Zane Sager and his prisoners—and they both needed training in the skills for their new employment. The logical solution would be housing them in one of the outbuildings at Daughtry House.

101

There they could shadow the hotel servants and simultaneously aid in preparations for guests to arrive in the fall. Elderly, wise, built of godly moral fiber, Mose and Horatia Lawrence—managers of the kitchen and grounds—had over the years maintained a strong influence over Aurora and her sisters. She could think of no more ideal shepherds for two lonely women cast adrift in the world.

But in the interest of realism, a couple of tripwires stood likely to blow her magical plan to bits. For one thing, Horatia was a busy woman and might not appreciate such a distracting assignment. Even more problematic, Irish-born Bedelia and Chinese Rosie would almost certainly resent understudying a Negro couple.

Aurora frowned at a weed pushing its optimistic way through a muddy patch in the pathway. Every problem had a solution, if one refused to admit defeat and applied a little thought. Just because she couldn't see it now didn't mean it wasn't there. What would Grandmama do in her place?

Everybody assumed Grandmama relied upon her considerable force of will when managing her circle of influence. But Aurora could vividly remember the morning her mother had left her with her grandparents and then ridden the train back to Ithaca with Selah and Joelle. Ithaca was too dangerous, Mama said, now that Papa had gone to fight the Yankees. Her grandparents wanted to pay her tuition at a new school for girls in Memphis. She would love it, and the family would be together again for Christmas, because the Confederacy was going to win. Mama snapped her fingers to show how quick that would be.

Aurora was ten, old enough to listen to reason and understand on an intellectual level. But she'd cried herself to sleep that night, in the pretty bedroom she always slept in when she went to visit. She wasn't scared, exactly. But every other time she'd been to McGowan House, Selah and Joelle had slept in the adjoining room. Aurora could walk through the door and climb in between her sisters if she had a nightmare or simply wanted to listen to them whisper together over boys or clothes or a book one or the other had read. Joelle might grumble about "Pete and her knobby knees," but Selah would smooth her hair and sing nonsense songs until she yawned. Or Joelle would tell a ghost story that was so ridiculous they'd all end up in a fit of giggles and Mama would come shush them and make Aurora go back to her own bed.

But that night. That awful night, she'd been alone. She'd lain awake, rigid as a corpse, staring at the darkness and feeling the sick, black unfairness of it all. They didn't want her. She was too young and too female to be any good to anyone—if she'd been a boy, she could have followed Papa to war—so she must live with grandparents she barely knew and go to a school with girls she'd never met in her entire life.

As soon as daylight came, she burst into the sitting room that was her grandmother's sanctorum, ready to tell Grandmama she wasn't having it. She'd be brave and useful and read Joelle's boring books—whatever they insisted on—but she missed her sisters and her mother and her room at Ithaca. She would walk all the way back if necessary. It was what she decided in the wee hours of that long night.

But Grandmama wasn't there. An empty cup and saucer sat on the desk under the window, a half-written letter scratched with her grandmother's elegant script left beside the inkpot and quill. Aurora caught the words bubbling on her tongue. She stood there a minute, looking around at the deserted room—a wall lined with shelves full of exotic foreign knickknacks, another wall stuffed with books, the empty fireplace, a brocade love seat in one corner, a rocker in the other.

Then she'd gone pattering through the house looking for Grandmama and couldn't find her anywhere. Grandpapa was gone to the hospital. Finally she went to the kitchen to ask Vonetta if she'd seen her grandmother. "In her sitting room, honey," Vonetta said kindly. "Go ask her if she wants some more tea, would you? Then come on back here and I'll give you some oatmeal for breakfast."

Aurora didn't want oatmeal. She wanted to go home. But she ran back up the stairs to the sitting room, ridiculously hoping she'd just overlooked her grandmother somehow.

The room was as empty as it had been before. Maybe more so. Frustrated, aching with fatigue and anxiety, she sat down on the hassock in front of the rocker and felt her face crumple. A wail came up from the pit of her stomach, and she folded over her knees. "Oh. Oh. Oh. It's so . . ." She didn't know what "it" was. But it hurt.

She didn't hear the door open, but she felt Grandmama's arms even as the scent of lavender enveloped her. She cried in Grandmama's lap for a time, until finally her grandmother gave her a handkerchief and told her to stop ruining her skirt.

Sitting up, Aurora blew her nose. "Where were you?"

"Prayer closet."

That was when Aurora noticed through aching, burning eyes that the door next to the fireplace stood ajar. She'd assumed it to be a linen closet or some such. "I thought that verse in the Bible was a metaphor."

"No reason it can't be literal." Eyes sparking with amusement, Grandmama stood and offered her blue-veined hand to Aurora. "Come here."

Following her grandmother, she stood back while Grandmama opened the closet door wide, revealing nothing more exciting than a simple wooden chair. It didn't even have a cushion. There wasn't room for a table or bookshelf.

Aurora looked up at Grandmama, puzzled. "Didn't you hear me come in the first time?"

"I thought I heard the outer door open, but I was busy with God. There didn't seem to be any blood or mayhem." Grandmama scowled. "Are you all right?"

Aurora looked at her feet. "I was just . . ." In the face of this prosaic concern, her misery seemed overblown. "I'm fine."

"You are now, but what had you in such a maudlin dither? I've never known you to behave this way, Petey."

Grandmama was not one of those squishy grandparents who gave one too much candy or spent money on elaborate, unnecessary toys. And she never, ever used Aurora's nickname.

She felt her eyes leak again and wiped them with the soggy handkerchief. "I m-miss my mama. And I know that's silly, because you'll take good care of me."

"Of course I will. But I'm going to teach you something that will stand you in good stead when you're confused or scared, or when people misbehave, or when you're just plain lonesome." Grandmama sat down in the chair in the closet and patted her lap. "Come on."

"I'm too big to—"

"Aurora, sit down!"

Aurora sat. Grandmama closed the closet door on the two of them.

It was very dark, and a little stuffy. But peaceful with lavender all around. Aurora relaxed and let her head fall onto Grandmama's shoulder, and she felt that graceful, beringed hand rest on her hair. "Grandmama, did you ever get left behind?"

"Honey, we all get left behind at some time or another. Only one Person is always there. It helps to be utterly quiet and undisturbed when you talk to him, but you're right—you don't actually have to be in a closet."

Aurora felt Grandmama's chest rise and fall with suppressed laughter. Her own heart lightened. Her grandmother had a well-hidden sense of humor. And suddenly she felt loved in the most tangible way. God had answered her prayer before she ever prayed it.

Sitting now on the steps outside her saloon, she remembered that sense of belonging to God, of being someone he personally saw and loved. He had probably—no, she *knew* he'd already provided a way for her to help Bedelia and Rosie and Zane Sager. Her first step should be a willingness to listen. And then she must have the courage to do what he told her to do.

Zane could feel the eyes on his back. Walking that gauntlet back to the jail with Riggins and Beaumont reminded him of June 1864, when his unit got caught in the bottleneck at Tishomingo Bridge. Come to think of it, that had been not too far from here, near Brice's Cross Roads. Overwhelmed by Forrest's cavalry corps, the whole Guard unit got swept

106

up and taken prisoner, signaling the effectual end of his service. He'd been marched to Alabama and treated to all the tender mercies of Cahaba.

Now he was free. In fact, in one of those ironic reversals of life, most of his duties involved escorting and guarding prisoners like Jefcoat and Moore. Still, sometimes he wondered whether he'd traded one type of incarceration for another.

Down near the end of the street, across from the railway station, he could see the outline of the Dogwood Saloon, where Riggins proposed hiding him and his two charges until the trial. A small dress-clad figure sitting on the porch steps almost looked like—

Zane stopped in his tracks. "You didn't bring her with you, did you?"

Riggins looked guilty, but Beaumont laughed. "Aurora doesn't like getting left behind. Looks like she didn't make much headway with her new employees." Beaumont raised a hand and yelled at the girl on the steps. "Hey, Pete, did they boot you out?"

She stood up and propped her hands on her hips, yelling back, "I left of my own free will!" She started stomping toward them. "Wait! I need to talk to Deputy Marshal Sager."

Beaumont elbowed Riggins. "You think he can handle it by himself?"

"I don't know." Riggins shook his head. "I feel like this is one of those 'every man for himself' situations. Let's go relieve Pickett and let the chips fall where they will."

Zane could not describe how much he wanted to follow the two of them to the jail, where at least his responsibilities were clear-cut and followed a military code of procedure. But as he watched Aurora Daughtry's purposeful approach, he asked himself when he'd ever voluntarily run away from anything that scared him.

Never. That was the answer. So he took a deep breath as he went to meet her.

Their paths converged in front of one of the two boarding-houses already doing business in Tupelo. Avoiding Aurora's big gold-shot eyes, he looked up at the plain clapboard facade to his right. "Why do we need another boardinghouse?" When she didn't answer, he made himself look at her.

Her lips were pursed, expression quizzical. "Why, good morning, Mr. Sager. I'm very well, thank you. And you?"

He felt blood rush to his face. This was why he hated women. Well, he didn't hate them. He just didn't know what to do with them. "I'm sorry." Was he doomed to spend the next week or so apologizing every five minutes? "But did you really think this out?"

"I actually did. You might not think it to look at me, but I'm told I have a shrewd head for business. Ask Schuyler. Never mind, don't ask him. He pretends to be stupid because he's too lazy to do what he doesn't want to do. Anyway, I had my lawyer make some inquiries about the potential for growth, and he discovered there will soon be a new railroad coming through Tupelo, to link Kansas City and Memphis to the coal fields of Birmingham. We've already got cotton growing all around us, and he believes there'll eventually be a compress here. All this industry will require housing, and I intend to have the cleanest, best-run boardinghouse, with the finest food in town." She took a step toward him and smiled. "I'm going to practice on you."

He looked down at her and stated the obvious. "You talk. A lot."

"Are you worried that I'll tell people you're staying with me?" Her beautiful winged eyebrows quirked a little.

"Mainly I'm concerned for your safety, not to mention your reputation. If anyone finds out you've got three unmarried men putting up in your house, you'll be ruined."

"That would be my problem, not yours," she said with sunny indifference. "But there is one thing you can help me with." She took his elbow and more or less towed him back in the direction of the Dogwood. "I need you to arrest one of my saloon girls."

Nine

As THE DEPUTY MARSHAL locked the cell door behind a sobbing Bedelia, Aurora hoped she hadn't just made a terrible mistake. When the idea hit her out of the blue, she'd assumed the inspiration had come from desperation.

But now she wondered if perhaps it wasn't just a bit devious. Not to mention misguided. Bedelia showed no signs of ceasing her theatrical objections.

"Thank you, Mr. Sager." Closing her ears to the saloon girl's hysterics, Aurora smiled at the deputy sheriff. He made quite an effective co-conspirator, once he saw the logic behind her method. "I didn't know how else I was going to convince Miss O'Malley that she cannot continue squatting on someone else's property."

"Rosamund!" Bedelia blew a blonde ringlet out of her eyes. "I can't leave her out on the street all by herself!"

"And you people can't leave this woman here overnight!" Constable Pickett hooked his thumbs at the opposite cells of Jefcoat and Moore, who stared at Bedelia as if a ban-

110

shee had landed in their midst. "This ain't no place for a female."

Sager sat down on his preferred seat and tipped it on two legs back against the wall. "Miss Daughtry has offered an alternative solution that our . . . piercing guest won't take." He put his head back, closed his good eye, and seemed prepared to abandon the subject in favor of a nap.

"That is true," Aurora said with a sigh. "I'm afraid Miss O'Malley insists on doing things her own way." Maintaining her composure with difficulty, she took Schuyler's arm and smiled at Levi. "Gentlemen, if you've concluded your business, I think we'd best return to Daughtry House. Selah and Joelle will be wondering if I've absconded with their men."

"Wait! What alternative?" Pickett moved to block their exit. "I didn't hear no alternative."

Aurora blinked up at him. "I'm surprised you could hear anything over all that caterwauling. Why, I offered to take Bedelia and Rosie home to Daughtry House with me. My staff and I could train them for jobs at the hotel, with the potential to return here to the *boardinghouse*"—she cast a significant look over her shoulder at the middle cell—"if they excel." She was pleased to note that the wails from that quarter had diminished to dramatic sniffles.

Pickett chewed on the end of his mustache for a moment, then walked over to Bedelia's cell. "All right, Deedee, that's enough. You've pitched your fit, now it's time to use your noggin."

Folding her arms, she gave him a resentful stare from dry green eyes. "It's outraged I am."

"I know you are." His nasal voice softened. "But you knew you couldn't stay at the Dogwood, not once old Rom turned up his toes. If it hadn't been this nice young lady, woulda been somebody else booted you out. At least you'll have a way of earning your keep."

"I got my own way of earning my keep, an' it don't involve emptying chamber pots," Bedelia said.

Pickett glanced over his shoulder at Aurora. "Never mind that," he said, blushing.

"Bedelia," Aurora said, "I know you don't particularly like me, and you have no reason to trust me—not yet, anyway. But remember my sister Selah? She's the nicest thing in the world, and she's going to—" She caught herself, unable to remember if Levi knew Selah's secret yet. "She'll need extra help with me here in town. Wouldn't you like to be useful, instead of just hoping somebody will come along and drop off food, as if you and Rosie were stray cats or something?"

"I ain't no stray cat!" Bedelia howled, for all the world like a tabby whose tail had been stepped on.

"No, I didn't mean—"

The chair against the wall thumped to the floor as Zane Sager surged to his feet, interrupting Aurora's backtracking. "Bedelia O'Malley," he said quietly, stalking toward her cell and giving Pickett a look that sent him scuttling back to his desk. Sager took hold of the bars and leaned in. "Are you listening to me?"

Aurora stood behind him, mesmerized by the contained power in his muscled body, as Bedelia was evidently mesmerized by his face.

"I'm listening." Bedelia sucked in her lower lip.

"All right," Sager said. "I'm going to tell you something I heard once that changed my life. I was going down for the count, but this made me get up and keep fighting. You're a fighter, I can see that. I know you're worried about your friend. But you gotta get out of here to help her. And when somebody offers you a hand out of the mud, you don't spit on it just because it doesn't land you exactly where you want to go. Maybe you don't believe in God, but sometimes he sends you off in a new direction for your own good. And you may not know how good that is for a very long time. But eventually you will. You're gonna have to trust me on that."

He waited, standing there, until at last Bedelia dropped her gaze and nodded.

"All right. I don't trust her. But I trust you." Bedelia backed away from the door, fists clenched at her sides. "Now let me out of here."

With a very small curve at the corner of his mouth, Zane Sager unlocked the cell door. "Miss O'Malley, you're free to go with Miss Daughtry. Consider yourself on parole. I'll be out to check on you in a couple of days."

As Bedelia passed her on her way to the door, Aurora walked over to lay her hand on Sager's forearm. "Thank you," she said softly. "That was brilliant."

He froze and looked at her. "I just told her the truth."

"I know. Very tricky." When he produced that rusty laugh, she joined him. "Selah may skin me when I show up with that harridan and her Chinese friend tonight. When are you going to—you know?"

"I still don't think that's a good idea. I was just helping you get rid of your unwanted guests."

She frowned. "But—"

"Look, Miss Daughtry. You're going to have to trust me, too, to know what's best for my prisoners. For now we're hunkered down here and things are just fine." He moved back so that her hand fell away from his arm. "Go home."

Stung, she restrained an ungracious retort. With a curt nod and a dip of a curtsey, she wheeled to follow her cadre to the carriage. *Arrogant boor.*

She sighed as Schuyler handed her up beside Bedelia. Zane Sager was the most interesting boor she'd ever met in her life. And if he ever fully smiled at her, she might be lost.

Zane waited nearly two hours, pretending to doze in his uncomfortable chair, before Pickett finally left for the noon meal. The constable had grudgingly offered to bring him something when he returned, and Zane had accepted. The man had most likely been the one to sic the dogs on him last night, but some vestige of basic manners apparently remained.

When Pickett had been gone for a good ten minutes, Zane rose and approached the cells. Now that the women were gone, he needed to get down to the business at hand. Once the judge arrived next week, he would have a lot less discretion in handling the prisoners. And he had some questions he wanted to ask, following up on what Beaumont and Riggins had told him this morning.

He squatted on his haunches outside Jefcoat's cell and reached into his shirt pocket for a tobacco pouch. He offered it to the prisoner. "Want a plug?"

Jefcoat's expression was suspicious, but after a moment he took the pouch, extracted a wad, and stuck it into his cheek. "Thanks."

"How about you, Moore?" Zane glanced at the light-skinned Negro. When Moore shook his head, Zane returned the pouch to his pocket. He'd never developed a taste for the expensive tobacco habit, but the price of buying it to get people to talk was justifiable. "You know this whole town is afraid you two are going to name names," he said conversationally. "They came after you last night."

"Pickett said they came after *you*," Jefcoat said around his plug. "Us Southerners don't like federals telling us how to manage our business."

Moore's smile was sardonic. "I think they'd be just as happy to turn us loose."

"Pickett could have done that this morning while I was gone," Zane said. "He's smarter than that."

Jefcoat snorted. "Not much."

"If that's so, how come you're in this cell and he's not? Weren't you both involved in that business over at the newspaper office?"

"That's not what this is about." Jefcoat spat into a corner. "This is about Schuyler Beaumont getting revenge."

"Well, the murder of a man's father is bound to make him a little touchy," Zane said. "He says you admitted it."

"He's a liar." Jefcoat's small eyes were hard. "He's the one attacked me. Didn't he, Harold?"

"I saw Beaumont leap on Mr. Andrew and try to choke him," Moore said. "He ought to be the one behind bars."

Zane pulled out his whittling. "Then what kind of revenge are you talking about? Why would he attack you?"

"I don't know." Jefcoat looked confused. "I told him it was an accident—whoever killed Mr. Zeke."

"How do you know that?"

"Because he—they—were just trying to scare those two colored rabble-rousers." He glanced at his half brother, who just gave him a stoic stare in return. "It was a wild shot not meant to hurt anybody."

Zane paused in the act of paring curling slivers into the twig to shape the raccoon's tail. "Jefcoat, I want to believe you. But you've got some high-powered influence between you and justice." Glancing at the bearded young muscle-head, he shrugged and went back to his carving. "Only way I see you getting clear—you help us pull some of that obfuscation down."

"I don't know what—"

"Smoke screen," Moore said. "He means you need to give names of the leaders."

"I'm not a rat," Jefcoat snarled. "Besides, they'd kill me if I talked."

"You're in protective custody," Zane said. "My job is to not let anything happen to you."

Jefcoat gave him a pitying look. "I'd watch out, if I was you. That little crowd last night was just a warning."

"I promise you I can take care of myself. Are you willing to go to prison for these people? Klan terrorism is a federal offense now."

"Prison?" Jefcoat smirked. "Nobody's going to prison. Judge Hill is well known for a twenty-five-dollar maximum fine and a thousand-dollar peace bond."

Zane's hand clenched the knife hard. He'd heard the same thing but hoped it wouldn't be true in this case. Marshal Eaton was convinced the presence of the US Attorney General would raise the stakes enough to force the judge to apply appropriate penalties. The president was serious about stopping Klan violence in the South.

He looked at Jefcoat coolly. "I wouldn't take that chance, if it were me." He transferred his gaze to Moore. "How about you? You going to let this white boy walk all over you? Beaumont told me he played you for a fool, trying to nail the white schoolteacher."

Moore just returned his stare. "I got nothing to tell you," he finally said with stolid blankness.

"See?" Jefcoat crowed. "Harold knows what side his bread's buttered on."

Zane rose and tucked the little half-finished raccoon into his pocket, making a production of folding his knife. "Well, you'll have plenty of time to think it in that cell. Would've thought you'd have a little more sense—"

The outer door opened to admit Pickett, followed by a bull-shaped fellow wearing a hat too big for his bullet-shaped head and a sheriff's badge pinned to his vest.

The sheriff stopped to knock the dust off his boots and check the environs of the building before following the constable inside. He walked over to Zane with a hand outstretched. "Sheriff Epinetus Gere," he said by way of introduction. "You must be Deputy Marshal Sager."

"Yes, sir." Zane shook hands. "Sorry about taking over your jail. Pickett didn't seem to know we were coming."

Gere responded with a dry smile. "Pickett don't know much of nothing." Dodging the newspaper wad Pickett threw at him, he walked over to the cells and checked the locks. Apparently satisfied that they would hold, he went to his desk and began to rummage about in a drawer. "Sorry I wasn't here to help with the take-in."

"Pickett explained," Zane said. "I hope everything is all right."

Without looking up, Gere shrugged. "Under control."

Zane waited. Usually people explained emergencies, loved to talk about their own heroic part in it. When Gere found a pipe in the drawer and proceeded to fill and smoke it without further comment, Zane made a mental note. He didn't trust any of these local lawmen, knew better than to take them at their word.

He was about to take the opportunity to walk outside and stretch his legs when the door slammed open. Zane recognized the balding head and ink-stained collar of the man whose shotgun had so bravely defended him yesterday. Aurora had introduced him as Wimus McCanless, Joelle's editor at the *Tupelo Journal.*

McCanless remained half in, half out of the doorway. "Is the deputy marshal still—oh, there you are. And Sheriff Gere—it's good you're back." He stepped inside, removing his glasses to wipe sweat off his forehead. "I just got word— there's been a murder."

Gere lunged to his feet. "In broad daylight? Where?"

McCanless shook his head. "Probably last night. Fisherman found Deputy Marshal Theophilus Redding washed up in the Tishomingo River early this morning. His throat was cut."

Zane's hand went of its own volition to his eye patch. Jones.

Ten

Dogwood Boarding House
Monday, June 6, 1870

Fixing people wasn't as simple a procedure as one might suppose, Aurora concluded, but at least she and Bedelia had reached what might be called an armistice.

Standing on the top step of a ladder to reach the chandelier over the bar, she adjusted the scarf tied about her head to better deflect flying dust. The upstairs mainly needed a good sweeping and a mop bucket to restore it to cleanliness. But the Dogwood's former male denizens seemed to have viewed the alarming amount of grime accumulated on the ground floor as part of the decor.

She applied her rag and brass polish to the chandelier with renewed vigor. The first part of her plan—introducing her charges to their new home at Daughtry House—had gone quite swimmingly. Bedelia took one look at Horatia's new grandson Benny, cooing in his swaddling in a homemade cradle on the hearth, and fell into a puddle of maternal bliss.

Rosie's interaction with Horatia's collection of cookware exhibited similar evidence of covetousness.

Moving the girls' meager belongings into one of the little outbuildings that had formerly housed plantation slaves had been accomplished with complete lack of drama. The cabin—along with a row of five others just like it behind the overseer's old cabin—had been reroofed, freshly painted, and furnished with simple bedsteads, table and chairs, and a couple of rugs. Professing herself charmed (prompted no doubt by memories of her recent brush with jail), Bedelia flung herself onto the center of the bed, while Rosie wandered over to inspect a small painting hung beside the door. Aurora left them amicably arguing over who would get to sleep next to the window.

The first sign of trouble came the next morning when Aurora knocked on the cabin door. "Wake up, girls, it's time to get dressed for church!" After a full minute of waiting with no response, she knocked again. "Bedelia! Open this door!" Finally she resorted to taking off her shoe and hammering with the heel. "Wake up! Fire!"

The door creaked inward half an inch. One black almond-shaped eye appeared. "Miss Ola?" Rosie, who struggled with Aurora's *r*-filled name had resorted to her own diminutive. "We sleepy. Day off you say."

"The day is free so that everyone can go to church. I thought you understood."

"I understand, but Bedelia—"

Aurora simply pushed her out of the way. "Bedelia! Get out of that bed!"

"You are not the boss of me!" Bedelia's voice came from beneath her pillow.

"Yes. I am."

"It's Sunday."

"Correct. This family goes to church on Sunday."

Bedelia came out from under the pillow. "Am I your employee or your family?"

Aurora stomped her foot, the one with a shoe still on it. "Both! Now get up or I'll have the deputy marshal come pay you a visit."

Bedelia sat up, blinking suddenly bright green eyes. "The deputy marshal can pay me a visit anytime he wants," she purred, stretching. Curls everywhere, she looked like a blonde Medusa.

"If you'll get up and get dressed, maybe he'll be at church." Aurora laughed as Bedelia scrambled for her robe. "Breakfast is in the manager's cottage kitchen. We leave at nine," she said and left the two former fancy women to clothe themselves in whatever strength and beauty they could muster.

As everyone piled into the carriage and wagon, a small kerfuffle over décolletage ensued, but Joelle solved the problem by loaning Bedelia a lacy shawl, pinned in place with a brooch Gil Reese had given her during the first week of their erstwhile engagement. Rosie's dress was modest enough, a striped cotton travel dress with a tight black collar.

Looking back on it, Aurora should have known that Gil—she couldn't go back to calling him Pastor Reese, not after the way he had treated Joelle—would recognize the brooch. She also could have predicted his objection to the presence of two former dance hall girls in his church service. She saw his eyes latch onto Rosie and Bedelia, seated on the Daughtry family pew between ThomasAnne and herself, saw his heavy eyebrows draw together over his Roman nose.

121

Consequently, she did her best to shunt her charges outside as soon as the last "amen" rang at the end of the closing hymn. "Come on, girls," she said, hooking her arm through Bedelia's, "we've got to get home to make the gravy. Rosie, you'll like that."

But Bedelia dug in her heels. "You said the deputy marshal would be here."

That was loud. And here came Gil, marching down the aisle, looking like a thundercloud about to rain on everybody in sight.

Aurora pulled harder. "I guess he didn't come after—"

"Good morning, Miss O'Malley," came a crisp baritone from behind her. "I'm glad to see you made it to the Lord's house after your upsetting day yesterday."

Aurora slowly let go of Bedelia and turned to find Zane Sager standing at the end of the pew she had just passed. Had he been there the whole time? She was notoriously squirmy in church, and wasn't that just charming?

Chancing a look at his face, she found him staring, not at Bedelia, but straight at her, a little sideways tuck at the corner of his mouth. He was freshly shaved, his hair slicked back with some kind of tonic, and his shallow-crowned hat was tucked under his arm. Of course he still looked like an outlaw in that eye patch. And she preferred his dark hair in its natural disheveled state.

"Hello, Deputy Marshal," she said with what dignity she could muster. "I told Bedelia you'd probably be here today." She hadn't really believed it, but he didn't have to know that.

Surprise flashed in his one good eye. "Did you?" He returned that quizzical gaze to Bedelia. "It was a bit of a last-minute decision. The sheriff offered to stay with my prisoners so I could leave the jail."

"Would you like to come home with us for Sunday dinner?" The words were out of Aurora's mouth before she could call them back.

"Oh, please come, Deputy Marshal," Bedelia said, clasping her gloved hands. "I'm going to make the gravy."

Before Aurora could dispute this bald-faced lie, Gil Reese reached around her to point at Bedelia's chest with a long, bony finger. "Where did you get that?"

Bedelia's face reddened. "It was a gift—not that it's any of your business."

"It *was* a gift," Gil said, "from me to my former fiancée. You must have stolen—"

"There's been a misunderstanding, Pastor," Sager said. "Miss O'Malley is a guest of the Daughtrys."

"That's impossible. I know Bedelia O'Malley, and—" Too late Gil saw his mistake. "I mean, *everybody* knows the nature of these unfortunate girls."

"Do they?" Sager asked silkily. "But hopefully everybody also knows how Jesus treated women who wanted a new start in life. Not to mention what he had to say about white-washed hypocrites."

That sounded a little off somehow, Aurora thought, but she wasn't going to split hairs. She'd look it up later. "Exactly. I'm not sure who's going to make the gravy"—she frowned at Bedelia— "but it will be good. We hope you'll join us."

Sager shook his head. "I'm afraid I can't be away from my duties any longer. Thank you for the invitation." His gaze lingered on Aurora's face for a second before he turned to Bedelia, picked up her hand, and kissed her knuckles. "Do your best, Miss O'Malley, and you may own a boardinghouse yourself one day."

And that was how it came to be that on Monday morning Aurora stood on a ladder polishing chandeliers, wondering why the deputy marshal hadn't kissed *her* hand. She appreciated his kindness to Bedelia, but what had Aurora said to send him back to the jail as if the hounds of hell were after him? At least he seemed to consider running a boardinghouse a worthwhile endeavor.

Despite the fact that he'd turned down the offer of staying here in no uncertain terms.

Overhead she could hear ThomasAnne tramping around, directing Bedelia in the art of bed making, while Shug Pogue's hammer tapped sporadically as he inspected the roof. She smiled at the thought of Rosie, who had remained at Daughtry House today, happily beginning her culinary training under Horatia Lawrence. The excitement on that small round face made every bit of sweat and sore muscles Aurora endured worth the effort.

An hour later, aching in places she didn't know she *had* muscles, dirt and brass polish smeared in equal portions from head to toe, she moved the ladder to the fireplace. That picture had to come down, and now. The bubble-covered woman's saucy stare was making the back of her neck itch.

Near the top of the ladder, she tested the weight of the frame and found it heavy, not to mention large and awkward, but she thought she could manage it by herself. Bracing her hips against the ladder, she lifted the frame off its nail.

"Here, let me get that."

As the weight suddenly shifted, she lost her balance and listed sideways with a startled little shriek.

"Hold on—I've got you." Zane Sager caught her around the waist, holding her fast while lowering the picture frame to the floor with his other hand. "You all right?"

Her hand rested on his powerful shoulder, her chin was on top of his head, and she could hardly breathe for his grip around her ribs. "I'm—I think so." The words came out in puffs of indignity. He was always sneaking up on her.

"Didn't mean to scare you," he said as if reading her mind. Letting go of the picture, which slapped backward against the floor with a *bang*, he braced both hands at her waist and set her upright on her feet. "There you go. No harm done."

Aurora looked down. "The pink lady looks a little jolted." She'd been calling her that in her mind but had no intention of saying it aloud. She bit her lip.

"I don't blame you for letting her go." Sager didn't look particularly scandalized. "Waste of bubbles," he said dispassionately, shoving the frame across the now gleaming floor with one booted foot. "I prefer women covered in . . ." He half-closed the extravagantly lashed green eye to examine Aurora's face. "Mustard?"

Blushing, she scrubbed at her cheeks with both hands. "Brass polish. I was cleaning the—" *What* were they talking about? Oh yes, the pink lady. "I could use a bubble bath myself, I imagine." She stared at him in horror, imagining what must be going on in his head.

And then a very slow grin appeared on his dark face. She had been absolutely right to fear this. It transformed him from grim to heartbreaking.

Pitched headlong into insanity, she said, "Don't worry, we're going to repaint her."

His eyebrow went up. The grin broadened. "So . . . orange? Purple?"

"Oh. My. Gracious." She grabbed an old curtain she'd unearthed from the attic, and tossed it over the naughty picture. "Please forget anything I just said. Did you need something, Deputy Marshal? I'm sorry I don't have anything to offer you to drink, since we're not yet open for business, but lemonade is probably not your libation of choice anyway. But since you're here, let me say thank you for sticking up for Bedelia in church yesterday. Gil Reese is a self-righteous, over-educated donkey and I never liked him, which makes it difficult to listen to him preach, but it also makes me even more thankful that Joelle finally woke up and realized Schuyler is the only man alive who can understand half of what she says."

A moment passed while he appeared to be sifting through her monologue to decide which part to answer. "You're welcome," he finally said, the eye still twinkling, though his mouth resumed its usual sardonic bend. "I came to see if the offer of housing is still open."

The sight of the ladder had disabled his brain.

Otherwise, there was no excuse for allowing an encounter with a young Southern gentlewoman to descend into risqué innuendo. But she would never understand—in fact, he couldn't even explain to himself—why the sight of an ordinary ladder landed him back in Cahaba, enduring the stretching of his shoulders and underarm tendons, the torment of hanging for hours from a rung so high his toes barely touched the ground.

Jones's term for that particular punishment was "On the

Ladder." And he made sure his victims never forgot its effect, even after five years.

Still, what kind of man stood frozen in a doorway, while a copper-haired elf like Aurora Daughtry hoisted a framed picture bigger than she was over her head? She could have taken a dangerous tumble if he hadn't snapped out of his mental episode at the last moment.

Now he watched her polish-stained, heart-shaped face as she considered his question. She should slap him, throw him out on his behind, *something* besides purse her lips and study him with those big brown eyes.

Finally she smiled and said, "Of course it's still open. Why did you change your mind?"

He felt crazily absolved. The death of his friend Theo Redding had changed his mind. But she didn't need to know that. Thinking about it Saturday night, he'd planned to send Riggins to work out the details with Aurora. But then Sunday morning came.

And Sunday mornings usually changed his perspective. Seeing the two saloon girls in church with Aurora, dressed and in their right minds, clearly happy to be accepted by a respectable family like the Daughtrys, had jerked another knot in his feelings.

Feelings he had previously been able to suppress. And he hadn't been able to keep his mouth shut when the preacher got all high and mighty about that ugly, gaudy pin. Of course he'd run from the invitation to dinner with her family—proving he was a coward after all.

But this morning he'd come over here to inspect the perimeter of the place for outside entrances, checked the front door and found it open. And when he took her by the waist—

sure enough, it was small enough to fit easily between his hands—she took his awkwardness with no apparent resentment or disdain.

He shrugged. "I thought about it," he said. "We can stay here without putting you in danger, but we'll have to be careful about the move. And of course you'll have to act like we're not here. Beaumont and Riggins both think I can trust you to keep quiet."

"I don't know why there's any question about that." She tugged off the calico scarf around her head, letting loose a mass of red-brown curls, and scratched her head. "I told you, I'm the best secret-keeper in the family. I knew Schuyler had Grandmama's ring in his pocket for over a week before he gave it to Joelle. I know Dr. Kidd is head over heels in love with ThomasAnne. And I was the first person to know Selah is—" She pinched her cherry lips together. "Never mind."

He had no idea what she was talking about, but then he didn't really care, so long as she kept her mouth shut about him and the prisoners. He nodded. "Fine. The marshal is going to wire me with instructions to get on the train with Jefcoat and Moore and head for Oxford. So I'll make a big production out of leaving tomorrow. We'll get off at the second stop and disappear."

"How are you going to do that?" Her eyes widened.

"Little trick I learned in the army." He waved a hand. "Anyway, we'll double back in the middle of the night. I walked around the exterior before I came in. There's a cellar at the back, where the ground slopes down toward town. Tonight before you leave, lock all the doors and windows, but leave that cellar door open."

"How exciting!" She bounced on her toes. "But I'm not leaving. ThomasAnne and I have moved in."

"No. I knew you'd be here during the day, but you can't—"

"No, *you* can't tell me what to do with my own board-inghouse. There's too much to do to keep traipsing back and forth between here and Daughtry House. But I hadn't realized there was a cellar. I'll go down there this afternoon and clean it out. I'm sure it can be put to some good use—"

"Miss Daughtry—"

"Oh, stop calling me that." She was beginning to get a pigheaded look that reminded him of his sister Jacqueline. "If you're going to keep bossing me around like—like one of my brothers, then you might as well call me Pete like every-body else."

He supposed she meant Riggins and Beaumont, the clos-est thing she had to brothers. But he couldn't call this vivid, sassy porcelain doll "Pete." If it made her unhappy to be "Miss Daughtry," then he wouldn't call her anything. But he wasn't going to argue either. He'd find another way to make sure she left every night. Folding his arms, he took a step back. "Fine. I just wanted you to be aware that I'll be back tomorrow night. I'll have Riggins or Beaumont give you any more details that come up. All right?"

Frowning as if she didn't quite trust his acquiescence, she nodded. "I packed us a lunch so we wouldn't have to go to the hotel. Would you like to—"

"No. Thank you," he added hastily when she looked hurt. "I have a lot to do today." He glanced at the empty spot on the dirty wall, where the picture frame had been. "And so do you. Good day, Miss—Good day." Wheeling, he left with what shreds of dignity he had left.

He thought he heard a thump behind him, as if something hit the wall. Probably his overwrought imagination. Ladies did not throw things.

The cellar smelled like old whiskey. Aurora couldn't decide if that was disgusting or fascinating. Maybe both.

Holding up a lamp at the top of the stairs, she tried to picture her father and old man Oglesby hacking this underground room out of the clay that formed the side of the hill. Her imagination failed. Papa had become a rather mystical figure in her mind—a horseback, gun-toting ghost with the thick brown beard, shaggy hair, and deep-set eyes she remembered from her childhood. Selah had tried to describe the man he'd become at the end—broken of mind, graying, and scarred by war and deprivation. She said Papa's eye had been blown out by shrapnel, so he wore a patch.

Zane Sager did too. Accidents happened—though war wasn't really an accident. Men put their lives in danger because of things they believed in. She didn't know how Zane had come by his wounded face, but she knew he was a warrior with a strong sense of justice and commitment to protecting those weaker than himself. She could still feel his hands, bands of iron at her waist, keeping her from falling off the ladder.

She wanted to think her father was a good man who believed in good things. But because she wasn't sure of that, she didn't like to think of him at all.

Looking over her shoulder, she smiled up at ThomasAnne, hovering at the top of the stairs with Bedelia. "Y'all can come on down. Nothing more dangerous than a few spiderwebs."

"I really don't like spiders," ThomasAnne said.

"Neither me," Bedelia said. "I'll just stay right here until they're gone, so."

"Bedelia, did you never come down here?" Aurora turned to climb back up the narrow stairs. Looked like she'd have to have one of the men clear out the creepy-crawlies before they could deep clean.

Bedelia, kneeling at the trapdoor, shuddered as Aurora emerged. "No reason to. My job was dancing and hostessing. Drinks was Old Rom's purview."

Aurora sat down on the edge of the opening, letting her legs dangle. Her dress was already filthy, so a little more dirt wouldn't hurt. ThomasAnne had pulled up a chair and seated herself, plying a fan made from an old beer invoice. She was only minimally less dirty than Bedelia and herself.

"Bedelia, how long have you worked here?" Aurora asked.

The saloon girl squinted. "Five years, maybe? I came with my husband—he worked on a rail crew right after the war."

"You were married?" ThomasAnne asked, voicing Aurora's surprise.

Bedelia nodded. "My Billy drank here every day. When he was killed in a knife fight, Old Rom came out to the camp and offered me a job." She shrugged. "I'd no place else to go. Rom kept me from starving."

"What about Rosie?" Aurora demanded. "She can't be more than sixteen! Surely she hasn't been here that long."

"She's fifteen. Ran away from home a year ago, didn't want to marry the man they picked out for her." Bedelia paused. "A friend of her da."

If that was true . . . Aurora's throat clenched on bile. She looked up and met ThomasAnne's eyes, which swam with tears. "Well. Bad things happen. My grandpapa says it's because human beings are free to make evil decisions, and God loves us enough to want us to come to him in humility." She got to her feet, dusting a cobweb off her skirt. "I have to say, though, if I were God, I would squash Rosie's father like a bug."

Eleven

Tuesday, June 7, 1870

Shepherding two prisoners back to Tupelo by himself on foot was considerably more difficult than the train ride in with Riggins. But having survived three days in the woods of northwest Alabama with hunting dogs on his trail, this little trek seemed to Zane like an afternoon tea party. At least he had on good solid boots, and he wouldn't be forced to sleep in trees and rub feces on the bottom of bare feet to hide his scent.

They'd taken the last train to Memphis out of Tupelo Monday afternoon. Riggins, smart enough to make it look as if they'd tried to sneak out, had purchased the tickets himself, then passed them to Zane as he, Jefcoat, and Moore slid onto the endmost car just before it pulled out of the station. The three of them got off at New Albany but neglected to re-board, instead heading off into the woods. Circling and doubling, but always in a southeasterly direction, they spent

Monday night camped in an abandoned hunting cabin. To be precise, Jefcoat and Moore slept, while Zane dozed fitfully.

The next morning, Zane woke his companions early. They traveled slowly toward Tupelo, along the rails but far enough away to avoid running into anyone.

Zane had brought along enough simple food to last them through the next day. As he bit off a hunk of the jerky that constituted his evening meal, he couldn't help thinking of Aurora's offer of her picnic lunch. Loaves and fishes, he thought wistfully. Major miracles often came from the most mundane things.

But you couldn't count on that. Exhibit A, nobody had swooped in at the last minute to rescue Theo Redding—proving this was a dangerous job that Zane could never inflict on anybody he cared about.

Not that he *cared* about Aurora exactly. In any case, he wasn't free to enjoy a polite meal with a young lady. He was a rambler, every waking minute consumed with either hunting down Sam Jones or safeguarding the worthless hide of some criminal. Forever in pursuit of justice.

Justice. Aware of the irony, he eyed Moore, sitting on a fallen log beside Jefcoat and morosely staring at the ground between his feet. Zane supposed all three of them had gotten what they deserved. But maybe God heard his prayers and would eventually deliver Jones into his hands. Well, the hands of the law.

He touched his badge. Wasn't that the same thing?

By suppertime on Tuesday, Aurora had had her fill of cleaning. She and ThomasAnne and Bedelia had scrubbed every square inch of the Dogwood Saloon—soon-to-be Boarding House—including the attic and the cellar. Finished with his inspection of the roof, Shug agreed to vanquish the spiders, while Schuyler walked down to the Rattlesnake to sell the cases of bourbon and kegs of beer left in the cellar. Thomas-Anne wanted to dump all the liquor in the street, in a demonstration of its worthless nature, but Aurora couldn't see the sense in sending good money after bad. Why not, she reasoned, use the proceeds to purchase real food, which would feed the renovators until paying boarders could be taken in?

Accordingly—dirty, hungry, and exhausted—the three of them heaved the Pink Lady into the boot of the carriage, covered her in a blanket, and headed for Daughtry House. Not that Aurora was caving in to Zane Sager's insistence that she not stay overnight. This was purely for her own convenience. She had to take Bedelia back to Daughtry House, and she really needed a soak in the bathtub. Tomorrow would be soon enough to move in.

Yesterday afternoon and all day today, Aurora had been so busy she'd had little time to worry about Zane Sager. Somehow, though, she'd made time to wonder how he'd accomplished his "little trick" of vanishing off the train. And what he'd found for food. And where he'd spent last night. And how he'd managed to sleep while guarding two prisoners.

Oh, all right. She was worried about him even now, as she pulled on the reins to draw the sorrels to a stop in front of the house. Last night she'd gone to sleep in her own little bed in the manager's cottage, picturing the tenseness of his shoulders, the tiredness in his green eye. Something bad had happened, or he wouldn't have agreed to stay at the Dogwood. Certainly his reversal couldn't have anything to do with her wish to have him there.

Before she could jump down from the carriage, Tee-Toc was running around from the back of the house to hold the horses while old Mose followed more slowly.

The front door opened and Selah came out to stand on the porch and wave. "Hurry, we're just serving supper!"

"Wait! Don't touch that!" Aurora cried when Mose moved to lift the picture.

Removing the pipe from his mouth, Mose looked at her over his shoulder, eyebrows up. "Som'n valuable, Miss Aurora?" He eyed the object with curiosity.

"No, it's . . ." She edged between him and the picture. "It's just an ugly old painting I want Charmion to cover up with something pretty. It's a—a surprise for Joelle's wedding gift. I'll take it to the barn until I can get it to Char."

Mose shrugged. "Whatever you say, Miss Aurora."

"Come on, Tee-Toc, you drive. I'm tired." Climbing back into the carriage, she waved off Selah's hands-on-hips frown. "I'll be back in just a minute. Y'all eat without me." She had to get rid of this picture before anybody else saw it.

Tee-Toc drove around the house, whistling. There was nothing the ten-year-old boy liked more than horses, and putting the reins in his hands gave him more joy than a pocketful of gold.

Quite a horse enthusiast herself, Aurora knew the sorrels would need to be unhitched, rubbed down, and fed and watered before being turned out in the pasture for the night. But as soon as the carriage rolled to a stop inside the barn, she jumped to the ground. "Wait, Tee-Toc, before you take care of the horses, I need a quick favor. Help me get this frame up in the loft out of the way, would you?"

"In the loft?" Tee-Toc's dark eyes widened.

"Yes. What's the matter?"

He shifted. "There ain't no more room up there. Let's put it in the tack room." He reached for the blanket-covered frame.

"No!" Aurora eyed him in suspicion, then glanced up at the loft, where sure enough, a wall of hay bales lined the edge from floor to ceiling. But the boy looked more than reluctant. He looked frightened. "What's behind those bales?" she demanded.

"Nothing!"

"All right. Then you won't mind if I poke my head up there to take a look around."

"Please, Miss Aurora, Mr. Levi said not to let nobody go up there. I needs my job!" Tears stood in Tee-Toc's eyes.

Aurora relented. But what on earth was Levi hiding in the loft? She'd just come back later and take a look for herself. "All right. Calm down. I just need a safe place to put this picture. Can we find a place in the tack room where nobody will come across it?"

"Yes'm." Tee-Toc wiped sweat off his dark brow. "Thank you for—I just don't know why I gots to know so many secrets. It's just plain dangerous!"

Truer words were never spoken, Aurora thought as she and Tee-Toc hauled the heavy picture into the tack room and slid it against the back wall under a shelf. The tan-colored blanket blended in with the wall. It occurred to her that if Levi was stashing witnesses in her boardinghouse, he might also be hiding them here in the barn. After all, not too long ago, Georgia and Lemuel Frye had found refuge in the schoolroom. Fortunately, just before the fire, Joelle had moved them out, sending them to temporary quarters in Doc Kidd's Tupelo office. Nobody said where they went from there . . .

She glanced up at the loft as Tee-Toc shut the tack room door and went to care for the horses. Maybe she'd better let well enough alone. What she didn't know couldn't be blurted out at inappropriate times. As Tee-Toc said, secrets were burdensome things.

She hadn't forgotten.

Carrying an oil lamp, Zane followed Jefcoat and Moore through the outside cellar door, carefully navigating the wooden steps. He could have broken in, but finding it unlocked saved a lot of noise and trouble. By his best estimate, it must be shortly after two in the morning, and there would be time to sleep for a few hours before dawn. He was so tired by now, he could have slept for two days.

The cellar was dank but didn't smell as putrid as he'd expected. In fact, it smelled like soap.

Not only had she remembered to leave the door unlocked, she'd cleaned the cellar. Reeling with that unexpected luxury, he cast his gear onto the plank floor and manacled his two prisoners to opposite sides of the tiny room. Once they were settled in for the remainder of the night, Zane lay down on his bedroll between them and composed himself for sleep.

Oddly, he found himself wide awake. It wasn't the accommodations, for he'd definitely slept in worse. Cahaba, with its bare wooden shelves attached to the walls, lice-infested and open to the elements. Muddy battlefield trenches during the war. And even before that, a Christmas in Nebraska during his Pony Express days, sleeping on the dirt floor of a snowbound way station.

Now he was . . . content. God had been good to rescue him from those privations, none of which he deserved exactly, but which constituted the bounds of living as a sinful, prideful human being. One of many. Now he had heaven to look forward to. One of these days he'd have another conversation with Judge Teague and talk it all over, and hopefully everything would make sense from the other side.

Lying there listening to Jefcoat snore, poking through what he knew, the people involved in this little conundrum, he knew he was missing something important. So he began to pray for wisdom. And for God's favor in seeking the judge's killer.

He was almost asleep when he heard Moore hiss through his teeth.

"Marshal!" Moore whispered. "Hey, Marshal!"

Zane had given up convincing Moore that he wasn't *the* marshal, just a deputy. "What's the matter, Moore?"

"I been thinking."

Well, then that made two of them. "About what?"

"About what's gon' happen when the army come down here and stir things up. These white folks ain't gon' take the government sittin' on 'em. They'll take it as an act of war. I was in that courtroom in Tuscaloosa. I was on their side, and I nearly got my head blown off."

Zane didn't immediately answer. It was true. The Memphis riots of 1866 had resulted from Irish policemen attacking, and uniformed black men peacefully congregating in the city in large numbers. It had taken three days for troops from nearby Fort Pickering to reestablish order. And then local and state officials had refused to bring indictments against any of the perpetrators.

Worse, now that Judge Teague was gone, Zane was very much afraid the Tuscaloosa riot might go unresolved.

But there was something personal in Moore's warning. Zane sighed. "I'm tired, Moore. Get to the point."

"Yes, sir. I just want you to know I'm angry. And I'm sorry I let old man Jefcoat and little Andrew over there play me for a fool. You been kind to me, 'spite of everything. If they's anything I can do to undo my part, I will."

"Exactly what are you saying? Are you willing to testify against them?"

"I am." The reply was plain, simple, quiet. "If you can keep me alive long enough to do it."

Twelve

HEART THUMPING against her loosely laced corset, Aurora unlocked the Dogwood's front door while Schuyler drove the loaded wagon around to the back entrance. The last time she'd seen Zane Sager, she'd looked like a chimney sweep in a Charles Dickens novel. She might not be the first stare of fashion today—dressed as she was for supervising a renovation crew in an outdated striped chemise covered by an apron—but at least she was clean.

"Hello! Anybody here?" Pausing to admire the rich red-and-blue design of one of the new braided rugs she'd purchased from the industrious women of Shake Rag, she wiped the dust off her feet, then looked over her shoulder at Thomas-Anne. "Sounds awfully quiet."

She'd left the cellar open for Zane but wasn't sure where to look for him. She couldn't quite picture the three men bunking in the cellar.

This time, while Bedelia stayed at Daughtry House with Rosie for housekeeping lessons, Schuyler had driven Aurora and ThomasAnne to town in the wagon. The Daughtry

House employees had loaded the wagon with the lumber requested by Shug Pogue. The Pogue family would arrive shortly, along with a crew of men from Shake Rag, engaged to repair rotten boards in the walls and floors and replace missing shingles from the roof. India Pogue, who possessed a multitude of creative skills, would assist Aurora and Thomas-Anne in painting the kitchen and measuring for new curtains throughout the house.

ThomasAnne crept inside, still somewhat leery of rats and spiders, while Aurora rounded the bar. The cellar trapdoor lay in place, which didn't necessarily mean anything. Crouching, she pulled it open and peered into the dark opening. "Deputy Marshal?" she whispered. "Zane?" When dead silence greeted her, she rose and leaned over the bar. "ThomasAnne," she said to her cousin, who hovered patiently beside the door, "will you go out back and direct Schuyler in unloading the lumber? If Shug and India arrive, you can put them to work too. I'm going upstairs to look for . . . our guests."

"Of course." Looking relieved to have something to do that wouldn't involve descending into the bowels of the cellar, ThomasAnne slipped back out the door.

Removing her hat and tossing it onto the bar, Aurora made a mental note to acquire a hat rack, then lightly climbed the stairs. The kitchen and common room, which she planned to divide into a cozy sitting room and bigger dining area, took up the entire ground floor. The second floor, however, boasted a large central bathroom flanked by six bedrooms, three on each side.

Aurora planned to share the largest bedroom on the rear-facing east side with ThomasAnne, leaving the other five for boarders, two to a room. All the rooms had been thoroughly cleaned, but Aurora was looking forward to repainting and decorating. Everybody said she'd inherited her mother and grandmother's gift for color and design, along with a knack for welcoming guests. She knew she had a lot to learn, but she did enjoy the homemaking and entertainment aspects of the hotel business (the part that both Selah and Joelle abhorred).

Wishing she had Grandmama here to provide advice, she turned left at the landing to peek into her own bedroom. It was large and airy, with windows on two sides, and she envisioned patterned wallpaper, moire drapes, and a thick Persian rug beside a four-poster canopy bed. She'd also like to import a dressing table and armoire to replace the simple oak table presently shoved against the wall to the right of the doorway, but that could come after she'd started clearing a profit. At least the two narrow beds had fresh sheets and a new blanket, thanks to ThomasAnne and Bedelia's work on Monday. She was going to sleep here tonight, if she could convince Schuyler to stay.

Finding the remaining bedrooms in a similar state of spartan cleanliness, she continued to the end of the hallway opposite her room, where a narrow stairway accessed the finished attic. Though it would be mercilessly hot in the middle of the summer, right now it should be bearable at night, and at least there was a small, narrow window for ventilation near the slanted ceiling.

Finding the door closed, she knocked. Silence greeted her. Knocking again, she leaned close to the door and said quietly, "Deputy Marshal, it's me, Aurora. I just wanted to look in on you and see if you needed anything."

The door opened so quickly she all but fell in. As she

righted herself, Sager backed away from the door with a gun in his hand.

He looked relieved to see her. "Miss Daughtry," he said, holstering the pistol, "you're here early."

"Of course I am." Taking a quick look around, she saw the two prisoners cuffed to the bedsprings of the cots on opposite ends of the long, narrow, low-ceilinged room. Both men appeared to be asleep. She turned her attention back to the lawman. "When did you get in? Did you have any trouble?"

"Sometime in the wee hours," he said, glancing behind him at the three chairs in the room, as if he wasn't sure whether to invite her to sit down. "No trouble, thank you. We slept in the cellar for a few hours, then migrated up here. We appreciate you ladies making us comfortable."

Far from comfortable, he looked like he'd been sleeping on the ground for three nights—one green eye bloodshot, black patch over the other, whiskers shadowing the lean jaw, and his dark hair as rumpled as his clothes. In fact, she'd be surprised if he'd slept at all. Her heart went out to him.

"Excuse me, I'll be right back." She backed out of the room, closing the door behind her with a snap.

She all but ran down the stairs to the kitchen, where she found ThomasAnne and India Pogue putting away supplies they had purchased at the Emporium yesterday. "Thomas-Anne," she said breathlessly, "I need a large breakfast of fried eggs with grits, bacon, and biscuits, as fast as you can put it together. Can you do that for me?"

ThomasAnne paused with the pantry door ajar and looked at the sack of hominy in her hand. "I suppose so. Who is it—"

"I'll tell you later," Aurora interrupted. "I'll owe you the biggest favor, if you'll just do it without asking questions right now." She rushed out the back door. "Schuyler!"

Schuyler tossed an armload of boards onto the pile already stacked against the back wall of the house. Swiping his forearm across his brow, he turned back to the wagon. "What?"

"I need you upstairs."

"I'll be done in a few minutes." He helped Shug take another load of lumber off the wagon.

"No, this is important. I mean *now*."

He gave her a brotherly grin. "Pete, everything is important to you, from hangnails to arson. Hold your horses, we're almost done."

Dancing with impatience, she clenched her hands in her skirt. Otherwise, she might've rushed over to strangle him with the string tie dangling at his open shirt collar. Finally, when the wagon was empty, Shug got in the driver's seat and set the horses toward the hitching lot on the other side of the courthouse.

"I'll be back in a whiles, boss," Shug called over his shoulder.

Schuyler walked toward Aurora, picking splinters out of one palm. "I don't suppose you have a needle, do you?"

"No, but India probably does." She hauled him by the sleeve through the kitchen. "We'll ask her when she brings breakfast upstairs."

"You are a hard, cold woman," he told her without rancor, following her into the common room and up the stairs. "What's got you in such a tizzy?"

"That man has got to have help, and I don't know what to do. I want you to talk to him and make a plan." They

145

reached the landing, and she charged toward the attic stairs, dragging her captive.

"'That man'? You mean Sager? He won't thank you or me for interfering." Schuyler forced her to stop. He towered over her by nearly a foot, and his generally amiable face bore an uncharacteristic scowl.

"I don't care. He's clearly dead on his feet, and it's not safe to have him up there jumping out of his skin. He nearly shot me!"

Schuyler rolled his eyes. "I doubt that. But I'll talk to him." He reached to knock on the attic door but paused when she made to follow. "Where are you going?"

"I want to hear the plan. This is my house."

Grumbling under his breath, Schuyler gave a sharp rap at the door with his knuckles. "Sager, it's Beaumont."

The door opened. Sager sighed when his gaze landed on Aurora, but he stepped back to let her and Schuyler enter.

Stooping as he encountered the low ceiling, Schuyler looked around for a place to sit.

Sager dragged over a chair. "Here." He pulled over another for Aurora. "Ma'am."

She planted her hands on her hips. "You're exhausted. Schuyler is here, so lie down and get some sleep."

"Watch out if she snaps her fingers," Schuyler said with a grin. "Disobey, and the flyswatter might come out."

Sager's mouth curled a little. "That sounds ominous. I appreciate the offer, but this is what I'm paid to do. I'll sleep after the trial."

Schuyler rocked the wooden chair back on two legs. "Deputize me. Can't you do that?"

"Of course he can," Aurora said, though she'd never heard

of such before. She stuck out her chin at the deputy marshal. "I knew Schuyler would have an idea."

To her delight, Sager didn't immediately object. He stared at Schuyler in a calculating manner. "I might," he said slowly. "But not to sleep. I've been thinking about our plan, and I want to alter it a bit. I know we set this up so that it would look like I left town with the prisoners—as far as anybody knows, I took them back to Memphis. For their safety, that's good. But I don't want that bunch of yahoos to think they intimidated me. Besides, the US Attorney, Wiley Wells, will arrive today, and I need to be free to meet with him. I also want to go over to the courthouse and look around at the location of entrances, windows, stairs."

Schuyler shook his head. "How are you going to—"

"Just listen." Sager glanced at Aurora, then the second chair, as he pulled over a third.

Realizing he wouldn't sit down until she did, she sighed and cooperated. He did have nice manners.

Sager took a seat and leaned forward eagerly. "I've thought it out. I'll find out when the next train comes in from Memphis, slip over to the station, and pretend to get off. That's where you come in."

When Aurora huffed, Schuyler laughed. "You'd already planned to deputize me, hadn't you?"

"Seemed like the best option." Sager folded his arms. "All right. Raise your right hand. 'I, Schuyler Beaumont, do solemnly swear . . .'"

Schuyler echoed the oath in its entirety, and within a minute or two became a duly sworn deputy marshal of the District of Mississippi. "So help me God," he finished and dropped his hand. "Is that it? Do I get a badge?"

"If I had one, I'd pin it on you," Sager said dryly. "You armed?"

Schuyler lifted the side of his coat to reveal the holster at his hip. "Since that day in Tuscaloosa, I don't go anywhere without it."

Sager nodded. "Good. Then I'll go downstairs and watch out the window for the train. They give you any trouble, shoot for a leg." He glanced at Jefcoat, who opened one eye and snarled. "Miss Daughtry, will you accompany me, please?"

"Of course." Aurora smiled at Schuyler. "Thank you, Sky. ThomasAnne will be up shortly with breakfast." She quit the room and waited for Sager to close the attic door. "If you change your mind about sleeping, you can have any of the three empty rooms on this end of the second floor." She turned to descend the narrow stairs.

He followed her closely, making her extremely aware of his catlike step, the lithe movement of his body.

At the landing, he paused and cleared his throat. "Miss Daughtry. Aurora," he added when she took another step.

Surprised at his use of her given name, she turned. "Is something wrong?"

His expression was odd, almost sheepish. "You and your family have been more than kind to me. I don't want you to think me ungrateful."

"I think you're tired and lonely. I think you don't know what to do when people serve you. You need to let them." She wrinkled her nose. "It makes them happy to do so."

"Them? Them who? You mean *you* are happy serving people. I don't know anybody else who acts this way. At least, I did once, but he's—he's dead now, which is what makes it hard to—" Zane swallowed and looked away.

Zane. That was how she thought of him all of a sudden. He had *almost* told her something personal.

In that instant, it became her mission in life to crack him open and get him to tell her about whatever had made him so defensive and broken. It might not happen right now, but it would happen.

She smiled up at him and said, "I know," though of course she had no idea what or who he was talking about. "It's all right. And it does make me happy to be useful. So here's what we're going to do. We're going to go through the kitchen first and get a couple of biscuits. Then while I go to the station to find out when the next Memphis train is due, you're going to sleep, because it will make me *happy*." She turned and headed for the ground floor. "I promise I'll wake you up in time to meet the train."

After a moment, she heard his step behind her. "You, Aurora Daughtry, are a managing female."

She laughed. "I know. That makes me happy too."

Zane sat in a clawfoot porcelain bathtub, up to the chest in hot, soapy water. His head lay back against a towel, and he was so close to sleep, he could actually feel his brain shutting down.

Aurora Daughtry wasn't just a managing female. She was a fairy godmother with magic skills beyond his wildest dreams.

Somehow, while he was sitting at the bar eating eggs, bacon, grits, and biscuits the size of a bobcat's head, loaded with fig preserves and melting sweet cream butter, she had arranged to have hot water sent up to the front left bedroom. Stomach full, he'd dragged himself up the stairs and arrived to find not only the full tub but a stack of clean towels and washcloths on the bed, and a new razor and soap lying on the pitcher stand under a small mirror.

What could he do but strip and fall in?

For the first time in his life, he began to understand why men tied themselves for life to one of those infuriating creatures. The amenities were pretty good.

He shifted in discomfort, thinking of Aurora's copper curls bobbing in a mad mess against the milky skin at the back of her neck. Yes, he had studied it as he followed her like a puppy down the stairs. That would be another amenity, one which he had no right to think about.

So he stopped thinking about it and began to scrub away three days' worth of grime. Jiminy, it was a wonder she'd been able to stay in the same room with him.

Clean, dry, and dressed in the extra underclothes in his bag, he got into the bed with a groan of pleasure. The pillowcase and sheets smelled like fresh air. He was going to have a very hard time getting up when it was time. Aurora had promised to send someone to wake him half an hour before the train arrived. Just enough time to dress and . . .

Someone touched him on the shoulder. He bolted upright, reaching for his gun.

He'd left it on top of his clothes beside the—

The Someone shrieked. "Don't shoot me! I'm just waking— Zane, it's all right, it's just me!"

Heart thudding like a bass drum, he looked around wildly and realized Aurora stood in the center of the room with her back to him. The door had been flung wide open. He was in a boardinghouse in Tupelo, Mississippi, not Cahaba Prison.

Thank the Lord the sheet was still over him, and he hadn't actually jumped out of the bed. Sinking back, he threw his arm over his face. "I'm sorry," he said. "I was in such a deep . . . I'm sorry. You should've sent someone else."

"Who else was I going to send? Schuyler's in the attic, ThomasAnne took dinner over to Doc, and the Pogues went home. The train will be here in twenty-five minutes."

"What is a Pogue? Never mind. You—you go on downstairs. I'll get dressed as fast as I can, and we'll—no, we won't. Thank you. Goodbye." He sounded like a moron, but his reaction to her was terrifying. How was it possible to have been that deeply asleep?

When he heard her leave the room and shut the door, he dropped his arm and swung his bare feet to the floor. In less than ten minutes he had shaved and dressed in a clean shirt and socks, with the same pants he'd had on—hopefully he'd find a way to get them laundered soon. Or purchase a new pair. He picked up the dirty clothes and wet towels and left them in a neat pile beside the door. Presumably there was a maid somewhere around here, perhaps the one who had brought up the hot water.

Buckling his holster around his hips, gun firmly in place, he took a deep breath and opened the door.

Aurora stood in the narrow hallway, chewing on her thumbnail. Jerking her hand behind her back, she looked up at him. "Are you all right?"

"Of course I'm all right." He knew he sounded gruff, but he was embarrassed. "I knew I shouldn't have gone to sleep in the middle of the day."

"You must have needed it." Her cheeks turned rosy. "You looked so peaceful, I almost didn't wake you up."

"Good thing you did. I'd have been very . . . unhappy if you hadn't."

The oblique reference to their earlier conversation seemed to please her, for she gave him that blinding grin. "I'm glad you approve. And in case you wondered, you don't snore." She turned for the stairs.

Laughing, he followed. What was she going to say next? "That wasn't on the top of my anxiety list. But please tell whoever brought up the hot water, I'm eternally grateful."

"I will." Her tone was odd.

"Was it one of the Pogues? Is that some kind of local Indian tribe?"

Aurora giggled. "India and Shug Pogue work at Daughtry House, but they live in Shake Rag, not too far from here. They're going to manage the renovations." She took the last two steps to the ground floor in one jump. "I brought the water."

He grabbed her by the arm and turned her to face him. He stared at her, horrified. "You did—*what*? You hauled all that water up the stairs by yourself?"

"Don't look so shocked. I'm stronger than I appear." She flexed one arm.

It did look surprisingly sturdy, encased in its blue-striped cotton sleeve. He could even see the outline of a firm little bicep. "I'm sure you are, but you are a lady, and ladies don't—"

"Oh, horse pucky! Ladies do what they have to do. I grew up in a doctor's household and had to do all kinds of tasks that you might consider menial or unladylike. I ride horses and muck stalls and scrub floors and do laundry when necessary."

152

"Well, don't get any ideas about emptying that tub by yourself. I'll do it."

"What a grump." She sniffed. "Fine. I don't have time to argue with you. The train will be here at 1:05, so I'm going to head on across to the station and stand where you can see me. I'll wave when you can get over there without anybody noticing you."

That sounded a little hare-brained and overly complicated, but she was so clearly pleased to be helping him that he hated to disappoint her. "All right."

Aurora nodded, reaching up to press her thumb to his chin. "You cut yourself. I wish I had some alum. Grandpapa used to—What's the matter?"

He could hardly tell her that he'd flinched because he hadn't been touched by a woman since a nurse called Miss Marks held his face while the doctor at Cahaba sewed up his eye. Swallowing, he took Aurora's small, soft hand and squeezed it before letting it go. "I just didn't want you to get blood on your dress."

"I told you I'm not squeamish." She produced a handkerchief from her apron pocket and handed it to him. "Here. At least press this against the cut until the bleeding stops."

He took the lacy bit of fabric and reluctantly pressed it to his chin. He would make sure to wash it before returning it. Or better yet, he'd buy her a new one.

Aurora nodded. "Press hard. And remind me to get some cinnamon powder out of the kitchen when we get back. That will help."

Managing. Bossy. And adorable. "I'm not walking around with cinnamon powder on my face."

She snorted laughter. "It's not as bad as it sounds. All right, all right, I'll leave you alone. Watch me out the window, and come when I wave."

"You said that already." But he followed her to the front door of the saloon. As she flitted out onto the porch, Zane moved to the now squeaky-clean window and watched her dart across the street to the train tracks.

She quickly fell into conversation with a lady on the platform, but he had a feeling she would have talked to one of the posts holding up the station roof if she'd found herself alone. The next twenty minutes passed quickly as he watched her hands animate her every word, imagined the bubble of laughter beneath her breath and the sparkle of joy in those golden-brown eyes.

Joy. That was the way he thought of her, and it drew him with the force of a tide to the seashore.

When the train came, she looked across the street at him, lifted her hand, and smiled. And he went to her.

By the time he got across the street and slipped past the engine onto the platform, the lady Aurora had been in conversation with had disappeared. The station was busy with travelers, making it easy to fold himself into the stream of passengers exiting the second car back from the engine.

He found himself following an elderly woman dressed in an elegant travel suit that even he recognized as the first crack of fashion. She supported herself with an ivory-headed ebony cane that affected neither the military posture nor the regal set of her head. A couple of tall feathers sprouted from a quite terrifying hat, firmly pinned atop a mass of upswept white hair. When Zane took her elbow to keep her from tripping on a loose board, she turned and raised a pair of winged reddish-gray eyebrows that looked oddly familiar.

He smiled and released her. "All right, ma'am?"

"Certainly." Smacking him across the knuckles with an ivory fan, the old woman smirked at him. "A bad boy with good manners. Married one of those, once upon a time, and turned him into a good man."

Resisting the urge to rub his stinging hand, Zane eyed her doubtfully. "Do I know you?"

Before she could answer, he heard a gasp from behind him. "Grandmama! What are you doing here?"

Thirteen

WHO INVITED HER? Aurora knew she hadn't done it, and she couldn't imagine Joelle or Selah subjecting the family to the presence of the Grand Inquisitor.

Grandmama bridled. "I came to make sure Schuyler and Joelle do not elope in some ill-bred fashion, as Selah and Levi tried to do. One simply cannot trust those impulsive Beaumont children, forever plunging the family into scandal—Camilla and her underground railroad, Jamie and his fishboat, and now Schuyler riding about at night in costume, pretending association with that Klan rabble. I told your grandfather, I'd better come down here and make certain Joelle has fully considered the consequences of allying herself with that unpredictable young cockerel."

"Grandmama, *you're* the one who gave Schuyler your wedding ring as a betrothal gift!" Aurora couldn't help glancing at Zane to make sure he was all right. Grandmama had given him quite a crack on the knuckles.

He had crossed his arms as if to observe the show, but humor lit that one green eye.

Grandmama sniffed and rounded on him. "Young man, since you seem reluctant to take your piratical gaze from my granddaughter's face, perhaps you wouldn't mind retrieving my trunk from the baggage car."

Zane bowed. "I'd be happy to, if you'll tell me—"

"Trunk!" Aurora's voice rose in dismay. "How long are you planning to stay?"

"Never mind, missy, I'll leave when I get good and ready. Or when I feel you can be trusted not to allow the entire operation to run amok."

"Operation? What operation?" Aurora stood her ground.

Grandmama thumped her cane against the platform. "Are you denying that you purchased a saloon?"

"As a matter of fact, I am. It was a gift." Aurora looked around at passengers hurrying to and from the ticket office. "And it is no longer a saloon. But perhaps we should continue this discussion indoors." She glanced at Zane, who was staring at Grandmama with the fascination of a mongoose eyeing a cobra. "Grandmama, this is Deputy Marshal Zane Sager, who will be staying at the boardinghouse for the next week or so. He is not a porter."

Grandmama looked him up and down. "Is he not? What an egregious waste of those shoulders."

Zane burst out laughing. "Ma'am, if you'll give me your name, I'll go look for the trunk and deliver it wherever you wish."

"I am Mrs. Winifred McGowan. It appears that I will be staying at the saloon"—Grandmama waved a hand— "boardinghouse, whatever you wish to call it—since my granddaughter has decided to flout all bounds of propriety."

"Grandmama! We are not open for guests—"

"But you just said Mr. Sager—"

Aurora stamped her foot. "That is a special circumstance!"

"Aurora, don't be childish." Grandmama frowned.

"And anyway, ThomasAnne is with me, so everything is perfectly aboveboard."

Grandmama made a disparaging noise. "ThomasAnne was patently ineffectual at curbing Joelle's proclivity to mixed bathing. I do not trust her to keep you out of trouble."

"Mixed bathing? Joelle? What are you talking about?" Aurora was beginning to fear her grandmother had descended into senility.

Zane cleared his throat. "Ladies, I think I'll just go retrieve the trunk." He hesitated, apparently weighing the comparative pigheadedness he was dealing with. "I'll take it to the boardinghouse, and we'll go from there."

Fulminating, Aurora watched him stride away toward the pile of trunks and cases that had collected near the baggage car. "I never saw such presumption in my—"

"I would say he has an uncommon degree of common sense. Where did you find him?"

Aurora took Grandmama's arm and began to steer her across the street, toward the boardinghouse. "I didn't *find* him, as if he were a penny in the crack of a sidewalk. He's been assigned to guard all parties of this high-profile trial that we are involved in. I believe he's been conferring with Levi."

As she'd hoped, mention of Grandmama's favorite took the focus off Aurora. "Hmph. Bad business, that fire. What is wrong with people—grown men destroying property willy-nilly like schoolyard bullies?"

Aurora shook her head. "I don't know. Maybe they're worried that our hotel will encourage a Negro uprising."

After a few moments of silence, Grandmama sighed. "It is fear. And misplaced, irrational anger. We fought a long war because of it, and I'd hoped that would settle it. But it appears we've still a long way to go toward reconciliation."

Politics and social unrest made Aurora uncomfortable, and she didn't feel she knew enough about it to write or talk about it like Joelle did. She just wanted people to get along. Still . . . "A deputy marshal just like Zane—Mr. Sager, I mean, was killed a few days ago. I worry about him."

Grandmama stopped her, right in the middle of the street. "Aurora Josephine Daughtry, you stay out of this imbroglio. It's bad enough that Joelle stuck her nose in it and brought all this mayhem down on us."

"Now that's not fair. Jo was only doing what she thought was right. *She* wasn't the one who went burning down people's churches!"

"Of course not. But she didn't have to draw attention to herself as such an outspoken critic."

Aurora could have pointed out that Grandmama had never been chary of speaking her mind, but in the interest of peace she held her tongue. After a moment, she said meekly, "Are you ready to continue? I think we can find you a cup of tea and a bedroom to take a nap."

Giving her a considering stare, Grandmama released a chuckle under her breath and resumed the slow walk. "I see you have gained a modicum of restraint, which is an encouraging sign. But I mean it, Aurora. That boy is in a dangerous position, and I don't like you harboring him during these politically tense times. For heaven's sake, don't encourage him to fall in love with you."

Aurora felt as if her head might explode with embarrassment. "Grandmama! Nobody is falling in love!"

"I wouldn't be too sure of that," Grandmama muttered.

Aurora chose to pretend she didn't hear it.

Zane dropped the trunk in the middle of the bedroom next door to the one he had slept in this morning. Rolling his aching shoulders, he thought of the old lady's oblique admiration and grinned.

No wonder she had looked familiar. Aurora was her spitting image, from winged eyebrows to that delicate cleft chin—minus a few decades, of course. And the two of them clearly adored each other, despite the brief hissing and extension of claws. Jiminy, he didn't want to get between them in a real disagreement.

He could hear them talking in the common room downstairs, along with a lighter, wispier voice he didn't recognize. This morning he'd met the black woman named India who'd made his breakfast, as well as her husband, Shug, and they seemed nice enough people. Pogue—a family name, not an Indian tribe. He'd only been teasing Aurora to get a laugh out of her.

Worked like a charm.

Still smiling, he went up to the attic to check on his prisoners and their deputized jailor.

He found Beaumont, against all expectations, sitting on the floor reading Zane's Pony Express Bible.

When the door opened, Beaumont looked up and got to

his feet. "I'm very glad to see you," he said, laying the Bible open on the chair where Zane had left it earlier. "I took the men out to the privy a while back, but now it's my turn."

"Any problems?" Zane surveyed the room. Jefcoat still lay on the bed, but he was awake and listening to the conversation. Moore sat on his bed, back against the wall, apparently in a brown study.

"Jefcoat and I had a little conversation," Beaumont said with careful neutrality. "I'll tell you about it later." He strode out of the room, leaving Zane to pick up the Bible, curious about what the dandified Southerner had chosen to read.

He sat down with the little Bible open to Matthew 18, where Peter questioned Jesus as to how many times he should forgive someone who had sinned against him. Four hundred ninety times still seemed like an excessive amount to Zane, because how could you keep up with a number that big? But maybe that was the idea—forgive past the point where you're still counting.

He looked at Jefcoat. Was that what the two men had been discussing? Offense and forgiveness?

"The judge will be here before tonight," Zane said. "And the US attorney. Do you boys have a lawyer?"

Jefcoat sat up, chains and manacles rattling. "General Maney has agreed to represent us. Pa talked to him."

"Yeah?" Zane stared. "When did that happen?"

"I got a letter, delivered to the jail while you was out jiggin' around that morning with Schuyler and Riggins." Jefcoat glanced at Moore. "He's even gonna represent Harold."

Zane absorbed that information. If Maney had agreed—or offered—to represent Jefcoat in court, he must have little fear of charges being pressed against himself. And he could be applying pressure against Jefcoat to keep his mouth shut. Both angles boded ill for the Attorney General's prospects of ending the Klan's reign of terror.

By the time Beaumont returned, he knew he had to do something about his ability to investigate the leads he'd already uncovered. He trusted Riggins, but he needed to go after Jones.

At Beaumont's entrance, Zane got to his feet. "I need another temporary deputy until Pierce sends a man from Oxford," he said abruptly. "As much as I appreciate your service, you've got other duties to attend to, and I need to be free to meet with the prosecutor and the judge later today. Who would you suggest?"

Beaumont's brows went up. "Wimus McCanless is a good man. You'll find him at the newspaper office—well, what's left of it. He's working on cleaning and repairing the equipment the Klan destroyed."

"Where is that?"

"Franklin Street. North of the courthouse."

"Fine. Can you stay here just a little longer, until I can get someone to relieve you?"

Beaumont sighed. "If it's going to help us get this bunch of hellions rounded up, I'll do whatever it takes."

"Thanks, Beaumont. When this is over, I'll owe you a great deal." Zane shook hands and left his deputy to whatever solace he could find in the Bible.

Nearing the ground floor, he heard raised voices, which jerked to a halt when he entered the common room. Aurora and her grandmother sat at opposite ends of an ugly horse-hair sofa that looked mighty uncomfortable. In a matching chair nearby sat a woman who matched the wispy voice he'd heard earlier—flyaway red-brown hair, faded blue eyes, hands clutching her skirt. He seemed to remember seeing her tip-toeing around the kitchen while he sat at the bar eating his breakfast. He'd thought she was a maid.

Aurora leaped to her feet. "Zane! Mr. Sager! I was hoping you'd like to take a trip to the courthouse while Grand-mama takes her nap." She shot Mrs. McGowan a tight-lipped look.

"I do not need a nap," snapped the old woman. "I want you and ThomasAnne to drive me out to Ithaca for a cup of tea with Selah and Joelle. I understand that I am soon to become a great-grandmother, and I want to see for myself that Selah is caring for herself properly. Also, we need to discuss getting this marriage under way. Long engagements are good for nobody."

Zane shook his head, intending to excuse himself from any part in the disagreement, but Aurora edged over and took him by the arm.

"I'm sorry, Grandmama," she said firmly, "but I already promised. I'm sure Dr. Kidd will be happy to drive you and ThomasAnne over to Daughtry House. Mr. Sager and I will stop by the doctor's office on the way to the courthouse and send him over to collect you."

"That's another thing!" Mrs. McGowan thumped her cane against the bare floor and fixed the wispy woman with a glare. "ThomasAnne, I do not understand your thinking, leaving Aurora here alone in a houseful of men all morning. It's a good thing I arrived when I did!"

"Well, ma'am," Zane said, glancing at Aurora's cousin, "to be fair, one of those men is Miss Daughtry's own cousin and future brother-in-law, am I not correct?" Zane could not have said what prompted him to stick in his oar, but Aurora rewarded him with a grateful smile.

The old lady's back went, if possible, even more rigid, her nostrils flaring as if she could not decide from which direction she wished to breathe fire. But she released a sudden cackle of laughter. "Tact and common sense as well as a pair of broad shoulders. I like you, boy."

"That's a relief, ma'am," Zane told her with a straight face. "Your trunk is safely in your room, should you need it before you leave for Daughtry House." Acutely aware of Aurora's fingers gripping his arm, he looked down at her. "I'd be glad of your company if you want to come, Miss Daughtry, but I have an errand to take care of before I go to the courthouse."

Her eyes lit. "Oh, I don't mind at all! Can we pop into the bookstore for a book for Joelle while we're out?"

Zane felt bizarrely as if he were negotiating a courting ritual. How had he gone from sleeping in the woods with a murderer and a riot-inciter to escorting a pint-sized Southern belle about town? "I don't see why not. Mrs. McGowan, I promise I'll take good care of—" He stopped as a couple of mental rail lines came to a sudden and violent intersection in his brain. McGowan. From Memphis. Aurora had mentioned that her grandfather was a doctor, and she had grown up in his house. He stared at the old lady. No wonder she looked familiar. She had been one of the nurses at Adams Hospital, married to the surgeon.

But Aurora was a Daughtry, no? His gaze jerked back to her face. She was beginning to look alarmed.

He forced a smile for the dragon. "Don't worry, Mrs. McGowan, we'll be back before dark."

Aurora could not forget Grandmama's absurd admonition. Zane had escorted her about downtown Tupelo—not exactly the greatest of metropolises—for the last thirty minutes without once indicating more than polite interest in her conversation, let alone her person. *Falling in love?*

Hah. No danger of that.

Demonstrating the proper behavior of a gentleman, he had offered his arm for her to cup her hand around. But he seemed fearful that her skirts might brush against him and kept quite a distance. As she commented on the businesses they passed, he would either simply nod or produce a laconic response such as "Ah," "Indeed," or "I see." Not exactly scintillating conversation.

As they approached Doc's home and medical office, which stood opposite the Gum Pond Hotel, she abruptly stopped. "Zane, have I done something to offend you?"

He gave her a cautious look. "No." When she didn't respond or move, he added reluctantly, "Why?"

"I get the feeling you resent the intrusion of my company."

He sighed. "Are my manners that bad? In fact, Miss Aurora, that's just it. I find it hard to believe a beautiful young lady like you wants to spend your afternoon walking around with an ugly, taciturn cuss like me."

Aurora's mouth fell open. He'd called her beautiful. But he thought *he* was ugly? "There's nothing wrong with being quiet and thinking your words through before spitting them out, as my family has made sure to remind me since I learned to talk. Which apparently was extraordinarily early." She waved a hand. "That's beside the point. It's just that you look over your shoulder a lot, as if you want to escape. If you'd rather be alone, I promise it won't hurt my feelings. I asked to come with you because Grandmama worries about me walking around by myself, but I'm perfectly capable of shopping without an escort. She'd never know, because she'll be gone to Daughtry House before we get back."

After one of those quick assessing looks around, he unexpectedly took her elbow and pushed her close to the nearest wall—which happened to be beside Doc's front door. She looked up at his face just a couple of inches away, her breath gathering high in her chest at the sudden intimacy.

"Believe me," he said, low and intense, "there's no one I'd rather be with, and your jabbering is like drinking a cool glass of lemonade after walking around in the desert. I'm looking over my shoulder because we're drawing attention, and it worries me. If something happened to you because some cur shot at me, I'd—" He clamped his white teeth together, the lean jaw working.

"What do you mean, we're drawing attention? How do you know?"

"There's a woman staring at us right now, out the window of the store across the street. Your grandmother is right to be concerned."

"How do you know she's—did she tell you to treat me this way?" Aurora stood on her toes to look over his shoulder at the Emporium. "That's Mrs. Whitmore. She stares at everybody. She may be a busybody, but she's not going to shoot you! And I don't jabber! Well, maybe I do, but that's not something you say out loud!" She pushed at his chest. "I'm having second thoughts about your manners."

"I tried to warn you. I'm no good at anything remotely

like courtship. Even if I wanted to. Which I don't." He glared at her.

It occurred to her that he packed more raw emotion into one eye than most people conveyed in two. She felt his perfect frustration and self-loathing radiating at her. Suddenly all her aggravation melted as she heard what he meant, not what he actually said. Although some of what he'd said indicated some pretty staggering ideas.

He had thought about courtship, even if he'd verbally rejected it. He worried about her safety. His instinct was to stand between her and danger. He found her excessive amount of talking refreshing.

Looking up at him, she said softly, "Zane Sager, just remember that what you want and what you deserve are not always the same thing. And what God has planned for those who love him is on another level entirely."

Fourteen

AFTER QUICKLY SETTLING with Dr. Kidd the matter of driving Mrs. McGowan and her niece out to Daughtry House, Zane followed Aurora into the newspaper office, still reeling from the rush of . . . something, he would not call it fear, and it wasn't anger, nor exactly excitement, but some mix of the three—the thing that still zinged through his body. It had built from the realization, as he spotted that woman's heavy, disapproving face in the window, that Aurora Daughtry's well-being and state of mind meant as much to him as the exterior difficulties in which he found himself.

Despite what he'd said, he *would* like to court her. He'd like to dress up in a good suit, find some flowers somewhere, approach her grandmother, and ask to take Aurora to a dance.

But first he'd have to learn to dance.

Never mind, it didn't matter, because the whole idea was ludicrous.

And what did she mean by *what you want and what you deserve are not always the same thing*? Was that a threat or a promise?

Deliberately setting the whole matter aside for one of those times when he lay awake in the middle of the night with nothing better to do than relive old nightmares and plot strategies to keep himself alive, he looked around the cluttered office. The damage perpetrated by the Klan—nearly three weeks ago, by his reckoning—had been somewhat restored to order. You could tell by looking at the two heavy desks that they had been put back together with some new pieces, that carvings had been sanded off. And the walls had been freshly repainted. He didn't see a printing press, but there was a door that presumably led to a production room.

Meanwhile, Aurora had been in animated conversation with the newspaper editor—one of the men Beaumont had brought to help disperse the mob that had threatened Zane at the jail. He was also the one who had reported the murder of Theo Redding. A small-statured man with a wisp of hair and a pair of rimless spectacles covering an otherwise bald head, purple ink stains on hands and chin, he was about as nonthreatening a deputy as Zane could imagine.

But beggars couldn't be choosers.

As Zane approached the editor's messy, paper-strewn desk, Aurora turned to smile at him. "Zane, you remember Mr. McCanless, don't you? He's been encouraging Joelle's writing for some time now."

Zane shook hands with the editor. "Yes. We've met twice now."

"And neither were particularly auspicious occasions," McCanless said with a shake of his head. Anger in his eyes, he looked around at the bare walls and empty bookshelves. "Same bunch of riffraff who tore up all my books, broke the desks, smashed windows . . . If the press hadn't been solid

169

iron, they'd've wrecked it too. Took me a week to get all the type sorted back into its drawers—" Truncating his rant, he folded his arms. "But if they think they've scared me out of printing the truth, they've got the wrong man."

Zane met Aurora's big eyes. She wasn't a child, and she had experienced the ugliness of political and racial division firsthand. "I admire your courage, McCanless," he said. "The Justice Department is working to stop that sort of violence. I know you're busy, but if you can spare a few hours here and there, I could use some help getting ready for the trial."

"Me?" The newsman grinned a little. "What can I do?"

"I understand you're to be trusted with confidential information. Are you willing to keep your mouth shut about what I'm about to say?"

"He kept Joelle's identity secret for over a year," Aurora put in.

Zane glanced at her. "That's a solid recommendation. But in this case, people's lives are at stake."

"I'm not afraid," McCanless declared. "And protecting sources is essential to journalism. Believe me, I'm determined to get to the root of this conspiracy."

"Then I'll be glad of your cooperation. What do you know about those two men that I had in the jail?"

McCanless scratched his head, knocking the spectacles sideways. "One of them was running around here with young Beaumont—Jefcoat, I believe is his name. The two of them made no secret of collusion with Whitmore, Perkins, and that bunch. T'other—all I know is his name is Moore. Don't know anything else about him. But Beaumont says he was collecting information for the law and has detached himself from the Klan. That right?"

Zane nodded. "Jefcoat and Moore were caught in the act of kidnapping Beaumont, at the behest of someone they called 'the general.' We suspect that could be either Alonzo Maney or Bedford Forrest."

"General Forrest was having dinner with us the evening of the fire," Aurora said. "In fact he spent the night with us. Do you think he set the fire?"

"That's possible," Zane said. "But I'm interested in this Maney character. Mr. McCanless, what do you know about him?"

"I've heard the name. He's a respected lawyer from Tennessee, involves himself in defending Klan cases all over the South. We ran an article once about military high-ups who fled to Mexico after the war and came back when Johnson issued amnesty. Maney's name was mentioned. Didn't seem to lead to anything unusual, so we never followed up."

"Reporter's name?"

McCanless smirked. "T. M. Hanson."

When Aurora choked on a laugh, Zane looked at her. "What?"

"That's my sister," she said.

These Daughtry sisters were something else. "All right, I'll talk to her." When McCanless seemed to have nothing further to add, Zane shrugged. "Well, if you hear anything else, interesting or not, let me or Riggins know. All I need from you now is a little of your time. I've got Jefcoat and Moore stowed in Miss Daughtry's new boardinghouse for safety, on the quiet. Beaumont has been with them most of the day, and I hoped you'd be willing to be deputized to relieve him for a few hours." He looked away, forcing out words. "With Redding gone, the Marshals Service is sending another deputy, but he won't be here until tomorrow. The federal prosecutor and judge are coming in this afternoon, and it will help if I'm free to assist them." He met the editor's gaze frankly. "There aren't many men in this town I trust."

McCanless's chest visibly puffed. "I'm honored you'd think of me. I've never been a radically political man, but when my business and family are threatened . . . Well, right is right, and wrong is wrong."

"Yes, sir," Zane said. "It is, and I appreciate your service. It might be that I can pay you—"

"Absolutely not! A man needn't be paid for doing his duty." McCanless stuck his glasses on his nose with indignant force.

"Thank you," Zane said, relieved. "Then would you please raise your right hand and repeat after me?" With the editor duly deputized, Zane pulled out his pocket watch and consulted it. "Mr. Wells's train should be here in a half hour or so. If I could get you to slip in the back door of the Dogwood, the prisoners are being held in the attic. Beaumont is expecting you, but it would be a good idea to call up the stairs before you knock on the door."

"Certainly." McCanless bent to fish around on his desk for a piece of paper. "Better send a runner to tell Mrs. Mac I'll be working late . . ." He glanced up. "Miss Daughtry, please tell your sister that we should be up and running again by next week. I'll want her contributions regarding the trial and anything else she has ready to submit."

Aurora nodded. "Of course."

Zane cleared his throat. "Thank you, McCanless. We're doing our best to put an end to the violence that put you out of business."

"Oh, I'm very far from out of business," McCanless said grimly. "If anything, I'm more determined that truth reaches the public—however much they dislike it."

"Glad to hear that." Zane tipped his head toward the door. "Miss Daughtry, how about if I escort you to the bookstore, so you can make your purchase? Then we can walk over to the station to meet the train."

"Of course." She took the elbow he offered. "Mr. McCanless, thank you for standing watch at the Dogwood. We'll meet you there later." As he held the door for her, she looked up at him with a smile. "The bookstore is right next door, and I'll be quick. Joelle wants—"

He never heard what Joelle wanted, for he and Aurora both froze in the doorway.

For the last ten minutes or so, Zane's hackles had been raised by a muffled commotion outside the brick walls of the office. Now he saw why the noise had sounded so familiar. Across the street, where a broad swath of green lawn stretched in front of the courthouse, a uniformed and armed Negro militia had mustered. Rifles shouldered, faces intent, they were drilling and marching on the grass, steadfastly ignoring the hoots and catcalls of white citizens who had gathered along the street to watch.

Zane pushed Aurora behind him. He could think of no possible way this scenario could end peacefully.

Aurora stood on tiptoe to peer over Zane's shoulder. She knew many of the men marching on the courthouse lawn. Levi had hired them to repair the Daughtry House roof and outbuildings during renovations in March and April. Some had stayed to work at the hotel when it opened for business in May, with the arrival of the opera star Delfina Fabio, the famous General Nathan Bedford Forrest, and of course his wife. All of the militia were residents of Shake Rag—a Negro community on the outskirts of Tupelo, where former slaves had drifted after the war—and belonged to the church that white supremacists had burned down when their pastor announced his candidacy for state congress.

Aurora and her family had assisted in rebuilding the church within a week of its destruction, donating lumber and other materials from the hotel sawmill and blacksmith. She had shared meals in the homes of the Lawrences and Vincents, and had participated in a quilting bee with the Shake Rag women at the Pogues' house.

Now a frisson of fear climbed her back as she realized where the tensions of the last month had taken them all. Not quite back to civil war, but certainly into racial animosity. Because she knew these men, she wasn't afraid of them. They were free, but their liberators—the Union army—had not been able to coerce goodwill in the hearts of the former masters. Rather, shame and resentment remained behind, taking root to grow up as bitter fruit.

It was the hatred of her own people she feared. *Her people?* Dear heaven, let it not be so. Her skin was white, but she could never align herself against these her friends.

She pushed against Zane's back. "Let me pass."

"No. Stay here." He looked over his shoulder. "Aurora, I mean it. Don't cross me this time. I've seen this kind of situation turn into riots. It happened in Memphis—"

"I know. I was there. But this time I can do something to stop it."

"No." He turned, and she saw that his right hand had moved to the grip of his gun. "Those men have a right to be there. The governor has given the militia orders to muster and drill, to keep order during the trial. Of course the white citizens have the right to congregate too, and the whole thing is a recipe for disaster."

"I know." Acknowledging his fear seemed to take some of the wind out of his sails. She put a hand on his forearm. "Listen. I live here, and I *know* these people. You saw what happened when the men at the jail saw there was a woman there. Their instinct, half the reason these men act so crazy, is this notion of chivalry—the protection of white women. If you and I handle this together—you as the badge of the law, me as the protected species of *female*—I think we can keep it under control."

As he studied her, clearly ready to shove her back into the office and shut the door in her face, something entered his expression. She thought it might be admiration, but he quickly hid it behind his more characteristic stoicism.

"Come on, then," he said, "but if I push you to the ground, cover your head."

She nodded and took his arm again—the left one, leaving his right hand free to pull his gun if needed. She could feel the taut muscle under her hand, the tension in his whole body as they crossed the street and entered the cluster of men at the edge of the courthouse lawn. People turned to look at them, frowns shifting to surprise at the appearance of one of the crazy Daughtry sisters. The three of them had developed a reputation for unorthodox behavior, and this wasn't going to help.

But she was tired of caring what hateful people thought.

Right now she was praying that every one of those motley-uniformed black men on the lawn would go home safely today. And she was praying for Zane and herself to possess the wisdom and grace necessary for whatever happened.

She smiled at Mr. Fisher, who had apparently abandoned the barber shop in favor of gawking at the militia. She didn't think he'd been part of the mob that came to the jail. "Mr. JJ, have you met Deputy Marshal Sager? I told him just this morning what a wonderful fresh shave he could get in your shop."

The barber glanced at Zane, gaze zeroing in with professional interest on the scab forming on Zane's chin. "I'm sure I could do a better job than that."

Zane self-consciously rubbed his chin. "I imagine so. I could use a haircut too. I'll stop in soon."

Fisher scowled. "I'd heard you were here about the trial."

"I am." Zane paused, then said deliberately, "Your name has come up in discussions of some of these events we're interested in. Anybody questioned you about it?"

"Which events? You mean the burning of that blasted radical church?" Tipping his head toward the militiamen, Fisher stroked a finger along his beard. "That's what this is all about. They're threatening to march on everybody in town."

Outraged, Aurora was about to respond when she caught Zane's eye. She closed her mouth.

Zane addressed the barber calmly. "You didn't answer my question."

"And you federal men don't know a thing about how things work down here. You think you can come in and shoulder your way around like you own the place. No, I didn't light no matches, if that's what you mean. But that don't mean

I want ignorant colored vagrants wandering around with loaded guns, when people are trying to walk past for a trim and a shave. It's dangerous."

"Here's the thing, Mr. Fisher." Zane's face remained relaxed, steady, though Aurora could still feel his tension against her arm. "By law, these men have as much right to protect themselves as you do. They have a right to vote. They have a right to a fair trial. They have a right to worship in their churches as they see fit. You say I don't know how things work down here in Mississippi. But as of last week, your very own governor, James Alcorn, requested that they muster for protective detail when federal officers gather for official duty. That's all they're doing. Nobody's threatening anybody—unless you force aggression on them."

Though Fisher didn't reply, Aurora could see the man's frowning consideration of Zane's words.

Perceiving a stir near the courthouse, she drew Zane's attention by squeezing his arm. "Please give my regards to your wife, Mr. JJ."

Taking the hint, Zane gave Fisher a nod and moved with her toward the officer directing the drills of the militia. When he turned, wiping a sweaty brow with a white handkerchief, Aurora was astonished to recognize Clancy Crumpton, the manager of the Daughtry House dairy. In a sober blue uniform, outlined with touches of piping and brass buttons, he looked both older and more impressive than he appeared in everyday work clothes.

A smile lit his dark face as he returned the handkerchief to his inner pocket. "Miss Aurora! What brings you to town today?" He issued a brief "At ease" to his little unit, then sent a curious look Zane's way.

Aurora dipped a curtsey to her employee, aware that she would be a topic of conversation among the white men milling along the street. Well, phooey on them. "I've begun renovations to my new boardinghouse," she said brightly. "I'm surprised Shug hasn't mentioned it to you. He's been managing the repair work."

"Ain't seen ol' Shug much lately." Clancy glanced at his men. "I've been busy training the new militia."

"So I see. It's a very fine group you've got here. And I hope nobody gives you trouble." She hesitated, glancing at Zane. "Deputy Marshal Sager, this is Clancy Crumpton. He and his wife, Neesy, manage the dairy at Daughtry House."

Glancing at the stripes on Clancy's sleeve, Zane shook hands. "Sergeant Crumpton. Along with Attorney Wells and Marshal Pierce, I'm grateful for your assistance."

Crumpton nodded. "I volunteered—all of us did—because we know what's gon' happen when we try to go to the polls in November, if the Ku Klux ain't stopped. I escaped in '63, and the minute I got to Union lines I signed up to fight. So I know what to do with a rifle—and what not to do with it."

"You look like a man with experience," Zane said. "I served off and on with Negro troops in the Guard, until I was taken prisoner in '64."

"That right? You's military too?" Clancy smiled at Aurora. "Got you a good man here, Miss Aurora."

"Oh, no, I—" Blushing, she swallowed her protest. Zane didn't belong to her, but he *was* a good man. "We should let you get back to your practice. The deputy marshal and I are headed to the train station. But anytime you want to stop by the Dogwood for a meal or drink of water, you're welcome—"

"Miss Daughtry, if you persist in this foolish tendency to insert yourself into dangerous situations, I'm afraid I will no longer be able to guarantee your safety. What do you think you're doing, my dear?"

Aurora dropped Zane's arm and wheeled to find Mr. Whitmore regarding her with the most patronizing smile it had been her misfortune to encounter. She stuck out her chin. "Well, I am certainly not here to purchase dress materials or cheese. I might ask, rather, what *you* are doing here instead of minding your store?"

Whitmore's eyes bugged at her impertinent tone, not to mention the sassy words. "How dare you—"

"Mr. Whitmore," Zane's deep, reasonable voice interrupted, "if it's me you wanted to talk to, you'll need to accompany me over to the train station. The marshal from Oxford, Mr. Pierce, and the US Attorney, Mr. Wells, are due to arrive. You got questions about militia activity, either of them could answer better than me." He turned to Clancy, offering his hand again. "Good day to you, Sergeant Crumpton." Tucking Aurora's hand into his elbow, he began to walk away.

Whitmore had no choice but to follow, gobbling like a Thanksgiving turkey. "Now, see here, young man—" He rushed around to block their path. "We told you, we're not going to stand for federal interference in the local peace process. We thought that when you left town, you weren't coming back."

"Well, you thought wrong. Now get out of my way. Sir." Zane's voice was polite but icy. "And try to remember there's a lady present."

Aurora was delighted to find that she had correctly predicted the ingrained respect for white women in men like

Oliver Whitmore. His mouth opened and closed a couple of times as he looked from Zane to Aurora and back again. He stepped aside.

Zane nodded, satisfied, but instead of continuing their walk toward the station, he turned and planted both feet in an aggressive stance. Shoulders back and chin level, he shouted, "Sergeant Crumpton, perhaps you'll give me a moment to address your audience."

The crowd, militia and white onlookers, hushed to an instantaneous silence.

Clancy smiled. "Absolutely, sir!"

"Thank you." Zane raised his voice to a battlefield roar. "It has come to my attention that there are some citizens of Tupelo concerned about the safety of their women and children, in the anticipation of law enforcement arriving. I wish to assure everyone that these fine uniformed state militiamen here will be assisted and supported by soldiers of the US Army, who will arrive shortly before the trial begins. Furthermore, you can rest easy that anyone caught threatening by word or action any participant in the trial will be promptly jailed and charged with disturbing the peace, at the very least. However, peaceable citizens have absolutely nothing to fear, and you can all go home or back to work. Immediately." He paused and looked around. "Have I made myself clear?"

Several moments passed, during which no one moved or spoke. Aurora held her breath.

Finally, Oliver Whitmore waved a hand. "I'm going back to work. I've got better things to do than stand around and watch colored boys march up and down the block." He walked stiffly toward the business district, looking straight ahead without meeting anyone's eyes.

One by one, then in pairs and little groups, other men began to follow, until no one remained except the militia.

Clancy saluted, Zane nodded, and Aurora executed a little hop-skip of victory.

Zane looked down at her as they walked away. "Brains and creativity, not hardware," he said with a glint of a smile.

Fifteen

THE GUM POND HOTEL'S RESTAURANT was doing a hopping business this evening, and Zane wished there had been another dinner option in this little town. Grated his soul to spend his money in Frank Brown's establishment for the second time. He supposed he was lucky they were able to secure a table for such a large party.

Zane held Aurora's chair as she gathered her skirts and sat down opposite two of the four men they'd collected at the train station. The US attorney and Mississippi district marshal had been expected, and Zane was relieved that the new deputy marshal, Virgil Mosley, had been able to come. He surreptitiously studied the fourth man who had stepped off the train behind Mosley.

Aurora had welcomed the bald, gray-bearded man with surprising warmth and introduced him to Zane as James Spencer, Oxford Justice of the Peace and friend of the family. On the way to the restaurant for dinner, Aurora had related the dramatic story of Selah and Levi's meeting during a train wreck outside Oxford. In the aftermath of the rescue, Spencer had facilitated the couple's budding courtship, as well as the Daughtrys' adoption of Wyatt Priester, a youngster who had been orphaned in the wreck. Later, he had played a more official role in Riggins's investigation into train robberies and derailings throughout Tennessee and north Mississippi.

Zane couldn't help wondering if there might be some connection between those robberies and the current Ku Klux Klan crimes that would bring Spencer back to Tupelo.

US Attorney Wiley Wells, a young man dressed in a natty suit and sporting a thick brown imperial beard and mustache, settled in his chair. "Miss Daughtry, Spencer spent the entire journey lauding the superior accommodations of your family's hotel. I wish we could put up there, but I'm afraid we'll need to stay in town for the convenience of interviews and meetings. As it is, Marshal Pierce and I have about a week's worth of work, preparing for Judge Hill's arrival." His deep-set brown eyes sought out Zane. "Sager, I understand you've unearthed quite a few leads for us."

"Yes, sir. I'll show you my notes first thing in the morning."

"I hope you've got a plan to find the dog that killed Redding," Pierce said. Even younger than Wells, with a freewheeling cowboy bearing and style of dress, he chomped angrily on an unlit cigar. "You'd worked together before, hadn't you?"

"Yes, in Judge Teague's district over in Alabama." Zane avoided Aurora's sympathetic gaze. "Theo was my friend."

"He was a good man, and we'll miss him," Pierce said. "But Mosley here is ready to take up where Redding left off."

Zane nodded at the deputy seated to his right. He and Mosley had met in DC back in May, when they both testified before Congress. Mosley wasn't the brightest of wits, but he was dependable and good with paperwork. "Glad to have your assistance." He looked around the busy restaurant. They were already getting curious looks. "But I suggest we save classified conversation for a less public place."

"Agreed." Wells looked up as Mrs. Brown waddled over to take their order. "Hello, madam. What's your special tonight?"

The woman's demeanor was a good bit stiffer than the last time Zane had seen her. "You Yankees can read, I presume. It was on the board at the front."

At this uncalled-for rudeness, Zane met Aurora's alarmed gaze. "Now, Mrs. Brown," she said, "these men only came from Oxford. But even if they were Yankees, their money spends just fine. They want to let rooms here for a couple of weeks, and that'll mean three meals a day as well. Do you really want to send them down to the Twin Tree?"

Mrs. Brown had the grace to look ashamed. "Mr. Brown said you folks are here to try to put him in jail, and he didn't do *nothing*." Glancing over her shoulder at the hotel's front desk, where her husband was busy signing in guests, she huffed. "Oh, all right. I'll talk to him. Smothered steak with mashed potatoes and fried okra for six it is."

"You sure we won't wind up with spiders in our beds?" Pierce asked with a wink at Aurora.

"Not entirely," she said, dimpling, "but I can guarantee Mrs. Brown's banana pudding is worth putting up with any number of uninvited bed partners."

To Zane's relief, the remainder of the meal passed uneventfully—one might even say pleasantly. Aurora's knack for leavening conversation with wit and skillful questions

184

resulted in all four men abandoning the heavy subjects of law enforcement and politics in favor of getting acquainted. He already knew that Pierce was a native Mississippian and an aggressive law enforcement officer. But he discovered that Wells had been born in New York, risen to the rank of lieutenant colonel in the Union army, and had practiced law in Holly Springs for three years before being tapped as the US Attorney for the Northern District of Mississippi. He was a logical choice for prosecuting federal crimes of racial violence.

The loquacious Mr. Spencer confessed to owning a music store in Oxford, in which he conducted weekly rehearsals of a community wind ensemble. He had personally tuned the grand piano at Daughtry House.

Aurora set down her after-dinner coffee cup. "Gentlemen, I'm going to insist that you all come out and have dinner with us at Daughtry House this week. You must hear our Levi play the piano, and we have quite a few singers in the house as well—no, not me!" She laughed. "And I'll just say that if you enjoyed this meal, our Horatia's cooking will send you straight to heaven." Dropping her napkin beside her plate, she looked at Zane. "Mr. Sager, if you would be so kind as to escort me, I need to return to the boardinghouse before Grandmama and ThomasAnne return."

"Of course." Pushing back from the table, he rose to assist Aurora. "Wells, I've found an office near the courthouse that we could work from. Maybe we could meet here for breakfast in the morning at seven, then I'll begin briefing you on what I've uncovered."

"Excellent." Wells stood along with the other men, in deference to Aurora's departure. "Miss Daughtry, it's been delightful to meet such a charming ally. We'll look forward to that dinner invitation at your convenience."

Aurora smiled. "Have a pleasant evening, Mr. Wells. Gentlemen." Dipping a curtsey, she took Zane's arm. As they exited the hotel, she looked up at him. "I like your friends."

"They're not my—"

"Zane." She shook her head and kept walking. "What do you think a friend is?"

He shrugged.

She sighed. "I know you lost Deputy Marshal Redding. But those men back there respect you and depend on you and *appreciate* you. They *would* be your friends, if you'd let them. So would Levi and Schuyler." The look in her eyes said *and so would I.*

That couldn't be what she meant.

"It's not just Redding," he managed. He wanted with all his heart to tell her about Judge Teague, but he was terrified that once that dam broke, he'd be washed away in grief.

She gave his arm a little shake. "There's someone else you're grieving for, isn't there? You've almost said so, more than once." She looked up at him, eyes suddenly wide. "Zane, were you married? Did your wife die?"

"What? No!" Zane's tanned face went as white as his shirt. "Don't you think I'd have said so a long time ago?"

Aurora glanced about. They were in a very public place, which lent propriety to their being alone together. But it made continuing a very personal, private conversation difficult. If anyone saw them enter the boardinghouse together and her grandmother wasn't there, she was going to create gossip.

"Come this way," she said, grabbing his hand and towing him toward the southern edge of town.

Zane followed, looking confused. "I thought you wanted to get back to the boardinghouse."

"I will. Later."

"Where are we going?"

"Church." On a Wednesday evening the building should be empty, and who would object to the two of them spending an hour or so in the sanctuary . . . praying? Of course she would pray with him. That made perfect sense.

"Aurora." His tone was the same one her sisters used when she was being mule-headed.

"Don't worry, I'm not going to make you get baptized or anything."

"I've already been baptized. I'm a Christian, and I don't object to going to church, as you already know. I just don't know why we have to go right now."

She turned down a side street that led to the back of the church. "Because we need privacy, and the church is the only place appropriate I can think of. Gil always has Wednesday dinner with a parishioner, but he leaves the building open for people to come in and pray if they want to."

"Does he live in the church?" Zane asked incredulously.

"No, of course not. He has a little house next door, though, and he'd come in and be nosy if he saw us in the sanctuary." Aurora blew out an unladylike noise that would have horrified her grandmother. "Gil is a pill. Yes, that rhymes, and isn't that satisfying?"

She heard Zane chuckle behind her, which made her smile.

One could be serious and have fun at the same time, a little-known fact that gave her a small edge in keeping a sunny attitude. Within a couple of minutes, they'd walked down the path between the church building and the parsonage and ducked around the corner to the front door. As she'd predicted, it was unlocked.

Aurora peeked into the entryway. Empty, also as expected. Pulling Zane behind her, she opened one of the double doors that led into the sanctuary. They stood at the back of the center aisle, facing the altar rail with its pulpit and choir loft. The piano, where Joelle played the hymns every Sunday, was over to the left. There was a sad arrangement of dying hydrangeas on the altar. Somebody should throw it out.

Now that she was here, she felt a little peculiar. She still clasped Zane's hand, and she would have let go, but his grasp was firm and warm. And very masculine, with long fingers, calloused palm, no rings of any sort. That should have been a clue that he wasn't married—although not all men wore wedding rings, most did.

Why had she blurted such a personal, awkward question?

Realizing she was staring down at their entwined hands, she took a deep breath and dared to look at his face. His expression was intent, as if he were memorizing her. The breath left her lungs. He lifted her hand to his mouth and kissed her fingers.

Then let her go.

She had no idea what to do now. Usually she could figure out a plan of action, bend people to her will, create a party. But this young-old man held himself tightly bound behind a screen of courtesy, discipline, and law that left her utterly mystified.

He turned and walked away from her. She watched his loose, slightly bowlegged horseman's stride, as he went to the altar rail, where a kneeling bench provided a place for prayer. He dropped down onto it, resting his elbows on the rail, and laid his face in cupped hands.

With tears in her eyes, Aurora followed and knelt beside him. She didn't think of herself as a particularly churchy kind of girl, though her relationship to God was comfortable and intimate. She read her Bible and prayed every day, and tried to listen for the promptings of the Holy Spirit. She had a feeling he was shouting at her right now. *Pray with this man. He needs me.*

So she laid her palm against his back, bent her head close to his shoulder, and told God in a whisper, "We're listening."

Stillness fell, a holy quiet that she might have found boring when she was a little younger. Shared with Zane it felt electric, and she thought of a verse she'd learned a long time ago, something about two or three gathered together "in my name." She'd never experienced this in church before, even on Sunday. *Especially* on Sunday, where Gil Reese held sway.

After a moment she heard Zane begin to murmur. She couldn't understand the words, but she heard his heart breaking. She didn't know real men prayed this way. Well, perhaps she was aware that Levi did—his blessings over meals were more than rote thanks for food. And Schuyler had begun to demonstrate a more verbal faith of late. But her father had never done so when she was small. She'd heard Grandpapa pray over his patients, in a stilted King James English that always struck her as more of an incantation than a genuine request for aid. Maybe she was wrong about that.

By the time she circled around to the absurdity of trying

189

to assign motive to anyone else's prayers, Zane was quiet again. She straightened away from him, knotting her hands in her lap.

He heaved a deep sigh and sat back on his heels, dropping his hands to the railing. As he looked at her, his eye was dry, his countenance peaceful. "You were in Memphis the night of the *Sultana* explosion, weren't you?"

Her mouth fell open. "Yes! I was living with my grandparents then. Were you there?"

He nodded. "We didn't meet, or I would remember it, but I think I met your grandparents at the hospital the next day."

"Is that when your eye was damaged?"

"No." He touched the patch. "This happened in prison. But I was on the *Sultana*—"

"You were *in* the explosion?"

"No, listen. I don't talk about this normally, but you were there, so you understand. I got on the boat in Vicksburg, feeling lucky to be going north, even though it was crowded as—well, overcrowded beyond belief. Then when we stopped for refueling in Memphis, we were allowed to get off for dinner. I went to the Soldiers' Home—"

"I was there! I may have seen you!"

"Maybe." He shrugged. "I wouldn't have been much to look at. Thin and weak and dirty . . ." His cheeks flushed.

She covered his hand with hers. "They all were. I couldn't believe how they had been treated." She gulped back the urge to cry, remembering those sorry, smelly specimens of humanity that her countrymen had so evilly misused. "Never mind—go on, I'm listening."

"All right. So I went back to the wharf to get on the boat, and I saw a fellow prisoner who'd been released a few weeks before me. He was an officer and a respected judge, a friend of General Grant—a bit more important to the Union command than a gimpy Provost sergeant. Judge Teague was . . ." He looked away. "Aurora, I don't know how to tell you what kind of man he was. If I'd had a father like him, no telling where I'd be now. I might be President of the United States!" His mouth curved as he pinned her with that intent green gaze. "He kept me alive at Cahaba, more than once. So when I saw him sitting on his luggage on the wharf, looking like somebody had sucker-punched him, I had to know what was wrong. He'd been in Memphis for nearly two weeks, working out details of a new assignment as a federal judge, but he'd just gotten word his youngest son had taken ill in St. Louis after mustering out of the army, and wasn't expected to live. No more trains going out that night, and the *Sultana* crammed to the gills."

Aurora gripped Zane's hand. "You gave him your place, didn't you?"

"Yes. After we arranged for the transfer of passage, I boarded to make sure Judge Teague was settled. As I was heading toward the gangway, past the boiler hold, I noticed a man coming out." Zane paused, his inner gaze clearly in another place and time. "The light was bad, since it was past dark and the lights on the boat flickered, but something struck me as odd—maybe the way he pulled his hat down over his face as he shut the door behind him and shoved his way through people crowding onto the boat. Anyway, it got my curiosity up, so I followed. I almost lost him a time or two before we got down to the wharf, but by then I thought there was something familiar about the way he held himself as he walked. Maybe he'd been at the prison."

Wrapped up in the story, Aurora blurted, "Where did he go?"

"He turned north along the landing, which runs nearly a mile up the Memphis riverbank. I had nothing else to do, so I went after him, staying back so he wouldn't hear or see me. I never got close enough to see his face, but there was enough moon to see his outline. Eventually we followed an old Indian trail up the bluffs, going through the woods with the river to our left. It had rained a lot, and sometimes we had to leave the trail." He blinked and looked at her. "Won't bore you with any more details, but I just wanted to give you the circumstances of how I wound up where I did."

"I'm not bored," she said. Far from it.

"Anyway, we slogged along for quite a while. Not sure how long, but probably a couple of hours later, the *Sultana* caught up and slowly passed us. I found out later she'd paddled over to the Arkansas side for refueling, which caused enough of a delay that we didn't get too far behind her. Clearly the man I followed was watching for her, since he sped up to keep her in sight for the next two or three hours."

"Zane. You walked through the woods, all that way in the middle of the night?"

"I've made harder treks." He turned to sit on the kneeling bench, resting his elbows on his knees, looking at his linked fingers. "Of course I was in bad shape from malnutrition, but I knew this man had done something while he was on that boat, that he was waiting for something, and so I pushed myself. And I'm glad I did. When the explosion came, the concussion knocked me to the ground. I don't know how long I was out, but by the time I came to, the *Sultana* was in flames, the stern was gone, and the current

192

was turning her so the wind pushed the fire to the bow. It was—it was like watching hell come to life. I relive it most nights in my sleep."

Aurora slid down to sit on the floor at his feet and reached up to grab his clenched hands. "Oh, Zane—I heard the echo of that boom from seven miles away. I don't know how anybody survived. Was Judge Teague hurt in the explosion then?"

He shook his head. "My first thought was of him lying asleep in my spot on the upper deck, and I couldn't move. But I made myself get up and see if I could find any survivors. Miraculously"—he swallowed—"by the grace of God, there were lots of them. Hanging onto trees, floating barrels, logs, doors, anything they could grab. I tumbled down the bluff toward the water and saw a Negro paddling a canoe just off the bank, trying to haul people out of the water by himself." He looked up, a slight smile lightening his expression. "I wish you could meet Lucky Tolbert. We became pretty good friends that night. I hollered and offered to help, so we worked together for some time, dragging people to safety as best we could. And to answer your question . . . about an hour into our work, we found Judge Teague—"

"What? But that's wonderful!"

"It was. I was never so glad to see somebody in my life. He'd had the sense not to jump into the water right away, with the crush of folks that wound up drowning each other or boiling themselves in steam. He pried off a piece of board from a stair, then made his way to the front of the boat, and stayed there until it started to go down. By then the crowd had drifted away, so he just jumped in and drifted downstream. At some point, he found an abandoned door, which was a lot more stable in the current. When we pulled him into the canoe, he was shivering with cold, bleeding from a head wound."

"But alive."

"Yes, thank God. Alive."

"Then—" She didn't understand the sorrow in his eyes. "What's the matter? What happened?"

Sixteen

AURORA DAUGHTRY had completely bewitched him.

To his memory, Zane had never spoken to anyone at such length in his entire life. But she made him feel as if her regard and respect would not suffer from hearing his pain. Her small, soft hands held his with such compassion that it was all he could do to keep from opening his arms and pulling her close.

That would be a disaster.

And now he'd reached the most difficult part of the story, which, for the life of him, he didn't know why he'd begun.

He sat there, telling himself to walk her home, give her back to her grandmother, and go back to doing the only thing that made his life valuable—which was hunting down criminals and putting them away where they couldn't hurt people like Aurora.

But she had prayed with him, prayed *for* him, and he owed her some sort of explanation for this display of emotion. So he controlled it. Leveling his voice, he went on with the story. "A Union supply ship picked us up off the island where Tolbert had been camping and took us to the Memphis landing.

Rescue wagons were shuttling survivors up to the three hospitals. We wound up in Adams—"

"My grandfather's hospital!"

He nodded. "I stayed there with the judge for three days, until he was well enough to go to a boardinghouse. People were so kind, people who a week before that would have spit on us. Women brought us food and clothes and other necessities."

"Of course they did! Southerners are not monsters!"

"I know." He looked away, absently stroking her fingers. "By the time the judge was able to leave the hospital, his son . . ." He sighed. "Well, he'd passed on."

"Oh, Zane."

The tears in her eyes moved him. "There was nothing I could do about it except be there. I think he was grateful. He treated me like a son." He wasn't going to tell her how many nights the judge woke him up from a screaming, cold-sweat nightmare in which he found himself back at Cahaba, either hanging from that accursed ladder or standing in waist-high water waiting to use the latrine. "When he realized I had no place to go, no real home, he recommended me for a position with the marshals service. I'd been Provost Guard in the army, and it was a natural fit. The judge had been recently appointed to the judicial district of northern Alabama, so I moved with him to Montgomery and lived in a boardinghouse there for four years."

"I see why you think of him as a father," Aurora said softly.

"And you can understand why I have to bring in the swine who murdered him in cold blood." He thought the brutal words would shock her.

But she rose onto her knees, leaning close, clutching his

fingers. "I do understand. That's how justice works. Judge Teague is the one who presided over that trial after Schuyler's father's murder, isn't he? Do you think the two are connected?"

"They have to be. And I think the man I followed when the *Sultana* exploded is responsible for one or both murders. I can almost prove it."

She frowned. "It sounds like you think he caused the explosion."

"I'm certain of that too. There's a connection somewhere between all three. The judge knew something that got him killed, and I keep thinking it had to do with my testimony before Congress—which makes me a mark too. What did Ezekiel Beaumont and Judge Teague, the soldiers on the *Sultana*—myself included—and these Frye people all have in common?"

"The Fryes?" Aurora stilled. "Why do you mention them?"

"Well, they were at the trial, and I know Teague was interested in what they had to say. They seem to have subsequently been the target of those fires at Daughtry House. Because I was in Washington during the trial, I was too late to gather whatever they know. If only I could talk to them . . ." He paused at the expression on her face. "What? Do you know where they are?"

"No . . ." Aurora looked away. "But if I find out, I'll let you know."

She wasn't telling him something, and to this point he'd thought of her as brutally honest, as open as a plate glass window in front of a candy store. Had his outpouring of personal backstory made her withdraw? He felt as though a poisonous wound had been lanced, but the thought of even a drop of it spilling onto her was galling.

He waited, watching her, wondering. Finally he said, "Aurora, I'm sorry if all that was more than—But you wanted to know—"

"Of course I wanted to know!" She sandwiched his hands in her small ones. "Now I understand why you're so all-fired intent on finding the judge's killer. So many things about you make more sense now."

To Aurora's relief, Zane did not withdraw. He even smiled a little. "Did you really think I was hiding a wife away somewhere?"

"I hoped not. But since we're on the subject, please tell me if you've got a sweetheart in Montgomery. Or Memphis. Or Nebraska or wherever you were in your Pony Express days. You were a Pony Express rider, weren't you?"

He laughed. Why did he always laugh when she asked him something? "Yes, I rode for the Pony. But trust me, there was no opportunity for a sweetheart during those days. Not many young ladies ventured out to Indian territory before the war. And no, I didn't leave a sweetheart at any point in my travels." Smile fading, he looked down at their joined hands. "Until you, I never met anybody who could look past this ugly mug long enough to carry on a conversation, let alone get to know me."

She had a feeling they had just leapt far beyond the bounds of proper church behavior, and it was completely her fault. After all, *she* had touched him first. He was a gentleman, and likely he hadn't wanted to embarrass her by repulsing her. Besides, he'd actually *said* she was beautiful and he'd like to court her.

Therefore whatever happened next would be at her own instigation. Gil would probably tell her she'd go to hell for it, though she believed Jesus would most likely understand.

However, she *could not* allow him to continue thinking he was ugly. So she let go of him and turned around to sit down on the kneeler beside him. "Close your eyes," she said.

"What?" He was looking at her like she was crazy.

"I mean *eye*!" She snapped her fingers. "Close your eye. I mean it."

He obeyed.

Reaching up under her dress, she untied the garters of her right stocking, then settled her skirts modestly over her legs. Then she removed her right shoe and the stocking and tucked them out of sight under her skirt. Her bare foot stuck out in plain view. "All right, now you can look."

Zane gingerly looked at her sideways.

"At my foot," she said.

She watched his gaze travel down her arm to her dress to the hem of the skirt, and she saw when he did a double-take and started counting toes. "You have—"

"Yes, I have six toes on my right foot. I guess that little one on the side hardly counts, but my sisters think it's awfully funny. Once I asked Grandpapa to cut the extra one off, but he spanked me and said not to ever say anything like that again." She looked thoughtfully at her own foot for a minute, then at his red face. "I've gotten used to it, but for a long time I was mad at God that he messed me up so badly. I used to pitch a fit when they tried to make me go swimming or even take a bath, because I didn't want anybody to see it. And I know what's wrong with letting a man see my bare foot, but—"

"Aurora, hush. I know what you're doing, and I appreciate it, but it's not the same thing." He reached down to brush one finger across the top of her foot. "Even with eleven toes, you're the most exquisite thing I've ever seen."

Shivering with some unidentifiable longing, she leaned over, put her palm against his face, and turned it toward hers. "Fair enough. Then let me tell you what *I* see. I see a man of courage and integrity and immense loyalty. I haven't known you long, but what I've seen makes me want to keep digging until I understand what has hurt you and what has rebuilt you and strengthened you." She let her thumb trace his lips. Fine, beautifully cut lips. "And I'm going to be so honest my grandmother would probably shut me up in a room for the rest of my life if she knew I said this, but you are far from ugly. And I really wish you would kiss me."

She watched his gaze drop to her mouth. She could see the war going on in his brain.

"Aurora, I can't."

"Then I will." She set her lips to his, felt the warmth spread as he responded instinctively, then he gave a low groan. He turned her across him, settled her comfortably in his arms, and seemed intent on learning every square inch of her face. Drowning in emotion, she eventually realized that one of them was going to have to put a halt to this feast of mutual pleasure, and unfortunately, it would probably have to be her. She cupped his face with her hands. "Zane. I don't want to, but I'm thinking we should stop, because Gil might come back from dinner any minute."

The green eye widened as her words blew away whatever fog he had been swimming around in. He looked horrified, which was a crime in itself, because he had demonstrated a superior talent for kissing that strengthened her determination to be the only sweetheart he possessed in any state of the Union. Now she was going to have to work even harder to break through the walls he'd established around his heart.

Hastily he set her away from him and pressed the heel of one hand against his good eye. "Hurry. Put your stocking and shoe back on, then I'll take you home. Aurora Daughtry, you are a menace."

Fine. She was a managing female and a menace. But he seemed to enjoy kissing her, and that was a step in the right direction.

Aurora entered the sitting room with Zane and found her grandmother sitting in the only wing chair there, drinking tea like the Queen of England.

"Come in, children," Grandmama said with extravagant civility. "How thoughtful of you to grace me and Thomas-Anne with your presence after all."

Aurora's stomach knotted. She glanced at Zane, hoping he would stay and buffer what was sure to be a brutal dressing-down over the lateness of the hour and the fact that they were unchaperoned. But muttering something about prisoners, he disappeared up the stairs, leaving her to face the dragon alone.

The coward.

Though she could hardly blame him.

She smiled at her cousin, who sat on the big horsehair sofa, knitting a scarf. Or maybe a sweater for a giraffe. "Good night, ThomasAnne. Grandmama."

"Just a minute, young lady." Grandmama set her cup down on the side table with a sharp clink. "I wish to have a word with you."

"Can it wait until morning? I'm very tired." Aurora sidled toward the stairs.

"No, it cannot wait."

Aurora dropped onto the sofa beside ThomasAnne. "In that case, I need to ask your advice about a dinner party I want to host at Daughtry House for the dignitaries who have arrived for the trial. There's a US attorney and a marshal and a couple of deputies—"

"You are not going to distract me with parties," Grandmama said. "We are going to discuss your obvious infatuation with the very attractive young deputy with whom you have wandered about town for half the day."

Aurora smiled, vindicated. "He *is* attractive, isn't he? I told him so, but he wouldn't believe—"

"You *told* him he is attractive?" ThomasAnne apparently stabbed herself with a needle, for she yelped. "Aurora, how could you!"

"How could I not?" Aurora clenched her hands. "He somehow developed the idea that no one could overlook such a minor defect as an eye patch. I simply disabused him of that notion."

Grandmama's perspicacious stare was unnerving. "Would you like to share the particular method with which you accomplished this feat?"

Aurora thought of Zane touching the top of her foot. "No, ma'am, I would not." She clamped her lips together.

"I would like to point out that a young lady is given but one reputation. Once ruined, there is no getting it back."

Grandmama glanced at ThomasAnne, who ducked her head and returned to knitting furiously.

Aurora resented the implication that she had behaved loosely—although maybe she had. "Grandmama, *I* would like to point out that only this afternoon you declared that you liked Zane quite a bit. And you seemed to have no objection to my 'wandering about town' alone with him."

"That was before you came creeping in after dark, sporting a significant beard burn about your mouth and one of your stockings drooping at your ankle!"

Aurora clapped both hands over her mouth and looked down, horrified to discover that the hurriedly retied garter had indeed come loose again, and her stocking sagged. "It's not what you think," was all she could manage.

"Then tell me what it is," Grandmama advised, "so that I won't continue to think the worst."

Humiliated, Aurora glanced at ThomasAnne. To her surprise, she found sympathy in her cousin's expression. So she put up her chin and described exactly what happened. All but the kiss, which any fool would have deduced from the rest.

Grandmama was no fool. By the end of it, the old lady had bowed her head and shielded her face with a delicate handkerchief, as though she couldn't bear to look at Aurora. Her shoulders shook. "You showed him your six-toed foot?" Grandmama asked, voice wobbling.

"Yes, but you needn't cry," Aurora said, beginning to feel some regret at last for so desperately disappointing her grandmother. "He didn't seem to think it was all that grotesque. In fact, he was very kind about it."

"I'm sure he was." Grandmama dropped the handkerchief and looked up, and Aurora realized her grandmother's blue eyes were alight with laughter. "I've never heard anything so nonsensical in my life, aside from Schuyler Beaumont jumping fully clothed into a pool to rescue a girl who swims better than he does." Grandmama laid her head against the back of the chair and closed her eyes. "Oh, my soul. You girls are going to be the death of me. I'm too old for this."

"But, Grandmama—"

"Never mind." Grandmama waved the handkerchief. "So you got your first kiss at the church altar. I suppose it could be a lot worse. ThomasAnne, take this goose upstairs and put her to bed, if you please. I'm going to write Dr. McGowan a long letter before I retire myself. And Aurora, you should be aware that I shall sleep with my door open. I will know if either you or the handsome deputy sets foot outside your room before breakfast. Are we understood, miss?"

"I'm not a child," Aurora said with dignity, but she rose and followed ThomasAnne up the stairs. Outside her bedroom door, she kissed her cousin's soft cheek and whispered, "ThomasAnne, I'm sorry to have embarrassed you. If you're not ready to go to bed, you don't have to mind what Grandmama—"

"She's right, you know."

Aurora drew back. "What do you mean?"

"May I come in and talk to you for a minute?" ThomasAnne's tone was diffident, as usual, but her light blue eyes were filled with concern. "If you're not too tired, that is?"

"I'm not tired at all." Aurora wanted nothing more than to crawl into bed and relive the source of her "beard burn"— heavenly days, the things that came out of her grandmother's mouth sometimes!—but she wouldn't hurt ThomasAnne's feelings for anything. "Come on in."

Inside the room, she plopped down at the head of the bed, tucking the pillow behind her back, and started taking off her shoes, while ThomasAnne curled up cross-legged at the foot. Aurora was reminded of days when she was a little girl, slipping into her older sisters' room to listen to them talk. She'd never thought about ThomasAnne needing companionship.

Apparently she did. ThomasAnne looked serious but genuinely pleased to be sharing a confidence. "Aunt Winnie means well," she began. "All her preaching and bossing is out of love."

"I know that." Aurora tossed her shoes into a corner and sighed. "It's just that I get tired of being treated like a five-year-old."

"It's hard for her to see you grown up and being interested in a—in a man." Tilting her head, ThomasAnne studied Aurora. "I think she thought she was going to have a few more years before she had to deal with this."

"Why? Just because it took Selah and Joelle forever and a day to make up their minds? I'm nineteen, ThomasAnne. Most girls my age have already got babies by now."

"Yes, but you don't have to rush." ThomasAnne bit her lip. "There's nothing wrong with waiting until the right man comes along."

"I'm not in a rush!" Aurora lifted her hands. "I know it looks that way, but Zane Sager is the first man I've met who is just that—a man, not a little boy, and if you'd heard him praying tonight you'd understand why I'm drawn to more than his looks. Yes, he's got big shoulders and an intriguing way of walking, and when he gives me that little half smile, I just want to kiss his face off—but that's beside the point. ThomasAnne, he is a *good* man, I know it in my bones. He

would make a good father and he would take care of me and
love me—if I can convince him he's worthy of being loved."
She leaned forward to grab her cousin's hands. "Have you
ever been in love like that?"

ThomasAnne hesitated. "Before I answer that, let me ask
you something. Pete, do you remember the first time I came
to live with your family? You were little more than a baby,
maybe four or five."

"I think so. But maybe I've just heard stories my sisters
have told."

ThomasAnne shook her head. "I doubt that. They were
both away at school at the time. At least, most of the time
they were."

"Oh. Then—" Aurora thought back. "I do remember you
holding me in your lap and reading to me at bedtime. Does
that sound right?"

"Yes, of course. Do you remember *Stories for Children*
by Cousin Sarah?"

Aurora smiled. "The book with alphabet poems. I must
have begged you to read that to me every night for a month."

"Several months," ThomasAnne said dryly. "Persistent
little thing you were, even then."

"Especially then, I would think." Aurora sighed. "I'm
afraid I was quite spoiled." She brightened. "But thanks to
you, I was reading and writing by the time I was six."

"Yes, you were. And you brought a lot of light into a very
dark time of my life. I'm sure you don't know why I came
to Ithaca. Nobody talks about it." ThomasAnne's eyes were
sad, but she held Aurora's gaze. "I had fallen morally. No
better than Bedelia or Rosie. Maybe worse, for I ran away
from my sin."

Aurora sucked in a breath, then didn't know what to do with it. "Did you—you mean, you were with child?"

ThomasAnne nodded. "I had become betrothed, without my father's knowledge, to a young man who came to apprentice in his shop."

Aurora did not want to know this. She admired quiet ThomasAnne, loved her like an older sister, and had thought she knew her. Never in her wildest imaginings would she have guessed such a thing. Quite simply, she didn't know what to say. So she said nothing.

ThomasAnne forged on. "When it became clear that I was going to have a baby, I told my sweetheart. He was gone the next morning."

"What? How could he—"

"Oh, honey," ThomasAnne sighed. "It's a story as old as time. I thought we were going to be married, and I let him sweet-talk me. My parents sent me down here to Ithaca, and in one of those weird twists of fate, your mama discovered she was with child shortly after I arrived. I gave my baby away when he was born, but if we'd known your little brother would die, I'm sure your parents would have adopted my son. But it was too late by then."

Tears sprang to Aurora's eyes. "ThomasAnne, how could you bear it? I've always wondered . . . you're so pretty and sweet, and I couldn't imagine why you never married."

ThomasAnne blinked. "Me? I'm nothing to look at. As to how I bore it, what was the alternative? Aunt Winnie said she needed me, so I moved to Memphis and I never went back home."

"Why did you tell me this? Especially right now?"

"Do you think I'm trying to kill your joy?" ThomasAnne

smiled a little. "Let's go back to the question you asked me—the one about being in love. I thought I was in love when I was sixteen, with a man who tricked me and used me for his own pleasure. That 'love' turned to bitterness and hatred overnight. I thought I could never trust another man. But there is a man who has kept my secret for fifteen years. He treats me with respect and tenderness, but he won't let me hide behind fear. That, little cousin, is love. I so pray you'll not accept less in the man you choose to spend your life with."

Aurora's mouth fell open. "Dr. Kidd? Was he your physician when your baby came?"

"Yes. He had just returned to Tupelo and opened his practice, after graduating from medical college in New Orleans. The upside-down thing is that I might never have met Ben Kidd if I had not come to ruin." ThomasAnne lifted her frail shoulders. "Maybe that's what the Bible means when it says that all things work together for good to them that love God. It doesn't negate my sin or the wrong that was done to me. I have certainly repented and paid consequences. But it does mean that God has a purpose for my life beyond what I could ever have dreamed."

Exhilaration flooded Aurora. "ThomasAnne, that is so beautiful! I can't tell you how glad I am that—wait, *are* you and Dr. Kidd going to marry?"

"Yes, but we want to wait until Joelle and Schuyler are settled. And this trial has things all disrupted. Please don't say anything yet."

"Of course not, if you say so. Does Grandmama know?"

"I'm sure she suspects, but I haven't told her in so many words. Listen to me, Pete." ThomasAnne scooted closer and took Aurora's hands. "The whole reason I brought it up is

as a word of caution from someone who spent a long, long
time in despair and regret. One careless, selfish decision can
literally shift your world. Even if Mr. Sager is the man you
think he is, you'll walk a straighter path to happiness if you
can exercise patience and follow God's plan."

"Even if I think Zane needs a little nudge toward knowing
his own mind?"

ThomasAnne laughed. "I think you can trust God to nudge
him when the time is right."

Seventeen

FRIDAY EVENING, Zane straightened his tie in the mirror, glad that he'd taken the extra trouble of packing a dinner suit.

It had taken him all night and most of the next day to realize that Aurora had never told him where Georgia and Lemuel Frye were hiding, nor where she'd come by such information. What struck him eventually was that, if *she* knew, then Beaumont and Riggins surely did too. And they had withheld it from him.

He found this both infuriating and frustrating. The first thing he would do when he saw the Pinkerton agent and his unofficial partner would be to demand an explanation.

If, that is, he could keep his eyes off Aurora Daughtry long enough to do so.

How had she done that? Completely derailing his good intentions of keeping his distance. Extreme measures, that was how. Taking off her stocking and shoe to demonstrate an imperfection. Kissing him at the altar of the church. No wonder he didn't stand a chance. She was fearless.

Better question, *why* had she done that? He stared at himself, mystified. There had to be more eligible men, even in a backwater like Tupelo, Mississippi—or Memphis or Oxford, come to that—who would fall at her feet, offering a life of ease and wealth. Why would she choose a broken-down, tongue-tied cowboy like Zane Sager on which to focus her considerable charm? Was she practicing for some larger, more important target? Playing him for a fool?

Maybe. And yet, and yet . . .

There was an intrinsic artlessness about her, a complete absence of prevarication. He didn't think she could tell a lie if it would save her life. She seemed to mean every word of those beautiful things she'd said to him. And that was the heart of the danger. How would he protect her, if she recklessly ran toward whatever she wanted? Especially if that was, unbelievably, himself?

Unable to reach any satisfactory conclusion, he turned from the mirror in disgust and picked up his hat from the side table.

Hiring a horse from the closest livery stable, he took the road out of town toward Daughtry House. Wells, Pierce, and Spencer had offered to take him up in their hired carriage, but he preferred traveling on his own. Mosley, his fellow deputy, had been more than happy to remain with the prisoners while he went to "hobnob with the aristocrats." Frankly, Zane would have taken the cowardly way out and stayed behind himself. But Pierce insisted on his presence as liaison with their prosecutorial allies.

So be it.

Fifteen minutes later, he reined up in front of the mansion Riggins had told him so much about. He knew nothing about architectural styles, but he knew wealth and privilege when he saw it. Restored to its antebellum glory, Daughtry House rose like a beautiful pearl in the middle of a grassy park, approached by a straight, brick-paved path under arching oaks. In front of the broad wooden porch, the lawn was dotted by clusters of azaleas and dogwoods and finished off by a massive magnolia with drooping branches. The blooms were all gone by now, but the brilliant green of the plate-like leaves made his throat ache.

He sat his horse, looking up at the tall columns that braced the second-story balcony, then tipped his head back to admire the rooftop cupola, setting the whole thing off like the uppermost tier of a wedding cake. He'd lived in Montgomery and then Memphis long enough to be aware of King Cotton lifestyle, and his unit had traveled all over northeast Mississippi, where these mansions spread across the land like exotic jewels sewn upon a canvas.

But this was *her* home. She'd been born here, spent her childhood under the watchcare of loving parents and older sisters, her every want and need provided. Now that the place was a thriving hotel—or would be soon—she could come back here any time she wanted and feel at home.

He was hit with a deeper sense of inadequacy at the distance between their life experiences. Even supposing—as he had admittedly done in recent midnight tossing and turning—he lost his mind to the point of asking her to share his life, how could he expect her to leave this luxury to become the wife of an underpaid tumbleweed of a lawman, who spent every waking moment with criminals?

His mind stuttered at the very idea.

He dismounted and was about to tie the horse to an iron

hitching post beside the path, when a Negro boy of ten or eleven years came running around the side of the house, waving.

"Hello, boss!" the boy said with a grin, skidding to a halt and taking the horse by the bridle. "Sorry I wasn't here when you come up—I took the carriage around to the barn. The other gentlemen, they already gone in the house. Just ring the bell and somebody will let you in."

"Thanks, son." Zane reached in his pocket for a coin and flipped it to the boy. "What's your name?"

"Tee-Toc. Don't worry about this 'un. I'll wipe him down and water him and make him real comfortable!" The boy smiled his thanks for the coin and led the horse away.

Zane bounded up the porch steps and found the bell pull. Momentarily a young Negro maid came to the door. "Come in, sir," she said with a smile. "You must be Mr. Sager."

"The one with the eye patch," he said dryly.

The girl giggled. "Yessir. That's what Miss Aurora said. Everybody's in the parlor. Dinner will be served in just a little bit. Can I take your hat? I'm Miriam. Just follow me."

Surrendering his hat, Zane entered a spacious two-story foyer with doorways to the right and left and a grand double staircase leading up to a second-floor mezzanine. Straight ahead, under the landing, a broad breezeway pushed toward the back of the house. Standing in the center of the marble rotunda, he looked up and up at a huge crystal-and-wrought-iron chandelier suspended two stories down, from the dome at the top of the cupola. When he got done gaping, he looked around and found Miriam waiting patiently. "Sorry," he said, embarrassed. "I've just never . . . sorry."

She smiled as if this were a normal reaction to her place of employment. "I know. It's real pretty, isn't it?"

He shrugged. The place was beyond words. And his chances of winning the hand of Aurora Daughtry had dropped to zero. Following Miriam through a doorway to the left, he found himself in a large double parlor stuffed with graceful upholstered furniture, polished tables, and a fine old carpet. Under the front window sat a grand piano, and he remembered somebody saying that Riggins played. He hadn't heard real music in a long, long time.

"Zane! Welcome!"

He wheeled from the piano to find Aurora flying toward him. Squelching the urge to catch her in his arms, he instead took her hand and carried it briefly to his lips. "Miss Daughtry, it's good to see you."

Jerking to a stop, she bobbed a curtsey, then looked up at him, eyes bright with secret joy. "Would you like something to drink? Lemonade?"

Still crushed with the awareness of the difference in their social stations, he shook his head. Then changed his mind. He needed something to do with his hands. "Lemonade would be nice."

Following her toward a buffet where crystal glasses and a sweating icy pitcher sat on an elegant tray, he watched her pour the drink. She was always beautiful, but tonight she wore a deep jade evening dress that picked up green flecks in her eyes. Her curly copper hair had been tamed into an upswept twist of braids, with soft tendrils left to brush her cheeks. He noticed delicate pearl drops in her small ears and a cameo at her throat, with a matching ring on her right hand.

He was suddenly aware that his suit was several years old, and he didn't have proper evening shoes—just the boots that he wore every day. But it was too late to do anything about it, so he accepted the glass of lemonade and drank it in one long draft.

Without a word of censure, Aurora took his arm and tugged him toward a group gathered in the center of the room. Everyone looked at him, so he tried to smile. He knew the Oxford contingent, plus Riggins, Beaumont, and the doctor. He'd also met Mrs. McGowan and Miss Thomas-Anne. The remaining two ladies bore a family resemblance to Aurora, so he knew they must be her sisters.

"Most of you know Deputy Marshal Sager," Aurora said. "Zane, the tall one is Joelle, Schuyler's fiancée, and this is Levi's wife, Selah."

He managed to bow without falling over, then shook hands with each man. "Thank you for inviting me," he said to Mrs. McGowan, assuming she was the hostess.

"Of course you're welcome," she said with a vinegary smile, "but you should know Aurora would have come to get you herself if you hadn't arrived."

"Grandmama!" Aurora said on a gasp.

Everyone else laughed, including Zane, breaking the slight constraint. Forcing himself to relax, he stood quietly and listened to the general predinner conversation, which Selah and Aurora managed in deft tandem. Beaumont also demonstrated a knack for asking questions that made Zane feel included without putting him on the spot.

Before he knew it, an elegant black-clad Negro woman—Horatia, the head cook and housekeeper, Aurora murmured to him—came to announce that dinner was served in the dining room. Because Aurora happened to be standing next to him, manners dictated that he offer her his elbow. Smiling up at him, she tucked her fingers between his arm and rib cage, and off they went. Half of him hoped he'd be seated next to her at the table, the other half wildly prayed he wouldn't.

It seemed God was listening. Aurora put him between Riggins and Joelle—the tall, blue-eyed sister, whose staggering beauty made him all but forget his name, until he realized how painfully shy she was. His efforts to set her at ease made him forget about his own discomfort, and gradually he realized what a droll sense of humor she possessed. He really liked her, and after she'd casually asked him how he'd injured his eye, she seemed not to notice his deformity at all.

He suspected that Aurora, seated across the table from him between Pierce and her cousin ThomasAnne, had designed the seating arrangement so that he could easily meet her laughing gaze whenever Joelle's vocabulary sailed outside his reach—a frequent occurrence.

Finally, as the entrée was being cleared, Joelle turned to speak to her grandmother, and Aurora leaned in to whisper across the table, "You're doing fine. Nobody else understands her either, except maybe Schuyler, and even he has taken to carrying around a dictionary in his pocket."

Suppressing a grin, Zane shook his head. Even a rube like him knew not to carry on cross-table conversation.

Instead, he occupied himself with studying the oil painting of the three sisters and their mother hung over the fireplace. Mrs. Daughtry had been one uncommonly beautiful woman, and it was interesting to trace which of her features her daughters had inherited. Aurora got the heart-shaped face, winged eyebrows, and small cleft chin; Joelle the tall, willowy shape; and Selah the dark brown eyes. He knew little about art, but he had to admire the painter's ability to portray the variations on the mother's flaming Irish red hair in that of the three girls—Selah's dark mahogany with reddish glints, Joelle's in the strawberry-blonde family, and Aurora's closer to copper.

The only minor kerfuffle of the evening occurred when Bedelia O'Malley brought in dessert. He'd all but forgotten the existence of the two saloon girls Aurora had rescued—at least in her mind.

Bedelia clearly remembered him. She let out a joyous shriek and nearly dropped a tray full of pudding dishes as she elbowed the small Asian girl who had accompanied her into the dining room. "Rosamund! It's Deputy Marshal Sager!" Bedelia righted the careening tray. "What are you doing here?" She was dressed, he noticed, in the modest black attire of a serving woman, covered by a starched bib apron. But nothing could quite eradicate the flirtatious tilt of her full red lips and fluttering eyelashes.

Except possibly the eagle eye of Horatia, who stood in the dining room doorway, fists on her hips. "Here now, what's all this ruckus? The dinner guests didn't come to talk to you, honey, so serve the puddin' and get on back to the kitchen, you hear?"

Bedelia pouted, but obediently flounced around the table with the dessert, while Rosamund refilled drinks. When Bedelia leaned over his shoulder with his pudding, Zane smiled and said quietly, "Nice to see you doing well, Bedelia. Would you be able to get free to talk to me later? I want to ask a favor."

"You can ask me anything you want, handsome, I'm all yours," she said, shooting a triumphant look across the table at Aurora. "I'll be in the kitchen washing up the pots."

Of course she had completely the wrong idea about what he wanted to ask, but at least he had her full attention. He could straighten her out later. "Thank you," he said and hid his burning face behind his napkin.

She winked and moved to serve Riggins.

"How do you know Bedelia?" Joelle asked. She looked more curious than shocked.

He cleared his throat. "I arrested her. I just want to ask her what she knows about local Ku Klux Klan participation over the last year or so. I'm guessing most of the planning of their activities happens in the bars and saloons. She's bound to have heard something."

"I imagine she has," Joelle said. She gave Zane a thoughtful look. "I'd thought you might want to talk to me too—though of course Schuyler knows more than I do, since he actually joined them."

"I do want to talk to you. I just didn't want to ruin your sister's party."

"That's thoughtful of you, but Pete's well aware of the nature of this gathering. In fact, I'm sure that's what she had in mind when she planned it." Joelle directed her gaze at her younger sister, who was listening to the marshal tell a story. Pierce was laughing, clearly charmed by Aurora's dimples and bright golden eyes. "I know she's young, but she is a wonderful hostess, just like our mama was, and she's very smart. She could be a brilliant political matron, if she met the right man." Apparently realizing what she'd just said, Joelle fixed widened blue eyes on Zane's face. "I mean—I didn't mean—"

218

Zane laughed ruefully. "I know exactly what you mean. I've been telling myself the same thing since I met her."

"Oh, please don't pay any attention to me!" Poor Joelle looked miserable. "I'm rotten at making conversation, because I say exactly what I'm thinking, and it always comes out at the most awkward moment."

"Miss Joelle, I wish we had more truth-tellers in this world. In fact, I hear you're the writer behind the articles that stirred up some of the controversy hereabouts. I wish you'd tell me about your school and how it's proceeding since the schoolroom burned. Have you begun to rebuild?"

She seemed relieved at the change of subject, and he found that he even understood most of what she told him about her correspondence with senators, congressmen, and educators, both on the state and national level, regarding the education of freedmen. It was a complex and fascinating subject that involved not just the legislation of making education available to all, but the knotty problem of funding it.

"I'm afraid I never had much opportunity to go to school myself," Zane confessed. "I finished the sixth grade, then had to go to work in the gunpowder mill."

"Really? Where did you grow up?"

"Mainly Indiana, though I was born in Delaware. My pa took us west when I was about fourteen, though, and we never stayed put much after that."

"Pete said you rode for the Pony Express. I loved reading stories about it when I was younger."

He sighed. "I did. It was a hard life, and fortunately didn't last very long. Bill Cody and some of those fellows make it sound more romantic than it really was."

She gave him a perceptive look that made him shift in

discomfort. "You are not at all what I would have supposed Aurora would fall in love with."

His mouth fell open. Literally, he couldn't think what to say. "Ma'am? I mean, what do you—"

"I mean that in a good way. I'm glad I'm wrong. But don't tell her I said so."

"I'm not telling her anything at all! Miss Daughtry, I mean Miss Aurora, is by no means in l—" He gulped, unable to say the word. "You are very much mistaken, is what I mean."

"Oh, no, I'm not. She can't take her eyes off you. And I thought she was going to hurl her plate at Bedelia. So I should probably warn you that if you're not serious about her, you'd better get out of town on the first train. Pete is very determined when she makes up her mind."

He could attest to that. Managing menace and definitely mule-headed.

"But back to the subject of education," Joelle said, overlooking the fact that she had just upended Zane's life, "I've been talking with the Fryes about it, and—"

"Wait." He grabbed Joelle's arm. "The Fryes? You mean Georgia and Lemuel Frye? Are they here?"

"Well, yes." She glanced uneasily at Riggins, who apparently didn't hear her. "Was I not supposed to mention that?"

"Aurora implied something to that effect." She hadn't said that at all, but Joelle didn't need to know that.

"Oh. Well, good, then. I thought you must know, since you're here, and . . ." She shrugged. "The talk was bound to get around to the case we're trying to prosecute. They're important witnesses."

"Yes, they are. I'd really like to talk to them. Tonight, if possible."

Joelle's perfect brows drew together as she glanced at Riggins again. "You should probably ask Levi first."

Oh, he would. He definitely would, and he would not take no for an answer. Aurora wasn't the only bulldog when it came to pursuing a goal.

Eighteen

Aurora squirmed all the way through the after-dinner entertainment. Not because she didn't like music. Not because she didn't admire her handsome brother-in-law, who could do anything from rappelling off a railroad bridge to memorizing a piano concerto.

She pretended to be enthralled with Levi's solo piano performance of one of his favorite composers—Mussorgsky or Liszt or Chopin or one of those other eastern European crackpots—while glancing over her shoulder to observe Zane's somewhat prickly reaction to his surroundings. He clearly was not used to being waited upon, and she found his astonished gratitude at the offer of a drink refill or a seat closer to the piano both heartbreaking and charming. She couldn't help feeling protective of his dignity, but she also knew better than to jump to his aid when he seemed confused or uncomfortable. He was a grown man, after all, and he would figure it out.

She just wished she had the right to sit beside him on the settee against the wall while he did so. But he was not her beau. He was not "her" anything. He was merely one of the invited guests, on a par with Mr. Spencer, Marshal Pierce, and Mr. Wells—guests she was responsible for treating with equal hospitality.

As it was, she and Grandmama shared the big sofa with Selah, who watched her husband lose himself in his art, a winsome expression of pride and pleasure upon her glowing face. Joelle and Schuyler sat close together on chairs brought in from the dining room, and even Doc and ThomasAnne proclaimed themselves a couple in the way their eyes met often in enjoyment of the music.

Levi was three or four minutes into his second piece, a dance he called a "mazurka," when Grandmama reached over to pinch the back of Aurora's hand. "Stop sulking," Grandmama hissed under her breath. "You're making a spectacle of yourself."

"I'm not sulking," Aurora said through her teeth. "I'm listening hard."

"You look like you ate something that disagreed with you."

"It's not polite to talk through a performance."

"Neither one of you is listening anyway. Just take Mr. Sager out to the barn to look at the new litter of kittens."

Aurora turned to make sure someone hadn't brought in a different grandmother when she wasn't looking. "And that wouldn't cause a spectacle?"

"The barn, Aurora. And take food with you."

"For the kittens?" Aurora was getting really worried about her grandmother's grip on reality. And Joelle was giving them both annoyed looks over her shoulder, even though she and Grandmama were whispering.

"Two plates of roast with potatoes au gratin. And take

dessert as well. Come, Aurora, Tee-Toc told me you found them. Mr. Sager will want to talk to them."

The barn. Where Tee-Toc had dissuaded her from storing her naughty painting. Undoubtedly it was a measure of her demented lovesick state that she had forgotten all about Mr. and Mrs. Frye hiding in the hayloft. "Oh. Yes, he will. Very well." Waiting until Levi finished the last crashing chords of the mazurka, she rose, applauding, and sidled to the back and side of the room. Zane looked up at her in surprise.

"Mr. Sager, I believe you had wished to speak to Bedelia before you left tonight. I'm sure she's still in the kitchen washing up, if you'd like to come with me."

"Really?" Brightening as if he'd been handed a stay of execution, he lurched to his feet. "I did want to talk to her. But maybe we shouldn't leave right now—"

"Grandmama said it's all right. In fact, she all but commanded me to rescue you." Pursing her lips, she glanced at her grandmother, who was studiously ignoring her. "So follow me, if you please, and hang the consequences." She could feel his quiet, powerful presence behind her, the noise of the party fading as they left the parlor and walked through the breezeway.

"Where is the kitchen?" he asked when they'd reached the back porch. "I thought it burned to the ground." Zane took a lamp from the hook beside the door and lit it. The sky was overcast, putting the natural light of the moon and stars behind clouds.

"The roof and wooden storeroom did burn," she said, taking his arm as they descended the porch steps. "We're working on getting it back to functioning condition. Meanwhile, Horatia has gone back to working from the small

224

kitchen in the manager's cottage. That's where Joelle and ThomasAnne and I live when we're on the property. Selah and Levi have the old overseer's cottage."

He was quiet as they walked the brick path through Mose's flower beds, the scent breathing about them. Finally he said, "This place is enormous. How many acres?"

"I don't know. Forty thousand, I imagine. Maybe fifty?"

Zane whistled through his teeth. "Aurora, you realize I have literally nothing to my name? I live in a rooming house, but I'm hardly ever there. I don't even own a horse right now."

She thought about that. "Jesus didn't own anything either. I think there's probably a good bit of freedom in that. A shift in responsibility, maybe?"

"Don't set me up on a pedestal, Aurora."

"I'm not! And I would turn that right back on you. I'm not the spoiled princess you seem to think I am."

"Yes. You are." His voice was hard.

Snatching her hand away, she whirled to stand in his path. "That was mean!" She tried to discern his expression in the flickering lamplight. "And I'm not as smart as Joelle, but I know self-defense when I hear it. You're just trying to push me away before you can get hurt."

"What if I am? Do you blame me?" He set the lamp on the path, putting his face completely in the dark, and took her by the shoulders. "I don't want to insult you, Aurora, but I'm working. I don't have time for parties. I have to interview a couple of prostitutes in order to find a murderer, and every minute I stand here arguing with you is a minute I can't spend putting Jones behind bars."

The feel of his hands on her bare shoulders, coupled with the iron tone of his voice, all but sent her up in flames. She pushed at his chest. "All right then—let me go! Find your own way to the kitchen! And I'll tell Georgia and Lem Frye you were too *busy* to talk to them tonight."

"Fine." He dropped his hands. "Wait. What?"

"Never mind." She bent to pick up the lamp. "I'm sorry I've kept you from your *work*." She started walking, somewhat at random.

"Aurora. Wait, come back. Where are you going?"

"To the kitchen to get some food for the witnesses we are apparently hiding in our barn." She could hear him following her. "Grandmama told me to take them some leftovers from the meal."

He caught up to her. "How is it that everybody except me knows where these people have been all this time?"

"Probably because you're so intent on talking to prostitutes, you haven't been listening."

"All right, all right. I deserve that. Stop. Aurora, listen, I'm sorry."

"You're what? I didn't quite hear you."

"I said I'm sorry! Jiminy, what a crosspatch!"

She laughed.

"You're not really angry, are you?" He sounded aggrieved.

She stopped and held the lamp up to search his face. "Oh, I'm angry all right. But I also understand exactly why you behave this way. Grandmama says men have to be taught how to talk to women. It took her nearly thirty years to train Grandpapa."

He didn't respond to that.

"See?" she said. "You're learning already."

Then he chuckled, that rusty sound that tickled her heart. "Come on," he said, "let's get the interview with the girls over with, then you can take me to the barn. Are you sure your grandmother doesn't mind?"

"I told you, she sent me. I think she trusts you. In fact, I'm sure of it." She flicked a look up at him as they walked. "Though I don't know why."

"I imagine she's aware I'm scared to death of you."

"Oh really?" She skipped a step, and Zane took the lamp from her.

"Here, you're going to set us both on fire."

She sighed. "I'm pretty sure that's already happened."

All right. So be it, Zane thought, following Aurora literally down the primrose path.

He wasn't sure what a primrose was, but it had to be characterized by the lure of this switchback journey in and out of delirious joy and utter despair. The astounding thing was, she saw right through his attempts to hide his feelings. He hadn't even known he *had* feelings until a couple of weeks ago, and he sure wouldn't have suspected they'd climb right out from under his hard-won self-control.

It looked like he wasn't getting rid of her anytime soon, so he was just going to have to get used to sleeping with one eye open—which, in his case, meant no rest at all. He would have found the thought hilarious, if it weren't so pathetic.

Fortunately, before he could succumb to the temptation to set the lamp down again and find out if her lips tasted as berry-ripe as he remembered them, they arrived at the small front porch of the brick manager's cottage.

Aurora opened the door and stuck her head inside. "Horatia, it's me," she called. "Are y'all still here?"

"In the kitchen, honey. I'll be right there."

Aurora smiled at Zane over her shoulder, then went inside. "I brought Deputy Marshal Sager to talk to—oh, there you are. Horatia, this is Zane Sager. Zane, meet Horatia Lawrence. She and her husband, Mose, have been co-managers of the business since the beginning. We couldn't do without them."

Zane followed Aurora into the tiny entryway and offered a courteous bow to the neat black woman who'd rescued him from Bedelia's attentions in the dining room. "I hope we're not interrupting your work too much," he said. "I had a question or two I wanted to ask Bedelia and Rosie while I'm here."

"We're just wiping things down a last lick before Mose and me goes home," Horatia said. "Miss Aurora, why don't you take him to the office, and I'll send the girls along in just a minute."

"Yes, ma'am, but could I ask a favor before you close the kitchen for the night? Grandmama asked me to take supper to the guests in the hayloft. Have you got anything left?"

"Yes, in fact I'd already packed a basket to take to them on our way home. I'll set it out on the kitchen table while you talk to the girls."

"Thank you, Horatia. Zane, come this way." Aurora turned right through an open doorway.

Zane found himself in a large, comfortable office furnished with three or four overstuffed man-sized chairs and a large built-in desk under a wall of pigeonhole shelves. Papers and ledgers had been filed there in orderly fashion, indicating that somebody cared about records and numbers. The remaining walls were lined with bookshelves, except for a cozy fireplace in the corner. The brown-toned rug was old and well-worn. He liked the feel of this room.

He sat down in the chair Aurora pointed at, stretched out his legs, and relaxed.

"This was my papa's office." Aurora turned the desk chair outward to face the center of the room and sat down. "I used to come in here when I was very small, to play with my dolls while he worked on the ledgers." She closed her eyes, as if remembering. "He was already teaching Selah how to keep books. I think she was managing the paperwork by the time she was ten or eleven. That's why they made her and Jo go to boarding school. He wanted her to have the science and math she needed."

"That's . . . fairly uncommon, I would think," he said.

"Yes." Aurora sighed. "Mama was very conventional, but Papa—he never did anything the way other people said he should. I do know he loved our mama, though, and came unhinged when he discovered he couldn't protect her. I think that's why he lost his mind." She shuddered.

Zane was silent. There were apparently some tragedies in life he had managed to escape. But he knew what she meant. "Wartime prisons can steal a man's humanity." He looked around. "He seems to have been quite a reader."

"I think so. But about half of these are Joelle's." She gave him a suspicious look. "Do you like to read?"

"Not particularly."

"Me either." She grinned. "Except fashion magazines."

"I do read my Bible every day. That's one thing the judge insisted on. He said the first voice in my head every day ought to be Scripture."

"That sounds like Selah. I try to do that, too, but I always get stuck on Leviticus and Numbers."

"Well, you know, I think once you've read those, you might get a pass on rereading them."

"You think?" She scrunched her nose. "Tell me more about the judge. How did you meet him?"

He froze. "I told you, I don't like to talk about prison."

"I know, but—Zane, it might not hold so much power over you if you'd tell somebody about it."

"Not right now." Not ever.

Fortunately, before Aurora could pester the daylights out of him, Bedelia burst into the room, followed by the Asian—Chinese?—girl, Rosie.

"Mr. Sager!" Noting that he wasn't alone in the room, Bedelia scowled. "Miss Aurora."

"Come in and sit over there." Coolly, Aurora nodded at an empty chair across the rug from Zane, then smiled at Rosie. "Rosamund, I understand you made the pudding tonight. It was delicious!"

"Thank you." Rosie took the remaining chair and sat back, her feet dangling an inch off the floor. "You going to have best restaurant in Tupelo, Miss Ola. I promise I learn everything good."

"I know you will." Aurora glanced at Zane. "The deputy marshal wants to ask you ladies some questions. I hope you'll provide him with whatever information he needs to catch some very bad men who burned down our kitchen and schoolroom and Horatia's church."

Rosie's eyes widened. "I don't know nothing about bad men. I'm a good girl!"

"I'm sure you are," Zane said soothingly. "Anyway, nobody's going to arrest you for anything you tell us. But what I'm thinking is that you and Bedelia might have heard some talk at the bar, about some of their meetings—maybe the reasons they wanted to hurt the black people in town." He saw Bedelia flinch. "Deedee, did Constable Pickett or any of the others threaten to hurt you if you talked?"

"No." But Bedelia looked down, picking at her fingernails, high color in her naturally florid face.

"All right, fair enough." He paused. "There's a man I'm looking for, name of Maney. Did you ever meet him? Either at the bar or . . . anyplace else?"

"I might have heard the name," Bedelia said sullenly, "but I don't remember where or when. I was at the Dogwood a long time, and I met a lot of men."

"Will you tell me if you remember anything? Or if you see him again, will you let me know?" He looked at Rosamund. "Please, Rosie. I have to find him before he hurts someone else."

The Chinese girl gave him a reluctant nod, then addressed Aurora. "No more men, Miss Ola? Only Deputy Zane. I like him. He nice."

Since he wasn't likely to get anything else out of either of the former saloon girls—though at least he'd apparently gained an ally in Rosie—Zane stood up. "Aurora, perhaps we should collect Horatia's basket from the kitchen and let these girls go to bed. They look exhausted."

"I ain't tired." Bedelia shimmied her shoulders. "I'm just gettin' my second wind!"

Aurora rose. "Good night, Bedelia, Rosamund. I'll talk to you both in the morning about coming back to the Dogwood permanently."

"Don't know as I want to do that no more," Bedelia said, apparently in a contrary mood. "I likes it here, so."

"Fine. We'll talk about it tomorrow." Aurora waited, arms crossed, until the two women had quit the room, then gave Zane a comical look. "She'll sing a different tune when she finds out you're a guest at the Dogwood."

He scratched his head in embarrassment. "All I'm trying to do is get her to talk."

Aurora gave him a thoughtful stare. "Well, you'll have to decide how far you're willing to go to accomplish that. But I'd be very careful, if I were you. Cross that one, and she's just as likely to scratch your eyes out as look at you."

Nineteen

EXCEPT FOR THE POOL OF LAMPLIGHT in which she stood with Zane, the barn was dark, warm, and redolent of the animal smells and sounds that had comforted Aurora since she was a small child. Breathing it in, she smiled, relaxing for the first time all day.

"Come here, I want you to meet someone." She took Zane's hand and headed down the center aisle of the barn, past the stalls on either side.

"The hayloft ladder is the other way." He sounded confused.

"Yes, we'll get there in a minute. This old fellow is my best friend, and we have to speak to him first."

She stopped at the last stall on the left and peered over the low door. "Shep! Wake up, Grandpa, I brought somebody to meet you." Her childhood Shetland pony blinked up at her, then lurched to his feet to eagerly poke his grizzled muzzle over the door. She laughed and fished in the basket hanging from her arm. "I brought you a carrot—be patient!" As Shep gobbled the treat, she looked up at Zane. He smiled and reached down to pet the miniature horse. "When Papa told me he was a Shetland pony, I thought he said 'Shepland' and insisted on calling him 'Shep,' as if he were a dog. That's how I treated him. Would have let him sleep in my room if Mama hadn't pitched a fit."

"How old is he?" Zane asked.

"About my age, I think. Papa gave him to me for my fourth birthday. Papa taught me to muck stalls, to feed and water Shep, brush him, and eventually handle the tack." She fed the pony another carrot piece. "Even though I was too big to ride him by then, leaving him behind when I went to Memphis was the hardest part of that ordeal." She sent Zane a self-conscious look. "I know it doesn't compare to what you went through, but it was big to me at the time. When the war ended, I was relieved to find out Shep hadn't been stolen or mistreated by the Yankees who came through here. They even fed him and exercised him."

"I can see why. Give me that carrot." Clearly enamored, Zane opened the stall door to make friends, and Aurora lost another piece of her heart.

They spent another five minutes with the little horse, Aurora putting Shep through his tricks—Zane's favorite being "Bow to the queen!"—and Zane demonstrating his ability to charm anything on two or four legs with a minimum of effort.

Eventually, however, Zane, who had seated himself cross-legged in the hay at the pony's feet, looked up at her. "We've got to get back to business. But can I come and visit another day?"

"Of course." She leaned over to stroke Shep's shaggy forelock and kiss him between the eyes. "Good night, old fellow.

Sleep well." She extended a hand to Zane, boosting him to his feet. Aurora picked up the basket, Zane took the lamp, and they left the stall. "I wish you could stay the night. I'd bring you back out here to look over the matched sorrels Levi and I bought for the carriage."

"That them?" Zane nodded at two curious noses poking over the tops of their stalls as they passed.

"Yes. Here's the ladder to the loft."

"You're in an evening dress," he said. "Can you manage it?"

"Of course I can. Hold the lamp. I'll go up first."

The climb wasn't as easy as she'd made it sound. The soles of her evening shoes were slippery, and she'd had Thomas-Anne cinch her corset so tight she could hardly breathe. But at last she emerged, huffing and puffing, and turned to sit for a second, with her feet dangling into the opening.

As Zane began the climb, she heard a scraping noise behind her and scrambled to her feet. "Psst! Mr. and Mrs. Frye, it's Aurora Daughtry. We haven't met yet, but Grandmama and Horatia sent me to bring you some supper."

After a moment of silence, a cautious male voice answered out of the darkness, "Who is that with you?"

"It's Deputy Marshal Zane Sager. He's assisting the prosecution of the Klan trials. He needs to talk to you."

"All right," Frye said. "Get behind me, Georgia."

Aurora moved aside to allow Zane through the opening. Zane set the lamp on the floor, then climbed out to crouch beside it, looking up at the small, bespectacled young man who greeted them from behind the barrel of a revolver. He lifted his hands in a gesture of surrender. "I don't blame you for being suspicious, Frye. Let me show you my badge." He slowly reached into the inside pocket of his jacket and pulled out his US Marshals badge. "I came for dinner tonight, but when I found out you and Mrs. Frye were here, I couldn't pass up the chance to find out what you know. Marshal Pierce and the US Attorney will want to talk with you as well, but I believe the Daughtrys are wise to keep your location a secret for now."

"It looks like everybody in the county knows where we are," Frye said dryly, lowering the gun. He reached back with the other hand for his wife's hand. "This is my wife, Georgia."

A light-skinned black woman, dressed in gray calico, stepped forward. She was very pretty, with big dark eyes and a sweet, intelligent expression that Aurora instantly liked. Already aware of the Fryes' interracial marriage, Aurora glanced at Zane.

His eyebrow rose, but fine manners quickly masked any shock, and he simply nodded. "Pleased to meet you, Mrs. Frye."

"We're ready to bring this situation to an end," Georgia said, "and we want to help in any way we can. But we've been ambushed more than once." She looked at her husband.

Frye nodded. "Tuscaloosa was our home, and we did good work there, until the Klan took exception to the Freedman's Bureau and the Union League joining to educate Negroes. I understand you have my wife's brother in custody."

"That's right." Zane moved to sit on a nearby hay bale.

Since he left enough room for Aurora, she sat down too, even though she was short enough to have stood upright under the roof. The Fryes sat nearby so that they could comfortably converse in whispers.

"He seems willing to turn on Jefcoat now," Zane said. "I think he realizes he was played for a fool."

"I don't know why he trusted the Jefcoats to begin with," Georgia said. "Little Andrew is a lazy drunkard, always looking for a shortcut to get what he wants." She stared at Zane in the lamplight. "Don't believe anything he says."

Zane nodded. "All right, duly noted. Mrs. Frye, according to Beaumont and Riggins, you and Moore are both children of Jefcoat Sr. and one of his house slaves, but you were sold off fairly young at the Memphis slave auction to a family from east Tennessee."

"That's right," Georgia said. "The Maney family bought me, and I became nursemaid to their children." She glanced at her husband. "Lemuel was their tutor."

"This is what interests me the most," Zane said. "Alonzo Maney seems to be the nexus of this giant spiderweb, with connections to everyone. I understand you think he is behind Ezekiel Beaumont's murder—that young Jefcoat's fatal shot was no accident."

"I'm convinced it was an assassination." Frye's expression was grim. "Crooks like Maney do not change their stripes. During the war—in the spring of 1864, to be precise—my wife came across a letter to Mrs. Maney from her husband, hinting that he had purchased intelligence from a Masonic brother—no names mentioned—regarding an anticipated Union invasion of Mississippi. Maney had in turn passed this information to Forrest's camp. Georgia felt safe in keeping the letter, which had been thrown away, but didn't feel it warranted putting ourselves in danger with immediate action. However, a few years later, we met Mr. Beaumont at a Union League meeting in Alabama. As we got acquainted,

we discovered a mutual interest in the financial shenanigans
of General Maney. Beaumont had apparently come across
proof that Maney was in the Senate just long enough to become involved in a highly unethical—if not illegal—money-
laundering scheme that is presently under congressional investigation."

Aurora wasn't sure she got the connection. "Do you think
the two things are related? Buying and selling intelligence
and congressional money laundering?"

"Beaumont's murder, followed by Judge Teague's, is the
key." Frowning, Zane tapped his fingertips together. "If Beaumont knew about it, there's a good chance Teague did too.
They were friends, despite having served on opposite sides
in the war. Which makes me wonder if Maney had been trying to take out the judge as far back as our imprisonment in
Cahaba. Sam Jones certainly did his best to do away with
Teague on more than one occasion. And I have evidence that
Jones was in the courthouse the day of your hearing, Frye."

"I'm not familiar with that name," Frye said. "Who is
Sam Jones?"

Zane glanced at Aurora. "He's the villain who served as
second-in-command at Cahaba Prison, where I spent the
last year of the war. Teague got there before I did and was
released ahead of me. We hadn't known each other prior to
that experience, but a brotherhood of sorts can be established
in circumstances like that. I saved his life—he saved mine—"
Zane spread his hands. "In short, we watched out for each
other, along with a handful of other men. We developed
a policing and judicial mechanism to stop prisoners from
attacking and robbing one another for small liberties and
luxuries—food, utensils, tools, and the like. Anyway, back to

Jones. He had his own pack of dogs that roamed the prison, stealing what they could and terrorizing the weak, mainly for the pure meanness of it. I saw him shoot men on the least pretext of stepping outside the deadline." He paused, clearly reluctant to say more.

Grieving all over again, Aurora now understood why he'd refused to talk about it before. Had she been wrong to push him to do so? "So you think Jones was Maney's henchman?" she asked quietly.

"Jones was in a Masonic order in New Orleans, where he was a bookkeeper for the slave market. He was very proud of his ring. And I know where the spur I found in the Tuscaloosa courtroom balcony came from. He took it from me at Cahaba. Mr. Frye, I know you couldn't have seen him, since Riggins says he got you out right after the fight broke out, but Jones was there that day. If we can discover the name of the Union officer who sold out to Maney, we might have the connection we're looking for."

She'd said talking about it would make him feel better. And it had until he'd been forced to talk about Sam Jones.

Like a poisonous snakebite, it got worse from touching it. He didn't know how to draw it out, how to rid himself of the venom. He hated Sam Jones with a depth that someone like Aurora Daughtry could never understand. Everyone in her life loved her and all eleven of her toes.

Heck, *he* loved her. That was another thing that wasn't going away this side of heaven.

He rode the hired horse back to town, letting his mount pick his way along the dark, dusty rutted road. Probably most of the surrounding countryside belonged to the Daughtry Plantation. Fifty thousand acres, over a hundred square miles. That had to be a quarter of the county.

Even if he came out of this trial alive and had the chance to woo Aurora as she deserved, he would look like a fortune hunter. He ground his teeth. No man with any pride or self-respect would come to the woman he loved with empty hands. Maybe she didn't mind, but *he* did. He remembered her grandfather well—dry, upright old stick that he was, even five years ago—and there was no question of Dr. Belmont McGowan giving his beloved granddaughter to a penniless adventurer, no matter how much Mrs. Winnie might personally like him.

He'd returned Aurora to the parlor just as the entertainment ended, watched her slip into her seat beside her grandmother and receive an approving pat on the knee. The men migrated to the back porch with cigars and port, leaving the women to do whatever it was women did when they were left alone. Probably jabber about babies.

He could easily imagine Aurora with a little one or two. She would be a delightful mama and would never send a ten-year-old away from home to live with her grandparents. Well, maybe to protect her from invading armies she would.

With a sigh, he rubbed the back of his neck. The actions people took under crisis probably shouldn't be judged. He'd sure made his share of cringe-worthy decisions.

In any case, he was glad Aurora would be staying home at Daughtry House tonight, her grandmother having vetoed her plan to return to Tupelo after dark. He'd told his superiors what he'd learned from the Fryes, and they'd formulated a plan to throw out a net for both Maney and

Jones. It was going to take some time, but he thought it should work.

Yes, it should work, but there was a major drawback.

Aurora was at the center of it.

"You and the deputy marshal were out of the room together for quite a long time," Joelle said, turning so that Aurora could unfasten her dress.

For reasons she couldn't explain even to herself, Aurora had elected to share Joelle's room tonight instead of Thomas-Anne's. She didn't respond to Joelle's remark until she'd twitched loose all twenty buttons marching down her sister's long spine and loosened her corset strings as well. Watching Joelle shimmy out of the beautiful topaz-colored dress Charmion had made to replace the one that burned in the house fire, Aurora plopped down on the bed in her chemise and drawers and folded herself cross-legged. "Nothing happened," she said, pouting.

"Nothing?" Joelle raised a red-gold eyebrow in patent skepticism.

"Well, we talked to Horatia and Bedelia and Rosie, then I introduced him to Shep, and we went up in the hayloft. But nothing interesting." Aurora propped her elbow on her knee and her chin on her hand in an inelegant posture she was certain would horrify Grandmama.

Joelle planted her hands on her narrow hips. "The hayloft?"

Aurora had to grin. "Not for, you know, canoodling. Mr. and Mrs. Frye chaperoned us."

"Oh. Don't misunderstand, you shouldn't be *canoodling*,

but I'm a bit disappointed that he didn't even try." Joelle took off the corset, tossed it to the other side of the bed, and reached to untie her garters. "Schuyler had already kissed me by the time we were fourteen."

"Bragging is not becoming in a lady, Joelle." Laughing, Aurora caught the garter Joelle threw at her. "Anyway," she added casually, "Zane has kissed me."

"Ooh. Tell, tell." Joelle jumped on the other end of the bed on her knees.

"It was . . . Well, Grandmama seemed to think it was funny and immature, ThomasAnne said I was incautious."

Joelle scowled. "You told them before you told me?"

"Don't be mad. They just happened to be there right after. You know me, I can't keep from blabbing to whoever is handy. Except . . . I didn't really tell them all of it. I didn't tell them that I love him and I want to marry him."

"I knew it! Aurora, you've known him less than a month!"

"Not everyone gets to marry her childhood sweetheart, Jo."

"I know, but—this is very extreme, even for you."

"True." She sighed.

Joelle stared at her in obvious concern. "Aurora, exactly how far did you go?"

"Oh, my goodness!" Annoyed, Aurora straightened. "It was a kiss, nothing more. I've got more common sense than people give me credit for. And don't call me 'Aurora' in that admonishing tone. It makes me want to go do something truly rash."

Joelle straightened her legs and started rolling down her stockings. "If you want to do something rash, talk Grandmama into letting me and Schuyler get married this summer. I don't want to wait until September."

8

"Sounds like somebody else is pretty fond of kissing and shouldn't be casting stones." Suddenly weary to the bone and frankly just a bit jealous of her sister's blatant happiness, Aurora climbed under the covers without bothering to change into a nightgown. "Good night, Jo. I'll see what I can do with Grandmama, if you'll do your best to help Zane get this trial over with in an expeditious manner."

"Expeditious! Pete, what a top-drawer word. I'm proud of you, honey." Joelle gave one of her husky chuckles and blew out the light.

Twenty

Friday, June 17, 1870
Dogwood Boarding House

On Friday morning, as he woke up with the sun streaming through the open window, Zane stretched muscles sore
from four days spent mainly on horseback. Responsible for
delivering court summonses, subpoenas for deposition, and
other writs as directed by Wells or Pierce, he'd taken statements which mainly ranged from "I ain't tellin' you nothing,
you blankety-blank Yank," to "Yeah, I was there, but I can't
remember what happened."

Frustrating, but not unexpected.

The remainder of his days and evenings had been spent
sitting in the attic with Jefcoat and Moore, while Mosley
stretched his legs and got some fresh air. He could hear the
sounds of hammering on the roof, workers tramping up and
down the stairs with ladders and cans of paint, women haul-
ing about mops and buckets of soapy water. Once or twice a
day, Bedelia or Rosie would drop in to bring food or empty

the chamber pots—a humiliating experience for sure—and exchange news. Apparently Aurora had convinced them both that they were needed in their old home and ready for the move back from Daughtry House.

He managed to keep himself from asking what their "boss-lady," as Bedelia called her, was up to. But occasionally, some hint would drop that she was hanging a new picture or ordering dishes or planting flowers along the walk. It wasn't enough, but it was all he was going to allow himself.

Last night, Zane had been particularly interested to hear that Schuyler had taken a train to Mobile. It was about time. Hopefully, he'd come back with those documents the Fryes claimed were in his father's possession. The trial was set for next week, Judge Hill would arrive on Monday, and they would need every bit of evidence available to connect Maney to the murders of Ezekiel Beaumont and Judge Teague.

Pushed by the urgency of today's assignment, dreading the strain of holding the girl he loved at arm's length, he rose and got about the business of shaving and dressing.

Thirty minutes later he came down the stairs, bracing for the inevitable encounter with his landlady. Still, he couldn't help looking forward to breakfast. One thing he'd say for Miss Aurora: she kept a spectacular table, and her kitchen staff functioned with the precision of a military chain of command. He found her setting a table for one near the front window, and she turned at the sound of his boots on the gleaming wood floor.

Her dimples appeared. "Good morning, Deputy Marshal! Did you sleep well?"

"I did, thank you." He caught her before she whisked away to the kitchen. "No, don't run off. I need to talk to you."

Her cheeks flushed in apparent surprise. "You've been avoiding me, so I thought—"

"I know, and I'm sorry. It's been a hectic week. But Riggins is meeting me here, and—"

"Is something wrong?"

"No, but we need your help and—Here he is." To Zane's relief, the front door had opened to admit Riggins, followed by Joelle. "I'll let him explain."

"Levi!" Aurora ran to kiss his cheek and hug her sister. "Jo! I haven't seen you all week. How is Selah?"

"A little queasy in the mornings, but otherwise well," Joelle said with a sigh. "Can't keep her off her feet. She's helping Horatia restock the kitchen and says we'll be back in business in a week or two."

Riggins nodded at Zane. "Morning, Sager. Have you told Pete what we've got planned for her? You'll like this," he said to Aurora with a smile. "It involves shopping."

Zane intercepted Aurora's questioning look. "I haven't said anything yet. Just got down the stairs."

Riggins frowned, looking from Zane to Aurora. "You've been together here all week."

Zane shifted his feet. "I've been . . . tied up with Wells and Pierce."

"All right," Riggins said with a philosophical shrug. "Then let's sit down, and I'll lay it out."

Aurora put a hand on his arm. "Have y'all eaten? Let me lay two more places."

"I'll help," Joelle offered.

As the women bustled about dealing with dishes, silverware, and food, Riggins sat down and filled Zane in on a variety of matters pertaining to Judge Hill's impending arrival.

By the time Rosie brought in the tray of steaming grits, eggs, biscuits, and ham, Zane felt confident that the awkwardness between himself and Aurora would be ignored.

After thanking Rosie, who backed out of the room with a smile and a bow, Aurora asked Riggins to return thanks.

Once he'd briefly done so, the Pinkerton agent laid his napkin across his lap and leveled a puzzled and somewhat amused stare at Aurora. "All right, Little Bit, what's the matter with you two?"

"I'm perfectly fine." Lifting her coffee cup to her lips, she cut her eyes to Zane. "I don't know what's wrong with him."

Gritting his teeth, Zane wondered how it was possible to want to kiss someone and strangle her at the same time. "Nothing is wrong with me. I have some documents I need to take to Judge Hill today, and I thought you and Joelle might like to go to Oxford with me. Wedding shopping, you know." If that sounded awkward and forced, it was because Riggins had written the script.

Aurora plunked down the cup. "And?"

"What do you mean, 'and'?"

"Finish the sentence, Deputy Marshal." Aurora stared at him, narrow-eyed. "Why are you offering to take two women you obviously don't want to be anywhere near you on a two-hour shopping excursion?"

Joelle patted her hand and scowled at Zane. "There's no need for all this tippy-toeing around. They need us, Pete. We're to go to the bridal shop and get Mrs. Clancy to introduce us to Mrs. Scully."

"Scully? The man Wyatt nearly electrocuted?"

Joelle smiled, unfazed. "Yes, his wife. They think she might know something about this Maney character. Right, Levi?"

Riggins nodded. "We've discovered that Maney is the attorney for these men we're charging for the Tupelo crimes, and we need every bit of background on him we can dig up. During the war, your father and Scully served under Maney in Tennessee. It's possible—we're hoping—there may be letters to Scully from Maney that his wife will be willing to part with."

"Why don't you talk to her yourself?" Aurora asked Riggins.

She wasn't looking at Zane, but he answered. "A lady like her is not going to talk to two Yankees—one a detective and the other a federal law officer. But she might talk to you. Look at me, Aurora." When she reluctantly turned her big golden eyes his way, he braced himself for the impact. "You've got a way with people. I don't know anybody else who could get this lady to talk. And we need her."

"Oh, so my jabbering might actually serve some useful purpose?"

Zane couldn't quite read her, until he saw a shadow of one of those dimples. He relaxed. "You jabber to your heart's content. If you get her to give you anything on Maney, I'll—I'll pay you with three wishes," he finished recklessly.

Aurora tipped her head. "Three? Perhaps we should negotiate."

"Fine. Two then."

She laughed. "All right. Three wishes is a deal. What time does the train leave?"

By the time their little party arrived at the Oxford station at noon, Aurora was hungry, stiff, and ready for a visit to the nearest privy. The long trip from Tupelo by rail had involved taking the SL&SF up to Holly Springs, then switching to a spur line for a short hop down to Oxford—a triangular, out-of-the-way pattern that made Schuyler's scheme for a connector between the two east-west towns make a lot of sense. She was going to encourage him to push for it, next time she saw him.

As it was, she hurried through the crowded station with Zane and Joelle toward a line of hired conveyances waiting to take weary travelers to nearby hotels and restaurants. Zane quickly made arrangements with the driver of a closed carriage, handed Aurora and Jo inside, and then jumped in himself.

"We're going to the Thompson House for lunch," he said, "then I'll deliver you ladies to the bridal shop while I meet with Judge Hill."

Aurora eyed him in surprise. "The Thompson House?" That would not be a cheap meal.

"Marshal Pierce has offered to pay our expenses today. After that miserable ride, you earned a nice dinner."

Aurora wasn't going to argue. The worst part of the trip had been Zane's monosyllabic responses to any comment she made to him. She'd finally given up and directed her conversation at Joelle, who at least answered her in complete sentences. Maybe he was preoccupied by his official duties of the afternoon, but she suspected another reason, perhaps a little more personal, for the wall he'd erected between them.

To her surprise, during the course of the meal he came out of his shell to a degree. He had beautiful manners, demonstrated in the courteous way he drew out chairs for her and

249

Joelle and his ability to charm waiters. He was never going to be a silver-tongued beau like Schuyler, but Aurora found his quiet confidence restful. In fact, she enjoyed the meal so much that as they left the restaurant, she impulsively tucked her hand under Zane's arm and smiled up at him. "Thank you so much! That was delightful."

He froze. "I—You're welcome. The food was good, wasn't it?"

"Yes, but I didn't mean just that." Trying not to show her hurt, she pitched her voice low so that Joelle wouldn't hear. "Zane, I'm sorry if I seem to push you where you don't want to go. I didn't mean to—"

"Aurora, there's nothing wrong with you," he said, just as low. "I wouldn't change a thing." He stared at her. "Nothing, do you hear me? I'm the one who's messed up. Just—please understand when I can't show you how I feel. Not right now."

Her breath stolen away by the feel of his heart thumping hard against her hand pressed against his ribs, all she could do was nod.

He gave her his slow half smile and helped her into the carriage.

Within just a few minutes, she and Joelle were descending in front of the bridal shop they'd visited at the beginning of the month—the day she'd found out she was a saloon heiress.

Mrs. Clancy remembered them, of course. No one who had seen Joelle would forget her.

"It's the Daughtry girls!" the plump matron exclaimed as they walked in. "Did you change your mind about your friend's homemade dress?"

Seeing the thundercloud forming on Joelle's alabaster brow, Aurora intervened before her sister could sabotage her plans. "Oh, we're keeping all our options open. I was hoping you would have a new sample or two that Joelle could try on while we're here in town for the afternoon. Maybe something a little less . . . busy than the one we saw last time? We'd also like to look at veils."

Mrs. Clancy brightened. "Certainly. Come this way, Miss Joelle, Miss Aurora."

As she followed the shopkeeper deeper into the bowels of the store, Aurora felt as if she were wading into a bowl of meringue, and she remembered Joelle's derisive description of the overdecorated dress she'd tried on last time. She had better figure out a way to truncate this experience, or Joelle was going to jump ship entirely. "Mrs. Clancy," she began the fishing expedition, "I remember when we were here before, you mentioned your friend Mrs. Scully. Doesn't she do some of the alterations for your customers? I have a dress that is a little too wide across the shoulders, and I'd dearly love to see what she could do with it."

"Alterations?" Mrs. Clancy glanced over her shoulder. "I don't know that she—"

"I'm sure I heard that somewhere," Aurora interrupted. "I've got such a short amount of time in Oxford this afternoon, I wonder if I ought to go and visit her while you and Joelle enjoy looking at wedding dresses. Could you perhaps write down the Scullys' direction for me?"

Aurora would never know whether Mrs. Clancy considered her overbearingly rude, missing a few screws, or simply misinformed (she was pretty sure what Joelle thought). But the poor lady complied without further protest, writing out a nice introduction on a piece of bridal shop stationery. Aurora tucked it into her reticule, gave Joelle instructions to "look at every piece of fabric and lace in the store," and sailed out onto the brick walkway.

Joelle would probably give up in about five minutes, borrow a book, and sit in a corner until Aurora returned. But she didn't care, as long as she got to Mrs. Scully. One thing she was determined not to do was let Zane down. One assignment. That was all she had, and it was exactly tailored for her best talents.

Talking, asking questions, making friends. She could do that.

However, ten minutes into a conversation with Dorothea Scully, she wondered if she had overestimated her skills.

The Scully home sat on a narrow street lined with identical cottages, inhabited mainly by rail employees, a short walk from the train station. Ford Scully, a Confederate veteran, had been the Oxford station telegraph operator since the end of the war. Aurora knew he had served under her father in Tennessee, but that was about all she had known until today.

Unfortunately, Dorothea Scully gave her little more as they sat in the small front parlor, sipping blackberry tea from chipped china cups.

"Mrs. Dorothea, thank you so much for your kindness in receiving me this afternoon. I don't know how I got so confused about your connection to Mrs. Clancy. I could have sworn she said you took in some sewing." Before the woman could so much as open her mouth to deny the misapprehension, Aurora gushed on, "But now that I'm here, I wonder if there's anything I could do to make your husband's incarceration easier to bear. People can be so mean when our loved ones come under the scrutiny of the law."

Dorothea's pale, doughy face didn't even twitch, and her sad gray eyes remained fixed on her tea. "It's been hard," she admitted. "In fact, I wish I did have more skill with a needle. I could use the extra income."

Flooded with unexpected compassion, Aurora set down her cup and reached for one of her hostess's chapped hands. "My sisters told me your husband was a good friend of my father's, and that he came to our house the day Papa died—to warn him, you know, that authorities were on the lookout for the survivors of their old wartime unit."

Dorothea nodded. "Your father had come to see my husband one night a week or so before that. Mr. Scully tried to keep it from me, but I insisted he tell me the identity of the mysterious visitor." She looked up at Aurora. "I could tell your father wasn't right in the head. I was furious with my husband for getting mixed up in those train sabotages. I don't think Mr. Scully set the explosives—that was your father's part in the scheme—but he did intercept and pass messages between Mr. Daughtry and their—" Catching herself, she snatched away her hand, rattling her teacup in its saucer. "I mean, I—don't mind me, I'm sure I misunderstood the whole thing."

Aurora had enough sense to know when somebody had said more than they meant to. But if she pressed too hard, she would scare the woman away. She smiled as if she'd heard nothing untoward. "Men are so odd about what they think we women can understand, aren't they? As a child, I used to sit right at my father's feet and listen to him talk to his managers and business contractors as if I were no more

than a porcelain decoration in the room. Later, I could—
and often would—spout off nearly word for word to my
mother what was said in that office." She took a sip of tea
and tried not to wince as she found it both cold and bitter.
God, help me to handle this right, she prayed. "I imagine
you heard General Alonzo Maney's name more than once,"
she said coolly.

Mrs. Scully stared. "How could you know that?"

Aurora restrained the urge to jump from her chair in victory. "The General was a well-known figure in Confederate
military circles in the Tennessee theater during the war. He
was my father's commander, as your husband was under
Papa's command. I believe my father went to Mexico with
him at the end of the war and stayed until President Johnson
declared amnesty, though I'm a little hazy about where he
went when he came back. Selah thinks he went to California
to look for gold." She tipped her head. "Perhaps your husband received correspondence to that effect? When did you
and Mr. Scully marry?"

"We got married towards the end of the war. I was a nurse
in a field hospital here in Oxford, and when Mr. Scully was
invalided home, I treated him for extensive injuries he'd sustained while escaping enemy fire at Vicksburg. That was when
he first told me of his friend Jonathan Daughtry, who had
been imprisoned at Fort Douglas and subsequently escaped."
Mrs. Dorothea paused, then blurted, "You are correct that
he escaped prosecution for military crimes and accompanied
the general across the Mexican border. I believe Mr. Scully
heard from him twice after he returned to the States and
went to the gold fields."

Aurora knew she had just uncovered important informa-

tion, but she hadn't Levi's experience in interviewing witnesses. Where on earth should she take this conversation
next? *Common sense, Pete.* "Poor Papa," she sighed, looking
down, but acutely aware of her hostess's uncomfortable posture. "He missed our mama so much, and he was so angry
over what those Yankees did to her. It's no wonder his mind
broke. Your husband was a good friend, trying to keep him
from further imprisonment."

"I don't know so much about that," Mrs. Scully hedged.
"I think he was trying to protect himself as much as anything else."

Aurora detected resentment in the woman's tone. "Do you
. . . do you feel that your husband deserves to go to prison
for what he did?"

Mrs. Scully folded her arms across her bosom. "No woman
wants to see her man humiliated. Like I said, it's been hard,
with Mr. Scully not here to take care of the man things
about the house—and I got practically no income, now that
the railroad isn't paying his salary. But . . ." She wetted her
lips and flicked a glance at Aurora. "I'd been a widow for
nearly ten years when I got married to Ford Scully—I'd got
used to living alone again and doing things my own way.
But I loved my first husband and I liked being married. So
when Mr. Scully came along and courted me, I jumped on
it. Maybe a little too quick." She sighed. "Besides, right is
right, wrong is wrong. I'm not sure my feelings have anything to do with it."

Aurora decided what she was going to do. "Mrs. Dorothea, I admire that sentiment more than I can say. So I'm
going to tell you something and hope you believe me. Alonzo
Maney is an evil, evil man. I've seen and heard evidence

that he manipulated both my father and your husband—and probably a lot of other people—for his own personal gain, mainly for power and money. If you can produce some letters or other documents that would help law enforcement take him out of a position to keep hurting people, you would do a very great service to your community and your country. Will you help us?"

Twenty-one

As the train lurched into motion, Aurora turned sideways in her seat and laced her fingers together in her lap. "I've decided on my first wish."

They had taken the last train out of Oxford, switching to the connector at Holly Springs, which was scheduled to arrive in Tupelo by eight. His afternoon had been full of tedious reports, expense accounting, and trying to convince Judge Hill to admit Mrs. Scully's testimony against her husband. The judge might or might not cooperate.

Resigned, Zane looked at Aurora. "Have you? What is it?" He had a feeling he was going to regret this rash agreement having to do with wishes. He had managed to head off her previous attempts to bring it up by probing the surprising depth of Joelle's knowledge about Mississippi politics, but with no warning Joelle had fallen asleep, leaving Zane to fend for himself.

"I want you to tell me about your family." Aurora stuck out her chin.

He frowned. "You didn't say talking would be involved."

"You didn't ask." Squirming, she settled her shoulder against the back of the seat. "Joelle told me you grew up in Indiana and worked in a gunpowder mill."

"Yes. I was born in Delaware, though. My father was of French Huguenot descent, employed by the Duponts. My mother, I believe, was a descendent of the Delaware chief Hopocan. She died during the move to Indiana when I was about three. I don't remember her." If he thought that depressing bit of information would stop her questions, he had misjudged her.

She simply touched his hand in sympathy. "I'm sorry. Sager doesn't sound like a French name, though."

"It was originally St. Gérard, but it got anglicized over the years."

"We're very English and Scottish," Aurora said, eyes twinkling. "Grandpapa turned up his nose at Frenchmen. Do you have brothers and sisters?"

"Just a sister, Jacqueline. She's a little more than two years older than me." She was going to ask, so he might as well give her the whole story. "After Ma died, our pa turned into a sorry drunk. Which is why I had to leave school and go to work in the mill. After a few years, Jacqueline started thinking it might help Pa to go west and start over. She'd heard about the Overland Express and wrote letters in Pa's name, applying to run a station."

"Your *sister* did that? How very . . . enterprising of her! She sounds like Selah."

"Or you." He couldn't help a grin. "Jack would like you."

"Jack?"

"She dressed as a boy for over a year, while she ran the station when our pa got drunk and passed out." He paused and shrugged. "That happened a lot. And I was gone most of the time, either riding my route or catting around over at Fort Kearney. I didn't take my oath of morality very seriously."

That didn't seem to bother her. "You're not like that anymore."

"No, I'm not, but—" He swallowed, met her gaze. "I clearly can't be trusted alone with you."

Her eyes sparkled with mischief. "That wasn't entirely your fault. What happened to your father and Jack when the war started?"

"By then she had married a deputy marshal named Micah Fitzgerald. They're still out west. Pa's dead."

"Hmm. Then you really are all alone."

"Yep."

"And you like it that way." Her tone was bland, and she looked away from him, at her sleeping sister.

"No. I don't like it."

Her eyes flashed back to his. "Then—"

"But that's the way it's got to be." He loaded the words, aimed them, and let them go. "Until Sam Jones is behind bars or dead, whichever comes first."

Aurora lay awake beside Joelle, wishing she could undo that wish.

Not that she didn't want to know about Zane's family. But perhaps if she'd waited a little longer, he might have told her on his own. Maybe he wouldn't have said in so many words that he had no intention of giving her space in his life. Instead, she had grown impatient again, forcing him to define boundaries.

She tried to think and pray through what God had already taught her about faith—and how she could apply it here and now. She seemed to remember reading that "faith is the substance of things hoped for, the evidence of things not seen." Usually she could live as if God had her best interests at heart, even when there was no physical representation of it. Sadly, she now realized, that might be because her life had been singularly blessed to this point.

It was hard to believe in what she couldn't see, when her heart stung with rejection.

Feeling that rejection, for the remainder of the trip home she'd withdrawn, and Zane had let her. He closed his eye—sleeping or pretending to sleep, she couldn't tell—leaving her bracketed in silence between him and Joelle. How anyone could sleep with the train bumping and jarring one's head against the seat was a mystery to Aurora, and her relief at pulling into the Tupelo station had her nearly sprinting for the exit. The three of them arrived at the Dogwood just in time to eat a late supper with Grandmama and the saloon girls. Rosie had cooked the meal—a rich, thick stew of chicken, Chinese-style dumplings, and rutabagas, the giant yellow turnip that grew in abundance at Daughtry House.

After the meal, Zane went up to the attic to confer with Deputy Mosley, leaving Aurora and Joelle to recount to Grandmama their adventures in dress design and interviewing reluctant witnesses.

Grandmama sipped her after-dinner Lapsang souchong tea (brought with her from Memphis) and asked incisive questions, which Aurora had to answer carefully in order to avoid incriminating herself.

"Did you promise this woman her husband would not go to jail?" Grandmama wanted to know.

Aurora picked at her nails. "I told her the judge would go easier on a man who repented of his sins."

"You don't know whether he has repented or not. Even if he does, you don't know how the judge will rule. And what does his wife's testimony have to do with Scully's repentance?" Grandmama scowled. "Truly, your papa's choice of companion always left much to be desired." She cast a disparaging look about her. "A saloon, for heaven's sake."

Finding nothing useful to add to that observation, Aurora changed the subject. "Joelle, what do you think of Charmion's reimagining of the painting? Isn't it lovely?"

All five women looked up at the framed canvas now rehung over the piano. Playing off the name of the saloon-cum-boardinghouse, Charmion had painted a graceful dogwood branch with delicate green leaves and lacy pink-and-white blossoms on a background of pale blue-washed sky.

"It's so pretty it makes me want to cry," Joelle said. "I asked if she'd do another for me, and she said she'd see what she could do."

Bedelia sniffed at the idea of crying over trees. "I kind of miss our bubble lady. Saucy look in her eye, that one."

Joelle rolled her own big blue eyes. "I doubt that's what the men appreciated about her." She stood up, yawning. "Trying on veils wears me out. I'm going to bed. Coming, Pete?"

Aurora wasn't tired, but she had no desire to make herself the sole target of Grandmama's disapproving remarks. "I suppose." She trailed in Joelle's wake up the stairs, rather randomly responding to her sister's remarks as they prepared for bed—until Joelle said with some asperity, "Pete, he is fighting so hard not to give in. Give him some room, and he'll land himself."

"*He*? What are you talking about?" Pausing in the act of braiding her hair into a long plait over her shoulder, Aurora stared at Joelle, who sat cross-legged on the bed, writing in her journal. "You weren't asleep on the train, were you?"

Jo sighed. "Of course not. Who could sleep with all that noise and head-jarring? I thought he might talk to you if I bowed out of the conversation."

"Well, I wish you wouldn't speak of him as if he were a large-mouth bass. I don't want to *land* him. I just want to understand why he's so touchy."

"He's afraid. They're all afraid. Afraid they won't be good enough. Afraid they'll be rejected. A million other 'afraids.'"

"That's—that's unchristian." Aurora twitched back the covers and climbed into bed.

"Isn't it?" Joelle set her notebook on the side table and clasped her arms around her knees. "But we're all afraid of something."

"What are you afraid of? You went into a burning house to rescue your friend!"

Joelle winced. "Not one of my brighter decisions. The roof nearly fell on us all. Good thing Schuyler came in and carried Charmion out. Anyway." She waved a hand. "I'll tell you what terrifies me. The idea of testifying in a courtroom in front of a judge and a bunch of lawyers and the entire town. I'm like Moses—talking makes my brain freeze. I asked if I couldn't just write down my testimony, but . . ." She shrugged. "Levi said no."

"Well, if you're Moses, then I'll be your Aaron. I'll be there and hold your arms up."

Joelle smiled. "That's so funny. That's exactly what Selah said."

"Then I'll be Miriam. Or something. Never mind, we'll both be in the courtroom praying. And so will Levi and Schuyler. You are brilliant, Jo. There's nothing to worry about."

After rewarding Aurora with a brief, affectionate hug, Joelle had blown out the lamp and instantly gone to sleep.

Aurora, however, couldn't so easily dismiss the conversation, and let the events of the entire day roll through her brain like a series of scenes from a dime novel. Though she hadn't told Joelle about her own fear of rejection, surely God knew about it. It was just so hard to know where faith and courage crossed over into presumption. *Lord, please give me wisdom.*

That was when she heard a noise on the stairs.

She froze. It could be one of the deputies, or it could be Grandmama, a light sleeper who had been known to ramble at night. It could be Rosie or Bedelia, heading to the privy.

But Zane's clear worry about some man called Sam Jones kept resurfacing. What if Jones had found Zane?

Should she stay in bed and let him deal with whoever had decided to walk around in the middle of the night? But what if he was asleep? Surely it wouldn't hurt to at least take a look around. Besides, if Grandmama or one of the girls had fallen ill, she should offer to help. No need to assume dramatic attacks by imaginary villains.

Still . . .

Slipping out of bed, she drew on the dressing gown hanging on the back of the door, tied its belt firmly, then reached into her reticule for the little pepperbox derringer she carried when traveling and slipped it into her pocket. Grandpapa had taught her to shoot it years ago, when the Yankees took Memphis. Feeling a tiny bit safer, she opened the bedroom door. She would just take a quick look downstairs, then come back to bed and go to sleep.

Otherwise, she'd look like a complete hag tomorrow.

Sleeplessness had become such an old friend that Zane no longer cursed the darkness. In fact, he found the small hours of the night a rich medium for confession, prayer, and contemplation. A season when he could hear God's voice without distractions.

That was before Aurora Daughtry, clad in a dress the color of sunshine, penny-bright hair curling beneath a frivolous straw hat, unloaded before him a basket full of drool-inducing food and dared him with a smile to eat it. Every day since then, walking beside her, hearing her laugh, splashed by the overflow of her joy, he saw glimpses of the mature woman of God she was growing into. Of course he didn't worship her as an idol—but he'd come to recognize a partner only God could have created for him.

Now, tonight, he begged God to remove this painful thorn of longing. He wanted to tell her more than his place of birth and who his sister had married. He wanted to bare his wounds and let her cauterize them with tenderness and passion. He wanted to cover her in his own strength, protecting her from anything that would bring her distress. He wanted to slay dragons for her favor.

In short, he was becoming a sentimental idiot.

So he got out of bed—why had he thought lying down would bring relief from useless wishes?—strapped on his gunbelt, and quietly opened the bedroom door. Just a walk around the perimeter of the building. One more check of the security of each door. Then perhaps he'd be tired enough to go to sleep.

Out in the hall, at the foot of the attic stairs, he stood listening. All was quiet. No reason to disturb Mosley and the two prisoners. So he continued down to the ground floor, placing his foot near the banister to avoid the creaks in the middle of the step. At the bottom, he paused again. Silence.

He kept going. Having already memorized the layout of the dining and sitting rooms—formerly the bar area—and practiced maneuvering through them without a light, he moved with silent confidence toward the front door in the dark. He was almost there when he heard a scraping noise behind the bar. He wheeled.

Veins icy, he stalked noiselessly back toward the bar and rounded it. By now his vision had adjusted to the darkness, and he saw that the trapdoor leading to the cellar lay open. He slid his gun out of its holster.

He weighed the danger of fetching a lamp against going down blind. If he rushed the stairs from here, with or without a light, whoever was down there could escape through the outside doorway. He could fix that. Grateful that some intuition had made him learn every weak floorboard, rug, and table that might trip him, he made it safely outside.

The night was clear and humid, with a half-moon to light his progress around the building. He wished he'd had time to get Mosley to guard the front door while he went around back, but he didn't want to give the intruder the opportunity to escape. The exterior cellar door locked from the inside, so there was no way for him to get in that way without creating a lot of noise. His only option, then, was to somehow block the prowler's exit.

To his relief, he saw that Shug had left a wagon full of lumber and bricks near the back door, so Zane simply moved them a few at a time until the cellar door was braced shut, impossible to push open from the inside, trapping the intruder inside. That task accomplished, Zane reentered the house from the front and again made his way around the bar to the trapdoor.

He had started to descend, gun drawn, when a light flared below, temporarily blinding him.

He froze. Had the interloper seen him? Or did he have some other bizarre reason for suddenly lighting a lamp? Swallowing, he cocked his revolver. "Who's there?" he whispered harshly. "I've got a gun on you."

There was an eternal moment of silence. Then, "Zane?"

"Aurora." Releasing the hammer and returning the gun to its holster, he realized his hand was shaking. What if he'd accidentally shot her? He sat down hard on the top step of the cellar stairs and covered his face with one hand.

The light came closer. "What are you doing?" she asked.

Lowering his hand, he stared at her and thought stupidly that he must have died and gone to heaven. Or maybe the other direction, at this point he wasn't sure. Did angels really have white robes, freckles, and long, copper-red braids? "It must be nearly two o'clock in the morning. I'm checking the perimeter of the building. That's my job. What are *you* doing? In the cellar? At *two o'clock in the morning*!"

She looked offended. "I know what time it is, you don't have to repeat yourself. I heard something, and I came to see what it was."

All Zane's relief coagulated into another wave of fear. "You heard something? Where? Down here?"

"No, I thought I heard something on the stairs. I was afraid one of the other girls was sick, or Grandmama might need something, so I came to check—"

"By yourself? In the middle of the night? Aurora, how could you be so stupid? What if there *was* an intruder? I've told you there are bad people looking for me and the prisoners. And why would you come down here, if you heard a noise on the stairs?"

Her lips pinched together, her eyes narrowed, and he thought she might start hissing. But she seemed to regain control of her temper—barely. "Don't you *dare* call me stupid! I brought my pistol. And I came down here because I saw the trapdoor open. I didn't leave it open. Did you?"

"No, of course not—pistol? What pistol?"

Her hand went into her pocket, and she showed him a tiny pepperbox revolver. It looked somehow familiar, but that didn't make sense. "Where did you get that?"

"I've had it since I was fourteen. One of the patients left it at the house after the steamboat explosion. Grandpapa said I could keep it, and he taught me how to shoot it." She held up the lamp and glared at him. "What difference does that make? I have it, I know how to use it, and you're being a boor."

"That's because—" He wiped his sweaty forehead. He felt as if he'd come down with a fever. "I'm sorry my manners desert me when I'm scared half out of my mind. I'm sorry I called you stupid, even though that's not exactly what I said. I told you I don't talk well. I just—I don't know whether I want to kiss you or—"

"Oh, you're not getting any more kisses out of me, mister, not until I get all three of my wishes."

"Is that right?" As he stood up, the blood rushed out of his head, leaving his brains addled, possibly accounting for the fact that he walked down the steps instead of hightailing it back to the safety of his room. "Let me have the other two. Let's get this over with right now."

"I'm not ready to divulge that information at the moment."

By now he was standing one step away from her, towering over her. "So you're just going to keep me in suspense, waiting for the other shoe to drop."

She looked belligerent. "Well, you haven't been exactly forthcoming with me either."

"Touché. I think they call this an impasse." Suddenly he wanted to laugh. This woman. "I have an idea. I'll guess your next wish, and you let me know if I'm right." He leaned down to whisper in her ear. "But no more talking allowed. Put the lantern down."

"You're going to guess my wish without talking?" She sounded skeptical. But she set the lamp on the floor.

"Shh. No talking," he reminded her, leaning down to take her earlobe between his lips.

She gave a sharp gasp and fell against him. He caught her around the waist, lifting her off her feet. The only sounds to follow involved breath and the sibilant contact of lips. He'd intended to teach her a lesson about sassiness, about visiting cellars in the middle of the night, and about the correct location for carrying a handgun. But it was hard to be hard-nosed, with an armful of Aurora to deal with.

"Zane," she breathed at some point, "I'm sorry but I've got to talk."

"Why?" He kissed her.

"Because"—she dodged his mouth—"I need to say, you're a very good guesser."

"There are a lot of things I'm good at." He kissed her again. "Talking isn't one of them."

"You win this time."

"I'm sorry, I didn't hear you."

"You win. Zane, stop. Grandmama's going to wake up and see the light and—"

"Do we really care?"

"Yes." She hummed a little nonsense word. "I see now that I should have come to get you when I heard that noise—"

He set her abruptly away from him. "Which I should be investigating." Ignoring the slamming of his own heart, he picked up the lantern and stepped around the red-haired angel who always seemed to be in his path. "Go back to bed. Go to sleep. I'm going outside to look around, and I don't want to see you again until daylight." He looked over his shoulder. "Please, Aurora."

Twenty-two

AURORA WALKED UP THE STAIRS, one hand trailing along the banister, the other in her pocket around the handle of the little revolver. She'd doused the lantern and left it on the bar for Zane, should he need it.

There was a certain satisfaction in having found a man she could not easily manipulate. That wasn't to say that Zane couldn't be led. After all, she had secretly hoped she'd find him making one of his nocturnal security checks. The fact that *he'd* found *her* was a moot point. They had found each other. And discerning her wishes, he had acted upon them without fuss or argumentation.

Which seemed to her to be a mutually beneficial out-come.

She paused. However . . .

He had successfully distracted her from her original intent of discovering the source of the odd noise she had heard on the stairs. And who had left that cellar door open? Of course it could have been Deputy Mosley making rounds, but that didn't seem like something he would do—carelessly leaving doors open. Grandmama certainly wouldn't have gone to the effort, not to mention the indignity, of going into the cellar. ThomasAnne maintained her conviction that spiders lurked in every corner, no matter how thoroughly the space had been cleaned, and Joelle had been fast asleep right beside Aurora. That left Bedelia or Rosie.

Grandmama was fond of the maxim that "curiosity killed the cat," but Aurora knew she would not go to sleep until she had eliminated every possible culprit and could report victoriously to Zane in the morning that she had solved the mystery. With quiet determination, she resumed her trip up the stairs.

The saloon girls shared a room at the end of the second floor near the attic stairs. The oiled doorknob turned noiselessly under her hand, and she poked her head in. The first light of predawn layered shadows around the furniture—two simple beds, where the forms of their occupants created the expected shapes, and a small mirrored dresser. A couple of dresses hanging on nails in the corner created spectral outlines, but nothing else looked remotely out of place. Aurora had no intention of waking and questioning excitable Bedelia or gentle Rosie—that could wait until morning.

So she backed into the hall and eyed the attic stairs. Zane would tell her she had no business going up there. The deputy had his assignment under control. Well, if she was being *stupid*, so be it. She had to know for sure that her guests didn't need anything. Standing in the landing in front of the attic door, she hesitated. Should she knock? Three men slept behind that door. Or didn't sleep. She put her ear to the door and listened—to nothing.

Eyes closed, in case someone were indisposed, she carefully turned the knob and opened the door a scant inch. The room remained quiet. She would have thought somebody would be snoring. Or rustling. Something to disturb that profound silence.

Heart beginning to thump harder, she opened her eyes and waited for her vision to adjust. The attic was so dark she could barely see her hand in front of her face, but she knew death when it greeted her. No living, breathing human being could be this quiet, let alone three grown men.

As a scream rose in her throat, she clamped one hand over her mouth, the other instinctively gripping and withdrawing the gun from her pocket. What should she do? If the killer was still in the room, he must already be aware of her entrance. If not, he could be anywhere in the house, or he could have already gone. He could be stalking Zane.

Better make sure. Finger on the trigger of the leveled gun, she entered the room and stood listening again. When nothing moved, she squinted at the chair under the narrow slit of a window, where Mosley usually sat. The empty chair filled her with foreboding.

She edged around to one end of the room, where Jefcoat slept. By now her pupils had dilated so that she could discern his huge bulk on the cot. He lay splayed on his back, arms and legs flung wide. She could see the whites of his eyes and a dark river running from the slit under his beard onto the bedding.

Her body fell into incontrollable shudders as she backed away. Inevitably she would find the same thing at Moore's side of the room, but she made herself look anyway, compelled to know the worst. The Negro lay on his side, still as in sleep, but his throat had also been cut, the blood pooled below his chin.

In the numbness of shock, Aurora's grip on the gun relaxed, and it clattered to the floor. She stared at it, unable to make herself do anything about it. She could only think that Zane had tried to warn her, that he was right of course, and there was some evil entity stalking everyone involved in this case.

Someone had gotten in the house, climbed all the way up to the attic without disturbing Zane, and had lured Mosley away—or maybe Mosley was part of the enemy?—to kill the two witnesses. Now what? She had to find Zane and warn him.

Despite all her assertions of confidence to Zane, she was just a citified girl with a meager amount of training in self-defense. Yes, she had common sense, but nothing prepared one for emergencies like this. She had no idea about the protocol of evading a killer experienced in the art of stalking, hunting, and war. If Zane was correct, and the killer was Sam Jones, then he was also capable of handling explosives, as well as evading detection in a variety of settings. What possible chance did she have against such a lethal antagonist?

But standing here crying was not an option either. Knees quaking, she bent to pick up the gun, then rose, juggling it like some entertainer at a fair. At last she got control of it by wrapping both hands around the small handle and taking a few deep breaths. She turned and made it to the door without vomiting. So far so good.

Out on the landing, she listened for Zane's return but heard nothing. Everyone else in the house must be asleep still.

Or dead.

The thought brought more bile to her throat, so she swallowed and made herself start down the stairs. On the second floor, she considered looking in on Grandmama, Thomas-Anne, and Joelle, but finally decided there wasn't time. Selah would have been useful—she was good with a rifle—but Joelle's skills being more esoteric, she was better left to sleep. One more deep breath and a frantic prayer for protection, and Aurora edged toward the staircase.

She tried to imagine where the killer might have gone. He couldn't have escaped from the attic window, which was both too narrow and too high off the ground to provide egress. That meant he had to have exited the same way he got in—via this same staircase. He could be hiding beneath her. He could be behind the bar by now, or even back in the cellar. For that matter, he could have gone *through* the cellar and gotten outside through the exit at the back, behind the building.

He could literally be anywhere, waiting to pounce on her and cut her throat, as he'd done to those two poor men.

One thing was for sure. She needed help. She needed Zane, but she didn't know exactly where he was. Somewhere outside. But if she left the house, against his express orders, he might assume she was the intruder and respond accordingly. Should she call out to him? If she did that, she would alert the intruder to her presence.

Round and round her frantic thoughts went until they came back to the truth that she was at the mercy of the Lord. If she survived the night, it would be because he willed it so. Except for the little gun in her hand, she was helpless. Gathering her nonexistent courage, she took one step at a time down to the ground floor and stood on the new rug at the foot of the stairs. Why had it mattered what color it was, how big it was, the thickness of its fringe? Life was precious, and if she survived to kiss her sisters again, she'd never worry about new dresses or hair ribbons or other frivolous things again.

What would a silent murderer, who possessed the gall and wicked callousness to send sixteen hundred people into a burning watery grave, do after slitting the throats of two more victims? Would he hide and watch the reaction of the survivors, daring law enforcement to apprehend him? Or would he escape, running as far and fast as he could? She didn't know Jones, except for what Zane had said about him. From what she deduced, the man seemed the sort who would enjoy the chaos and sorrow he'd left behind. Judging by the calling cards he'd left behind in previous atrocities—the spur left at the courtroom, for example—he might even *want* to be recognized for his cleverness.

The thought brought anger boiling to the surface, an oddly steadying emotion. She extended her arms, the gun firm in both hands. "I know you're here," she said with quiet grit. "But you're a coward, squatting in some hiding place, letting a girl clean up your dirty work. I know who you are, Sam Jones, and I dare you to show your face, you miserable—"

"Shut up!"

Aurora wheeled, aiming the gun at the bar. The harsh, somewhat high-pitched male voice had come from behind it. She was exposed, but at least she hadn't lit the lantern and felt some protection from the darkness. "You might as well come out. Deputy Marshal Sager will be back any minute. It's him you want, isn't it?"

"Oh, I'll get him eventually." The voice was still angry, but she heard a measure of returning control. The barrel of a large-caliber pistol appeared at the top of the bar, followed by unkempt graying hair. As the man continued to rise, she saw that he was of medium height, with a barrel chest. She couldn't tell much about his features in the dark, but he casually laid his gun on the bar and reached to light the lantern. "I been following Sager for a while now, waiting for the right time. I saw y'all in the church that night, you slut. You gonna shoot me with my own gun?" he sneered.

"Yes." She pulled the trigger. The revolver went off, deafening her, jerking her arm to the side.

Just then the wick flared in the lantern, and she saw Jones's surprised expression. Her shot had gone wide, the bullet smashing into the mirror behind the bar, shattering it with a second ear-splitting sound of breaking glass.

But the noise couldn't touch the shock that jolted her as she realized what he'd meant by his last question. She had seen him before. Sam Jones had been a patient in her grandparents' house after the *Sultana* explosion, and he had left the pepperbox pistol behind. She had actually tended his wounds—injuries he'd sustained in the process of killing hundreds of people.

Several things happened in the next minute, so many that later Aurora could hardly separate them into individual incidents. She steadied the gun and aimed it at Jones's chest.

He dove to the side and onto the floor, rolling twice before scrambling to his feet and running for the kitchen and the back door.

She fired again. The bullet must have hit some part of his body, for he yelped and kept going.

Crashes came from upstairs, doors slamming open against walls, feet on wooden floors and stairs.

The front door burst open, and Zane ran in with his gun drawn. Seeing Aurora standing at the foot of the stairs with her pistol still aimed at the kitchen doorway, he jerked to a stop. "Are you all right?" he shouted.

"Yes." At least she was still alive.

"Jones?"

"Out the back door."

Zane took off running.

She burst into tears and sat down on the bottom step. Burying her head in her lap, she wrapped her arms about her head, sobbing. She had done everything wrong.

Zane stared at the body of his fellow deputy, lying at the back of the cellar in a puddle of his own blood.

Jones had gotten away again, and this time it was his own fault. He'd let himself get distracted by Aurora. Less than ten minutes—that was all the time Jones needed to kill Jefcoat, Moore, and Mosley.

Although, by the looks of it, Mosley had been dead long before he and Aurora got down here.

His gaze went to the top of the stairs, where she and Joelle sat, arms around each other. Aurora said she had found the dead prisoners, with Mosley missing, then had come downstairs to confront Jones with that ridiculous little derringer, waking the house in the process. She claimed she'd clipped him before he got away. While he himself went after Jones, she and Joelle had taken the lantern down into the cellar, where they searched for and found Mosley.

He couldn't imagine why she wasn't lying curled in a ball on her bed, other than the fact that she was a girl with an iron-clad constitution—a bit like her grandmother, who had somehow managed to calm everyone down before Zane got back from his fruitless chase. Mrs. Winnie had shooed the saloon girls and ThomasAnne into the kitchen to prepare breakfast for the mob of lawmen and attorneys who would inevitably come down on them.

"You had the lantern when I found you down here the first time." He bent down to close Mosley's staring dead eyes. "Why didn't you find him then?"

"I didn't have time to go all the way to the back before you arrived. Then, I was . . . busy." She glanced up at Joelle, who patted her shoulder and scowled at Zane as if he were responsible for her sister's trauma.

Which, in many ways, he was.

If he'd gone on into the cellar before going outside to block the back entrance, he'd have stopped Aurora on the stairs and sent her back to bed. Any number of alternate scenarios would have played out. But what was done, was done. He'd have to play the hand he was dealt.

Dizzy with weariness and disappointment, he approached the two women and looked up at them from the bottom of the stairs. "Aurora, I'd give anything to change what happened tonight."

She stared at him, her eyes big in her white face. "Me too."

"I'll be busy today, cleaning all this up, giving statements. Pierce will want to interview you too, I'm sure. Can you manage that?"

"Of course I can."

"I'll go with her," Joelle said.

"You're up for a deposition anyway," Zane said. "I'll send somebody for you when they're ready for you."

"I wish Schuyler was here." Joelle's expression was suddenly vulnerable.

"I know. He'll be back from Mobile in a couple of days." He looked at Aurora, wishing he could be her knight in shining armor for a change, instead of the man who sent her headlong into murderers and dead bodies. "You should both try to get some sleep. It's going to be a long day."

Aurora looked at him as if he'd told her to jump into a vat of boiling oil, but Joelle nodded. "I'll take her up and put her to bed. Thank you, Zane. I'm sorry about Jefcoat and Moore. And Mr. Mosley, of course. What are we going to do about—"

"I don't know," he interrupted, unutterably depressed. "We'll figure something out. At least we still have the Fryes. And you and Schuyler."

"Yes, you do," Joelle said. She rose and extended a hand to Aurora. "Come on, baby, let's get you into a bathtub and clean clothes. You'll feel better."

Aurora glanced at Zane as if she wanted to argue, but she sighed and grabbed Joelle's hand to haul herself to her feet. "I'm not the baby anymore," she grumbled.

Joelle smiled. "I know. I'm proud of you."

The two of them disappeared into the kitchen, leaving Zane to follow at his own pace. He stood with a hand on the bar, irresolute. His next move was to summon his superiors and the coroner. Then have the three dead men moved to the morgue. The responsibility of his job had never seemed more onerous, but at least he had a clear-cut plan of action.

In matters of love, he was so far in over his head that he didn't know up from down, right from left. Never had he so missed Judge Teague's wisdom.

Twenty-three

MOROSE, AURORA occupied a supremely uncomfortable chair next to Joelle in the temporary law office of the federal prosecutor. Zane sat in a corner, chair tipped back against the wall, whittling something and assiduously avoiding her gaze.

Everything was ruined. A triple homicide had blighted her beautiful new boardinghouse. Saloon? Dance hall? What had once scandalized her entire family now seemed tame. Who was going to want to live in the Dogwood now?

No one, that was who. At least, no one sane.

Marshal Pierce and Levi had helped Zane study the crime scenes, then comb the entire building from attic to cellar, in search of clues as to how Jones managed to get in. Because Aurora had seen his face—twice, as it turned out—there was no doubt as to the killer's identity. Zane said she was now an important witness, and she would be under federal protection until Jones was apprehended and brought to trial. She was waiting to find out what that meant.

Suddenly the door flung open to admit prosecutor Wells, followed by Levi. Zane let his chair fall to four legs. Wells flung himself into the chair behind the desk, while Levi took the only remaining seat in the small, crowded office.

Not sure what was expected of her, Aurora clenched her hands in her lap. Joelle put an arm around her.

"Miss Joelle, Miss Aurora." Wells began to shuffle through the papers on the desk. "Thank you for coming in. I imagine it has been a most trying twenty-four hours for you and your family."

"I won't pretend otherwise," Aurora said, seeking Levi's reassuring gaze. "But Jo and I will help in whatever way we can. I slept some this morning, so I'm feeling better."

"All right, then." Wells nodded and dipped a pen in ink to take notes. "Miss Aurora, let's start with you. Perhaps you'll be so good as to recount the events of the night for me."

"Yes, sir." She had no idea how much Zane had already told the attorney. She glanced over and found him staring at her, expression unreadable as usual. He didn't seem angry, but then he was good at covering his emotions. How could he kiss her until her brains dissolved, then turn into this awful stranger? She blinked away a rush of ridiculous tears. Crying wouldn't help anything. "The three of us—Joelle, Deputy Sager, and I—got back from our trip to Oxford around eight o'clock. After supper, Joelle and I visited with our grandmother for a few minutes, then went on to bed. Around ten, I suppose. But I couldn't sleep. It must have been well after midnight when I heard something funny on the stairs. So I got up to—to check on things."

Wells looked up sharply. "Something funny? What did it sound like exactly?"

She thought about it. "A scrape maybe? Could have been boots, but it was irregular."

"Jones limps," Zane said. "He was thrown from a horse as a boy, and one leg is shorter than the other."

Wells made a note. "Yet he got away from you this morning?"

Zane's cheeks reddened. "He's an experienced tracker. He knows how to disappear."

"Not an accusation, partner," Wells said, not unkindly. "Just an observation. What happened next, Miss Aurora?"

"I got my derringer out of my reticule and put it in my pocket. I went to Rosie and Bedelia's room to see if it might have been one of them I heard. They were both sound asleep."

"Why didn't you come for me?" Zane burst out.

From this side of everything that had happened, it seemed she *should* have awakened him. But at the time, pride had prevented her from thinking logically. She couldn't say, *You shut me out*, in front of all these people. "I didn't want to be the hysterical female, hearing bumps in the night. But I have exceptionally good hearing, always have." She looked at Jo-elle for corroboration. "You can ask anybody in my family."

Zane closed his pocketknife with an angry click and stuffed it into his pocket. He looked at Wells as if to say, *You see what I've had to deal with?*

The prosecutor's mustache twitched over a faint smile. "You didn't hear anything, Sager?"

Zane frowned. "I'm honestly not sure. I don't sleep well under the best of circumstances, and I was especially restless last night. But I didn't get dressed and go downstairs for a look around until after Aurora—I mean Miss Daughtry—did. I didn't even know she was up. I found her in the cellar."

Wells's eyebrows went up. "The cellar?"

"The trapdoor behind the bar had been left open," Aurora said.

"But you didn't see Mosley's body at that time?" Wells's skepticism remained clear.

"No, sir. Deputy Sager . . ." She flicked a doubtful glance at Zane. "He saw the light and engaged me in conversation."

Wells's gaze traveled from Aurora to Zane and back again. The mustache quirked again. "I see."

"Unfortunately, sir," Zane said, "I assumed Miss Daughtry was imagining things—"

"I *told* you the cellar door was open!" She glared at him.

Zane sighed. "—so I sent her back to bed. Even more unfortunately, she ignored me. While I went outside to complete my rounds, she went straight up to the attic."

"You paid for that decision, didn't you?" Wells frowned at Aurora. "Most women would have screamed at the sight of two dead men in their attic."

"I almost did," she said. "But I was afraid the killer was still nearby."

Wells stopped scratching notes to give Aurora a puzzled look. "What made you go back downstairs?"

"I was terrified, and I can't really explain it, but I knew I needed to find Deputy Sager. I couldn't just stay where I was—there wasn't a good place to hide, and there were four other defenseless women on the second floor." She looked at Zane, willing him to understand. "I'm no heroine, and I try not to be stupid. But what else was I supposed to do?"

It was all Zane could do to maintain his seat. He did not want to hear Aurora describe the confrontation with Jones. He wanted to be on a horse going after that piece of human debris that had dared to enter his home and threaten his woman.

Yes, he thought of the Dogwood as his home. It was the first place he had ever lived where he'd had more than a couple of consecutive hours of peaceful sleep. And he most definitely thought of Aurora as *his*, though she would never know it.

But he hadn't been given leave to pursue Jones yet. In fact, he wasn't sure he had enough information.

Bracing himself, he held her gaze. "What exactly did Jones say to you, Aurora?"

"He said he'd g-get you eventually."

Zane knew she was rattled, because she never stammered. "Me? He meant me? Why would he say that?"

"Because I said I knew it was Deputy Sager he wanted, and that you'd be back any minute. Or something to that effect."

Zane let out a whistle between his teeth and sat back. "That was red meat to a dog."

Aurora lifted her chin. "By that point I was so angry, I didn't care. He'd called me a slut! Anyway, it's what made him finally come out from behind the bar. After he said that— after he said he'd get you—he saw I had my pistol aimed at him. So he laughed and asked me if I was going to shoot him with his own gun."

"His own—*What* did you say?"

"I shot him with his own gun." She looked at him blankly. "Didn't I tell you that?"

285

"No! You said—you told me earlier that you've had that gun since you were fourteen!"

"Yes. As soon as I saw his face, I recognized him. Sam Jones was a patient in our house after the steamboat explosion, though I didn't know his name at the time. Remember, I told you I found the gun after everybody was gone and Grandpapa let me keep it? It must have belonged to Jones."

"That's why it looked familiar to me," Zane said, rubbing his forehead, trying to connect all the dots. "He had it at Cahaba, and I probably saw it two or three times a day when he'd take it out and clean it." He realized he'd taken over Wells's interview. "Sorry, sir, I didn't mean—"

"Go ahead. You know what to ask." Wells sat back.

Zane turned his attention back to Aurora. "What do you remember about him? About what he said? How long was he there?"

She wrung her hands. "It's his voice I remember most, sort of high-pitched, you know? He was physically a . . . nondescript man. Medium height, big in the chest, long arms. Graying hair, scraggly beard. He had brown teeth and lots of red veins in his face." She shuddered.

Zane nodded. "That's him. Addiction to alcohol caused some of that look you describe. What type of injury did he have?"

"Some men from the soldiers' hospital brought him in." Aurora closed her eyes as if trying to remember. "I remember thinking that he seemed unusually well-fed, and he wasn't soaking wet or—or burned, like everyone else that had been brought in. But he'd been cut across the hand. In fact, the artery across his palm was severed. Grandpapa was worried that he was going to lose the whole hand. He was in a fever and delirious for a day or two, which was when he . . ." She opened her eyes and stared at Zane. "I heard some things that didn't make sense at the time. But now they do."

"Did you? Like what?"

"Maney. The general. Hatch. Safe. He kept saying those things, over and over. When he came back to his senses, I asked him if he had family that he wanted me to contact . . ." She swallowed. "He said Maney was a friend who died in battle, but he claimed he didn't know anybody by the name of Hatch—that I must have misunderstood him."

Electricity pulsed through Zane as he met the wide-eyed gaze of the prosecutor. "Hatch is a name mentioned in the papers Aurora obtained from Mrs. Scully. You have them, sir?"

Wells grabbed a pile of documents at the corner of the desk and began to riffle through them. "Here it is," he muttered, extracting one and running his gaze over the paper. "Looks like Scully, as a courier through the telegraph, secured information about some sort of collusion between Maney and Reuben Hatch."

Something niggled at the back of Zane's brain. "Wonder if he's the same Union quartermaster in charge at Vicksburg at the end of the war, who loaded two thousand prisoners—me included—onto the *Sultana* and sent it upriver? Seems odd that he would be connected to a Confederate officer like Maney."

"Has to be," Wells said. "His brother Ozias was Illinois Secretary of State, a friend and financial supporter of Lincoln. Reuben Hatch was comparatively a bit of a ne'er-do-well. He started out as quartermaster at Cairo, Illinois, and got caught embezzling and falsifying records. At Ozias's request, Lincoln intervened before Reuben could be tried, and the judge advocate had him reinstated and transferred to New Orleans. As to the connection with Maney, Scully makes a note here that the three of them—Maney and the Hatch brothers—were connected through a Masonic order before the war."

"That makes sense," Riggins said, entering the conversation again. "We've been looking into Maney's background since the onset of this investigation. We suspect this mainly has to do with Maney's political ambitions. He was a Tennessee congressman, and there's evidence that Ozias Hatch's influence got him there."

Without thinking, Zane grasped Aurora's hand. "That's what was missing from the information Frye and his wife gave us when we interviewed them—the identity of Maney's Union informant!"

Wells rattled the document in his hand. "Scully claims that in the spring of '64, Hatch—Reuben, that is—leaked information about Sherman's plan to send troops into Mississippi to break up the M&O. And that created Maney's hold over the Hatch brothers."

Zane shook his head. "Why would Hatch do such a thing?"

"Money. Debt. Remnants of loyalty to the Masonic lodge." Riggins shrugged. "You and I can hardly comprehend such self-interest, but believe me, cowardice and greed trump patriotism more often than you'd think."

Zane frowned. "All right. So Maney got his seat in Congress and held his tongue about Hatch's treason. But why do you think they arranged to cram all those Cahaba prisoners onto the *Sultana* and then sink it? I *know* that was Jones I saw getting off the boat in Memphis. Also, he continued trying to kill Union Cahaba prisoners who survived. Aurora saw him there. And he killed Judge Teague later."

Wells stroked his mustache. "Follow the money. Let's say Maney did extort reward for his silence from one or both of the Hatch brothers, and got support for his congressional run in return. I guarantee it didn't end there. If Maney is twisted enough to betray the Hatch brothers for his own purposes, I'm willing to bet he's hiding other crimes."

"This Klan violence, for one thing. And we've been trying for months to prove his connection to the railroad scam involving the Crédit Mobilier," Riggins put in. "We're hoping Schuyler will bring back whatever evidence his father was holding against Maney and his co-conspirators."

"What if it's not that simple?" Zane felt as if there was some truth just out of reach that he should remember. His head was pounding in agonizing throbs. "Maybe it's not just Maney getting greedy and Ozias Hatch protecting his brother. Yes, there was a lot of money involved in federal payoffs to get all those Union soldiers back home. But Jones might have had his own agenda for sinking the *Sultana*. It's not likely he was after the judge at the time, because Teague wasn't even supposed to be on the boat. I got off at Memphis and gave him my spot. But I keep thinking all of us at Cahaba knew something that Jones had to get rid of." He lunged to his feet. "That spur, for example." He looked at Aurora. "Or the gun. Aurora, where is the gun?"

"It's right here." She showed him the little handbag she carried when she left the house.

"Hand it to me—carefully. Is it loaded?"

"Of course it's loaded. What good would an empty pistol do me?" She opened the bag and took out the derringer. "What are you thinking, Zane?"

"I'm thinking he's been looking for this thing since the

disaster in Memphis." Zane took the little pistol and quickly unloaded it so that he could safely examine it. "If he thought the judge or I had it, that could be why he's been on a five-year rampage." Once all six chambers were empty, he examined the wooden grip. The screw securing the steel back plate fit snugly, but the engraving across it didn't match, which told him it was a replacement. "One more thing," he said to Aurora with a wry smile. "Do you have a coin?"

Reaching into the bag again, she fished around and produced a penny. "Here. Don't spend it all in one place." She handed it to Zane with a saucy smile.

"Thanks." Using the coin to unscrew the pin, he proceeded to dismantle the gun's grip. A typical rounded pistol grip would be in two pieces, fitting flat together on the inside, but when he had the first wooden side piece off, he could see that the insides had been carved out to form an interior hollow space. Cunning and diabolical—the perfect hiding place for something small, like a secret message or a bank note. He wished he and Jacqueline had thought of this when they were kids, hiding things from their drunken father. Hands shaking, he withdrew a tiny roll of paper from the chamber and showed it to Riggins and Wells. "This is what he's been looking for."

Aurora stared at the scrap of paper she had apparently been carrying around with her for the last five years. That little gun had traveled in her luggage from Memphis to Daughtry House several times, and then to the Dogwood when she moved in there with ThomasAnne. She wasn't a violent, aggressive person by nature, but her grandfather had impressed upon her the need to practice with the gun so that she could defend herself if necessary. And she did feel safer when it was on her person.

Now she realized that piece of hardware had entwined her life with that of Sam Jones, as well as Zane's. She would never be free of Jones until she discovered why that paper had been hidden there.

She watched Zane lay the gun pieces on Wells's desk, then unroll the paper. His hands were steady, capable. Trustworthy.

Afraid? Of Jones? Of course she was afraid. But there was no doubt in her mind that Zane would guard her with his own life. She stared at his face as he turned the paper over. "What is it?" she blurted. Everyone was so quiet.

Zane looked up, frowning. "Numbers. Looks like a safe combination." He handed the paper to Wells.

Wells nodded. "I agree. Until we apprehend Jones, though, there's no way to understand its significance."

Aurora sat up. "Wait. Remember what I told you Jones was muttering while he was in delirium at Grandpapa's house? He said 'Hatch' and 'safe.' Maybe he didn't mean that Hatch was safe, but that there was a physical safe involved with his interaction with the Hatch brothers. Or Maney, or—"

"She's right," Levi said. "If all of that belongs together, maybe the safe is somehow related to the steamboat conspiracy."

Aurora nodded. "My grandfather was one of a handful of people in Memphis who investigated the explosion in its aftermath. I heard him say that there was a safe on the boat, containing the payment for all those thousands of fares, but it was never recovered from the wreckage. People began to say that it must have never been there to begin with. Or that someone stole it."

"That's a good theory," Wells conceded, "but no way to prove it at the moment. Let me hold onto this." He slid the tiny paper into a file on his desk. "Meanwhile, we have to locate Jones before he hurts anyone else." He looked straight at Aurora. "I don't have to tell you, Miss Aurora, you are in grave danger."

"I'll guard her around the clock, sir." Zane's voice was grim.

Aurora looked at him. He did not look happy with his self-assigned task. "You've got more important things to do," she said with assumed carelessness. "I'm sure Levi and Schuyler will—"

"I said"—he picked up the pieces of her revolver and began reassembling it—"I will guard you. Jones will find us, and I will either arrest or kill him, whichever seems right at the time."

She absorbed that. Yes, he was trustworthy. But he was also as cold and deadly as the gun in his hands. Zane would guard her not because of his regard for her but because of his hatred for Sam Jones. It was a sobering fact, and she couldn't change it.

She felt Joelle's arm around her again. Looking up at her quiet, beautiful sister, Aurora wanted to fold into that strength and love. Some part of her even wished she could become Pete again, the entertaining little shadow who made everyone laugh and roll their eyes. But the realization hit her that many lives besides her own depended on her taking up the challenge ahead. Jones would kill and kill again until he got what he wanted or he was stopped.

She must help stop him.

Twenty-four

ZANE STOOD AT THE WINDOW of the boardinghouse parlor, watching Wells and Marshal Pierce cross the street to the train station to meet US Attorney General Amos Akerman and defense attorney Alonzo Maney, scheduled to arrive on the last train of the day from Oxford. He understood why, under the circumstances, Wells could hardly have allowed Zane to come along, but it was frustrating to find himself relegated to the role of observer. He deeply desired to confront Maney, the central figure in all this chaos. Instead, he had to content himself with the thought that he would have his day in court.

Assuming he could keep himself and Aurora alive.

He looked over his shoulder at her. She sat in her favorite chair, listlessly picking at a mangled piece of handwork in some sort of hoop in her lap. All her sunny personality seemed to have dimmed to moonglow within the space of twenty-four hours, and he suspected—no, he *knew*—it was entirely his fault. He should have been guarding her door when she went downstairs the first time. He should have awakened someone to make sure she didn't come back down the second time.

He should never have kissed her at all, let alone twice. In the cellar. In her nightgown. He was embarrassed and chagrined and angry with himself. This time he would keep his distance, be the professional lawman he'd been trained to be.

"I wish you would sit down," she said without looking up. "I know I'm not a paid deputy of the law, but that seems a stupid place to stand when one has a killer's target on his back."

She was right. He stepped to the side, putting his back against the wall. "I'm sor—"

"If you say that to me one more time, I'm going to come poke your other eye out with this needle." She jumped to her feet, tossing the hoop and fabric into her chair. Staring at him, she clapped her hand over her mouth. "Oh, dear Gussie. What is wrong with me?"

He laughed. There was his Pete. "You're tired and scared. And aggravated with me for good reason. I know you don't want me around—"

"Yes. Yes, I do." She clenched her hands into small fists. "Can't you understand, you're the one person who knows how I feel? I just don't want you *forced* to stay around. Like I'm some—some horrible obligation!"

He reminded himself that he needed her to feel this way so that she wouldn't walk over here and destroy all his good intentions. "Pete, we can't change the circumstances. Even if we could be, you know, regular friends, I'm never going to be anything other than a seriously damaged fellow with responsibilities. You're a lady who needs feelings, and I can't give you that." He paused. "I won't."

A heavy silence fell. He watched Aurora breathe, saw the moment when blank acceptance drew a shade over her expression. "All right," she said colorlessly. "I have to go upstairs for a few minutes."

He followed her.

She wheeled. "Where do you think you're going?"

"I'm going with you."

"Are you out of your mind? You can't—"

"I'll wait outside the door."

"Zane, this is humiliating!"

"I'm sorry"—he put up his hands—"keep your needle in its pincushion! I know it's awkward, but it's got to be this way until Jones—"

"And don't say his name again! I can't bear it!"

He racked his hands on his hips. "Now you're being childish."

"No, I'm not! I'm being normal! I don't want the man I love waiting outside the door while I use the—" Her golden eyes widened, and she collapsed at the bottom of the stairs to bury her head in her arms. "Oh! Oh! Dear God in heaven, just take me home in a chariot of fire right now."

Electrified, Zane stared at her, listening to her soft sniffles, watching her shoulders quiver. He knew he hadn't misunderstood her. But she couldn't have meant that. She was simply overwrought with fear and frustration.

"What in the name of everything holy is going on down here?" Mrs. Winnie stood at the top of the stairs, both hands resting on her cane. She thumped it on the next step for emphasis. "Can't a person take care of correspondence in her room in peace, without all this shouting and sobbing and histrionics?"

Zane looked around to find Rosie and Bedelia standing behind the bar, Joelle at the kitchen doorway. He was surrounded by angry women. "I was just . . ." He shifted his shoulders. "Will somebody take her upstairs just long enough to . . . I'm going to wait right here." He met Joelle's narrowed eyes.

"What have you done?" she hissed, marching past him.

"I don't know. Please—"

"All right, that's enough." Joelle put a hand on Aurora's shoulder. "Come on, we'll talk about it."

"I don't want to talk."

"Then we'll sit and meditate. That'll suit me better anyway."

At last he was alone with the two working girls. Rosie regarded him in bewildered silence, while Bedelia busied herself wiping down the bar, her expression a masterpiece of disdain.

"What?" he said, daring her to criticize.

Bedelia rolled her eyes. "For a smart man, you sure act like a simpleton. I coulda told ya that train wreck was comin', so."

"For your information, I knew it was coming too. It's better this way."

"Oh really? Feeling good about the outcome, are we?"

Tight-lipped, he just stared at her. Something occurred to him. Bedelia was mighty good at listening in where she wasn't supposed to be. "How long did you say you worked here at the saloon?"

"Boardinghouse," she corrected automatically.

He waved a hand. "I mean when it *was* a saloon."

"I moved in about four years ago. Before that I lived in the rail camp with me man."

"I'd be willing to bet you know more about the inner workings of the local Klan than anybody in town. They ever meet here?"

Bedelia shoved a lock of curly blonde hair out of her eyes with her arm. "Maybe."

"Would you be willing to testify? Name names?"

Alarm flashed in the green eyes. "Those men carry some weight around. They'd be like to squash me and Rosie"—she glanced at her friend—"like a coupla ladybugs."

"The marshals could protect you."

"Like you did Jefcoat and Moore?" she sneered. "No thanks."

"Fair enough." Zane sighed. "Then we'll get you out of town, send you out west with a nest egg to start over."

That might have been a spark of interest that crossed Bedelia's blowsy face. "I dunno. What you think, Rosie?"

Rosie looked troubled. "I like eggs. I like to cook."

Zane grinned. "I'm fond of eggs myself. Bedelia, did you ever hear the name Maney or Forrest out of Whitmore or Brown or any of that gang?"

"Not sure. They was more like to call each other boy-club names like Grand Titan or Grand Cyclops and such nonsense." She scrunched her face. "The moniker Maney might ha' come up."

Zane nodded. "Good. I'll let the attorney know he can call you in, if that's all right with you."

Bedelia shrugged. "Sure."

It was a long shot, but . . . "What about Jones? Sam Jones? You ever hear that name?"

This time pure terror suffused the woman's face. "No! Absolutely not!"

"But—are you sure—"

Bedelia twisted the rag in her hand. "I never seen him, nor heard anybody here mention him."

He approached her carefully, slowly, as though she were a feral cat. "Listen. Deedee, this is important. Jones is the man who broke in here last night. You know that. Aurora shot him—clipped him, at least—but he's running loose and could come back here at any time. Tonight even." He was close enough to touch her, but he simply held her fearful gaze. "If you know where he might have gone, maybe another booze joint or flophouse—someplace he'd go to recover from a wound—I need you to tell me so we'll have a chance to grab him before he hurts anybody else."

Bedelia wrung the rag as if it were the throat of some antagonist. Moments passed before she flung it onto the bar with a groaning curse. "He said he'd hurt Rosie."

"Who? Jones?"

Bedelia nodded, teeth gritted. "I know where he is. But you got to get Rosie out of town tonight, before you do anything." She glared at Zane. "Promise me."

Aurora lay supine, arms and legs flung wide, upon her bed. There were no more tears left in her body. She was wrung dry as a chamois left out in the sun for a week. Rolling over, she saw Joelle sitting sideways in a chair under the window, catching the last rays of sunlight in order to read some tome she'd brought with her from Daughtry House.

The man I love . . .

Of all the things she had ever said—and wished she had the magic ability to reel back into her mouth—that one won first prize. There were some thoughts a girl simply didn't say aloud.

She cleared her aching throat. "Joelle. I'm going to live."

Joelle swung her feet to the floor. "Of course you will," she said gently. "They don't mean to be so stupid. They just can't help it." She smiled. "You'll learn to overlook the stupidity and find the things he's good at."

Aurora sat up. "That implies there might be some universe in which Zane Sager and I are on speaking terms again. I'll get to heaven and ask God for a mansion on the other side of eternity from him."

Joelle laughed. "You know he loves you."

"Of course God loves me."

"Well, yes, but so does Zane."

"He's had every opportunity to say so. But he hasn't." The last word cracked off on a miserable wobble. "I find that I don't care."

"Pete, don't be silly. Not every man is a fountain of urbanity like Schuyler or Levi. Hasn't he *shown* you that he loves you?"

"I don't know. Maybe. But then again, maybe it's my imagination." She folded her arms. "I want the words."

Joelle sighed and shut her book. "No wonder he's losing his mind. You're quite a pill sometimes. Come on, I promised I'd bring you back so he could keep an eye on you after you'd calmed down."

"I'm far from calm."

Aurora continued to resist until Joelle finally resorted to opening the door and shouting, "Zane! Come and get her!"

Humiliated all over again, Aurora brushed her hair, glared at her sister, and marched downstairs.

Zane met her halfway. He looked at her with that tensile muscle working in his jaw, the one that said he was a breath away from yanking her close. A thrill of something delicious bounced from her stomach to her throat, terrifying in its power.

"Are you all right?" he growled.

"Just dandy," she said, lifting her nose and sashaying past him down the stairs.

He followed. "You have a surprise guest."

She kept going. "I find I'm quite tired of surprises."

"I think you're going to like—" Zane stopped on a grunt as Aurora threw her arms wide, whacking him in the chest.

"Grandpapa!" She picked up her skirts and pelted down the last three steps. Her handsome, elegant grandfather stood in the entryway, issuing instructions to a porter from the train station as to the disposition of his luggage. When she reached him, she flung herself at him. "Oh, Grandpapa! I've missed you so much!" He gave her one of his lovely, strong hugs, and she held in fresh tears. Knowing he wouldn't appreciate getting his shirt front wet, however, she stood on tiptoe to kiss his cheek, then stepped back to grin at him. "Why didn't you tell us you were coming?"

He glanced over her head. "Your grandmother knew."

Aurora looked around to find Grandmama observing the reunion with a small smile.

"To be precise, I insisted that he come." The smile gained a touch of vinegar as Grandmama approached. "It seemed to me a rather firmer hand on the yoke might be needed under the circumstances."

Unable to conjure a firmer hand than her grandmother's, Aurora smiled at Grandpapa and tugged him to the settee. "Come tell me about your trip. How are Vonetta and Alistair?" She had missed the McGowan housekeeper and butler as much as anyone she'd left in Memphis.

"They are well and send their love." Grandpapa sat down beside Aurora with a tired *oof*. "The trip was noisy and uncomfortable, and I'm glad to finally be here. Now explain to me this nonsense I hear about saloon girls and whiskey cellars and home invasions." He scowled at her.

Aurora glanced at Zane, who stood like some stoic statue under the chandelier in front of the stairs. "Did you meet Deputy Marshal Sager?"

"I did. Actually met him a long time ago, after that steamboat disaster in '65. Seems to be a sensible, hardworking young fellow, and Duke Teague, God rest his soul, held quite a high opinion of him. Your grandmother thinks you're going to be very happy together."

All the air exploded from Aurora's lungs, and she needed several seconds before she regained the power of speech. "She thinks—happy about what?"

"Marriage, of course. Young women cannot go cavorting about in the middle of the night in their undress and expect to maintain a proper reputation. You were not reared with such low morals, Aurora. Surely you know what is expected of you." He glanced at Zane. "Young Sager seems aware of his duty."

"But Grandpapa!" Aurora tried to untangle one coherent thought from the mass of boiling protests that surged through her brain. "I was in my nightgown because there was a killer in the house! Surely I can get a pass—"

"It's possible that you might have. But your sweetheart admits that there passed some physical intimacy between you." Grandpapa's expression softened. "Aurora, you may not believe it, but your grandmama and I were young once, and I'm not so prudish as to believe that modern young people observe the stricter tenets of morality we once adhered to."

"Sweetheart?" Aurora said on an embarrassing squeak. "Grandpapa, it's not like that—"

"But under the circumstances," he continued, "I believe the deputy's offer of protection mandates the blessing of God and church upon your remaining in the same house, let alone the same room." He patted her knee firmly. "Your only alternative would be to return to Memphis with me and Winnie, where we could place you under our own protective custody."

Aurora grappled for dignity. "Grandpapa, I'm not a child. I'm almost twenty, a grown woman."

"You are a young and beautiful woman of good birth and fine reputation. I won't allow you to throw it away." His gnarled, clever surgeon's hands grasped hers. "Aurora, if you love me, you'll respect my wishes."

She had one more ace in her hand. "But Zane doesn't want to—"

"Zane does want to." Zane's quiet, deep voice reached the muddle in her head. She saw now that he had moved close enough to kneel at her feet. "We have to, don't you see? Your grandfather is right. I need to stay with you at all times or I'll—I'll go out of my mind with worry. If you think anyone will be willing to stay in your boardinghouse after you've forfeited your reputation, you don't know Southern bigots and snobs very well."

"I hardly think I should be required to marry every gentleman who offers to serve as my bodyguard, Grandpapa! This is absurd." She couldn't make herself look at Zane. What he must be thinking—after telling her in no uncertain terms that he had no feelings for her.

"Dr. McGowan, may I have just a few minutes alone with your granddaughter?" Zane's voice was grave and respectful.

Ooh, he could put on the charm when he wanted to.

And Grandpapa fell for it. "I suppose I could allow it."

"Not the cellar, though," Joelle called. She sat at the top of the stairs, observing the action as if it were a stage play.

Giving her sister an exasperated look, Aurora rose. "Come in the kitchen, then, Zane, and let's settle this farce. I can't think of a less romantic location for . . . for . . . anything."

The kitchen, long deserted since supper, had been scrubbed clean by Rosie and Bedelia. Hopping onto the butcherblock table, Aurora folded her arms across her middle and swung her feet.

Zane approached, looking wary, and stood silent for a long moment.

"This was your idea," she prompted him. "So talk."

"I'm trying to pick words that won't get me stabbed in the eye with a needle."

"Would you please forget I said that?" Reluctantly she laughed. "Forget *everything* I said."

"Some of what you said was pretty wonderful."

She peered up at him.

"The part where you said you love me."

Putting her fingertips to her temples, she squeezed her eyes shut. "Oh . . . my . . . goodness. Zane, you have turned me into a raving lunatic."

"Aurora, I've never known anyone like you. You're so

bright, you make my head hurt, but I can't look away. You scare the life out of me, but you make me braver than St. George."

"Who's St. George?"

"The fellow with the dragon."

"Oh. Never mind, I'll ask Joelle later." She lowered her hands, and he took them. There was a brief tug-of-war, which he won. Admittedly, she didn't try very hard. "All right, then, St. George. Carry on."

He stroked her fingers. "That's all I've got. I know I botched this thing, but when your grandparents brought up my obligation to your reputation, I knew this might be my one and only excuse to inflict myself on you. You simply don't know what you'd be taking on, and I didn't want to risk leaving you alone with a b-baby or—" He stumbled into silence. "Do you know what I mean?"

She stared at him, fascinated, drawn and confused. "I have no idea what you mean. But I don't care. Joelle asked me if you'd shown me that you love me, and I think you just did." She chewed her upper lip and watched his gaze fall to her mouth. So she sucked in her bottom lip and then let it go. He leaned a little closer. "Zane, do you love me?"

"I wish I could spend the rest of my life with you, not just the next few days."

That was a douse of cold water. "Wait. Where do you think you're going? After all this is over, I mean?"

He shook his head. "Let's worry about that when the time comes."

There was something very off about this whole backward-inside-out proposal. But then, she'd seen her sisters' courtships and engagements begin in unorthodox ways, then proceed satisfactorily. She had to have faith that God was going to work this thing out between her and Zane as well.

"All right," she said. "As long as we are laying cards on the table, you should be aware that you'll be getting a pretty shady deal too. I have it on good authority I'm managing and bossy. And a little spoiled."

He nodded. "Noted."

"And I wake up cranky."

"I'll keep my distance until noon."

She laughed. He still hadn't said he loved her, and maybe he never would. But he did have a nice sense of humor. And that eye patch was downright alluring. "I think I deserve a kiss after the trauma you've put me through in the last day or two."

"I'd be happy to oblige, but your grandmother is in the next room, and she scares me more than any dragon. And more than you."

"Good point." As he let go of her hands, she slid off the table and landed so close to him that it was a simple matter to slide her arms around his waist and hold on. "You don't have to say words. I've got enough for both of us."

Twenty-five

AURORA MIGHT CLAIM TO BE TIRED of surprise arrivals, but her sister clearly was not. As Schuyler Beaumont walked in the Dogwood's front door, Joelle's squeal of joy echoed throughout the entire ground floor. The M&O train from Mobile had just arrived.

Leaning on the bar, watching Aurora supervise her employees in serving a late supper of fried chicken with field peas and boiled okra, Zane surveyed the gathered company. It occurred to him that he had gone from a dearth of relatives—exactly one sister and one brother-in-law, on whom he hadn't laid eyes in years—to a plethora of in-laws, out-laws, and shirttail kin. There were people everywhere.

The elderly Dr. McGowan and his consort reigned from the head and foot, respectively, of the long custom-made oak table in the dining room. Next to the doctor sat the younger Tupelo physician, Ben Kidd—whose massive intellect and eclectic style of dress no one seemed to find either unusual or humorous—and wispy cousin ThomasAnne, who clearly adored him with quiet ferocity. On ThomasAnne's other side

sat family friend James Spencer, the justice of the peace from
Oxford, and a youngster named Wyatt, apparently a foster
son of someone—whether Spencer, Kidd, or Riggins, Zane
couldn't be sure. Everyone seemed to regard the teen as a
younger brother or nephew.

Across the table from Kidd and ThomasAnne, Levi and
Selah Riggins carried on a teasing conversation about the
"reformed" painting over the piano. Homesick for his wife,
Riggins had gone to Daughtry House to retrieve her as soon
as he'd gotten wind of Aurora's betrothal. The two of them
held hands under the table, a public display of affection that
seemed to shock no one except Zane. Meanwhile Joelle and
Beaumont billed and cooed in the parlor, apparently too
love-starved to be interested in real food.

Zane had to ask himself why he resisted joining them at the
table. The warmth of his acceptance as their beloved Aurora's
betrothed both astonished and gratified him, especially as he
remembered his worry about seeming to be a fortune-hunter.
What a difference just two weeks could make.

Now he understood that wealth was relative in all sorts
of ways. Beaumont was the most financially well-off of the
bunch, but no one treated him any differently than the penniless young Wyatt or fragile, dependent Cousin ThomasAnne.
Furthermore, he saw that within the circle of this room,
mutual affection, humor, courage, faith, and generosity held
more value than any amount of money.

Despite the circumstances of his hasty proposal and Aurora's coerced acceptance, her sisters and the rest of the
family professed to assume his good intentions. In fact, to a
person they seemed to see something in him that he barely
discerned himself. *Was* he what she needed for now? Could

he provide for her physical needs? Could he guard her from enemies with his body? Could he protect her, at least during the short time he'd be with her, from the damaged parts inside himself?

He wasn't at all certain of any of those things. But he was going to try.

Apparently that was going to begin tonight, after supper. His gaze went to Aurora. He knew he'd disappointed her with his refusal to say the words she wanted to hear. But once they were said, they couldn't be withdrawn. And he needed her to have a reason to hate him if he had to leave. He needed her to forget whatever perverse attraction he held for her. Some women, he'd noticed, admired dangerous men, and perhaps that was what she saw in him—someone off-limits.

Well, his failure to hold her entirely at arm's length meant he would have to endure the torture of her nearness, knowing the consummation of his love would never happen. It was like standing outside a candy store with his nose pressed to the window and not a nickel in his pocket.

She turned at that moment and gave him her scrunch-nosed, dimpled smile. He did love her. Maybe she'd never know that for sure, but he comforted himself that it was for her protection.

Zane took a seat at the table when Aurora did. She sat beside Selah, which put him at the foot of the table next to Mrs. Winnie. He'd only been half kidding when he claimed she scared him.

He sure didn't feel like eating, so he pushed his food around on his plate and listened to everyone else talk. Across from him, fifteen-year-old Wyatt, apparently something of a prodigy, fielded questions about electromagnetics and astronomy, which he planned to study at Ole Miss next year. Zane understood just enough to wish he could stay around and get to know the boy better. Seemed to be a likable kid.

"He's an orphan, you know," Mrs. Winnie said, delicately dabbing at her mouth with her napkin. "His father was killed in the train wreck where Selah and Levi met. But he's landed on his feet and doesn't feel sorry for himself."

"Admirable." Zane eyed her, wary. "But not all orphans are created equal. Some are forced to grow up so fast they skip over important things."

"Such as?" Her icy blue eyes challenged him.

He grimaced. "Like table manners. I swear I don't know which of these three forks I need to use for my dessert."

"It's tiramisu. You'll need the spoon above your plate. But just so you'll know next time, with the forks you work your way from the outside to the inside. The big one next to your plate will be last."

He nodded. "That makes sense. I wish somebody had explained that a long time ago."

"All you had to do was ask." The old lady paused, glanced at Aurora, engaged in a whispered giggle-fest with her sister. "But you were not speaking of forks. What else did you skip over?"

He didn't want to talk about this with Aurora's grandmother. He should have kept his mouth shut. "Nothing," he muttered.

"I wouldn't have supposed you to be such a coward, Mr. Sager."

He looked at her, jaw clenched. "I beg your pardon?"

"You're afraid you won't be able to hold her. You're afraid everyone else is too educated, too refined, too well-dressed for you to keep up with, and that Aurora will grow ashamed of you." The blue eyes narrowed. "I can see it in your face. The minute the crisis is over, you plan to dive out of the way—assuming everyone, including Aurora, will forget all about you and go on with their lives. Hear me well, young man. You underestimate my granddaughter, and you underestimate yourself. I can't imagine another man who would be able to keep the girl from rolling right over him. She needs more than a protector. She needs a lover and a partner. If you leave her, she will never recover. And neither will you." Laying the napkin on the table, she picked up her tea glass and sipped it, watching Zane across the rim.

Coward? Leave? How had the interfering old bat leapt to that conclusion? He wasn't *planning* to leave, he was simply giving himself permission to accept the reality of—

He grappled for control of his anger. *Coward.*

No one had ever called him that before. Was that how he appeared to Aurora? Even in all his teasing about his fear of her grandmother lay a grain of truth. He was afraid of being *less than.*

"Excuse me," he muttered, pushing back his chair. "I have to—"

Shots rang out, windows shattered, glass went everywhere.

Zane grabbed Aurora and shoved her under the table. "Stay down!" he roared. "Everyone take cover!"

While her immediate surroundings exploded into chaos for the second time in as many days, Aurora lay under the table with Selah and Joelle. She had a pistol in her room. Why had she not brought it to dinner? She had shot a man already—a fact that she might have found astonishing, even absurd, if her life hadn't taken an irreversible turn for the bizarre the day she inherited a saloon. If she were a man, though, she would carry the gun in a holster, like Zane did. She would be ready to defend her loved ones, not cowering under a table like a—like a . . . girl.

And wasn't that a useless thought. God had created her a woman, for his purposes.

Peeking around the side of the table, she felt someone grab her by the skirt.

"Get back!" Joelle shrieked as more gunfire popped and another window smashed.

Counting voices, Aurora returned to cover. Though her ears rang from the gunfire inside the room, she could barely distinguish shouts from outside. There were at least ten men out there, maybe more. She would bet it was the same mob who had threatened the jail on the day Zane arrived with the prisoners.

She leaned over Joelle to address Selah, who crouched with her arms curled around her belly. "What do you think we should do?"

Selah looked at her blankly. "Stay here. Levi told me to."

"I think we should find a way to get out." Aurora looked around to Grandmama for corroboration. Her grandmother was missing. Panic rose, but then it dawned on her Grandmama must have already recognized the danger of sitting in one place. She grabbed Joelle's arm. "Where's Grandmama?"

Joelle looked wildly behind her. "I don't know! I thought she would have—Maybe she went behind the bar?"

"Probably." Aurora looked for ThomasAnne and found

her at the far end of the table, curled into a ball with her arms over her head. "That's where Bedelia and Rosie would be too. They'll be guarding the kitchen door. But I think we can get out through the cellar and go for help."

Joelle looked like she might argue, then gulped and nodded. "Selah, do you want to come?"

Selah looked as if she might vomit. "I'd better stay here with ThomasAnne. We'd only slow you down."

Aurora didn't like the idea of leaving her sister and cousin here, but there was danger in leaving too. In all likelihood, none of them would make it out of this situation alive. "All right. Pray."

Selah nodded.

Taking a deep breath, Aurora briefly clasped Joelle's hand. "Let's go." Hiking up her skirts, she got into a crouching position, while Joelle did the same. When the gunfire paused, she darted out from under the table, keeping her head down, and headed for the bar.

A bullet zinged past her as she dove around the wall of the bar into safety. Joelle followed a second later. They lay facedown for a moment, gasping, shivering, then Aurora lifted her head.

"Why, Miss Daughtry, fancy meeting a lady like you in a place like this," Bedelia said with a husky chuckle.

The two saloon girls crouched under the inside corner of the bar, taking advantage of the greatest protection from the mayhem in the dining room. It occurred to Aurora that Selah and ThomasAnne would be safer here, if they could make it across the open space between here and the table. Too late for that now.

"Grandmama's not here!" Joelle stated the obvious.

"Maybe she had the same idea we did. Jo and I are going out through the cellar," she told Bedelia. "Y'all want to come?"

Bedelia's green eyes widened. "I ain't daft! What if that bunch of thugs is guarding the cellar door? For that matter, what if they come in through the cellar?"

"I doubt anybody knows it's there. We're going to give it a try. The only option is sitting here waiting for some stray bullet to hit." Aurora shrugged with assumed carelessness. "I'd rather die trying to do something."

Bedelia shuddered but clutched Rosie's shoulders. "Not me. I ain't no hero."

Aurora might have argued with her, but Joelle pulled on her sleeve. "Let's go, Pete. The longer we wait, the greater the chance somebody will discover that cellar entrance."

Crouching, the two of them duck-walked toward the cellar trapdoor and wrestled it open. Gunfire opened again in the front of the house as Aurora slipped through the opening, Joelle close on her heels. The noise muted as they went underground, and Aurora felt a corresponding rise in confidence. She stopped to listen. If anybody waited down here, they were awfully quiet.

Looking over her shoulder a couple of times to make sure Joelle was still behind her, she crept across the dark cellar. It gave her pause to think of Deputy Marshal Mosley's dead body having been dragged here by the vile Sam Jones. And when Zane discovered she'd flouted his orders, he was not going to be happy. But going back was not an option.

At last they reached the rear stairs.

"Wait." Joelle grabbed Aurora's hand. "We don't have any kind of weapon. What if there's somebody out there?"

Aurora looked around the shadowy cellar. A faint stream

of light came from the bar and kitchen areas, but she could distinguish few details in her surroundings. "I remember when I was cleaning this place out, before Zane came. I was going to get rid of all the whiskey, but I kept a couple of bottles for cooking. Horatia likes to put it in her bread pudding sauce."

"Bread pudding is going to save our lives," Joelle said with a sigh. "I love it."

"Do you have a better idea?"

"No. Where are the bottles?"

"Next to the kitchen stairs." Aurora retraced her steps and came back with two bottles. She gave one to Joelle. "If someone threatens you, throw this at their head and run."

Battling genuine terror, she climbed the steps. What if the exit was still blocked from Zane's attempt to trap Jones? She couldn't remember if anyone had removed the boards and bricks he'd piled on top of the door. At the top of the steps, she shoved on the door with her free hand. When it moved, she pushed harder and felt it give upward. Cautiously, she peered out. Heavy darkness had fallen—she thought the time must be close to nine o'clock by now—but starlight revealed a sliver of the back alley behind the house. Across the alley lay the slope down to the town square. At least they would emerge well beyond the back door, and thus, theoretically, bypass any attackers guarding the kitchen.

"Looks like we're clear," she told Joelle and pushed the door open. It fell back onto the ground with a frightening thud, and she paused, heart pounding. Nothing else happened, so she climbed out and squatted beside the opening as Joelle followed suit.

"I neglected to ask where we're going," Joelle whispered. "I assume you have a plan."

"We could go for the sheriff or the constable, but I don't trust either of them."

"Don't you think the sound of gunfire would have brought them anyway? This whole thing smells really evil."

"I know." Aurora tried to think who their allies might be. "Mr. McCanless would come," she said doubtfully. "There's the marshal and Mr. Wells, staying down at the Gum Pond. Surely they'll hear the noise and come to investigate."

"We should have invited them to supper."

"Too late now. Jo, we're running out of time. We've got to do *something*."

The two of them crouched, thinking. Aurora feared she'd launched herself and Joelle out of one desperate situation into another one even worse. She didn't even know what to pray for.

Finally Joelle said quietly, "I have an idea. But it's going to be pretty scary."

Twenty-six

GUN RELOADED AND READY TO DISCHARGE, Zane stood with his back against the wall between the front door and the shattered window beside it. His physical control over his own mental violence was in an equal hair-trigger state. He didn't know why Wells and Pierce hadn't come to investigate the source of gunfire just down the street from the hotel, but surely they would have arrived by now if they were coming at all.

He glanced over at the big oak table, which Riggins had flipped onto its side to protect the women. He hadn't heard a peep out of them in quite some time. That seemed odd—he hoped no one had fainted—but he dared not leave his post. The seven men in the room—Riggins, Beaumont, young Wyatt, Spencer, the two physicians, and himself—should have been able to repel the attack. But they were already nearly out of ammunition.

Surely the enemy knew that.

A couple of quick attempts to discern the identity of the attackers revealed torch-lit figures in black robes and hoods spread across the lawn—evil costumes disguising evil intent.

They had been shouting incoherent insults and threats since the first shots broke up the dinner party. Zane had hoped firing back at them would send them running.

It had not. Now his main fear was that one of them would decide to set the house on fire.

It was time to act.

He caught Riggins's eye. "Cover me."

"What are you going to do?" Riggins asked.

"Negotiate." He slid to the other side of the door and stood behind it as he opened it an inch or two. "Whitmore!" he shouted, taking a stab at the identity of the ringleader. "I want to come out and talk."

The response was a bullet whizzing into the opening.

Zane slammed the door. Shaking with rage, he moved to the window. "You realize there are seven women and a boy in here, don't you?"

"A bunch of Negro-loving sluts," Whitmore yelled. "We've put up with them long enough. Nobody wants to hurt them, we just want them gone—and you government flunkies with them."

"Whitmore, there will be federal troops here next week. So far you haven't hit anybody, which is miraculous. It's almost Sunday. Give us a day of peace, then let's gather on Monday at the courthouse to talk. None of us wants bloodshed, but it's my job to apprehend the men who killed my fellow officers—and make sure they're prosecuted according to the law."

A shotgun fired, presumably into the air. "And I want the scum who murdered my sons in cold blood!" That rough, countrified voice was not Whitmore. In fact Zane was sure he'd never heard it before.

The crowd of cloaked men parted to reveal a solitary gray-bearded figure, dressed in an old-fashioned suit and string tie, advancing with a hunting rifle at his shoulder.

Zane opened the door and stepped onto the porch. "I'm Deputy Marshal Sager. Please identify yourself."

The man aimed his gun at the center of Zane's chest. "You're the one I want. I hear it's your fault they got to my boys."

"You must be Mr. Jefcoat," Zane said coolly. "If you shoot me, there are six guns aimed at you from inside, and one of them is bound to take you out for the murder of a federal officer."

The rifle wavered. "Where's my son's body?"

Zane noted the reference to one body this time. Perhaps his half-black son didn't rate a Christian burial. "At the morgue awaiting your arrival. Mr. Jefcoat, I did my best to protect them. I would have done so anyway, but you should know that Andrew and Harold had separately agreed to testify against terrorists like these men around you—men who dress up like children in costume and ride around at night, burning down the houses and churches of innocent people. Threatening and beating men doing nothing more than attempting to exercise their legal right to cast a vote. Destroying the property of the free press—which, if I'm not mistaken, is a right guaranteed by the Constitution to every American citizen."

Rage suffused Jefcoat's face. He seemed a broken man with very little left to lose. "It's *our* votes that don't count! We were the ones invaded by raiders stealing our property. Now my son is dead. I want justice."

Voices in the hooded crowd shouted, "That's right!" and "Tell him, Jefcoat!" and "Murdering Yankees!"

Zane madly picked through possible responses. Why had God put him here at this time? He was no orator. Riggins or Beaumont should come out here to address this rabble. Or even venerable Dr. McGowan. Maybe one of them could calm everybody down.

But *he* was the one with the badge. He'd sworn to protect the people in this house. Maybe he had failed in the past few days, but that didn't mean he should give up now.

He lowered his gun, released the hammer, and put it in its holster. He would not raise his hands in surrender, but left them loose at his sides, where all could see. "Mr. Jefcoat"—he raised his voice to be heard above the growing clamor of the mob—"your son was killed at the behest of a man manipulating this bunch around you. They're all scared the same thing will happen to them if they turn on him."

The noise of the crowd turned off like a spigot.

"What are you talking about?" Whitmore roared. "Nobody's scared of nobody."

"Take off your mask, Whitmore," Zane said wearily. "Everybody knows who you are. You say you're not afraid, but disguise is a mark of fear."

The storekeeper reached up and whipped off his hood. The torchlight revealed his bald head and sweaty, scowling face. "I told you—"

"I'm not done," Zane said. "Think about what you folks are protesting here. You know who's in this room? Your neighbors. Your doctor—the man who delivers your babies and sets broken legs and sews you up when you open your hand on a plow blade. A justice of the peace, who settles disputes and marries young couples. A young inventor who might discover a way to get you on the other side of the

319

country in less than a day or figure out how to cure smallpox. And that's not to mention the women who turned a rundown plantation and a seedy saloon into thriving businesses. You run them out of town, and you'll be the poorer for it." Zane took a breath and kept going. "Put that aside for a minute, and let's go back to Mr. Jefcoat. I'm sorry for your loss, sir. I'd bring those two men back if I could. I'd bring back Judge Teague, Ezekiel Beaumont, Deputy Redding, and Deputy Mosley. But I'm not God, so I can't. Best I can do is stop the violence right here and now.

"I say that, not as a Southerner or a Northerner or even a federal officer. I say it as a man who wants to marry one of those ladies in there and live here among you. I want to be your neighbor. I want to go to church with you and eat in your hotel restaurant and walk down the street without being afraid somebody's going to knife me in the back. But that can't happen if we can't settle our disagreements in the open, in daylight—and, if necessary, in a court of law."

"The law's not on our side!" someone shouted.

A roar of agreement went up.

Zane waited until it abated, then took a step forward. "Think about what you just said! If the law's not on your side, then whose side are you on? Anarchy? Violence? Screaming and mobbing and tearing each other apart make you less than human. If you don't like the laws, vote to change them! That's what Americans just fought a war over—the right for every man to have an equal say in his destiny. In the meantime, give one another room to disagree. Keep arguing—verbally or in print—but keep it civil. Come to the trials, if you wish, listen to the testimonies and decide for yourselves. Don't let a handful of men with personal agendas, like greed or revenge or hunger for power, twist us against one another. Don't let them destroy our humanity."

Had he said enough? Too much? Zane felt as if some powerful current had taken over his body and mind, turning him into a new version of himself. Even with one eye, his vision clarified.

As he looked at Jefcoat, pity filled him. "Mr. Jefcoat, somebody here knows who ordered your sons' murders. Maybe your political views differ from mine, but we both want that monster brought out into the open and prosecuted."

Jefcoat wheeled toward the crowd. "Is that true?" he cried, faced twisted in grief. "One of y'all know? Take off those hoods, you cowards, and let me see your faces! I joined the Klan myself this spring, out of fear. I sent both my boys to fight against what I thought of as tyranny—but if I'd known they'd turn on Andrew and Harold—if this is what they do, how can I—how can we bear it?" He sank to his knees, keening, cradling the rifle.

Zane bent to put a hand on the man's shoulder and, as he did, looked over the robed mob. Behind them had gathered a darker group, dressed in plain homespun and denim, ragged and quiet—but also armed.

The Negro militia had arrived.

Aurora looked down and realized she still carried a full bottle of whiskey. She wondered if she might have to use it after all.

Surrounded by Negro militia, she had stood beside Joelle, bursting with pride and love as Zane finished as eloquent and courageous a speech about constitutional liberty as she'd ever heard.

After escaping from the besieged house, the two of them had hurried down the street to the north end of town, then across the railroad tracks to the gum swamps of Shake Rag. Aurora and Joelle had helped their families rebuild the Negro church there after it burned, had eaten with and worshiped alongside its members—and thus had begun to establish a new and better relationship after the ravages of slavery and war. Perhaps miles remained to go. But steps had been taken in both directions.

Now. Now, it turned out, her family needed them. She and Joelle went first to the pastor, Reverend Boykin, and he called in other men to meet at the church. They listened to her hurried description of the events of the day. And they responded. They went for their hunting rifles and accompanied her and Joelle back to town.

In their company, at this moment, she felt secure, though she couldn't guess how the crowd would respond to Zane's plea or Jefcoat's agonized challenge. She thought the white mob still hadn't realized they were surrounded. At any moment they could turn, unleashing violence.

She looked for her sister. "Joelle, I think we should slip around to the—"

A rough hand went over her mouth. "Oh, no, missy, I think you'll stay right here." She felt something sharp dig into her throat. "Move and I'll slice you in two where you stand."

Her blood went to ice. Rolling her eyes to get a glimpse of her captor, she saw nothing but the edge of the beard and long, unkempt hair pressed against her cheek. But the hoarse, high-pitched voice in her ear had given away her captor's identity. Her arms were fastened to her sides by Jones's sinewy ones, and she knew if she wiggled, he'd do what he said.

He raised his voice to a harsh rasp. "Everybody shut up and give me room, or I'll kill her!"

Where was Joelle? Had someone else grabbed her? Was Jones going to kill her in the middle of a hundred people, right there in front of Zane and her family? What did he want? She couldn't give him the safe code, since she didn't have it anymore.

She still held the bottle, but it dangled from her numbed hand, useless beneath the powerful arms holding her motionless.

The Negroes around her didn't seem to know what to do. They moved back, muttering.

"Maney!" Jones shouted. "Where are you? I have her."

The robes in front of Aurora parted, shuffled, a bizarre dance she would have found amusing if she hadn't been scared spitless. She found herself held prisoner in the center of a macabre ballroom of hatred, confusion, violence. Torchlight flickered above and all around, with the lamps blazing through the open door and broken windows of the boardinghouse in front of her.

Zane stood on the porch, horror in every line of his face and body.

"Maney!" Jones roared again. "Get whatever you want out of him. He won't touch you now."

Nobody else moved.

Then an elderly female voice said quietly, "But I will. With your own gun."

A gun went off over Aurora's head, crashing into her eardrums. She fainted.

It took him less than ten seconds to reach her. He dropped to his knees, ignoring the mess that had been Sam Jones's head and the robed miscreant who had shot him. There was blood dripping down the side of Aurora's neck, remnants of gore sprinkled on the top of her head.

Oh, God, let her be alive.

He lifted her, held her limp body against his own crashing heart. Putting his mouth on the pulse point under her chin, he felt the steady throb. Relief flooded him.

Standing with Aurora in his arms, he turned and headed for the porch at a run. "Doc!" he shouted. "I need you!"

The noise of the crowd on the lawn—black, white, robed, armed or not—now signified less than nothing. Taking the porch steps two at a time, he stumbled past Riggins and Beaumont into the sitting room. He laid Aurora on the sofa and knelt there looking frantically at her grandfather, who had dropped his gun and rushed to meet him.

Pushing Zane aside to crouch beside the sofa, Dr. McGowan looked up at Doc Kidd, who had grabbed his medical bag from a corner. "Stethoscope?" Kidd produced the required instruments as McGowan asked for them and examined Aurora.

Praying, Zane watched, staying as close as they would allow him. Dr. McGowan gently cleaned her face, taking particular care as he examined her ears. Blood streaked her hair and spotted her dress, but Zane couldn't see obvious wounds, except for a red welt across her milky throat, left by Jones's knife.

At last McGowan sat back on his heels, wiping his hands on a clean cloth ThomasAnne had handed him.

Zane suddenly realized the women had come out from under the table to offer aid and whisper prayer. Selah now stood behind the sofa, held in her husband's arms, with Rosie and Bedelia hovering in the dining room doorway. Joelle and Mrs. McGowan were nowhere in sight. Questions clamored for answers, but Aurora came first.

He looked at her grandfather. "Why isn't she waking up?"

"Trauma." The old man looked worried. "Her eardrum burst, so there'll be some hearing loss. Other than that—she seems to be fine." He looked around. "Does anyone know what happened? Where's my wife?"

"Right behind you."

Zane kept his place beside Aurora but turned in time to see Winnie McGowan enter the room. She cast off a dark hooded cloak and tossed it across the back of a chair.

"Grandmama!" Selah eyed her grandmother in suspicious astonishment. "What have you been up to?"

"Shooting villains." The old lady stalked over to lower herself creakily to her knees and lean over Aurora. "Is she all right?"

Aurora's lashes fluttered, then her eyes opened wide. She looked around wildly until she found Zane. Reaching past her grandmother, she flung her arms around his neck.

And nearly strangled him. He didn't care. He pulled her close, cupping the back of her head, pressing his cheek to hers. "I love you," he muttered in front of everyone. Another thing he didn't care about. "I love you, I love you."

She pulled back. "What?"

He looked at her blankly. She hadn't heard a thing he said. So he repeated it, mouthing the words slowly. "I. Love. You."

She gave him her Aurora-grin. "I thought so. I just wanted you to say it again. Second wish just came true."

"You're yelling."

"What?"

He laughed and climbed onto the sofa, where he drew Aurora into his lap. He was so giddy with relief, he had trouble focusing on the dwindling violence on the lawn. Bemused, he stared at Winnie McGowan. "How did you do that? Please explain to me what just happened."

The old lady gave her hand to her husband, who helped her to her feet and shepherded her into the nearest chair. Maintaining her usual disciplined posture, she regarded Zane with eagle-eyed approval. "While you cowboys were shooting things out, I went upstairs for a cloak and Aurora's pistol." She frowned at Aurora. "I'm surprised at you, young lady. One never knows when a gun might be required at a dinner party."

Aurora looked confused. "What?"

Mrs. Winnie shook her head. "Never mind. Then I went out through the cellar and slipped around the house and into the crowd. I knew Jones wouldn't be able to resist insinuating himself into that mob. Nor would Alonzo Maney. So I simply watched for one or the other to make his appearance." Her glance fell on Zane's knuckles gently stroking Aurora's cheek. "Didn't count on Miss Sunshine here taking matters into her own hands." The old woman shuddered. "We almost lost her."

Zane tucked Aurora closer, wordless at the very thought.

"Where's Joelle?" Aurora said loudly. "She was right behind me."

"On the porch with Schuyler," reported Kidd from the

dining room, "dealing with Mr. Jefcoat and the marshal. They managed to get the crowd to disperse and go home."

"The marshal? When did Pierce get here?" Recalled to his duty, Zane beckoned Bedelia. "Please, Deedee, take Pete upstairs and help her get bathed and put her to bed." He looked at Aurora, letting her see his affection. "I don't want to see you again until morning."

She cupped a hand behind her ear. "I'm sorry I can't—"

He kissed her, cutting off the apology, then said slowly, so that she could read his lips, "I love you. See you in the morning."

She smiled and let him go.

Zane rose and followed the sound of voices to the front entryway. Shattered glass and splintered wood lay everywhere, and bullets had pierced the walls in several places. A massive clean-up operation would be necessary to get the place back in condition again, but he had no doubt his Aurora would be up to the task before long.

Only a small group remained in conversation on the porch— Pierce, Schuyler and Joelle, plus Spencer and a glassy-eyed Jefcoat. Zane noted the conspicuous absence of local law enforcement. No doubt they had been among the robed trespassers.

As Zane stepped outside, Schuyler saw him first. "How is Pete?"

"Deaf as a post, but otherwise as feisty as ever." Zane addressed his boss. "Marshal, I did my best to control the violence. Do you think that crowd will stay gone for the night?"

Pierce eyed him with approval. "I'd say you did a good job of impressing them with what would be for their own good. By the time I got here, Beaumont had wrapped up the matter and sent them on their way." He shook his head. "Mrs. McGowan is quite the virago. I think this bunch of cowards were afraid to cross her further after what she did to Jones. The militiamen have agreed to take shifts guarding the property for the rest of the night."

Zane looked around and realized that what he'd thought were shadows of trees in the dark were armed sentries stationed at intervals around the house. "Huh. Then it's over. Jones is dead." Hardly able to make it seem real in his own head, he looked at Jefcoat. "I know you wanted him to come to trial, but—"

"I wanted him dead," Jefcoat said flatly. "I would prefer to have killed him myself, but . . ." He hunched his shoulders, looking away. "I suppose you understand how I feel, Sager. Beaumont says you do."

Zane didn't answer. There had been a time when he certainly did understand the thirst for revenge. But now that Aurora had come into his life, everything was different.

He was different. Now he just had to convince her that was so.

Twenty-seven

AURORA'S FIRST THOUGHT upon waking Sunday morning was that the world had gone mighty quiet. Even the birds neglected to sing on this bright, shiny Lord's day. The sun streamed through Charmion's charming filmy white curtains, laying puddles of light across the sheet and making her squint and blink. Even Zane Sager would have a hard time worrying on such a—

She sat bolt upright. Now she remembered why this feeling of peace and well-being suffused her spirit. And she remembered why she felt as if cotton wadding stuffed her ears. Her grandmama had shot that vile Sam Jones, right across the top of her head, deafening her for the time being.

Jumping out of bed, she listened hard. Maybe she could hear a bit of noise coming from downstairs. She hoped it wasn't her imagination. She very much wanted to hear Zane repeat those three magical words a few hundred times today.

As she hurriedly got dressed, she tried to remember falling asleep last night. Bedelia had helped her wash her hair and get into a clean nightgown—mercy, her entire body had ached in every muscle and joint, as if somebody had run over her with a wagon—and she'd climbed between fresh sheets hoping to stay awake long enough to get another kiss from Zane. Before she knew it, though, everything had jumbled into a silent, cloudy dream. Probably Grandpapa had dosed her with something to make her sleep, which also explained why she didn't have a migraine.

After a futile minute spent attempting to tame the wild curls snarling about her head, she gave up and wadded the whole mess into an old-fashioned snood she found in a bureau drawer. Calling it a job well done, she stuffed her feet into slippers and pelted down the stairs.

She found the family in the dining room, finishing a large Southern breakfast. Her stomach responded to the lovely aroma of oatmeal, bacon, and toast with a rumble so loud that even she heard it. However, food would wait.

"Where is he?" she demanded of nobody and everybody.

"Well, if it isn't Sleeping Beauty," Schuyler said, slathering fig preserves on his toast. "I win. Levi said noon, Joelle thought eleven. But I"—he crammed the toast into his mouth and chewed—"I knew you wouldn't be able to wait past eight before inflicting yourself on the poor fellow. Don't pout, he's gone down to the hotel to see Mr. Spencer about a marriage license."

"I'm not pouting, and I can hear you," she said, taking a bowl off the bar and helping herself to oatmeal.

"What have you done to your hair?" Joelle frowned. "Even I know snoods have been out of fashion since 1863."

Aurora sat down next to Grandmama. "I may cut it off like yours. All these curls are so tiresome."

"Don't you dare!" Joelle looked horrified. "I'm growing mine back as fast as I can."

"Let me know how you're coming along with that," Aurora said. "I can help with a little pulling, if you like."

Everyone laughed except Grandmama, who placed a gentle hand on Aurora's arm. "Did you sleep well, love? How do your ears feel?"

"Stuffed up, and I slept well." She tried to sound cheerful and not pouty. Zane would eventually come back. "Are we not going to church?"

"I think we're going to become Baptist," Joelle said. "I'm pretty sure Gil Reese was in that mob last night, and I don't like the idea of my pastor standing on my front lawn in a black robe, holding a torch. I don't think there's a penny's worth of difference between Baptists and Methodists anyway."

"I don't like the idea of listening to Gil Reese pontificate under any circumstances," Schuyler growled. "Self-important twit. I hope he's convicted and put in jail with the rest of those bigots."

"Now, Schuyler." Joelle patted his hand.

"And another thing," he continued, warming to his topic. "I don't want him pronouncing our wedding vows. What do you think about getting married in Reverend Boykin's church, Jo?"

Joelle's lovely smile bloomed. "That's a brilliant idea! Let's do it today!"

"Today?" Schuyler glanced at Grandmama. "What do you think about that, Mrs. Winnie?"

"What difference does it make what she thinks?" Joelle demanded. "No disrespect intended, Grandmama, but *we're* the ones getting married. We're both adults." She shoved back her chair and stared at Schuyler. "But maybe you'd rather wait? Your brother and sister wouldn't be here—"

"No, of course I don't want to wait." He laughed. "After all, I didn't attend either Jamie or Camilla's wedding. I always thought all this wedding-dress, bridal-wreath hoopla was unnecessary." He took Joelle's hands and kissed them. "The sooner the better. Let's get married today!"

Aurora looked at the front door, through which Zane would arrive at some point. She would like to get married today too, but as she tried to remember what her last interaction with Mr. Sager had been upon the subject, things got very fuzzy. Grandpapa had insisted she say yes to some proposal, but when she'd pressed Zane in the kitchen, he'd said something like *I wish I could spend the rest of my life with you, not just the next few days.*

In fact, those had been his exact words. What had he meant? It occurred to her that he'd only agreed to marry her because he was being forced to spend all of the next few days, including the nights, as her protector. Which implied that when the crisis was over, he'd consider himself free to leave.

Would he take off and never return? He certainly could. She knew plenty of women who'd had their men go to war and never come back. Zane might even think he was doing her a favor, considering his sense of his own "damage," as he put it.

But . . . but . . . the crisis had come and gone before they'd said any vows. Now he wouldn't *have* to marry her.

On the other hand, he said he loved her last night. Four times. Although that might have been part of her wonderful relaxed dream.

She pushed away from the table. "Excuse me," she mumbled. "I have someplace I need to go."

He had looked for her everywhere. When Zane came back from the Gum Pond Hotel at nine o'clock with the marriage license in his coat pocket, he'd burst into the dining room, hoping to find Aurora settled at breakfast with the rest of the family.

Yes, they said, she'd come down a little after half past seven, wide awake and making jokes, back to her normal sunny self. Somebody thought they'd been talking about Schuyler and Joelle tying the knot that very day at the Negro Methodist Church when Aurora said she had to go somewhere.

Nobody remembered where.

So he'd rushed throughout the house, calling her name like a fool. He even went down into the cellar with a lantern—though he couldn't imagine Aurora voluntarily pursuing any errand down there alone—and then all the way up to the attic. Again, the bloodstains on the floor made that a crazy idea for a hiding place. Finally he returned to the dining room and sat there alone, hoping she might realize how worried they all were and come back on her own.

The rest of the family didn't seem concerned. Joelle checked the bedroom, said she wasn't there, and none of her belongings seemed to be missing. So he didn't know what else to do but wait.

An hour went by, then two. Now genuinely concerned, he decided to take a walk around town. Maybe she'd decided to stretch her legs and got lost.

In her own hometown. That was absurd, but he couldn't sit here any longer. He trudged up the stairs to his room for his Bible. Maybe he'd go sit in the empty church—surely church was over by now—and read and pray. And worry.

He started to open the door to his room but paused with his hand on the knob. It was ajar. He always closed the door when he left the room. It was a personal habit, and he never changed habits, a fact that had saved his life on more than one occasion.

Sliding his gun out of the holster, he pushed the door open a little at a time.

He stared at the bed, where Aurora lay curled on her side, fast asleep, with his Bible flattened open beside her. Her hair was loose, spilling like flame across his pillow, and he was stricken with a surge of longing so deep he nearly fell to his knees. Before he could do anything so dunderheaded, he returned his gun to its holster, then unbuckled the whole thing and dropped it on the bedside table. It made a large thud, which caused Aurora to turn over with a ladylike little snort.

Which made him laugh and sit down beside her hard enough to bounce her nearly off the bed.

She sat up, wide-eyed. "Zane! I fell asleep!"

He nodded. "You're not shouting. Your ears must be better."

She yawned and knuckled her eyes. "Some. You still sound like you're in another room. I think Grandpapa drugged me good. I tried to stay awake."

"I've been calling and calling. Did you not hear me?"

She gave him a reproachful look. "I just told you—"

"Right, right. It's just that I was worried. I was about to go look for you in town."

"Why would I go to town?"

"Why would you come up to my room and go to sleep like Goldilocks? And what are you doing with my Bible?"

"I was reading the parts you marked. And what you wrote in the margins." She peered at him from beneath her lashes, her cheeks flushed like a rose. "I found my name several times. Are you angry with me?"

He looked at her, that beautiful hair curling into her eyes and over her shoulders, golden eyes still drowsy, and he couldn't find one iota of anger within a hundred miles. "I'm very angry. I'm afraid I'm going to have to marry you to make you pay."

She grinned. "Oh, goody. I was hoping you'd say that. Especially since we're sitting on your bed and you shut the door. Grandpapa wouldn't like that at all. Also, since you mentioned it, Joelle and Schuyler have arranged to get Reverend Boykin to pronounce their vows this afternoon, and we might as well kill two birds with one—"

He took her lips with his, burying one hand in that glorious red mane tumbling down her back. Coming up for air, he said gruffly, "You talk entirely too much, Miss Pete."

"Well, if you're going to be critical, maybe you can think of something better to do."

He could. And he did.

"I might have known I'd have to share the altar with you," Joelle grumbled as she pinned Aurora's curls into a simple knot at the back of her head. "I should have bought that monstrosity you made me try on, in your size."

"Now you're just being mean," Aurora said, craning her neck to see the back of her hair in the mirror. "Besides, there isn't going to be an altar. We're getting married in a saloon."

Joelle laughed. "That's my favorite part of this whole

thing. Besides, you know, getting to marry my childhood sweetheart."

Aurora laughed. "Everyone but me thought you hated him, right up until the day he proposed."

Joelle bent over to brush her own hair, conveniently hiding her face. But her ear was scarlet. "He was pretty charming, for an adolescent prankster who made my life miserable."

"I knew it!" Aurora snatched the brush. "Here, sit down at the vanity and let me do that. You're making a mess."

Taming her sister's red-gold tresses into an elegant twist and loaning her a pearl-studded comb for decoration, Aurora stood back to study Joelle in the mirror. The bronze medieval-style dress Charmion had made for Joelle after the fire played up her fiery coloring, and its elegant lines emphasized her statuesque beauty.

"Nobody will even see me when you walk down the stairs," Aurora said with satisfaction. "You look like a queen."

Joelle made a rude noise. "You know there's one person who won't be looking at anybody else."

Aurora took Joelle's hands. "I'm glad we're getting married together, Jo. Otherwise, I might be just a little . . . nervous."

"You? Nervous?" Joelle looked incredulous.

"Yes. I—I love him so much, it frightens me. But everything will be so different. I'm used to telling other people what to do. What if he tries to boss me around?"

Joelle's blue eyes twinkled with sly humor. "Of course he will try sometimes. But you'll find ways to convince him he wants what you want."

"Jo!"

"Oh, I'm just teasing." Joelle's tone grew more serious.

"Pete, you're marrying a godly man. You pray for Zane to follow Jesus Christ, and then you can confidently follow him."

"That sounds right. But it sounds messy."

"I'm sure it will be. Aurora, none of us is perfect. We're going to make mistakes and struggle through things. But isn't it wonderful that God gave us a partner to struggle with—and have fun with?"

"Oh, it is!" Aurora flung her arms around her sister. "Let's go get married!"

Twenty-eight

AGAINST ALL LAWS OF PROBABILITY, Zane found himself married to the youngest of the three beautiful red-haired Daughtry sisters. They'd made it through the ceremony—filled with laughter, a few tears, and Reverend Boykin's sonorous blessing—to a full-blown wedding supper, served by two former saloon girls.

After dessert, the entire party crowded around the piano, where the elder bride sang a lilting, romantic art song accompanied by Levi. During the ensuing uproarious applause, the younger bride made Schuyler boost her onto the bar—apparently a permanent fixture in the Dogwood Boarding House.

Zane stood below, looking up at Aurora's laughing face as she lifted her glass of ginger beer and winked at Schuyler. Still dressed in her white-and-gold-striped wedding dress, with her hair coming down in wavy hanks at her ears and the back of her neck, she embodied joie de vivre.

"A toast!" Aurora giggled. "I want to toast my newest brother-in-law. May he be endowed with all necessary patience for long bouts of creative moods and unpronounceable words. Long live Mr. and Mrs. Beaumont!"

"Long live Schuyler and Joelle!" "Hip hip hooray!"

Shouting with laughter, Schuyler pounded on the bar. "And may the good Lord protect my new brother against the tidal wave of conversation which is about to overtake him and drag him under! Long live Mrs. and Mr. Sager!"

With a deep sense of gratitude and belonging, Zane endured the back-pounding, toasting, and general hilarity that would heretofore have sent him diving into a lonely corner. How had he gotten so lucky?

As Levi launched into the "Fairy Wedding Waltz" on the piano and Schuyler swung Joelle into his arms, Aurora crouched to offer Zane a sip of her drink. Putting his lips where hers had been, he met her sparkling eyes.

"Are you happy?" she asked, looping her arms around his neck.

"Do you have to ask?" He set the glass aside and leaned in to put his forehead to hers.

"I was afraid you might take the next train out." She looked around. "We're a loud bunch."

"I'm not taking any trains unless you're on it with me. Besides, I find I'm getting used to a little bit of noise."

She wrinkled her freckled nose. "I can be quiet when I need to."

"Don't make promises you can't keep." He grinned at her.

She laughed. "Dance with me, Zane."

Zane hated dancing, but he loved his new wife, so he let her teach him. As in most things, he was a quick study and found he didn't hate it as much as he anticipated.

But he couldn't help wondering what other lessons Aurora

would feel compelled to teach him. It was a fairly terrifying thought.

The party broke up at eight or so—the wedding guests yawning prodigiously and claiming to be exhausted. The bridal couples, having been assigned to bedrooms at opposite ends of the second floor, retired neither knowing nor caring where the rest of the company went.

Following Schuyler and Joelle up the stairs, Aurora walked arm in arm with her groom. Her husband. She glanced up at him. His expression was pensive, but that nerve jumped in his jaw. He must be as nervous as she was. After all, as he said, he'd never been married before either.

At least he'd already been exposed to her extra toe. There wouldn't be that to contend with.

They walked to the door of her bedroom, which stood open. Somebody had come in and freshened it with a vase of flowers on the nightstand and a couple of extra candles on the bureau. The bed was turned down.

She swallowed and looked up at him. He smiled down at her, dropping her arm. Then he bent and scooped her up. Held close against his chest, comforted by the slight scratch of his whiskers against her temple, she felt her fears slip away. This man cherished her and would not let anything bad happen to her.

She pulled his head down to whisper in his ear, "I just got my third wish."

Zane lay beside Aurora, listening to her even breathing. He prayed he would stay awake through the night. *Just this*

once, Father. Let our first night be perfect. No nightmares. No ladders, no lice, no rats, no Jones.

Sooner or later they'd have to talk about his night terrors. But not tonight.

As he'd carried her into her room, he'd been so nervous that he almost asked if they could sleep together on the little cot in the room he'd inhabited for the last two weeks—the cot where he'd found her asleep this morning. But Aurora deserved better than a cot for her wedding night.

The Lord knew she deserved better than *him*, but it was too late to go back now.

Now she belonged to him in every sense of the word.

The utter joy of that thought took him afresh. He turned onto his side and looked at her, pillowed on his shoulder. The candles had guttered, but a shaft of moonlight came through the open window to light Aurora's sleeping face. He would spend the rest of his life beside this woman, growing a family—a real family with children, a family that went to church together and sang and danced together. He might have to travel some, but—

The thought stopped him. His job was in Memphis, a fact he'd discussed with her grandfather but which, in the rush of ensuing events, he'd failed to mention to Aurora. She was not going to be happy about leaving her sisters and the boarding-house and her employees. He winced. And returning to the proximity of her grandparents might be a contentious issue.

He smiled, reaching up to brush his thumb across her beautiful eyebrow. Perhaps he could think of mutually en-joyable ways to convince her the move would be tolerable. Relaxing, he curled his arm around his wife.

Sometime later, he awoke with Aurora hitting him in the

chest. "Zane! Wake up! It's me. I'm not going to hurt you. Please, sweetheart. Oh, wake up!"

He jerked to a sitting position, stared at her in the moonlight. She lay against the pillow, tears streaking her cheeks. He shoved himself off the bed and stood on the rug, shaking. His knees felt like rubber, his shoulders like concrete, his hands clenched into fists. One finger at a time he released them. "What did I do?" He found he could hardly move his lips.

"Nothing. But your face . . ." She sat up and swiped her hands down her cheeks. "Zane, what did you see? I've never seen such pain. Not ever."

He fell to his knees beside the bed and took her hands. His trembled so that he had trouble grasping hers. "You're crying. *What did I do?*"

"I swear, you didn't hurt me. I was just so worried. You were holding on to me so tight and praying and shaking—"

"I was afraid this would happen. I tried not to go to sleep—"

"Zane! That's absurd! You can't go the rest of your life without sleeping!"

"No, but I can leave you to sleep without me." He jumped to his feet, then flung himself into the chair in the corner. "I tried to tell you—This is why I—They come and there's nothing I can do about it." He folded over, elbows on knees, his head in his hands. "Aurora, I'm sorry. I should have known better, I just thought, I was so happy, surely it would be all right with Jones gone."

She was quiet for a long moment. Finally he looked up.

She sat cross-legged in the center of the bed, looking exactly like the angel he'd once compared her to. A sleepy-eyed, copper-haired angel. "It may take a long time," she said, "but it *will* be all right. Because I'm not going anywhere. You are mine, Zane Sager, do you hear me? Do you remember when I said it's probably your scars and broken places that make you who you are? Well, I love those scars. And I love that you endured so many breakages and survived to help other people, when it costs you everything every day of your life." She gulped, and he saw that she was crying again. "I want you to heal. I don't want you to have nightmares. I think we can work through it together. We may have to have some help, but I'm willing to try if you are. Please tell me you love me enough to try."

He stared at her. "Aurora. I have no words for how much I love you. I just can't bear to hurt you."

"Then come hold me. Come love me with your body if you can't say it with your words."

He stood up. Considered gathering his clothes and moving down the hall. Then he counted the cost. He would sacrifice everything, including his dignity, for this woman.

He went to her, gathered her into his arms, and kissed away her tears. "I'm not going anywhere either," he said and lay down with her.

Twining herself about him, she sighed and relaxed. "I don't mind moving to Memphis," she murmured after a moment, "but there will be rules about Grandmama's visits."

He chuckled. "I might have known you've already thought this through. Who's taking over the boardinghouse?"

"ThomasAnne and Doc. They're getting married next week. But I imagine it's more likely to become a hospital." She rose on an elbow and flirted her eyelashes. "One person can't think of everything."

"No? I have yet to see you give in to indecision."

With a smile that reminded him of the erstwhile bubble-bath lady, she laid her cheek against his chest. "As long as we have that straight, I acknowledge that you outrank me in the big things."

He touched her nose. "Magnanimous of you, Deputy-Deputy Marshal Sager."

Thinking she might want to talk more, he waited, stroking her back, twirling a ringlet gently around one finger. After a moment, he opened his eyes and peered at her.

She was sound asleep.

Zane held her close as he rolled onto his back, stared at the ceiling, and smiled. He wondered how many days it would take before the potion her grandfather had given her last night wore off. Soon, he hoped. It had better be really soon.

A NOTE TO THE READER

THE DAUGHTRY HOUSE SERIES began as a simple historical romance about three sisters trying to hang on to their family plantation in the aftermath of the Civil War. As the characters developed in my mind, and as I researched the period, suspense and mystery elements began to surface. In *A Rebel Heart*, Pinkerton agent Levi Riggins tracks down the perpetrator of a real-life train wreck in north Mississippi. In the process, he connects his own wartime history—which includes Grierson's raid through Mississippi and the battle of Tupelo—to two different rape-and-pillages (one in Mississippi and one in Tennessee).

Suspecting that the train wreck is related to Ku Klux Klan terrorism across the South—including a series of race riots, church burnings, and the murder of a federal judge—Levi enlists the help of the Daughtry sisters and his new friend Schuyler Beaumont, son of an assassinated gubernatorial candidate. By the end of *A Reluctant Belle*, several of the lower-level criminals are unmasked and rounded up, but the powerful and mysterious mastermind behind the cabal remains to be caught.

In *A Reckless Love*, US Deputy Marshal Zane Sager assists in making sure the criminals face charges, while pursuing his own agenda related to the murdered judge. The overarching storyline involves the imprisonment and mistreatment of Union soldiers at Alabama's Cahaba Prison, the explosion of the Mississippi River steamboat *Sultana* off the bluffs of Memphis (which may or may not have been sabotage), and a corrupt congressional money-laundering scheme.

You can imagine how complicated all that got by the end of the third installment of the series! Keeping all those criminals, accomplices, heroes, red herrings, and sundry townspeople straight involved significant lists, charts, and maps. With the help of a slew of editors and beta readers, I think the central storyline got resolved to the reader's satisfaction, but I want to confess right here that I'm aware there may be small loose plot threads I simply didn't have space to tie up. Perhaps there will be future books to take care of those! If not . . . well, chalk it up to creative license. In the words of one of *my* favorite writers, Lois McMaster Bujold, "the author reserves the right to have A Better Idea."

Now, moving on to requisite research . . . judging by the emails I receive, many of my readers are eager to learn more about the history of post–Civil War Reconstruction behind this series. If that's you, keep reading.

First, I'd like to take a few paragraphs to point out which characters in *A Reckless Love* are "real people." As I mentioned in the reader note attached to *A Reluctant Belle*, Nathan Bedford Forrest was a celebrated Confederate general with well-documented exploits during and after the war. Because he owned plantations and ran a couple of businesses in the north Mississippi and Memphis area, and because he was unarguably involved in the Ku Klux Klan for a number of years, he seemed a logical choice for a background character. There is some disagreement about how long he remained in leadership of the organization (records of his own testimony before Congress contradicts that of contemporary witnesses), which is why I elected to leave him mostly out of the conclusion of my series.

Frankly, I was much more interested in law enforcement and judiciary figures of the day. President Ulysses S. Grant was in the White House, and though he clearly was a flawed human being, he seems to have tried to bring justice and order to the chaotic political culture he inherited from Andrew Johnson, who assumed the presidency upon Lincoln's assassination in April 1865. In May of 1870, Grant signed into law the Enforcement Act, defending the rights of formerly enslaved persons and making sure they could vote. The men Grant appointed to his cabinet, as well as the establishment of the US Marshals Service, indicate that he was serious about quelling the violence rampant in the Deep South.

One of Grant's earliest cabinet appointments was US Attorney General Amos Akerman, who came into office in June or November 1870, depending on which source one consults. Having served as a colonel in the Confederate army, Akerman joined the Republican Party during Reconstruction and became an outspoken civil rights advocate for freedmen in Georgia. After serving for a year as the Georgia US Attorney, Akerman accepted Grant's appointment to the cabinet, creating the new Justice Department, and oversaw the successful prosecution of more than 1,100 cases against the Ku Klux Klan.

On-the-ground prosecutors of the time period included swashbuckling Mississippi US Attorney Wiley Wells, who makes a brief appearance in *A Reckless Love*. A Northerner and US Army veteran, Wells was responsible for bringing charges against Klansmen and had to regularly deal with the kidnapping, harassment, and murder of witnesses and deputy marshals.

Moving on to the judiciary, my deceased judge Marmaduke Teague—Zane's mentor—is loosely based on Alabama federal judge Richard Busteed. Busteed had risen to the rank of Union Brigadier General during the Civil War. Because of his defense of freedmen's rights, his fellow Alabamans tended to look upon him with skepticism to hatred. After being shot on the street in Mobile in 1867 (the attacker escaped and evaded prosecution), Busteed recovered, only to face trumped-up impeachment charges in 1873, after which he resigned.

Robert Hill, federal judge for the Northern and Southern Districts of Mississippi, functioned pretty much as I've portrayed him in this story (though the Tupelo case I've invented never happened). I'm fascinated by the practical ways people of the time dealt with the nearly impossible scenarios into which they were thrust, doing their best to be fair and just—but also to keep themselves out of hot water! Hill presided over hundreds of Ku Klux Klan trials during Reconstruction, enabling nearly unanimous convictions—though the general penalty was a $10–25 fine and a $1,000 peace bond. Not exactly a great deterrent.

The new United States Justice Department—headed by

the aforementioned Amos Akerman—was supported by the reorganized US Marshals Service, which had previously operated in a sort of free-wheeling fashion under the Department of State. The two US district marshals who figure in my story are Lucien Eaton of Tennessee and young James H. Pierce of Mississippi. These men functioned during the Reconstruction period in a dangerous atmosphere of Southern resentment and recalcitrance. They and their deputies, while given great latitude in pursuing criminals, were burdened (as have been law enforcement officials through the centuries) by lack of funds and excess of paperwork. However, in developing Zane Sager, I found research indicating that the marshals and deputies of the Reconstruction Era were surprisingly well-trained and inured to difficulties by their service in the United States Army. Many were injured or killed in the line of duty, as I've pictured in *A Reckless Love*. For more information, please see Stephen Cresswell, "Enforcing the Enforcement Acts: The Department of Justice in Northern Mississippi, 1870–1890," *Journal of Southern History* 53, no. 3 (1987): 421–40, doi:10.2307/2209362; and *The Ku Klux Klan in Mississippi: A History* by Michael Newton.

I imagine the reader will find intriguing the explosion of the steamboat *Sultana*, as described in the prologue. It is based on a real event, the greatest maritime disaster in American history. For a fascinating treatment that traces the background of a major player and the aftermath, see *Sultana: Surviving the Civil War, Prison, and the Worst Maritime Disaster in American History* by Alan Huffman. You'll find information about Ozias Hatch, who served as Illinois Secretary of State and friend of Abraham Lincoln, and who apparently covered up the actions of his slacker younger brother Reuben on multiple occasions. There is little doubt that Reuben's greed is apparently at the root of the *Sultana* disaster. I took the bare facts of his crimes and tweaked them a bit to layer into my own story. It didn't happen. But it *could* have!

There was no real General Alonzo Maney, the main villain of my story, though some of the details of his backstory are based on the life of General Earl Maney of Tennessee. The rape-and-pillage of the Tennessee plantation during the war, as I noted in *A Rebel Heart*, was a real event, and Confederate generals really did move in and out of state legislatures and the United States Congress. The Crédit Mobilier congressional fraud scandal, involving the Transcontinental Railroad, really happened, though it was not uncovered until around 1872. For more information, see https://en.wikipedia .org/wiki/Crédit_Mobilier_scandal.

Confederate Lt. Col. Sam Jones, second in command of Cahaba Prison, was unfortunately a real person. Court-martialed for cowardice and falsifying military records, Jones was assigned to Cahaba and later suspected of murdering prisoners, along with assorted minor cruelties as pictured in Zane's memories. Alcoholic, often drunk and brutal, Jones loathed Yankees. He doesn't survive my story (ha!), but in real life, he reportedly fled to Mexico, then returned to New Orleans. Most of my information about him and Cahaba derives from a fascinating book entitled *Cahaba: A Story of Captive Boys in Blue* by Jesse Hawes, MD.

A couple more minor elements I'd like to mention here: There were real black militias that operated in Southern states, attempting to defend themselves and their families against the violence of white supremacists like the Ku Klux

Klan. I found *The Freedmen's Bureau and Reconstruction: Reconsiderations*, edited by Paul A. Cimbala and Randall M. Miller, a valuable resource. Regarding women's property rights laws, records indicate that a woman named Betsy Love made Mississippi the first state in the union to legalize women's property rights as separate from their husbands or fathers. Surprising, no? Other readers might question Levi calling Aurora "Polly Pry," a pseudonym taken by reporter Nell Campbell in 1878–80 by fellow reporters at the *New York World*. The reference goes back to a popular 1825 three-act farce by John Poole about a comical, meddlesome eavesdropper, so the reference would have been common by 1870.

That's all I can think of for now, but questions via my website contact are welcome. Drop by bethwhite.net and say hello!

LOVED THIS BOOK?
KEEP READING FOR A PREVIEW
OF ANOTHER CAPTIVATING
STORY BY BETH WHITE!

One

Massacre Island
Mobile Bay, 1704

The fifty-six-gun frigate *Pélican* lunged as Geneviève Gaillain dropped six feet over its side before the canvas sling jerked her to a stop. Clutching the sodden rope above her head, she looked up at the dark-skinned mariners straining to keep her from plummeting into what they charmingly called "the drink." The sling swung with the motion of the ship, setting the sky tilting overhead in rhythm with the ocean's slap-slosh against the hull.

Queasy, she searched among the women still aboard until she found her sister leaning against the rail, cheeks as pale as the belly of a sea bass. If Geneviève yielded to her own terror, Aimée would refuse to get into the sling when her turn came.

And if her sister didn't get off that pestilential ship soon, she was going to die.

Geneviève looked over her shoulder at the scrawny, wind-twisted pines staggering along the shore like teeth in a broken comb. She'd begun to wonder if she would ever see this

Louisiane that she was to call home—the New World, God
help her.

She shut her eyes as the jerky, swaying descent resumed.

"Hang on, miss!" shouted the mate in the longboat below.
"Almost down."

The seamen above chose that moment to release the rope,
dumping her unceremoniously into a pool of seawater in the
bottom of the longboat. Laughter erupted from the ship, but
she caught her breath, ignored the merriment at her expense,
and began the awkward business of untangling herself from
the ropes.

The mate in the longboat reached down to help, grinning.
"Welcome to Massacre Island."

She resisted the urge to jerk from his grasp. "Thank you,"
she muttered, recovering her dignity by scooting onto one of
three narrow planks crossing the center of the boat. As the
sling was hauled up, she looked up and cupped her hands
around her mouth. "Aimée! Come on."

Her sister recoiled from the sailor waiting to help her into
the sling. "I can't."

"Don't be ridiculous." Geneviève forced sympathy from
her voice. "You can and you will!"

The sailors grabbed Aimée, stuffed her into the sling heed-
less of petticoats and shrieks, and dropped her over the side.
Geneviève supposed they had little choice, but it was mad-
dening to see her little sister treated like just another item
of goods for sale. Although, essentially, she was.

After swinging through the air like a sack of sugar on a
string, Aimée fell into the boat with a solid thump and a
muffled squeal. "My skirt's wet!"

The mate chuckled as he extricated her from the sling. "You'll get a lot wetter than this before the day's out, *m'selle*."

Aimée's blue eyes widened as she struggled to keep her balance in the reeling longboat. "What do you mean?"

"Sit down before you pitch us all into the bay." The sailor shielded his eyes against the sun and gestured for the sling to go up for another passenger.

"Geneviève, what does he—"

"Aimée, sit down." Geneviève grabbed her sister's clammy hand. "You're going to faint."

Aimée crumpled onto the seat. "I wish we'd never come," she whispered, leaning against Geneviève. "I want to go home."

Geneviève put her arms around her sister's quaking body. There was no home to go back to. Tolerance in France for Huguenots had come to a flaming end. Here in Louisiane there was at least the promise of marriage, a chance of gaining independence, a home and children. The pouch of coins in her pocket pressed against her thigh, reassuring her. So many unknowns about this venture. She had promised to marry one of the Canadians who had already come here to explore and settle, and Aimée, as young as she was, had promised as well.

Yielding herself was inevitable, part of the bargain she had struck, as was hiding her faith. She and Aimée would have to make the best of it.

Another girl landed in the rocking boat, displacing her anxious thoughts, then one by one, with varying degrees of noise and struggle, four more. Finally the mate in charge roared, "No more room! We'll get the rest on the next trip."

The sailors hauled up the empty canvas seat, tossed it

onto a pile of rigging, and noisily saluted the departure of the longboat.

Thank God she and Aimée had been chosen to depart with the first group. They would have the choice of accommodations for the night—though who knew what that would be like. *Massacre Island*. She shivered. What a name for their landing place. But at least they would not have to stay here long. Tomorrow they were to travel up the river to their final destination, Fort Louis.

By the time they were halfway to shore, she and Aimée were both soaking wet from salt spray. Still, incredibly, her sister's cheek against her shoulder burned with fever.

Geneviève anxiously brushed her hand across her sister's damp, curly blonde head. Poor baby, she was lucky to be alive. One of the sailors had been buried at sea only yesterday. Geneviève herself still trembled from the fever they'd all picked up in Havana, but at least she was upright.

As the longboat drew closer to the beach, she lifted her hand to block the stark glare of sand as white as spun sugar. She began to make out human figures—male figures—gathered to watch their arrival. Her stomach tightened. Was her future husband among them? Some unknown Canadian with pots of money as they had been promised?

With every stroke of the oars she came closer to meeting him. Would he be like her father, a good man who had failed to protect his daughters? Or would he be like the rude and vicious dragoons who had been quartered in their home? Could she be so lucky, so blessed, as to find a man as kind and resourceful as Father Mathieu? As brave and principled as the great *Réforme* warrior Jean Cavalier?

Still several yards out from the beach, the boat grounded

against sand with a bump. Aimée whimpered and stirred in her arms. Geneviève looked up and found herself encircled by grinning, bearded men standing hip-deep in the water. Her overpowered gaze took in a variety of faded, ragged clothing, sunburnt faces, and twinkling eyes.

The young man closest to her, the only one in uniform—the blue, white, and gold of the French marine—removed his tricorn and bowed, all but baptizing himself in the chopping surf. He rose, plopping his misshapen headgear back into place, and scanned the passengers of the boat as if surveying goods in a market. "Welcome, *mademoiselles*. We've come to carry you ashore."

Geneviève stared at the boy. He couldn't be more than nineteen or twenty years of age, his cleft chin emphasized by a dark beard still thin and fine. Indeed he was broad of shoulder but built on lanky lines.

They were all slender, she realized, looking around at the other men. Gaunt in fact. Another sliver of apprehension needled her midsection. "I can walk, *monsieur*. But I would be grateful if you would help my sister. She isn't well."

The young man transferred his gaze to Aimée, who lolled against Geneviève like a rag doll. "We'd hoped the fever in Havana would be gone by now." He slid his arms gently under Aimée's knees and around her back, lifted her with surprising ease, and turned to slosh toward the beach.

Ignoring the rough voices and equally rough, reaching hands of the men surrounding the boat, Geneviève hauled herself over the side.

And found herself underwater. She thrashed, tried to find footing as she sank under the weight of her skirts. Just when she thought her lungs would burst, a pair of steely hands clamped her around the waist from behind and hauled her into sweet, blessed air. She coughed and vomited.

"Let go!" Choking, she shoved at the sinewy arms around her middle. "You're squeezing the life out of me!"

"Stop kicking," the voice rumbled against her back, "or I'll let you swim."

"I *can't* swim!"

"Then relax and enjoy the ride." He hoisted her over his shoulder and turned toward the beach.

Geneviève shoved a hank of sopping hair out of her eyes. She had lost her cap in the water, and her braid had come loose. All she could see was a rough shirt of a faded, pink-tinged brown, plastered against hard lateral muscles flexing as her rescuer half waded, half swam with her. He gripped the back of her thigh with one large hand to hold her in place and extended the other for balance.

Lifting her head, she peered at the *Pélican* floating in the distance, sails flapping against the steely sky in a brisk northwest breeze. No more worm-ridden hardtack for breakfast. No more briny bathing and drinking water. No more malodorous cabin shared with three other fractious women.

She realized she had much to be thankful for.

A noise must have escaped her. The man halted. "Pardon. Are you uncomfortable?"

She hung upside down with her hair dragging in the water, her thighs tucked under a strange man's chin. "Oh, no, monsieur, I was merely wondering what time tea will be served."

A rusty chuckle erupted against her knees. "Forgive us, mademoiselle. No one thought to warn you about the sinkholes." He continued slogging his way toward shore.

Sinkholes. What other unexpected dangers awaited her in

this alien land? As the water got shallower and clearer, she could see sea creatures swimming amongst bits of brown, foamy algae. The gentle roll of the surf was wholly unlike Rochefort's rocky, choppy seashore, as were the long-legged, wide-winged white birds swooping in the distance. They were big enough to carry off a small child.

The bay was big, the wildlife was big, the men were big. She and Aimée would be swallowed whole.

The man stopped. "You can walk from here," he said, shifting her into the cradle of his arms. He held her a moment, looking down into her face.

Boldly she returned his stare. His bony, angular face was outlined by a neatly trimmed dark beard and mustache, with black eyebrows slashing above a pair of fierce brown eyes uncannily like those of the boy who had carried Aimée ashore. Dark hair curled to his shoulders and blew back from a broad, intelligent brow.

"You should know," he said, "that I only came to pick up supplies. I'm not here for a wife."

ACKNOWLEDGMENTS

HERE'S THE PART where the author gets to say thank you to a bunch of people who (a) keep her sane, (b) keep her from making some serious mistakes, and (c) make the book not only publishable but more entertaining.

Chip MacGregor has been my agent almost since I began publishing at the turn of the century. Good gracious. That's a long time! Thank you, Chip, for continuing to believe in me and being my advocate.

Lonnie Hull Dupont has been my acquiring editor at Revell since the beginning. What an honor to work with such an erudite and wise woman full of soul-deep kindness. And I continue to be grateful for Barb Barnes's eye and ear for words and story. You have made me a better storyteller and writer.

My best friend Tammy Thompson never fails to ward off the dragons of illogic and toxic snarkiness that lie in wait for the unsuspecting manuscript. She also provides advice regarding the American legal and justice system (especially in a historical context), where I apparently know less than I thought I did. Thank you, my brilliant friend, for the rescues. If I misunderstood anything you told me and got it wrong, I apologize.

I have this son who, to my everlasting delight, enjoys history and story as much as I do. Thanks to Ryan White for contributing plot elements, little-known military history, and early reading. Your quirky sense of humor, your grasp of dramatic progression, your fine encouragement and ability to catch inconsistencies—all those things make your mom very, very glad she survived your teenage years. Burying you in the backyard seemed like a good idea at the time, but I think we're even now.

My thanks again to my friend Alabama State Trooper Ronnie Redding for answering questions about on-the-ground law enforcement stuff. As I wrote about a working US deputy marshal, I often found myself wondering, *How do they really do that?* Honestly, I'm still kind of scratching my head. Men like you, who keep ordinary citizens like me safe—dealing with the crazy and tragic events and people in the world so we don't have to—are the real heroes. You and your brothers in uniform have my complete admiration and respect.

Final thanks to my neighbor and friend Kim Carpenter—and of course my husband, Scott White—for early reading of the manuscript. You provided feedback that helped me shape characters and plot. I'm sorry you have to endure typos and clunky prose, but I couldn't do without you.

Beth White's day job is teaching music at an inner-city high school in historic Mobile, Alabama. A native Mississippian, she writes historical romance with a Southern drawl and is the author of *The Pelican Bride*, *The Creole Princess*, *The Magnolia Duchess*, *A Rebel Heart*, and *A Reluctant Belle*. Her novels have won the American Christian Fiction Writers Carol Award, the RT Book Club Reviewers' Choice Award, and the Inspirational Reader's Choice Award. Learn more at www.bethwhite.net.

GET TO KNOW

Beth White

Visit BethWhite.net to

• Discover More Books

• Sign Up for the Newsletter

• Connect with Beth on Social Media